In memory of Alice Young

Death by hanging, 1647

ONE OF
WINDSOR

ONE OF
WINDSOR

The Untold Story of America's First Witch Hanging

To Ray Nichols

Beth Caruso

BETH M. CARUSO

One of Windsor

The Untold Story of America's First Witch Hanging

Copyright © 2015 by Beth M. Caruso
Cover art by Lori Truly
www.trulyartandsol.com
Facebook: Art & Sol. Art, by Lori Truly
Family tree art by Claire Meucci
Maps by Dr. Yunliang "Phil" Meng, Geography professor,
Central Connecticut State University
Book designer: Susanne Aspley, www.aspleywrites.com
Editors: Susanne Aspley and Dr. William Harris
All rights reserved.
Printed in the United States of America
By Beth M. Caruso, Hartford, Connecticut.
Lady Slipper Press

ISBN: 13-9780692567036
ISBN-10-0692567038
Library of Congress Control Number: 2015906604
First Edition, October 2015
Second Edition, April 2016

Dedicated to my loving parents,
Dr. Joseph A. Caruso (1940 - November 2015)
and Judy Caruso,
for their never ending support.
Thank you for believing in me.

FOREWORD

When I first heard about Alice Young several years ago, I was shocked to discover that she was the first American colonist hanged for witchcraft. Until that time, I had only known about the witchcraft trials in Salem, Massachusetts. Since then, I have had the chance to learn about so many other accusations and trials throughout New England and especially in Connecticut. Upset that such an important historical event and person was so largely unrecognized and unacknowledged, I decided that one day I would tell her story to the best of my ability.

The problem was that very little was known about Alice Young. Every time I started my quest to capture her elusive story and her essence I ran into the proverbial brick wall that so many others before me encountered. It almost seemed like a historical cover-up of sorts. The identity of this unfortunate soul was not even known until the late 1800s when James Hammond Trumbull discovered it on the inside cover of the Matthew Grant Diary. Until that time, she was only known as "One _ _ _ of Windsor" as referenced in the John Winthrop Diaries. Dates in both entries matched, allowing Trumbull to identify her positively. And even then, he only shared the information with a few other historians. In any case, the records were sparse at best.

However, one day in the spring of 2013, when I was reading about the importance of neighborhoods as a vital part of Puritan society, the idea struck me. Since I couldn't find information about Alice, I decided to research the lives of her neighbors to see if any clues about her would surface. Fortunately, James Hammond Trumbull had already compiled a map for Windsor from that time, but with a large range of years for that early colonial period instead of a specific year. On the map, he listed the Young property at Backer Row.

I delved into the lives of every other family living on Backer Row in 1647, the year of her hanging. With the help of old land records from the town of Windsor, genealogical records, and many other historical documents, I was able to recreate the map for Backer Row specific to 1647. Some of the landowners changed from the original map because the new one was so specific. The pattern of people that came to life before me on Backer Row amazed me, and a possible story and theory quickly evolved about what might have happened to her and who she was. What astonished me the most was that the story was hidden only by the fact that the women, the wives of the men on Backer Row, were largely ignored, as so often happens in early American history.

Writing about Alice was a rich and interesting experience. From the beginning, I wanted to convey that she was not just a victim of an unjust witchcraft accusation but was a human being with a full life who was dearly loved and tragically lost. I always sensed that there was so much more to her humanity than the unfortunate events that led to her hanging.

It was not until after I finished writing the book that I came across the article entitled, "One Blank of Windsor," published in the *Hartford Courant* on December 3, 1904, by Annie Eliot Trumbull, James Hammond Trumbull's daughter. It was the avenue through which the public first became aware of Alice Young and America's first witch hanging. Annie Trumbull also made sure that the

Matthew Grant Diary was placed into the care of the Connecticut State Library so that the only piece of evidence that gave testament to Alice Young's life was never lost. Interestingly, a close friend of mine, Liz McAuliffe, my biggest confidante in writing this book, also crusaded to make sure that the same document went online for further safekeeping a few years before we met.

In reading her article, I knew that Annie, too, had sensed another Alice, an Alice who had a rich life full of varied experiences and raw emotion. Indeed, Annie Trumbull surmised,

"It may be permitted to us to guess that her death was ennobled by something in the grand manner–that she was too fair to be safe from jealousy–too young to have lost the magic of voice and laughter. To some minds such a victim snatched from warmth and color may seem the sadder picture, but it is not so for it has the swift brightness of one whom the gods love..."

It was profound to find another writer who had been touched by Alice in the same way that I had been. It was also remarkable to me that we both understood the importance of nature in her life's narrative.

"It is so difficult to bring back with any emotional veracity the picture of that May day of 1647. There is painful irony in the very season: May, the month when the miracles of spring have been performed to the benefaction of man! May, when the powers of darkness that governed the long winter and taunted man in the bitterness of early spring, had been totally banished. May, when if ever the bewitchment of sun and scent and blossom has turned a barren New England into a wonder of beauty! May, when, if ever, life is precious and earth is dear, Alse Young was brought across the blue, broad, benignant river to be executed for the sin of witchcraft. For was it not written in the Capital Laws that one should not suffer a witch to live?" Annie Eliot Trumbull poetically described in her article.

With this novel, I hope that the spirit of Alice Young will also touch you, the reader, in some meaningful way. I encourage you to look at the family tree and the maps placed at the end of the book with the Author's Note to help understand this complicated story.

Beth Caruso
September 1, 2015

Prelude

BOSTON, MASSACHUSETTS BAY COLONY, 1692

The elderly reverend knew it was crucial to stop Satan. As if in unison with the Dark Lord's latest antics, tremendous bolts of lightning and deafening thunder heralded the ensuing rainstorm of that early autumn day in Boston. The reverend's dedicated son would have preferred that he stay home by a fire and rest. Still feisty in his later years of life, he refused. He was fervently determined to discuss pertinent matters at hand concerning the witchcraft calamities in Salem and surrounding towns. As a minister, albeit a retired one, he felt responsible for guiding younger ministers, such as Cotton Mather, to make their congregations understand the menacing threats of witchcraft.

The aged minister was someone who had personally suffered through a demonic incursion in Windsor, a river town of the Connecticut Colony, back in 1647. He was fully cognizant of its evil impacts. Satan had infiltrated Windsor through a consort and witch whom he knew all too well. The Great Demon had been stealthy in his trickery. But this time, the respected pastor hoped to arrest the Devil's mischief before the same level of destruction and harm could occur. Accordingly, he was there to offer his assistance to Cotton Mather in dealing with witchcraft presently taking hold in Massachusetts Bay towns and villages. The young minister welcomed him into his home.

"Good day, dear Reverend. You must come in quickly out of the rain and take comfort by the hearth. I will have my servants bring you my finest cider and freshly baked, delicious cakes to eat. I have so much to share with you. By your experience, you have been the inspiration I have needed to start the work that we were speaking of the other week," spoke Cotton Mather.

"Thank you, Cotton. It will warm my body as well as my heart to sit by the fire and hear of the inspirations that took hold of your soul. I hope it helped you to do the honorable task of warning our people of the great wrath of Satan," replied the elderly reverend.

With that pronouncement, the old reverend took off his soggy cloak and sat down at a table next to the hearth. He paused and grew distinctly somber before continuing.

"Satan must not be allowed to advance further into our New England wilderness, for we have painstakingly worked at taming it over the years. Yet our young people lapse into disobedience of the commandments of Jesus Christ. Our current admonishment by the Lord through the events in Salem and beyond act to bring us back to the righteous path," explained the aged pastor as the rain poured down.

He looked wide-eyed and serious at Cotton.

Cotton Mather nodded at the old reverend in agreement and replied, "You see, honored Reverend, by your histories of the very earliest acts of war first waged upon these colonies by Lucifer, I have been able to put the current difficulties in Salem into a broader view of understanding for our present government. I hope it will aid those justices that would weigh their opinions upon such cases of bewitchments. It is also for the benefit of younger generations. I know you prefer not to be mentioned by name, but hear what it is that I have reiterated concerning those times," he implored.

Cotton quickly pulled out a satchel full of papers written upon with a righteous and eloquent hand and requested, "Please tell me what you think, Reverend. This is from the introduction of my commentary. These words were taken directly from our lengthy conversations of what is transpiring now at Salem and in our congregations in relation to the Devil and his armies' frustration of defeat in Connecticut so many years ago. I am naming this commentary *Wonders of the Invisible World*."

"*Wonders of the Invisible World*," nodded the old reverend, speaking loudly over the storm.

A servant came in and poured warm cider for the two ministers. At being interrupted, the elderly pastor pursed his lips, staying silent, but met Cotton's eyes with a secret understanding. They waited until the servant left before continuing their discussion.

Cotton continued, "This is part of the Introduction, Enchantments Encountered".

He read, "*We have been advised by Credible Christians still alive, that a Malefactor accused of Witchcraft as well as Murder, and executed in this place, more than Forty years ago, did then give Notice of An Horrible PLOT against the country by WITCHCRAFT, and a foundation of Witchcraft then laid, which if it were not seasonably discovered, would probably Blow up and pull down all the Churches in the Country.*"

"Yes. Yes!" agreed the agitated old minister, and added, "The young people need to know how, if we had not ferreted out the witch that spawned all others on the shores of the Great Connecticut, all of our churches in the colonies would have failed indeed. Nothing would have pleased Satan and his legions more than to see those intent on building a godly and pure Utopian state in this wilderness beaten down and forced by evil to return to England. We, the people of Windsor, agonized much in bringing to light of day the bewitchments brought upon us by a naughty and wayward woman. She who made a pact with the Devil allowed him to nearly destroy us. By the Grace of God he did not, thanks to the watchful vigilance of God's dedicated and steadfast servants!" he howled with the tempest.

The aged pastor continued, enraged, "No one likes to speak her name. She deserves no recognition for her defamation of this country by unleashing devils that would dare claim this corner of the earth for their own in an affront to the Lord Jesus Christ. By her hand, a great pestilence of disease infiltrated the daily life of the fledgling colony of Connecticut, especially in the town of Windsor. We had settled into our homes only about twelve years when the Devil was overcome with venomous jealousy that we had claimed formerly heathen territory and tamed wilderness for our Lord Jesus. Satan saw a prime opportunity to permeate and upset our small community through the wickedness and unfaithfulness of that woman," he spoke as the sky rumbled.

The old reverend took a sip of cider, wetting his dry lips.

"Such was the power that Satan infused her with that a great many people died, including many young children, for the Devil has no conscience and no compassion. Upon her death, she did swear in a fit of lies that she was innocent. She cursed those whose testimonies and swift actions led her to the hangman's noose. The good Reverend Thomas Hooker was presiding at the First Church in Windsor for the Reverend John Wareham during the time of her bewitchments," recounted the old cleric.

He clenched his fists as he took a deep breath.

"He helped to expose her and was touched by her wickedness in such a way that he died less than one month later of the same dreaded disease that she helped to proliferate and use to kill other devout soldiers of Christ," the old reverend said.

Cotton Mather spoke again intensely, "Yes, I understand, Reverend. I preface the first reading I recited just now with this...*The New Englanders are a People of God settled in those, which were once the Devil's Territories; and it may easily be supposed that the Devil was exceedingly disturbed, when he perceived such a People here accomplishing the Promise of old made unto our Blessed Jesus, that He should have the Utmost parts of the Earth for his Possession."*

Cotton continued, "*I believe that never were more Satanical Devices used for the Unsettling of any People under the Sun, than what have been employed for the Extirpation of the Vine which God has here Planted, Casting out the Heathen, and preparing a Room before it, and causing it to take deep Root, and fill the Land, so that it sent its Boughs unto the Atlantic Sea Eastward, and its Branches unto the Connecticut River westward, and the Hills were covered with the shadow thereof. But in all those attempts of Hell, have hitherto been Abortive and Having obtained Help from God, we continue to this Day. Where fore the Devil is now making one Attempt more difficult, more Surprising, more snarled with unintelligible circumstances than any we have hitherto encountered.*"

The senior cleric nodded his head approvingly. Their conversation continued for the better part of two hours. The time was interspersed with prayers as well, imploring the Almighty Father to empower them in their fight against the Prince of Darkness. Cider was refilled several times. They discussed the importance of weeding out all of Satan's imps and witches in Salem and other nearby villages and towns so that New England could be as pure again as that first generation of godly wayfarers who led the ultimate religious Utopian experiment into the wilderness.

When the conversation eased, the thoughtful and grave old minister stared into the fire. He wondered if she were burning in hellfires in that very moment. And what of the souls of the family who had forever fractured in their defense or blame of her, the first colonial witch? He was becoming quite old now. Soon, he hoped to be called to God's kingdom. Until that time, he would continue to be of service to the younger generations of ministers trying to guide their lost flocks away from Satan.

Abruptly, there was a knock on the door that jerked the ministers from their pious imaginings. It was the elderly reverend's son. He had come to retrieve his father. He paid his respects to the Reverend Cotton Mather and then gently guided his father out into the streets of Boston, newly drenched from the rain. The elderly pastor turned around and shouted to Reverend Mather.

"Please feel free to call for my assistance again. For an old man such as I delights in nothing more than making his last acts upon this earth ones that are dedicated to bringing God's people closer to Him and away from the wretches of the Devil. I shall be honored to continue to help you with your mission," offered the old cleric.

"Thank you, honorable Reverend," answered Cotton with a slight bow.

Chapter 1

NEW WINDSOR, BERKSHIRE, ENGLAND, 1615

The infant was soon to enter the world. Alsie's increased labor pains and a sudden wave of panic made a swift announcement of her baby's imminent arrival. Gwendolyn, the midwife, motioned with a wise smile and nod to Alsie's cousin. Mrs. Mary Merwin Tinker and her daughters were to make the final preparations for the newborn. The lines embedded under Gwendolyn's eyes, eyes still bright after many years of life, were a testament to her wisdom and experience.

"Girls. It's time. Quickly…Sarah, bring the rest of Gwendolyn's supplies to the bedside table. She'll need the string and knives shortly. Little Mary, come and support Alsie's back. You too, Ellen. Assist Mary. Margaret, make sure the linens are warmed and everything else is ready for the babe! We must all give our support to cousin now," spoke Mrs. Mary Tinker, their mother.

"Yes ma'am," they replied in unison as some sisters hurried about making sure everything was in place for the birth, and the remaining sisters stayed at Alsie's side to comfort her.

Despite the excitement inside, a branch softly and hypnotically continued to hit the leaded glass window of the thatched cottage in a steady cadence. Alsie had already been in a trance for the past hour, the trance a woman's body and soul become held in toward the end of labor.

She entered the spiritual void that all mothers go to just before birth to psychically retrieve her child. But as the baby's head came down farther, she was jolted out of her trance and became frantic to have the experience end.

Alsie started retching and shaking all over, yet felt increasingly hot. The physical pressure of the baby about to be born became almost unbearable.

"Please, dear God, release me from my pain," she desperately cried, wanting the labor to be over.

The old midwife peered down and nodded again. Mrs. Tinker beckoned Sarah and Margaret to come close for the birth. Little Mary and Ellen were already giving Alsie cool compresses and holding her leg.

"It will be alright, dear cousin, Alsie," said the voice of a sweet young girl.

It was Ellen, who was now eleven and preparing for her own womanhood. She was a little nervous and couldn't help but doubt if she could ever survive such an ordeal as this in her own future.

Little Mary, her younger sister, was nine. She was very interested in what was going on and had no shortage of questions for the midwife about how the process of coaxing and leading a baby out of its mother's womb was done. She was naturally curious and intelligent, and if they let her, would have readily taken charge.

Margaret was Mrs. Tinker's stepdaughter and already an adult at eighteen. She had attended several births in the past. She directed the younger girls in ways to be helpful, yet she knew enough to caution them when to stay out of the way.

Sarah was thirteen and was curious but really had no idea how to assist. She patiently looked on and waited for her cues. Consequently, she acted as a runner when sister Margaret told her to fetch something.

Alsie had now fully awoken from her trance despite the branch still rhythmically tapping on the window.

"Alright, now Alsie, just a little more to go. The baby's head is crowning and wants to come out. If you give us just a few wee pushes, your little one will be out. Slow, easy pushes," coached Gwendolyn, her experienced midwife.

Despite feeling the quivering of her body and the excruciatingly intense contractions, Alsie was strong and remembered delivering her other babies. The girls were each shouting their own encouragements for her to go on.

"Push, Alsie!"

"Push the baby out!"

"PUSH!"

She was able to muster the needed strength and gave those few last pushes. A minute later, a screaming, wiggling pink mass of precious life slipped into the midwife's hands. The baby was a vigorous little girl, a lively one. Gwendolyn lovingly handed her to her mother, Alsie. After she settled down, the baby looked into her mother's face with an otherworldly gaze.

Alsie, in turn, looked deeply into her newborn's eyes, searching for any sign of the same gift of sight that she herself possessed. In hushed tones, out of earshot of the others, she addressed her little one.

"Are you like your mother, little one? Will you be privy to things that others cannot foretell? Ah, yes. I see it in you."

The baby stared back at her as if she understood the sentiments expressed by her mother.

"Pray that it will serve you and others well. Pray 'tis not a curse. But we must not think of that now, dear babe. You shall be cloaked in your mother's love, my little sign of heavenly light," she whispered to her precious newborn daughter.

Even though Alsie's own ability to foretell was welcome, at times it seemed more like a heavy burden. She used her clairvoyant talents to know how to heal someone or to forewarn about undesirable future events, but she knew to employ them ever so carefully. She had heard the stories of others who also had clairvoyant tendencies. Those that had been used in questionable or suspicious circumstances sometimes led to accusations of witchcraft and associations with the Devil himself. She knew fate was often grim for those accused of such a crime. She could not bear the thought of any such event happening to her girl and resolved to banish such dark thoughts out of her mind for good. After all, this baby girl signified hope, not death.

As she smiled down upon her new daughter, their souls embraced profoundly. She was pleased to have her wish for a girl fulfilled. This precious infant was her last child, her last living connection to her husband, Richard, who had recently met his death.

Richard, normally a man of robust health, died quickly from a horribly infected carpentry injury that stubbornly and dangerously refused to heal. The heat and bad humors from the wound on his hand spread to the rest of his body, where they took over with a hot rage. He woke up one day with a heavy sweat and never got out of bed again. By the next morning, he was dead.

Alsie was no stranger to grief, for she had already lost two sons to the Black Plague. Ultimately, this baby was her closest kin. Her only other living relations were Mrs. Mary Tinker, her wealthy cousin, and Mary's children. The baby was a welcome and joyful salve to subdue the pain from her other losses.

Alsie, her husband, and their deceased sons, Richard and Thomas, were from the town of Chesham bordering on the outer edge of Amersham in Buckinghamshire County where they had worked for the Merwins, wealthier kin and the parents of Mrs. Mary Tinker. The Merwins were cousins who had improved their station in life with the success of their family woolen business. After her parents' deaths, Mary Tinker and her husband, Robert, invited Alsie to live with and work for them and their large family.

As Gwendolyn and Margaret cleaned up Alsie, Mrs. Mary Tinker and the rest of her daughters took the baby and bathed her in weakened sweet wine. They swaddled her and brought her to nurse at another servant's breast that also had a young child. Custom required that another woman feed the baby until her mother's milk came in. After Alsie was clean, the midwife wrapped her thighs and her belly with fresh linens to ensure that she would not take in or catch any chilled air. Everyone took turns caring for Alsie's baby girl while she rested.

"So Alsie, what will you name the baby now that you've had some time to dwell on her?" asked her cousin, Mrs. Mary Tinker.

" 'Tis not a hard decision, cousin. 'Tis befitting that the girl child be named Alice to honor both my mother and her mother before her. She will be another Alice in a long, proud line of eldest daughters." Alsie was also given the name Alice by her own mother but went by her nickname.

"I understand. We, as women, cannot carry on our family names in perpetuity, but at least our Christian names can be passed on to future generations of our girls and their descendants," stated Mrs. Mary Tinker.

"And, in honor of her late father, I am happy she will receive the family name Ashbey. I can sense them all, Richard, Mother, and Grandmother, smiling down at us from their heavenly places."

She inhaled deeply and smiled as if to take in their love being sent from an unearthly dimension. Then she looked seriously at her cousin, Mrs. Mary Tinker. She grasped her hand as a slight tear escaped from the corner of her eye and she spoke again.

"Dear cousin, I am so thankful to have a healthy child to remind me of Richard, but I am even more thankful that you have been kind enough to allow us to stay with you and your family. I am truly grateful for the invitation given to Richard and me to live and work in your home. Dwelling in this cottage behind your lovely home has been wonderful. I cannot imagine what would have become of us if you and Robert had not taken us in," she cried. Now the tears cascaded down her cheeks in steady streams.

Many widows like Alsie did not share the same circumstances and were met with the brutal reality of roaming the streets with children after their husbands died. Sometimes they ended up in housing provided to the poor by towns with improved, yet still deplorable conditions. Alsie knew that her generous cousin and her lovely children would never let them go out into the streets to beg or be prey to highway robbers. Alsie was lucky compared to other widows, and she knew it. For even though she had no more immediate living family besides her newborn infant, she had the Tinkers.

Mrs. Mary Tinker responded to her cousin's emotional display of gratitude, "Robert and I were more than willing to take you and Richard in to work for us after my parents passed on. Robert has been so blessed as a textile merchant, and he truly needed the help. He was busy managing his properties as well as serving the churchwarden in New Windsor. Richard served to ease his burdens. And you, cousin, have assisted me immensely by caring for my family. Besides, you are a part of this family. You and baby Alice belong with us. I am only sorry that Richard, her father, and her brothers did not live long enough to meet her."

"Thank you. I will always remain your dedicated, loyal servant and your loving cousin, and I will teach my daughter to be the same," Alsie responded in kind.

Alsie was thus able to keep her daughter at her side. And baby Alice would be lucky to grow up with her doting cousins in a wealthy textile merchant's home. Her mother hoped that her baby would love the Tinkers as much as she did.

Just then, like a sudden flurry, the two youngest Tinker children, Rhody and John, burst into the cottage with their older brother, Robert. They were anxious to meet the new baby. Rhody eyed baby Alice suspiciously, as if an intruder was threatening her home. But two-year-old little John could not help himself and ran up to the baby, kissing her on the forehead.

"Ah, what a sweet little one he is! He loves his wee cousin already," laughed Alsie.

True to Alsie's wishes, Alice did grow up to love and adore the Tinkers as much as her mother did. She matured into a kind, pretty young woman who was steadfastly loyal and completely devoted to her extended family. They were so much a part of her that she could not imagine life without them or sense her own identity apart from them.

At the same time, her intuitive abilities developed. She, like her mother, found herself merging with the thoughts and feelings of others, sometimes unwittingly knowing things about their past or their future.

Chapter 2

NEW WINDSOR, BERKSHIRE, ENGLAND, 1635

B aby Alice, now twenty years old, looked carefully and meticulously at her surroundings again. Her mind was racing. Her gait proved to be unsteady. The day felt surreal, and she was woefully unsure of herself. Reality had finally set in. She only had a few precious hours to soak in the memories of her childhood home. In just a short time, she would be living with the Holman family in London as they awaited their New World journey.

So much had changed since her early years growing up in this comfortable merchant's home. The stately Tinker dwelling became more vacant by the day. Over the years, children either died or married, taking away their precious spirits from the revered family home.

During most of her childhood, Alice remembered the house erupting in growing gardens and uncontained laughter. Joy and celebrations marked the years, as did sadder moments when the entire family gathered for vigils of prayer around the sickbed of a loved one. Now it seemed so noticeably silent by contrast.

Mrs. Mary Tinker had managed her family and her household well, like a talented captain on a large ship. She had been firm and respected amongst her children, yet warm and caring to them over the years. She had eleven children in all, counting three stepchildren she helped to raise. Together, she and her husband Robert, ten years her senior, had eight children of their own, six girls and two boys. With almost everyone gone now, the house felt eerily vacant.

Alice dejectedly remembered the recent conversation she had with Mrs. Tinker about the changes in the family household. Mrs. Tinker's countenance had grown more severe with her personal losses. Even though she was still the domineering mother of her brood, she had fallen into depression and melancholy. She was not the same happy, welcoming cousin who had opened her doors to Alsie and her daughter. Between the loss of her husband and economic declines in New Windsor, she felt less secure than ever before.

"Alice, I must talk with you in earnest." She paused and gave Alice an exhausted look before continuing.

"With the advent of most of my girls marrying and leaving for the Massachusetts Bay Colony, I am not sure that I will stay here for much longer myself. Only Sarah and Rhody and her two young daughters are here now. As you know, Sarah is engaged and soon to leave for the colonies also. Rhody, now widowed, is considering joining her sisters as well," she explained.

"It seems so drastically empty compared to how it used to be before mama died," commented Alice sadly.

"Aye. " 'Tis sadly so, Alice. And now, what will become of you? I do not know. I promised your mother I would provide for you, and I have. But you are now twenty and at every gesture I have made to pair you with a desirable suitor, you have spurned my suggestions. Alice, you leave me in such a quandary. You cannot stay here forever dear. Sadly, our fortunes have changed amidst economic collapse in this region," she enlightened her.

What Mrs. Tinker did not reveal was her wariness of Alice. She kept Alice at a distance ever since the young girl foretold her husband Robert's death many years before. In truth, the child had meant no harm, and Robert's death was already expected, though unwelcome. But Mrs. Tinker never came to terms with it.

Alice froze. She did not expect this confrontation. She felt shaky as Mrs. Tinker continued.

"Since John is my only living son now, I will wait until he completes his education and then follow him as his career unfolds. I have no idea when or if I will ever see all my remaining children in the same place again. This house and land may soon be completely empty and sold. You are grown up now and must be responsible for yourself. I cannot coddle you any longer," she clarified firmly.

Alice finally spoke, barely getting the words to come out.

"But what shall become of me? This is the only home that I have ever known."

Alice felt hurt and disoriented at the thought of being separated from her only family.

Mrs. Tinker sighed dejectedly and questioned her.

"What do you want of me, Alice? Short of arranging a marriage, the only other option I have is to secure an alternative position for you with another family. What can I do?"

Alice was visibly upset as she paced the floor. She took quick, shallow breaths and nervously stroked her hair back away from her face. She knew that, as dismayed as she was, she had to think clearly about her options.

"What about my dear cousins, your daughters, near sisters to me, already in the Bay? Could I stay with them and their families until you and John can join us?" asked Alice hopefully. "I will gladly continue to serve you once we are together again."

She anxiously tugged a strand of her chestnut brown hair as she awaited Mrs. Tinker's response. The matron's reply was not as positive as Alice had desired.

"Alice, I cannot pay for your passage because John must finish his schooling. Furthermore, I do not know if my daughters or their husbands would be able or even willing to care for you. The best I can do for you is to look for passage with another family that would take you on as their servant in the colonies. In this way, you may eventually be able to find your cousins again," she suggested.

Alice was feeling overwhelmed and confused, but she understood that her cousin was in a precarious position concerning her own future. Alice was determined to make the best of the situation.

"If that is my best option for reuniting with my family again, then that is the one I choose," she responded without hesitation.

Mrs. Tinker actively looked for placement for Alice after their conversation. She felt obligated to do so as a last responsibility to Alice's mother, her departed cousin Alsie, who had worked for her for many years. It did not take long before a close family friend, Robert Keayne, also from New Windsor, told her about someone in need of help. William Holman was the head of a respectable family who was waiting in London for a ship to transport him and his family to New England.

Alice was feeling sorrow and anguish. It was the day that dramatically closed the door on her childhood forever, yet it opened the gate to the rest of her life. Robert Keayne was coming to pick her up and take her to meet the Holmans. It was arranged for her to accompany them in passage to the New World and serve them for a term of six years during their initial settlement in the colonies. They were staying temporarily at an inn in London as the final preparations were being made for the journey. She was nervous even though Mrs. Tinker agreed to go with her to meet the family.

Alice still had a couple of remaining hours that final morning in New Windsor before the appointed meeting time. All her last chores were finished in an orderly and timely fashion. She had the luxury of wandering through the Tinker household and property one last time, indulging her most sacred remembrances as she went. She looked at and felt her surroundings intently, to savor every last sight and smell. She placed and held them in an internal treasure chest of keepsakes of the good times she shared with her cousins and her departed mother. At least, no one could ever take that away from her.

Having grown up in the Tinker household nearly a sibling to the Tinker family brood, she became very close to them. Alice and her cousins, Rhody and John, were closest in age and often played together. Two more daughters were born shortly after Alice's birth and became playmates as well. The older Tinker sisters, Ellen and Mary who were at Alice's birth, remained close to her throughout her childhood.

It was a happy upbringing for the most part. The Tinker siblings never thought of their cousin as a servant, and she never felt like one in their home. Alice loved participating in many activities with them. The girls had lessons in music and foreign languages. They learned the practical arts and skills of weaving, embroidery, spinning, and stitchery. They taught Alice how to make little clothes for her homemade doll and how to stitch pretty pictures on cloths used for napkins, covers, and tablecloths. The girls also spent many hours in the stilling room under Mary Tinker's direction and Alsie's tutelage. There they learned to experiment with drying herbs, brewing ales and beer, and making pharmaceutical formulas to place in tinctures and syrups.

The gardens and orchards were largely under the direction of Alsie, but everyone participated in tending them and harvesting their produce. With the bounty from the gardens, she cooked for the entire family with her little daughter often at her side.

One of Alice's earliest memories was the preparation for Margaret's wedding that took place when she was still very small. Margaret married Walter Merwin, who was also Mary's great nephew. The Tinkers and Merwins were elated because the two families were joining again.

Alsie helped Mrs. Tinker prepare for the big celebration for weeks. In reality, Alice was too little to be of much assistance, but she dutifully stayed at her mother's skirts as she polished silver, arranged the pewter, and folded napkins. Her mother let her pour sugar, milk, and flour in measured amounts into mixing bowls while she made the many desserts for the upcoming affair.

When Alsie was too frantic with preparations, the older Tinker siblings watched little Alice. All the older girls loved to dote on her. The year of Margaret's wedding, she was the littlest one of the clan. Margaret, Sarah, Ellen, Mary, and Rhody held her and played with her like she was a baby doll.

"Come now, dear Alice, let us fasten you with colorful ribbons like a beautiful young lady of the court," the girls exclaimed.

They were taking many brilliant ribbons and making bows to decorate for the winter nuptials. They played with her, making bridges and Maypoles out of the same ribbons and also out of the vivid fabrics used to beautify and adorn their house for the occasion.

The girls practiced their music so they could perform the ceremony as a special heartfelt gift to Margaret. They loved playing the lute and the virginals. And they sang beautifully together in harmonies embodying their sweetness and innocence. Little Alice was mesmerized as she twirled and danced throughout their private recitals, making everyone laugh, which encouraged her further.

The sweet memories of that winter gradually transformed to remembrances that were much more sorrowful from the spring that followed. Sarah, the oldest child of both Robert and Mary Tinker, died in May that same year. Alice remembered how frightened she was seeing Sarah confined to bed. Sixteen-year-old Sarah had always been somewhat frail and more vulnerable than the other children after suffering from scarlet fever as a young child. She was never able to run as fast during childhood games and often needed to catch her breath. The weakness in her constitution and heart became more apparent each year despite remedies to balance and give her strength.

One day she became quite pale and despondent, collapsing suddenly during music lessons. Everyone prayed around her bedside, but no amount of prayers or herbs would help to bring her back into balance. In the final act of Sarah's life, with her spirit struggling to stay with her family, Sarah took her last breath. Mrs. Tinker said that God must have taken pity on Sarah and called her to his side.

It was not easy for Mrs. Tinker. She was seven-months pregnant with her seventh child and was greatly fatigued much of the time. Devastated by the loss, she could not pull herself out of her grief until another daughter, Anne, was born that summer. Two years later, her last child Sarah was born, whom she named in honor of her well-loved first daughter. She was grateful this baby was healthy and strong, in contrast to her first-born.

Alice decided to take one last glance at the garden. So much of her time had been spent there helping her mother or playing with the Tinker children. She remembered them fondly. There was one game she recalled vividly and smiled.

"...Twenty-eight, twenty-nine, thirty! I'm coming to find you, girls. I'll catch you quick as a wolf catches sheep strayed to the woods!" cried out John Tinker, leaving the hall, tossing a swathe of dark, wavy hair to the side of his face.

Anne and Sarah, the littlest ones, were hiding together and giggling away in a pantry. John wanted to let them think they were skillful in their choice of a hiding place, so he looked at the cupboard and spoke loudly.

"Where are Anne and Sarah? I can't find them anywhere."

Further uncontained laughter erupted.

He smiled, continuing on his mission to find one of the older children, Rhody or Alice. Rhody took her task seriously and remained as quiet as still air behind some stored barrels.

Alice, on the other hand, upon hearing him and the giggling in the cupboard, headed out to the garden. But she quickly became lost in what she saw, completely forgetting about everyone else and the game. Alice was a dreamer and sometimes got lost between two worlds. A spectacular little hummingbird of brilliant colors had caught her eye.

The children had been playing this game and others together since they were very little. Sometimes they wandered back near the larger gardens and the small grove of fruit trees near the back wall of the property and pretended they were homeless children in the forest surviving heroically and cunningly. Other times they pretended to run away from the clutches of evil witches or a cruel queen that had kidnapped them. Summer was such a lovely time. It always flew by so quickly, as childhood often does.

The Tinker gardens were magnificent. In summer, the flowers were abundant in every shape, size, and color imaginable. The one she found now was in an inner courtyard of the house that gave way to a carriage entrance. Beyond the inner courtyard garden were several outbuildings and a couple of small cottages with a stone path that meandered through them, eventually leading to the larger gardens and orchards.

The beautiful hummingbird that distracted her so much was flitting in and out of a crimson red bellflower. He was sampling sweet nectar and could never get his fill of it, going back for more until the triumphant yell of John scared him away.

"Hah! I caught you, Alice! Now you're mine!" he said and hugged her tightly before letting go with a grin.

Rhody and the younger girls heard John's jubilant voice from their hiding places and stood on the edge of the garden watching the scene.

"Oh, of course! The game! Silly me. I guess I have to be the one to find you now," smiled Alice awkwardly.

Just then Mrs. Tinker ran outside and shouted.

"Enough of this revelry, children! John and Alice, you are too old to play such a foolish game!"

Rhody then appeared.

"As are you, Rhody!" she continued.

"Leave these pastimes to the younger children. Come along and make yourselves useful. There is plenty of work at hand. Alice, go and help your mother in the kitchen, and John, I have other work for you. You must be the man of the house while brother Robert is away. Mummy needs you more than ever now that father is so ill".

Mrs. Tinker knew that her husband would never get better. He had been bedridden for several months and was deteriorating even more with time. She came to rely heavily on John and was protective of his time when he was not in school. In that moment, she had little recognition of the magnitude the course of events would have over her family's lives during the following year. The consequent repercussions of those events made her even more reliant on John.

The patriarch of her great family, Robert Tinker, finally succumbed that summer. He left her and the children well off and was generous in his will, but nothing prepared her for what came next just a few months later. Robert, her oldest son and her husband's namesake, died in the winter of the following year from a serious wound at seventeen years old.

At twelve years of age, John Tinker was the only remaining single male in the immediate Tinker family. Randall, his stepbrother, was largely estranged from them. He was on distant terms with Mrs. Tinker and was not very reliable. His stepbrother, Thomas, was also married and was busy with his young wife, Anne, and his new family.

Mrs. Tinker grew to rely solely on John. He was always viewed as her favorite but became even more cherished with time. She instilled in him obligations to care for his family. He undoubtedly knew at a very young age that it was necessary to achieve a certain level of success so that his family could continue to prosper. His whole family, especially his mother, was counting on him.

Mrs. Tinker sent him to one of the most prestigious boarding schools in England and made sure he had as many opportunities as possible to meet influential people to mentor and guide him on his journey to success. Alice and his sisters saw relatively little of him after the burials. Occasionally, he came home for school breaks but was largely busy training to ascend into the world of commerce and trade as his father had done before him. Mrs. Tinker observed his fastidiousness with a nod of approval as the head of her household. Alice missed her cousin horribly, but life continued.

Life soon changed abruptly for Alice as well. Walking on the flat stones beyond the inner gardens to the little thatched cottage at a hedged border, Alice recalled the last time she ever heard her mother's gentle voice or felt the squeeze of her hand by the light of a flickering candle.

She started to sob when she remembered the circumstances surrounding her mother's passing. A few months after Robert

Senior's and Junior's deaths, Alsie was on her way to the market to pick up a few items for the evening's dinner. It was a very foggy morning as she made her way along the curving medieval passages to the main market square of New Windsor, England. The fog was so unyielding that the driver of a cart with a spooked horse could not see her, and as a consequence, Alsie was fatally struck down.

Some compassionate men of the village dutifully carried Alsie back to her cottage on the Tinker estate. Alice was shocked and dismayed to see her mother bloodied and suffering, and would have done anything to help her. She ran to her.

"Mother! Mother! I'm sorry, Mother! I should have come with you to market!" cried Alice, reaching for her.

Mrs. Tinker gently commanded Alice to retreat to the other end of the room while she and her older girls carefully removed Alsie's blood-soaked clothes and bandaged her as lovingly as they could with herbal poultices of comfrey and adder's tongue applied to her injuries. But Alsie became weaker with each passing hour. She motioned for little Alice to come closer to her. Alice was sullen and scared but determined not to leave her mother's side. After several hours, Alice knew her mother was slipping away from her and the time was precious.

"Come, daughters. Let cousin be alone for a time with her own dear daughter." Mary Tinker spoke with tears in the corners of her eyes.

"Little Alice, stay close to your mother. It will bring her comfort," she added and patted her softly on the head, leaving the cottage for a while.

Alsie reached out her hand toward her vulnerable little girl who was about to become an orphan. Every word she spoke had to matter for she only had a few good breaths left to impart her wisdom. With the gentleness, warmth, and familiarity that only a mother can convey, she grasped Alice's small hand in her own and began to speak her last words to her.

"Sweet Alice. Know that I love you dearly and will always be with you in spirit. Try to remember that you are never really alone. Above all, do not fear. Fear is the guise of evil that separates people. It makes people forget who they are and misunderstand who others are. Act always in love and be kind and generous with your gifts. Never forget you are my strong, smart girl whom I will always be proud of," she finished.

As she spoke these last words, the sounds started to become faded. Her breathing slowed down, and all she could do was nod with a faint smile and hold Alice's small hands as tightly as she was able. Alice was overwhelmed with the impending loss of her mother and kissed her work-worn hands. She remembered that these were the hands that stroked her hair, cradled her, and applied healing medicines with great care and tenderness during her childhood illnesses. These leathery hands had nurtured her and the entire Tinker family with the love they infused into her cooking and her gardening.

Alice recalled the horrible agony she felt watching her mother Alsie suffer severely through part of the night. Alsie often moaned in pain, pleading for relief. Alice dutifully sat at her mother's side and gave her sips of water with a spoon. She stroked her hair lightly and caressed her arms, but felt helpless that she could not do more. Mrs. Tinker continued to try to nurse Alsie back to health, and a local doctor was called to help, but her internal injuries were too extensive and too serious. Sadly, young Alice became an orphan at the age of ten.

Alice often blamed herself for the incident. She struggled with the thought that if only she had gone to market with her mother when she asked for company, instead of insisting on continuing her games with some of the Tinker children, Alsie might still be alive. But unfortunately, when she asked to stay and play, Alsie indulged her and even promised to buy her a favorite treat, a hot cross bun, at the market.

The guilt would stay with Alice most of her life. She tormented herself by thinking that perhaps she would have seen the calamity coming down the road at the last second and pulled her mother out of the way. And lastly, she lamented that if she only had remembered to recount to her mother the dream she had a few nights before and warned her not to go the way she was going, the tragedy could have been prevented.

Alice took over her mother's duties as well as she could, but she was grief-stricken and had a hard time focusing on them. The other children took pity on her and often helped her finish her chores. Mrs. Mary Tinker, the family matriarch, let her stay on out of duty. She had her own children to care for, but she was the only family young Alice had left. The older girls, Ellen and Mary, showed her great affection and took care of her well after her mother died. With time, Alice slowly regained her footing. She grew into a beautiful young woman with the clairvoyant talents that her mother had when she was alive.

Alice took one last look at the cozy thatched cottage and blew a final kiss toward her mother's spirit that she could feel lingering close by.

"I will always remember you, Mama, and your last words to me. I will be strong and generous because of your memory," she whispered under fleeting breath.

After several bouts of tears, Alice composed herself and inhaled the last lingering fragrance of the lilacs in the central flower garden. She felt more at peace now. They were Alsie's favorite flowers. As she sauntered back to the main house, she knew that the time was drawing closer to her departure to London. The sun had almost reached its zenith in the sky. Eventually, she found her way back to her packed belongings resting near the dining table in the hall.

As she sat deep in thought and looked at the places of the table where each person of the family had sat, she recalled the evolution of each family member.

Rhody, the most dramatic and striking of the sisters, always had a place at the table directly next to her father. She had demanded it. Rhody was really named Rhoda, but she preferred the nickname that her father called her since she was a very little girl. She and her daughters had been living with her mother again since her husband died. She noticed Alice's diminutive frame in the hall and went to join her. She put her elegant hand on Alice's shoulder.

"Alice, now you as well. Another one to the colonies!" she remarked.

Alice studied her beautifully etched face for a moment. Darker hair and eyes matched the intensity of her personality. Alice was often entertained, yet sometimes intimidated, by Rhody's fierce intellect. At times, they squabbled, but it was nothing more than occasional sibling rivalry. Overall, they loved each other immensely. Rhody continued, "I planned to stay in England after wedding Thomas Hobbs, you know. He helped to ground me and secure me to my life for the first time. Yet now I feel like Mother after losing Father. Why did Thomas have to die and leave me with two young daughters to care for without him?" She released her arm from Alice's shoulder and directly faced her.

"My lawyer husband has left me with enough financial means to survive for a time, but I feel increasingly unsteady in his absence. I suppose I will follow the rest of you to the colonies very soon," she confided.

"You and your mother have had a difficult couple of trying years," soothed Alice, always so compassionate to the sorrows of others.

A few years after her husband's death, Mrs. Tinker allowed herself to marry again to a man named Humphrey Collins from a nearby church parish. Both mother and daughter Rhody became widows within the span of a few short years. Mrs. Tinker was now known as Mrs. Collins, but to Alice and others that knew her for many years, she would always remain "Mrs. Tinker".

Alice looked at the empty chair of the oldest remaining and gentlest Tinker sister, Ellen.

"Do you remember what started it all?" recalled Alice.

Ellen had married a man named William Hulburd who, like her father, was a wool merchant. He came from Reading, England just slightly upriver on the Thames.

"You mean the full-scale exodus of most of our family to New England? Of course! William with all his stories! He enticed the others with tales of prosperity and a simple and more authentic life with the religious reformists," remembered Rhody clearly.

"Poor sweet Ellen. She worried so much those initial years that William went to the colonies alone, attempting to spare her the initial hardships of early settlement. By the time he came back to retrieve her, Mary and Anne were already married. Their husbands became captivated by his enthusiasm and promises of vast economic opportunities that awaited them. We had no chance of keeping any of them here," sighed Alice, who would have preferred that they all stayed together forever.

"Yes. William's enthusiasm for the New World venture was contagious," responded Rhody.

Alice thought of cousin Mary. Mary, more than any other sister, had been completely accepting and supportive of her. She married Mathias Sension, an easy-going and personable man from Silver Street in London.

"Rhody, do you remember when we went to visit Mary and Mathias at their first home in St Nicolas Cole Abby in London?" asked Alice.

"I do indeed," recalled Rhody wistfully. "It was a wonderful day. One of the last days that you, my other sisters, and I were able to spend together. It brought Mother such joy to visit Mary with all her girls along. It was shortly after that when Anne met her husband, Thomas Thornton, from Staines."

She continued, "Imagine Mother's surprise when our quiet and introspective younger sister met such a serious man eight years her senior," she recollected.

It was Thomas Thornton, who was mesmerized the most by William Hulburd's tales of the New World at his return to England and the dissenting view of church teachings. He and Anne left England together with the Sensions, following the Hulburds that same year.

Suddenly, the swift sound of horses' hooves with cart approached the carriageway.

Rhody looked up at Alice.

"It's really time," she said tearfully and hugged her.

Rhody quickly left the hall to find her daughters whom she wanted to say goodbye to her cousin.

"Alice! Alice! Are you ready?" shouted Mrs. Tinker from a second-floor chamber.

"I see Mr. Keayne. Hurry now! We must not keep him waiting!" she added as she rushed down the stairs.

Sarah, the youngest Tinker child, ran to give Alice a last embrace.

"Fare three well, dearest cousin. I will miss you. May we find each other again in the Bay."

Even fifteen-year-old Sarah was enticed to the New World. She was betrothed to a man named Thomas King and was about to leave for the colonies that summer as well.

Soon Rhody appeared again with her two young daughters in the entryway and held a small, red velvet cloth bag. "I almost forgot, Alice. Here is a gift for you."

"Thank you kindly," smiled Alice as she started to open it.

"No. Please, Alice. Don't open it here. Wait until you are most homesick," Rhody implored.

"May God protect and hold you, Alice. Do not forget your family," she admonished and hugged her tightly, whispering something into her ear.

"Rhody, I have a strong feeling we will see each other again," said Alice, tearing up once again and hiding the little velvet bag within her personal belongings. Then she lovingly hugged her two small daughters, Anne and Hannah.

Mrs. Tinker rushed to the door to greet Mr. Keayne. His servant helped Alice with her small trunk. She gave one last wistful glance at the Tinker home and blew a final kiss to the remaining sisters at the threshold. The family was soon to be more separated physically than they had ever been. Alice was heartbroken.

Chapter 3

LONDON, ENGLAND, 1635

Robert Keayne was a merchant tailor living in London whose father had been a butcher. Having grown up in New Windsor in Berkshire County, he had known the Tinkers his entire life. He was the same age as Randall and had apprenticed with Mr. Tinker in his youth. Becoming particularly close to Mrs. Tinker, he visited her often to check on her after Mr. Tinker died. The Tinkers, a merchant family, had fueled Robert's own ambitions to become a merchant himself. In recent years, he became interested in the dissenting religious movement. It was through this movement that he met John Winthrop, one of the original founders of the Massachusetts Bay Company in London. Robert Keayne had his own plans to immigrate to New England. It was for this reason that he met William Holman.

As Robert Keayne's carriage pulled into the Dragon's Inn in the Cheapside District of London on a foggy spring day, Mrs. Tinker looked visibly relieved. But Alice looked dazed. She had lost her bearings by having to say goodbye to the only home she had ever known.

"Here we are, Alice," she said.

"Yes, my dear, we have arrived at your destination," confirmed Robert Keayne in a deep and authoritative voice.

"Come now, let us meet the Holman family."

Alice nodded with apprehension and gave him her hand to help her out of the carriage. As she looked tentatively around her, she could see that the inn was bustling with activity. Mr. Keayne's servant dutifully unloaded her belongings.

William Holman had run downstairs from their second-floor rooms upon noticing the carriage. He was lean with fair skin and walked up to the carriage with a steady gait. He was handsome, yet his expression was serious, making him less attractive than he really was.

He bowed to Mr. Keayne and Mrs. Tinker, now wearing her finest clothing of doublewide laces and a finely stitched collar. He nodded at Alice, who was fitted with a simple light-blue woolen dress that was made specifically to adhere to her new employer's godly dress standards. Alice shyly curtsied to him.

Mr. Keayne gave the initial introduction.

"This is Goodman William Holman, a farmer of comfortable means from Northamptonshire. He just recently sold everything there and moved to London with his family to make arrangements for a ship to the Massachusetts Bay Colony. He and his family will be joining me and other families on our journey to New England. We met in godly circles."

He turned to the ladies.

"Goodman Holman, I am delighted to introduce you to Mrs. Tinker, a long-time family friend, and her distant cousin, Alice, who will now be serving you."

Alice studied his face carefully for any clue as to what she might expect in her new situation.

"Mrs. Tinker, thank you for helping us find Alice. She is greatly needed here. Alice, I am pleased to meet you. My wife will certainly be comforted to see you." His voice was low and soft, which conveyed a basic kindness under his solemn exterior. He gestured to all of them.

"Please come up to our apartments, and I will introduce all of you to my wife, Winifred. It has been so difficult for her here in

London without the aid of her mother and sister to help her with our five small children."

Mrs. Tinker spoke directly to Alice, "Oh, Alice. This is a family in great need. It will be rewarding for you to give your help to them."

Alice couldn't think. She found it impossible to see herself as being a part of another family even in the role of their servant. But Alice tried to steady herself and remain calm, attempting to give her new employers a chance.

Once in the apartment, Winifred greeted them warmly.

"It is so lovely to meet all of you! I am so grateful you are here, Alice. My children range from eight to the babe sleeping in the cradle. They are well-behaved children. Even so, it has been so difficult to care for them without the usual comforts of home," she explained.

Winifred was the opposite of her husband. They balanced each other perfectly. She was gregarious and warm, often smiling at her visitors and her new servant. She was thirty-five but looked much younger. She seemed to epitomize grace, despite the many stressors that engulfed her. Alice couldn't help but feel a little better in her presence even though she was already homesick for Berkshire.

"I could not imagine how I would care for all five children with the upcoming Atlantic crossing and beyond that in the Bay, in a fairly uncivilized settlement. That is until my dear husband told me the wonderful news that he had found a girl to help us. Why, it's been hard enough trying to make all the preparations for the trip as well as take care of everything else," she said, smiling at Alice.

Alice felt her heart opening towards Winifred. The empathy that she felt for this young woman with five young children adventuring to foreign lands allowed Alice to let down her guard and connect with her.

"What is it that is leading you to New England?" Mrs. Tinker asked both Winifred and her husband, William Holman, curious to see if they were the same reasons that half her children had used before also leaving for the colonies.

William Holman answered her, "I want to try my hand at cultivating the rich soils of the New World. Everyone says land and opportunities are plentiful there. And, like other godly men, I want the liberty to practice my beliefs in a way that will not be admonished by the King and his bishops."

Mrs. Tinker nodded. She understood.

They spoke together for a little while longer until Mrs. Tinker was certain that she could walk away from Alice guilt-free, knowing that she had left her with a nice family and a suitable calling as their nanny and servant. She found Winifred to be charming and William to be honorable. And she knew Robert Keayne would also be nearby. She thought Alice would be fine.

Mrs. Tinker rose from her chair satisfied that she had done the right thing.

"This is good-bye now, Alice. Fare thee well, dear cousin. May a new life of satisfaction and purpose find you in the Bay. Only God knows if we shall ever meet again. May He keep you well."

She gave Alice a perfunctory embrace. In contrast, Alice held on to her tightly. She was the last of the family she had ever known, and now Mrs. Tinker was leaving her to find her own way in the world. Alice could not stop the flow of tears and only managed to say, "And you as well, ma'am. Fare thee well and send my love to your son and daughters, my near-siblings, when you see them again. Thank you for allowing me to grow up with your family. I love them so."

And just like that, it was over, the only life she had previously known. Mrs. Tinker and Robert Keayne disappeared into the carriage and then out of sight into the London streets. Alice was quite emotional and torn. She wished she knew what lay ahead. But her gift of sight was for her to share with others only. She was never able to see her own future as clearly as she could often see the impending events in the lives of others.

Initially, the days were dreary and routine with the Holmans. Alice scarcely left the inn. She was so engrossed and obligated with the care of the children that she had little time for anything else. Her heart longed for its old connections, but there was nothing she could do except hope that the New World also meant second chances.

At least Winifred was there and comprehended her predicament with great compassion. She eased Alice into her routine with understanding.

Winifred was appreciative to have the extra help and took advantage of it to meander the markets of London and find precious treasures needed for the voyage. William was relieved that burdens were a bit alleviated for his wife so he could focus on the serious task of organizing their passage and new start in the Bay.

Spring turned into summer, and soon they would be embarking on a great ship, the *Defence* that was amassing passengers and supplies to take to New England from London. It was arranged that the Holmans, their children and their new maidservant, Alice Ashbey, were soon to be listed on its manifest. Robert Keayne and his family were also to sail on this ship.

The task of preparation for the three-month long journey across the Atlantic was arduous. Attention to detail had to be absolute. Requisitions for supplies and food stocks needed to be precise and carefully calculated. The travelers knew that life was very undeveloped in the colonies, and people frequently died from cold exposure, disease, and lack of food. They understood the importance of compiling a complete list of provisions that were needed for the voyage to the colonies and the first months of starting anew. Previous immigrants underscored that some resources were available there, but most items needed to be transported over.

William Holman explained the plan for resettlement to his wife as Alice listened closely.

"We plan to leave England as soon as enough passengers are enlisted and sufficient supplies are procured to fill the ship. It is set to cast off in June or July. That way we can take advantage of the fair ocean breezes normally plentiful that time of year. We intend to arrive with the mild early-fall weather."

Winifred nodded but, in thinking of the children, posed some questions about basic needs.

"What will we do for shelter at such a late time of year? How long will the weather be fair? Will there be housing enough for everybody?"

"Do not worry, my dear. The climate should still be temperate when we arrive, allowing us time enough to build our first rudimentary homes before the harsh New England winter sets in," William Holman assured them.

"How will we ensure there are food and drink enough to last us through the first winter and spring? We must prepare to ensure our children do not go hungry," she emphasized.

"Of course, Winifred. The ship will be well supplied with food enough to last through the winter, and by spring we should be able to settle on fertile land to start our farm."

His wife brought forth another concern, "And what of the Indians, dear husband? How do we ensure our protection living amongst them?" Winifred asked.

Alice listened to the conversation intently. The few returning travelers they encountered at the inn caused them to fear for their safety with tales of a wild land inhabited by people who were savage and dark.

"Our armaments for defense are in place should they be needed," he consoled them again.

"Although it is hard to imagine or know if Indian tribes will want to harm us or help us, I have also heard that there are some who are obliging to the English. Perhaps they will even support us in finding fish and game," he added.

"God be with us so that we should have temperate weather and the absence of pestilence or hostilities from Indians. May He guide us to find food and water when it is most needed," Winifred implored.

William Holman and Alice nodded in agreement.

Most of their questions remained unanswered, and they understood that leaving life in England to tame the unfamiliar lands of the colonies had its share of risks. Theirs was certainly not a venture for the faint of heart.

The plan did not sound like a sure strategy to Winifred, but she placed faith in her husband and quelled any remaining worries with her own preparations for the trip. Alice also felt uncertain but was determined to help Winifred make the best of the situation. She worked diligently to that end. After all, surviving life in the colonies was the only chance that she had to join her beloved cousins again.

Winifred had already amassed a collection of seeds from her favorite cooking and healing herbs as well as from her favorite vegetables: carrots, parsnips, cabbages, radishes, and onions. She wisely gathered their seeds from the kitchen garden that she left behind in Northamptonshire. These were the seeds that she would transport with her to start new gardens in the Bay. She was quite well versed in how to use herbs and had many old family recipes that she brought with her from her stilling room. Her skills were greatly needed in a land almost devoid of doctors.

William Holman took care of organizing the basic farming and culinary tools and utensils that were essential in their endeavor. He also arranged for the transport of a few valuable head of livestock.

As the time approached, William Holman and the other men from the emigrating Puritan families gathered food and other essential supplies in a warehouse near the port. They loaded the stored barrels of salted beef and pork, dried peas and oats, bread, biscuits, cheese, butter, ground flour, salted cod, and dried herrings for some days prior to boarding the ship. For drink, there was a supply of beer, weak ale, cider, and stronger waters of gin and brandy. They were confident that they had prepared for their journey to the best of their abilities. By mid-July 1635, the ship was fully supplied, and all the families who planned for the journey were ready to depart.

The day they left London was sunny and bright. It was full of promise for a new life. The carriage from the Dragon's Inn that dropped them off at the waterfront quickly disappeared from view as William Holman helped his family and his maidservant descend the stone steps leading to the Thames River. At the bottom of the steps, a water taxi, a wherry, was moored and waiting for them. It was only one of the thousands of wherries, barges, and tilt boats on the Thames that brought Londoners to their destinations in the great city. Their belongings had already been sent ahead and were waiting for them on the great ship.

Their destination in the main port area was farther downriver between London Bridge and the Tower of London at a series of quays. They timed the journey to the port perfectly, when the tides were high and passage under the London Bridge was most accommodating.

As they traveled the Thames River to the port, Alice marveled at the vast display of thousands of timber-framed homes, shops lining the waterway, and the many steps that went down to the river. Some of the homes she observed were stunningly grand, such as those built four- or five-stories high, with clear glazed-glass windows, and were gilded of gold or painted in bright colors. Others were more humble, being small with thatched roofs and shutters but no glass. Steeples from the churches of the different parishes were seen, and small gardens, dunghills, and orchards were interspersed with homes and markets.

Soon they approached London Bridge and all its magnificence. It was lined with houses and shops of immense proportions, including the brightly painted Nonesuch House over the largest passageway. The bridge spanned twenty arches and was built on huge pillars of stone shaped like boats. It was of an enormous expanse and dominated the London scene.

But, for all of its splendor, there was one sight on London Bridge that made Alice tremble. At the Great Stone Gate, several heads of traitors were on brazen display for the benefit of citizens to view and, consequently, note the mortal demise of those who went against royal authority. Some were fresh and rotting to decay, and some were dipped in tar for preservation. But most were just hollowed out skulls whose contents birds had scavenged long ago. Their souls seemed to be hovering around them and eerily calling out to her. It left her cold and wary. She hoped it was not a gruesome sign of things to come.

Just beyond London Bridge, the travelers arrived at the bustling port. The children were now extremely excited and pointed at the towering and magnificent tall ships. They were much higher than anything else around them, with big bright sails to show the way. They were seen coming in from the horizon for miles away.

There were great cranes in place that helped to transport cargo in and out of ships and big, burly, unkempt men to operate them. Over twenty wharves and quays with big ships were stocked with goods of different sorts such as tin, lead, wool, wine, or livestock. All of these sights gave the travelers no doubt that

London was one of the finest, most cosmopolitan and populous cities anywhere.

William Holman, with his family and Alice, disembarked from the wherry.

"Hold on to each other tightly, and especially the children," he commanded over the din of the crowd on and near the wharves.

He cautiously led them through the maze of buildings of the general landing place, lined with many brick or timber shops sided with wattle and daub. Wooden signs hung over various establishments with pictures of barrels, bottles, dragons, unicorns, cauldrons, fish, and other images that advertised the purpose of each enterprise. Alice and the Holmans meandered through the maze of shops belonging to glovers, tailors, fishmongers, apothecaries, butchers, wine merchants, and others.

Alice noted that the most popular among establishments seemed to be the many alehouses and taverns. Many travelers stopped at them to partake of their last real meal of fresh meat, bread, herbs, pies, and fine spirits before boarding their ships to diverse destinations. William Holman had provided his family with their last fresh dinner at the inn, preferring not to mix his children or his wife with some of the rougher sorts of people at the taverns.

Indeed, all kinds of people had come together in this lively place: sailors, merchants, harlots, jugglers, old women with baskets of herbs or baked goods, bewildered travelers, and soldiers. They moved about with an air of either excitement or fear of things to come. Many street people were hawking their wares, adding to the clamor and clatter of the port.

"Meat pasties for your travels!"

"Hot cross buns! Delicious hot cross buns for sale!"

Alice, Winifred, and William Holman continued to weave their way through the stalls of vendors, gripping the children with their firmest grasps. As the morning wore on, the wharves became so packed full of people as travelers arrived that it was challenging to find one's way to the end of the quay. They used the tall masts of the ships as their guide through the labyrinth of laden drinking cups, iron kettles, brassware, sweet meat and savory pies, dried figs, herbs, breads, biscuits, shawls, shoes, and other goods. They inhaled aromas of roasted meats and sweet fruit pies that filled the air. They could not help but hear the tunes, both bawdy and irreverent, that street musicians played for the merry crowds.

After having successfully navigated through the crowds with great care, they met their parties at Galley Quay. In all, there were a little over a hundred people boarding the *Defence*. Their fellow travelers were easy to find along the dock. In contrast to so many of the people at the quay sporting flamboyant and festive fashions, the Holmans and other godly men, women, and children were in drab, dull and simple clothing of sad colors and looked much more austere than other characters at the port. Many had Bibles in hand.

"Ah look, there is Mr. Keayne." William Holman approached him with a greeting.

"Good day, Mr. Keayne and Mrs. Keayne. It is so nice to see you and your family again. I see we have all managed to find each other despite the suffocating throngs of people everywhere."

"Aye. God has given us a fine day to start our journey. It's an auspicious sign from the Divine. Good day to you as well, Goodwife Holman," replied Mr. Keayne.

"You remember our maidservant, Alice, I should think," spoke Winifred.

"Why of course," responded Mr. Keayne.

"The young cousin of the Tinker family. Are you adapting quite well to life with the Holmans? It was just last week that I ran into your cousin, John. He is doing quite well in his studies and recently returned from the Continent. I believe he hopes to take his mother to the colonies in the next year or two."

Alice nodded in deference and blushed. She was polite and shy in these situations.

"I hope that we will all meet again in New England," she said, longingly thinking of her family.

"Don't you worry. You're bound to cross paths again someday," Mr. Keayne said to reassure her, not really knowing if fate would be that kind.

Others from the group arrived and greeted each other heartily, relieved to have found the proper point of departure. They crowded together as a respite from the chaos they saw all around them. There they met the ship's captain, Master Edward Bostocke. He called each of them by name or head of household to come and board the ship. Sailors quickly grabbed any of their excess belongings that were not already on deck.

"Mind your daughters well," remarked some of the fathers, holding their girls close after noticing some of the sailors staring lewdly at them. Other sailors seemed like they were mocking the families. The rough and irreverent sailors would soon be forced into close quarters with the pious. It would be a long journey, with a whole host of different personalities to contend with.

By noon, everyone had boarded, and the ship started to set sail with the tide, going out on waters flowing toward the channel. As the last call for departure sounded, the passengers gathered on deck to say a final prayer in England. On bended knees, a young preacher said the following prayer, "We beseech thee Lord to protect us on this journey if it is Thy will."

They continued to kneel with heads bowed.

"We offer ourselves up to Thee as Christian servants in a new land. It is our solemn vow that we will uphold and spread the truths of the Bible to the pagans and heathens there who have not had the benefit of Thy holy words."

The prayers continued until the great ship started to float down the Thames.

As they left the quay, the sounds of the street vendors and musicians became more muffled. Instead of looking forward, Alice looked back, back towards London Bridge and the ghastly, decapitated heads on iron spikes.

She could not forget that image. She wondered who those poor souls had been. The tales told to her about them were ones of cruelty: tales of merciless acts done to traitors of the English state, traitors to King Charles. She questioned if they all really deserved to die. Taking one last glance at the bridge, she shuddered and then resolved to look forward. She reasoned that it was better to focus her mind on the journey ahead. She had five small children to help care for.

Chapter 4

LONDON, ENGLAND, AND THE ATLANTIC OCEAN, 1635

With the first movement of their ship down the Thames and out of London in favorable tides, the passengers of the *Defence* were giddy with excitement. However, it was not clear until the initial sightings of the ocean that the dream of a new life in New England started to turn into reality. It was their faith and hope in a better future that guided them to cross a vast ocean in a journey that would take almost three months.

The best days of the passage to New England were the first and the last days of the voyage. Alice hoped settlement would work out in the colonies because she had no intention of ever boarding a ship again unless it was forced upon her. But that first day was sunny and filled with anticipation and excitement. She enjoyed watching people from the deck before departure.

Alice still had her sea legs as they slowly floated down the Thames and into the Channel before hitting the Atlantic. She held firmly onto the children in her keep as they passed by many villages and beautiful pastoral countrysides with tempered fields of many shades of green. The Holman children waved as they drifted by farmers tending their fields. They pointed in awe at gracefully gliding swans, so plentiful along the ancient waterway.

Their merriment was contagious and gave even the sternest among the godly a reason to grin. Alice was uplifted by their childhood joy. Gentle ocean breezes also raised their spirits. But the revelry in majestic scenery and new experiences did not last very long.

"All passengers below deck!" shouted the captain abruptly.

"Quickly, all passengers below deck. To your cabins now!" he reiterated.

Swarms of sailors climbed the masts and took hold of the rigging. They hoisted and unfurled the remaining sails. The swarthy sailors rapidly focused on the task at hand, getting the ship through the Channel, out to the ocean, and on the right course.

Passengers had to be out of the way or a boom or some other massive part of sailing apparatus could strike them down. They filed in unison to find their accommodations below deck.

One look at their puny-sized cabin and Winifred stated, "I suppose we shall get to know each other very well. Pray we have the patience and the fortitude to endure," she despaired.

Her words reflected the unvoiced sentiments of her new maidservant.

The cabins were tiny allotted spaces that barely allowed any room for movement. Alice inhaled deeply and gingerly entered their temporary dwelling space. By the captain's orders, they were obliged to spend most of their time below deck in the dark, lit by candles and fireboxes in this tiny space. At least it was better than being knocked overboard by moving rigging or falling into dark ocean waters during a deadly storm with high seas.

Once her boisterous charges were herded and confined to their cabin, Alice was not sure how she and Winifred would manage all five young children. They were already restless and irritable in the constricted space. Out of necessity, they learned to entertain them with stories and song. Winifred brought their family Bible. She opened it much of the time and used it not only for religious teachings but also for aiding the older children to practice reading.

One night, when the seas were howling and spraying their curses, with land still many leagues away, Alice became so ill and so homesick that she could barely go on. Then she remembered the beautiful red velvet pouch given to her by Rhody. Alice pulled out the little bag and, with great anticipation, loosened its silk strings.

Inside, she found an intricate and beautiful strand of broad bobbin lace. In addition to this, there was a lovely length of white silk ribbon woven with tiny silver threads.

The beautiful and thoughtful gift immediately pulled Alice out of her hopelessness. She was so elated that she had to show Winifred.

"Alice, the lace is lovely, as is the silk ribbon woven with a silver thread. A gift from your cousin?" she queried.

"Yes, ma'am, fine Flemish lace from Bruges," she beamed.

"I shall fasten some of it to my garments ever so modestly and save the rest."

"It will be a pleasant way to remember your dear cousin," Winifred acknowledged her.

From that night forth, after the children were soundly sleeping, Alice worked on stitching and fastening some of the fine ribbon and lace to her clothing with devotion. She worked carefully and happily while Winifred did her own embroidery and sewing. The more time they spent with each other, the more apparent it became that they were kindred spirits.

As they sat together for long hours in the cabin, Winifred told her stories about her early life in Northamptonshire. Winifred's mother had taught her skills to heal people with her hands. She was also gifted at employing herbal medicine for just about any illness or imbalance. Her talents helped her patients to be cured as well or better than any practicing male doctor. Even though some skills were taught, they also came naturally to Winifred. People almost always seemed to improve in her competent care. Alice thought of her mother. She would have been pleased that her daughter was now under Winifred's wise tutelage.

During the journey to the New World, Winifred often used her techniques to help her own children and some of her fellow passengers on the ship. She assisted many victims of rough seas and upset stomachs with doses of powdered cinnamon and candied ginger.

Unfortunately, most conditions on the ship were not treated as easily. Putrid aromas of vomit and diarrhea from dysentery created an ever-present stench in their living quarters of almost three months. The children held onto wooden buckets with all their might. Alice's most dreaded task was to empty the slop buckets overboard for her family. At least it brought her to fresh air and away from the confinements of the Holman cabin.

For Alice and others, one day passed into another on the ship. It was difficult to keep track of the vessel's progress through the seas because each day looked like the previous ones. And every day was surrounded by ocean wave after identical ocean wave. A tempest with thunder and lightning could break up monotony, but usually the price was increasingly damp bedding and clothing that could never completely dry out.

Food was sparse and unappetizing. Alice was not in the mood to eat much. The rats and cockroaches on board were more than happy to take her share. Many passengers paid for this journey not just in sterling, but also in their vigor and the breath of life itself. The dearly departed who did not make it to new shores were sent to their ocean-floor graves for all eternity with nothing more than some simple prayers and forlorn shrieks from a loved one.

It was astounding to Alice that anyone would ever leave England at all. Yet, there she was amongst the rest of the passengers, often longing for the familiar and questioning herself more than once about the wisdom of leaving her homeland. Her one hope was that she would meet with the Tinkers again. At least she knew that her adopted sisters, their husbands, and children were already in the Massachusetts Bay. By God's grace, it would not be too far from the place where Winifred and William Holman were going to settle down.

William Holman spent his time making arrangements and finding out anything he could about living in the Bay from the other journeying men and sailors on the ship. Robert Keayne and his family had plans to stay in Boston. He was one of the original financiers of the colony, and the governor had made arrangements for him to settle in the main harbor town. It made sense for him to stay in Boston so he could continue to pursue his interests in commerce.

After much deliberation, William Holman decided that he would settle his family in Newtown, a village a few miles from Boston up the Charles River and on the opposite bank. Even though Boston was not much of a town, most people assumed it would grow as a port, and good farming land was already becoming scarce. Settling in Newtown ensured better farmland to choose from and bigger lots available for purchase. The plan gave them something to dream about during the many boring days at sea with nothing to do.

Finally, one early day in October at dawn, everyone on board ship heard the bell signaling the news that they had longed to hear since they left London.

"Land in sight. Land ahead! We've reached the colonies!" shouted a sailor.

Winifred and Alice looked at each other, grinning like excited young girls. They hugged each other first, and then they embraced each child.

"Land, land! They've spotted land!" Alice repeated in amazement.

"Yes, land!" reiterated Winifred excitedly.

"Praise be to God. We are here, children! We've reached our new home! Can you believe it, Alice! We are finally here! Land is actually in sight!" The children were jumping excitedly at the news and begging to see it.

"Our new home..." spoke Alice, not quite sure of what that meant.

William Holman was already on deck that morning, unable to sleep. As soon as he heard the clanging of the bell and surveyed the horizon for himself, he ran to his cabin to bring his family on deck. Normally a man of few words, he was unable to contain his excitement.

"Come now, family. Come up and see for yourselves! 'Tis land out there plain as the new day. Our long journey is almost over!"

Immediately, prayer was called. The small mass of devoted religious dissenters kneeled on deck and prayed in thanksgiving for having reached the distant Atlantic shore, as snickering sailors looked on. Alice's prayer was for the familiar, for family. Seeing her family again was the hope that she continually clung to.

It took a full day and then part of another before the ship was close to land. Patience was running thin. Everyone was cross and fatigued after being crammed into such a confined space for nearly two and one-half months. They were hungry and malnourished. Reddened gums, loosened teeth, and skin covered with tiny red spots, sure signs of scurvy, visited many of the ship's passengers toward the end of their journey.

Everyone tired of the unpleasantness of the ship's captain and his crew. On the third day, the ship was only a few hours from the port of Boston. It hugged the coastline for several hours. Everyone was allowed on deck again so they could study the land for themselves. They saw no one ashore except for several workers on scattered farms along the way. Empty and desolate of humans, there was nothing but towering trees. Eventually, the fledgling port of Boston appeared.

In just two and one-half months' time, the *Defence* had reached another port on the opposite shore of the Atlantic Ocean, the one in Boston Harbor. The novice travelers quickly discovered what a stark contrast it was to the lively London scene they had left behind at their departure. The day they arrived in the colonies, it seemed sparse and wild and, at the least, disorienting.

Boston was even less than Alice had expected. There was one other ship in the port at the time of their arrival. The day was blustery, and a cool chill was in the air. An inn and a few small shops came into view from the dock. A rough-hewn meetinghouse was in the common area. Several streets of scattered modest homes with thatched roofs stood beyond the small port, and more continued along a muddy pathway leading up a great hill. From there, they could see a larger home, the governor's, at the summit along with a few other more stately dwellings. The place seemed forsaken compared to the bustling port of London. It was hard for Alice to imagine what was in store for her in this strange new world.

Soon the people of Boston heard that the ship was fast approaching. Her sails were coming closer and into crisper view. Several traders boarded shallops, smaller two-masted vessels and light boats that could be rowed in shallow waters. They raced each other, paddling furiously to meet the *Defence*, more than eager to discover her cargo. Each trader hoped to reach the ship first to haggle for desperately needed supplies from the motherland.

"What cheer, new friends! What Cheer? Welcome to the Bay and our humble port in the wilderness!" shouted the traders from their shallops.

Everyone clapped and laughed, greeting each other with great joy. The journey had finally come to a close, with a much bigger one on the horizon about to begin.

Alice folded her arms to keep warm from the chill in the air while she waited to board a shallop. She sincerely hoped to adjust to this new desolate home, at least long enough to find the outstretched arms of her cousins again.

Chapter 5

BOSTON HARBOR, MASSACHUSETTS BAY COLONY, 1635

The first day in Boston was hectic and exciting. Shallop owners paddled everyone to shore. The Holmans and Alice had to suppress their eagerness and wait their turns to touch solid earth again, as did other passengers. Carts carried personal items and supplies to the homes or inns where they would be residing. At the harbor, the Holmans said their farewells to the Keayne family, whose friends had come to greet them and help them settle into Boston.

For the Holmans, who had no connections in Boston, Cole's Ordinary served as their first stop. Near the waterfront, it provided accommodations and the first tastes of the New World. They recognized it by a hoop of barley near the door and a bench outside where regular customers sat. The inn was full of passengers in merry moods, relieved to have reached their destination. The proprietor, Samuel Cole, was gracious and full of cheer.

The Holmans and Alice stayed together in a small room with two small bedstands and another featherbed on the floor. It was cramped, but still an improvement from their quarters on the ship. Eventually, their few goods were placed with them at the inn, and their animals that survived the passage stayed at a stable just behind the main building.

Once landed ashore, Alice sincerely tried to be open and appreciative of new experiences. Consequently, she never forgot her first American meal in the New World. The initial dinner at the inn was simple but special. It was a unique occasion featuring an assortment of American foods. Everyone was seated at a long table on wooden benches in front of an enormous hearth with a roaring fire. The new immigrants bowed their heads and gave thanks for their safe deliverance to a foreign land.

They were about to participate in a completely different gastronomic experience. A delicious stew placed before them was made of corn, fish, and pumpkins. Bowls with ample amounts of hickory nuts and roasted chestnuts sat on either end of the table. The diners had their choice of a stout ale or cider to quench their thirsts. The cook made plenty of baked beans for all to share. For dessert, pies were filled with native berries.

A more traditional pork stew cooked with parsnips and carrots evoked one of the few comforts of home and of fond recollections that were becoming exceedingly distant. Alice had no idea at the time what a luxury it was to eat the English pork stew. Peas porridge would soon become the daily staple.

Alice observed with keen interest the group of many memorable characters who sat at the dinner table. Among them was a man named Goodman Morgan Humphrey. Apparently, he thought himself to be the resident expert on the colonies. He was coming back to New England for a third time in-between his sojourns to other places. He had spent time in Barbados as well as Virginia and had finally decided to settle permanently in Massachusetts. He was a theatrical sort of man and was eager to impart his wisdom with no shortage of dramatic flair to anyone who would listen. He longed to stir up raw emotion in all. He was glad to take center stage and dominate the dinner conversation.

"The first time I came to this place, Boston was nothing more than a muddy village. Now it's a muddy little town with all types of odd fellows from all over the place. When I first came here, people were dying continually for want of food and medicine. Each woman had to do work for four men, not just her husband, because there were so few womenfolk. I remember one family in particular. Aye, 'twas the Carter family from Essex. They came one fine autumn day such as this. By the springtime, the whole lot of them was dead. Even though the Indians helped us some, the harshness of winter was too much for most," he said and belched.

Continuing, he said, "Mind you, one must be prepared to make it in these parts, for danger lurks around every corner. Pestilence, hunger, loathing of the hard work, boredom, and missing the homeland will surely kill many more. You had best hope you are all among the lucky ones and you've the smarts to survive here."

Goodman Holman spoke next.

"Why surely a vast wilderness must take its toll on some poor souls, but I know that most of those who come now have already heard tales such as yours, and we are hardier and more prepared to endure by the sheer strength of our faith and the experience of those that came before us."

"Nay. Faith. Hah! 'Tis not enough, good man. You'd best be relying on the education you get from the savages. They know more than anybody what it takes to survive here. They've been doing it for hundreds, if not thousands, of years. Pride in this colony has damn near killed as many as the plague and the spotted pox altogether!" Goodman Humphrey responded.

Alice looked on wide-eyed, determined to absorb any useful pieces of survival information.

Another stranger at the table spoke, a Goodman Parker who had also recently come.

"We shall see about that! I don't take kindly to relying on savages for advice. Why surely we will do well. God is on our side because so many of those natives have already perished from the pestilences that you speak of. God has paved a path for us here. So many English have come and settled before us. It will surely be easier now."

"You had best remember that when you're cold and hungry and dying for want of good medicines," retorted Goodman Humphrey. He continued, "What you speak of is not as simple as you'd think. Much of the land in the more settled parts has already been taken. So if you want the lots that you desire and want them on good soils, you need to go farther away to the west. It's becoming more necessary to settle even further out into more remote and perilous wilderness. Unless of course, you are like me and content with a trade that needs a bigger population and just a small plot for tilling," he chuckled.

The conversation among the men continued well into the night with all kinds of questions posed and answered in regard to settlement, commodities, behavior of the Indians, and the state of the godly people in America. There were all sorts of personal stories of those that came to settle: some who thrived, some who could not endure and returned to England, and some who met their early graves. Winifred and Alice took their leave early to care for the children.

As soon as Alice recognized that the last child had fallen asleep, she looked at Winifred seriously and asked, "Will we survive in this strange new land, Mistress Winifred?"

"Now Alice, you must not even ask that question. Of course we will, my dear. You will just have to see how well. We will heed the flamboyant Goodman Humphrey's advice to some degree. We will both learn what we can about this foreign land, but don't forget we have our precious seeds from home and the knowledge of how to use the plants that grow from them. I have no doubt that they will help us a great deal! And, of course, we have what will help us the very most, Alice. The Creator will guide us and strengthen us. Certainly there will be tests, but I have no qualms about them and, in fact, total confidence that we will make our mark. My husband is a man of much resourcefulness. He would not have brought his family here to a vast new land unless his faith absolutely dictated it. You must stop worrying. Now, be a fine girl and help me with some mending," Winifred assured her.

Alice nodded and smiled, but deep down in her soul she was not as optimistic. She would have to keep her concerns to herself from now on and learn as much as she could from Winifred, settlers who were her predecessors, the land, and especially the natives when possible.

***

Alice enjoyed venturing out into the streets of Boston with the Holman family. The first days were startling for her, as they were for many other travelers new to the Bay. Despite its humble beginnings, she was impressed by how much had been done to make Boston livable in just a short amount of time. She also relished observing the adopted habits of their new homeland.

It was a frontier like no other Alice had imagined. It was here that they had their first encounters with the natives of the region, Indians from various tribes such as the Massachusett and Nipmuck. It was Alice's first contact with people who seemed so drastically different from everyone she had ever known.

As native people came into Boston to bring furs to traders that filled the returning ships, Alice looked on, mesmerized. Everything about them was dissimilar to her countrymen. They appeared to be so much stronger and healthier than the English. Bronzed Indian men wearing buckskins and moccasins for attire, with adornments of feathers and strings of wampum, seemed exotic to her. She could not help but find them beautiful.

"So these are the men that the ministers call heathens," she thought to herself.

She noticed some of their woman who came with them carrying baskets of unfamiliar roots and herbs that she did not recognize. The women were sitting near the harbor together with handmade items of clay pots, woven baskets, or wooden bowls, in hopes that settlers might be interested in buying them.

Alice gravitated toward them. She could not stop herself. She paused and exchanged glances with them. Other sights distracted the Holmans. The Massachusett tribal women motioned to Alice to experience and touch. Her hands caressed the woven baskets and picked up various roots. She smelled the different herbs and berries and stared into the faces of those who brought them. They were a mystery to her. Yet for some unknown reason, they felt hauntingly familiar. She longed to know the secrets these women held close to their hearts.

"Come, Alice. We must continue," spoke William Holman, pulling her out of her reverie. "We have much to do today."

Alice nodded and caught up with him and the rest of the family, continuing to observe her surroundings. Even the English in their attire were outwardly different in this strange place. Gone were the brilliant and bold colors of England. Instead, these were replaced by tamer, more toned-down, sad colors of dull greens, mustard, russet, tawny, browns, pale blues, and other subdued and modest natural hues. The only exceptions were the scarlets and purples reserved for the garments of the wealthy. They noted to each other that the men had chopped off locks and sported plainer garments, except for the ministry or wealthy magistrates that wore the finest of intricate clothing.

Alice longingly searched their faces, looking for any sign of a missed family member or old friend.

As they meandered the streets of Boston, Goodman Holman stressed his eagerness to stock up on supplies in the days before they left for Newtown. Boston, being one of the only harbor towns along with Salem, had more commodities than most of the other frontier settlements. He helped his family take advantage of the opportunity by leading them into a trading establishment owned by Goodman Hall near the harbor.

"Come, family," he gestured to them. "This may be one of our last opportunities to increase our supplies before the harsh New England winter sets in."

"Some of these goods were probably just taken off our ship," remarked Winifred. She glanced at the shelves momentarily before exclaiming, "But look at the prices!"

Goodman Hall must have overheard their conversation and introduced himself. He felt the need to clarify the reasons for the drastic markups for the glass, ceramics, linens, iron and tools that had just come in from England.

"Indeed, the prices are higher, but we have scant supplies. Even though we trade for fish, furs and lumber with both England and the West Indies, the goods are still scarce. There is not much I can do to change that," he said and went on to explain the situation further.

"You'll also notice we have some tobacco, sugar, and rum, the likes of which you'd never find in England at such good prices. They arrive from our sister colony in Barbados. Mind you, I am also willing to trade for the right exchange. I have more American items in the shop bartered by ordinary farmers. Cheese, milk, greens, and root vegetables are all here as well," he added.

"I see," noted William Holman, observing his shelves.

"I can tell you are new to these parts. Where do you plan to settle?" he asked.

"We are shortly on our way to Newtown, but we want to enhance our stores before we go."

As they were talking, a minister entered the shop of provisions. He had a stern look plastered on his middle-aged face and an air of importance. He was dressed completely in a fine black doublet and breeches. Only the ruling wealthy and the religious elite were permitted to wear black. It was considered too bold for an ordinary person to wear. His clerical collar was enhanced with the most delicate of lace of a very fine quality.

Alice felt uneasy. She looked away and tried to ignore him. He seemed to be honing in on the little group speaking with the shopkeeper and listening in on their conversation.

Suddenly he spoke, "So you'll be going to Newtown. Have I heard correctly?" he questioned Goodman Holman.

"Yes sir. That is our final destination," answered William Holman as the others looked on.

The stranger introduced himself, "I'm Reverend Nathaniel Ward. I lead the congregation in Ipswich, but I am well acquainted with Reverend Stone and Reverend Hooker, who lead the congregation in Newtown. Then he turned and glared at Alice, speaking again.

"May I assume this is your daughter, sir?" he interrogated, continuing his series of questions.

By this time, Alice was feeling more than uneasy. She was downright nervous and knew that something was amiss.

"She is our maidservant, sir. She came with us to help take care of our children," William Holman further explained defensively.

"Shameful! What can be the meaning of this!" the pastor admonished with a condescending scowl.

They looked at him blankly, not understanding.

"Dress such as this deserves nothing less than several lashes at the whipping post! She is in blatant noncompliance with our sumptuary laws! Such frivolous comportment for a servant! Why have you and your wife allowed such a scandalous display?" firing his next question at them.

Alice felt rigid and could scarcely catch her breath.

Even though Winifred and Alice came over with simple dress as instructed, they quickly discovered just how rigid Massachusetts laws were concerning clothing.

"Please explain to us what she has done wrong!" implored Winifred, grasping her hands. "For we have only just crossed over and landed on your shores yesterday. I assure you, we mean no harm."

William looked on, red-faced and ready to intervene at any moment. Alice cowered, wanting to disappear out of his sight forever, but was grateful to Winifred for choosing to act as her protector.

Reverend Ward's rough exterior hardened even further.

"Why, don't you see? She has stitched silk ribbon imbued with silver thread on her coif and fastened broad lace along the edges. She has even added the same lace to the ends of the sleeves of her waistcoat as cuffs. This is not fitting for a servant. Only very narrow, modest lace is acceptable here. Even the upper classes are forbidden to wear such embellishments for dress. Where did she find such delicate adornments? For all I can see, they could be stolen property! They must be removed!" he commanded.

Alice was now trembling. The only remembrances she had from her cousin were now illegal. If only she could run away from his horrible tirade.

"They...they were gifts from my family. It is the only token I have of my dear cousin," she stuttered and struggled to find air.

William Holman looked at Winifred with an inquisitive expression.

Winifred addressed the cleric once again, standing up for her servant and new friend. Her voice became stronger as she spoke.

"I assure you, esteemed reverend, 'tis true. Alice received the adornments from her dear cousin. I watched as she sewed them into her garments on the passage. None of us had any idea that this would be met with disapproval or viewed as an abomination on these shores. I guarantee that we will have her remove them. Please spare her the whipping post. She is innocent of any contempt for the laws passed by the magistrates of this colony," requested Winifred, looking at him firmly and with conviction.

"Very well. But this is your one and only warning to obey the laws that we have placed to discourage unnecessary extravagance in dress," admonished the minister. "I trust that your servant will dress more modestly from this day forth as is required by our laws. It is your duty to see that she does!" he added, nodding his head at Winifred and then William Holman.

Finally, he left in a huff, completely forgetting why he came into the trading establishment.

Winifred looked at Alice, who appeared shocked and could not quite hide the tears that were starting to roll down her cheeks. Winifred took her gently by the arm. She whispered to her.

"I am so sorry, Alice. I know how dear those cherished gifts were to you."

Alice nodded, not uttering a word. She felt as if she were about to collapse or even die from the undeserved vicious and personal attack. She could still scarcely catch her breath. She was so shaken to the core.

It became even clearer to them now that the slightest hint of the superfluous, showy, or unusual was frowned upon and, in fact, legislated harshly against. As they walked back to the inn that afternoon, Alice sullenly stared at the groups of passing steeple hats and wool cloaks, remaining silent, hiding her voice... hiding her true self.

The Holmans maintained their accommodations for three nights at the inn in Boston until they were prepared to take a shallop, a smaller vessel, upriver to their preferred place of settlement in Newtown. The Holmans received additional advice about settling into the colonies from friendly strangers they met in town, and finished their purchases for the winter ahead. They were just beginning to acclimate to their new life in New England.

Alice, for her part, carefully removed the white ribbons embedded with silver threads and the broad lace that was so offensive to the ministry and magistrates. She did this in front of her employers to assure them there would be no further disruption in this regard. Once finished with that endeavor, she told them that she had discarded all of it into the fire of the large hearth at the inn.

But secretly, in her first act of rebellion in this strange godly place, Alice stitched the cherished gift of silk ribbon and broad Flemish lace onto the inside of her petticoat and more in her shift. She was conflicted about lying, but could not bear to part with the precious gifts from her cousin. Nor would she release the deep devotion she held in her breast.

She sewed the lace into place by moonlight at a window overlooking the glistening ocean bay when everyone else was fast asleep. The moon shined more brightly than usual that night. It had willingly become her accomplice in keeping her treasures close to her and safe from harsh judgment.

Chapter 6

NEWTOWN/CAMBRIDGE, MASSACHUSETTS BAY COLONY, 1635-1638

Just before the Holmans left for their new town, the ship that had come so far to drop them off on new shores departed. It was a bittersweet feeling to see its full masts and sails becoming minuscule as it headed deeper into its course along the seas. The ship's master wanted to reach London again before chilly wintry gusts of wind hampered its progress back home. For Alice, it was a relief not to be on that ship of misery anymore. Seeing it go away affirmed that they had reached the other side of the Atlantic.

"That's the last of her. The last of England, slipping away from us," spoke William Holman thoughtfully.

"Say farewell to her. It's the beginning of our new life in the colonies, children," he added.

It was the last bridge to their homeland and everything they knew. In a few hours, it would completely dissolve from their view, along with their former way of life in England.

"Our fair ship is slowly going away from us, back to shores that we may never see again," confirmed Winifred. The thought of never seeing her mother or other family members again made

Winifred unusually wistful and tearful. Alice, too, could not have tolerated the thought of a final family separation, but was more at peace hoping that she would eventually reunite with them in the colonies.

"We will flourish here with God's help. Of that I have great faith. Let us not forget why we came so far," William Holman reminded her and the rest of his family.

With his pronouncement, Alice nodded and remembered her own reasons for coming to the Bay.

The other ship from the West Indies, in port the day they arrived, had left the day before. There was no escape from the realities of their new life. They were in the colonies for the duration and would have to adapt no matter what was in store for them. There was no way to leave for the time being.

Later that day, Alice and the Holman family boarded a shallop with their belongings. It was only a few miles down the Charles River, but it would take them to their new life in Newtown. They stayed at first in a community building that helped new settlers become acclimated and gave them a place to stay for the winter while William Holman arranged for the building of their own home and outbuildings. There were many hardships and sacrifices along the way, but they were all determined to succeed in their new endeavor.

In due time, the Holmans built their home in the traditional English style. It was a farmhouse with a foundation in the shape of a rectangle that was wood-sheathed and timber-framed with a steeply pitched roof. It consisted of four rooms with a central chimney for warmth in the middle.

There were two larger rooms downstairs: a kitchen and a parlor, and two smaller chambers upstairs along with the small garret where Alice slept. Eventually, there were small leaded-glass windows in every room. It was simple but completely sufficient for the growing Holman family and their servant.

Alice had already become part of the Holman family. Many neighbors thought she was Winifred's sister because they did not have the typical mistress-indentured servant relationship. Winifred was completely comfortable with Alice helping to take care of her children. Feeding them, dressing them, bathing them from time to time, tending their sickbeds, and teaching them the basic skills needed to survive were ongoing and endless tasks.

Alice, for her part, had eventually opened up to the Holman family. It was something that she had never imagined was possible at her departure from the Tinker home. Over time, she learned that her heart possessed enough space to hold others dear.

Alice and Winifred planted a kitchen herb garden together, utilizing the seeds brought from home. Even though the garden took some time to become well established, the first summer proved to provide enough bounty to keep both women quite busy. Their neighbors were very generous and shared perennial plants that flourished well in their own gardens.

In this kitchen garden, they toiled under a mild New England sun to plant plenty of carrots, parsnips, red beets, radishes, turnips, lettuce, and cabbages. Herbs for seasonings in the kitchen and for medicine were plentifully planted in the garden as well and included: parsley, sorrel, marigolds, chervil, both winter and summer savories, thyme, sage, spearmint, southernwood, rosemary, lavender, and coriander. Some flowers they cultivated that were medicine and pleasing to the eye were roses, hollyhocks, and clary sage. The women added a variety of colored Canterbury bells to give a little comfort from home.

In the main farm fields, William Holman tilled and planted the core crops of peas, barley, and oats with the mutual aid of other farmers and with temporary labor. Since wheat grew poorly, he also planted rows of corn to make sure that they had the security of a food he knew thrived on American soil. Next to the corn, patches of native pumpkins, beans, and melons gave testament to the drastic changes of ordinary life in their new settlement.

Over time, William Holman added a few fruit trees of apple, plum, and quince to this mix of crops. However, they took several years to bear fruit. So in the earliest years, they relied primarily on the numerous berries that grew wild. Sometimes they picked them, but other times they would trade them from passing Indians wanting to barter goods. The Indians brought them wild strawberries, cranberries, raspberries, blackberries, and blueberries that grew in nearby bogs and meadows, and at the edges of woodlands.

Alice learned to cook and prepare meals with Winifred that were completely new to everyone. The children became accustomed to eating sampe or hominy grits every morning. To prepare them, Alice boiled cornmeal made from mashed corn. After cooking it, she added some butter and milk for extra flavor when it was available. It was delicious and sweet and unlike any English meal she knew of at the time. Another Indian favorite called 'sequotash', which was a mixture of corn, beans, and sometimes fish, became a staple in the Holman home.

They also lived on delicacies from the sea instead of meat in the summer. William Holman and other neighborhood men hunted deer, fowl, and other wild game in the fall and winter of their first settlement years. Meat from sheep, cattle, and pigs was scarce because the imported animals often died on the incoming ships. Overall, Alice and the Holman family learned to adapt quite well to their new home and circumstances.

The part of her time with the Holmans and, more specifically, with Winifred that Alice treasured the most was her education in the arts of herbalism and healing. Winifred could easily make concoctions to address any kind of ailment that arose in the family, be it a salve, tea, or tincture from the plants in her garden or the wild. But Winifred also had respected medical expertise that others outside the family eagerly sought.

Spring was Alice's favorite time of year. It was the time that the green ones started to come out of the ground or blossom from the trees and bushes. As they shot up through composting leaves, past the Earth's crust and upward toward the sunlight, they unfolded and unfurled themselves in a myriad of marvelous and spectacular ways, leaving both woodland and meadow in a vibrant sea of color. They made their appearances proudly or simply in varied and unique arrays of leaves and flowers. Winifred taught her that these green ones, both in the New World and in the English countryside, were in place to subtly and magically assist humans who were in need of help.

Winifred explained that plants were put on the Earth as part of God's gifts to humans to aid them in health and balance on their journey along the path of life. The sun, the moon, and the stars infused them with healing essences. The rich soils of the Earth nurtured them as they matured to become green allies. But the love and care that they put into them potentiated the strongest part of their healing effects as they made them into tinctures, ointments, teas, and poultices. Prayers and ritual, intermingled with the plants' own healing properties at bedsides and by hearths, enhanced their curative powers.

She taught that the green friends could come from both the wild and carefully planted gardens sown with treasured seeds brought from home. In this spirit and with intentions of passing on the goodness of the herbs that were starting to show themselves again after a rest of several months, Alice and Winifred busied themselves with caring for and harvesting from their splendid garden apothecary.

They went into wild portions of woodland and meadow, gathering the herbs that they recognized from England as well as those that they learned about in Massachusetts. The children also became part of the delightful and lighthearted undertaking. Little ones were hoisted on hips or led with gently held hands.

Lessons about healing with different herbs and techniques dominated the season and lasted well into the summer and early autumn.

With five children to care for and more that would be born over the next few years, Winifred was constantly treating one illness or another. Neighbors who heard about her expertise showed up at her threshold and asked for recommendations and recipes to cure loved ones.

They begged for samples of herbs for themselves and their families if they did not have what was required. Winifred gave them willingly if she had some to spare. In no time, Alice and Winifred were even making herbal formulas and salves to sell on market days.

At the market, Winifred and Alice became known for their herbal concoctions. Overall, selling their medicinal creations was a positive experience that earned them both much respect and many repeat customers, except for one disgruntled man. He became suspicious of a remedy his wife bought behind his back. Even though he was highly unpleasant and threatening, he soon moved to another colony and the roar of controversy became quiet. Winifred and Alice soon forgot him and focused on their important medicinal endeavors.

As they sat in the garden one mild summer morning, Alice listened intently to Winifred. She already knew the uses of many of the more widely used herbs, but Winifred had such a pleasant way of teaching and telling her stories that she always loved to hear more about them. Winifred picked up a sprig of thyme and inhaled deeply.

"Such a gift is this, Alice. Once again, one of the children has the chin cough. This dear herb we can make into syrup with some sugar to ease the cough or make it into an ointment to spread on the chest. It will strengthen the lungs and ease breathing. A tea of it will kill worms in the stomachs of young children. I've even used it to help deliver the afterbirth of one of my children. I can't imagine life without it."

"Such a sweet, spicy smell! I love it, too," said Alice smiling and continued.

"But if you can't imagine life without thyme, then I know you would be lost without sage for certain," Alice said, grabbing a soft oval leaf from a sage plant.

"What is possibly better for a mother than to have the aid of sage to treat hoarseness and sore throats in her children? And it can also do so much to heal their little wounds by cleaning them well and stopping the bleeding," recited the pupil.

"So true!" exclaimed Winifred.

"Let us not forget that sage can help a grieving mother to expel a dead child and afterbirth from the womb or bring on her courses when humors are unbalanced," she thoughtfully remembered. Alice nodded.

Winifred approached the lavender plants.

"And what do you remember about lavender?"

Alice followed her, walking over to the small patch of lavender and sitting beside it. Again she inhaled the pleasant aroma.

"The smell helps me remember its properties."

She gave a huge sigh.

"It is calming in cases of nervous excitement. It can be a gargle in cases of toothache and a rub for rheumatic conditions. It is a dear friend indeed as a poultice or ointment for many disturbances of the skin, including burns."

Winifred smiled and gave a nod of approval to her student, adding, "And to aid in falling-sickness and aches of the head. Excellent. Come, Alice. That's enough teaching for the day. We must bring in thyme for Mary, who has awoken. I still hear her coughing upstairs."

"This afternoon, I want you to gather enough herbs to prepare some tinctures, ointments, and teas for the colder seasons when more of the children will surely become ill. Let us attend to little Mary first. We will discuss them later."

For Mary, Alice dutifully prepared tea from a decoction of horehound, coltsfoot, and elecampane root sweetened with honey. She assisted Winifred to give little Mary frequent sips of it throughout the day. Alice helped Winifred make a strong liniment of acorn oil infused with thyme and lavender that they rubbed into Mary's chest morning and evening. Little Mary soon healed and became their number-one helper as they prepared for winter.

They gathered wild elderberries at the beginning of September and either pickled them and stored them in earthen pots or made them into syrup. They dried many herbs in great quantities, including sage, mints, yarrow, and rosemary. All of these were indispensable for treating fevers, sore throats, colds, and influenza. Winifred taught Alice her favorite recipe for treating the phlegm of consumption or deep cold, so often a visitor in winter: equal parts licorice, elder, and drops of anise in a strong decoction or syrup. Winter was always a challenging season, but they felt ready.

Children often needed first aid after tumbles and scrapes. Winifred stocked her winter and summer pantries accordingly. For these, she taught Alice to make ointments and salves consisting of plantain, heal-all, yarrow, comfrey, and adder's tongue. Alice worked tirelessly, crushing gathered herbs in a mortar and pestle to make the remedies. She soon became as devoted to her new calling and her mentor as she had been to the Tinkers.

A couple of times a week, local Indians approached the farm and village with baskets heaped full of curious foods and medicines. Alice and Winifred paid particularly close attention to the roots, barks, leaves, and flowers brought for trade.

Late one afternoon at the end of summer that first year was when Alice first noticed Assanushque. She dressed in moccasins and a buckskin dress that hung off her body like an empty burlap bag. She wore two braids that were starting to turn from charcoal color to white snow. Her skin was wrinkled, but her eyes were bright and vibrant.

As the old Massachusett Indian woman passed by the Holman place, she clutched a large woven basket. She called out to Alice in a language that she could not understand. But Alice instinctively knew that she wanted to trade the contents of her basket for other items. Alice was enticed to come over to her and quickly became enthralled with the captivating charm of the Indian grandmother.

Alice motioned to her to wait while she urged Winifred to come outside. Together, they looked at the contents of Assanushque's basket. Deep blue whortleberries drew their attention. They looked like bilberries from home. The elderly woman had dried them in the sun. Alice and Winifred recalled other settlers using them to make puddings and tarts. By putting them into syrups and making them into medicine, the berries could dispel the burning heat of a fever. They also had binding actions in cases of the flux.

"Splendid!" cried out Winifred. "What can we trade? I would like to try some."

"English herbs!" said Alice pointing to the garden.

"Perhaps she wants us to pay with wampum," Winifred noted and pulled out a string of crafted shell beads.

The settlers here often used wampum as tender for their own transactions with each other because coins were scarce. Indians used them to purchase European items from the whites.

The old Indian woman nodded and smiled, gently noticing that Winifred was very pregnant. She pointed to her belly and smiled. She gestured to the forest and the sun.

"Tomorrow."

They guessed that she would come back, but they weren't really sure. Assanushque gladly took the wampum beads that were offered to her as well as a small batch of herbs Alice had gathered for her from the garden, and tried to explain their use in mime.

Assanushque started to go back to where she came from with her empty basket when she observed the small leaves of plantain that were growing low to the ground. She said something in her language and kept pointing to their feet.

"English, English," she said and gestured to everywhere.

Just then her grandson, who had been following her to make sure she was not in danger, joined her. He knew a little English.

"Grandmother say plant follows the path of English wherever they go. Is it English medicine?"

"Tell her we use it as medicine for many reasons. We stop bleeding with it both inside the body and on external wounds. The juices from it are comforting to the stomach and digestion," she said as she pointed to Alice's stomach and gave a gentle pat. Winifred did not want to pat her own stomach and have the herbal usage of plantain confused with pregnancy.

"I am Winifred, and this is Alice," Winifred introduced herself and her assistant.

Alice smiled warmly at her. She was eager and curious to enter the door to a new world that was now slightly ajar in front of her– Assanushque's world.

Assanushque's grandson translated the essence of what they had tried to communicate. Assanushque nodded and pointed to herself, "Assanushque."

Then she pointed to her grandson with obvious pride and said a term they could not quite understand.

He interrupted. "My name is Quinuqussumittuck," repeating what Assanushque had just said.

They looked puzzled.

"English say John Indian. Grandmother Assanushque want to trade."

From that day forward, Assanushque came back with mystery items from the wild places nearby. She liked to trade with Alice and Winifred. They were much kinder to her than some of the other English living nearby. Alice waited in anticipation of Assanushque's visits. Each day with her was a day of new discoveries. And at the end of each native plant lesson, Alice felt a little more secure and comfortable in her new home.

The very next day, she came back with two roots that neither English woman had ever seen before. She pronounced them "cohosh". She pointed to Winifred's belly. One was blue cohosh and one was black cohosh. While she knew a few simple words in English, it was impossible for her to explain their uses except through miming and gestures.

Winifred understood that they were mainly used to help women in labor, to help expel an afterbirth, or to regulate courses. She traded them and some sumac berries for a small, pewter cup.

Assanushque was kind-hearted yet perplexing. She came often and greeted them sweetly.

"What cheer, English?" She did what she needed to do and left. She was fully present and helpful when they were together but would suddenly decide there was nothing left to say and take off back into the woods. Her grandson must have decided that his grandmother was safe in the presence of the English women and rarely showed himself again.

Through Assanushque's generosity, they discovered a whole other world of herbs and healing. Winifred now added wild cherry bark to her repertoire of medicines to ease coughs.

'Kinnikinnik', which the settlers soon came to call bearberry because of bear's natural fondness for them, could easily alleviate suffering and symptoms of scurvy, as did sumac berries.

She also brought 'Indian sage' which showed itself in white flowers every year as summers progressed. It became a treasured medicine to sweat out bad chills or break a fever. Later settlers eventually came to call the plant boneset, and depended upon it heavily in cases of malaria, typhoid, and influenza. Alice was astute and became even more skilled than Winifred in Indian healing ways.

One day, Winifred's oldest son, Jeremy, staggered to the house after he had fallen out of a tree. He was always a little too daring and gave Winifred and Alice many opportunities to practice their skills. After his tumble from the tree, he was scuffed up and bruised badly, but had luckily not broken any bones. Some of his cuts from the fall were deep. Winifred worried about his condition. Alice was desperate to find a way to help ease Winifred's concerns about her son. Assanushque was there the day he showed up with his many wounds and injuries. She scurried off to the woods, seeing that they would be busy.

Jeremy was quickly put to bed and made to rest for a couple of days. Alice and Winifred darted to their garden to pick out the best tissue-healing herbs for his wounds as well as those that would keep dark humors away. The crushed seeds of southernwood and plantain leaves helped draw out the thorns and splinters embedded in his skin from hitting a tangle of briars. The yarrow was bruised and made into a poultice along with comfrey and more plantain. They quickly wrapped the remedy poultices around his wounds and changed them thrice daily. During his recuperation, they gave him decoctions of heal-all to drink throughout the day.

He healed well over time, but being the restless boy that he was, he reinjured the largest leg wound. It became red, swollen, and filled with pus. It was not responding to the usual remedies. Winifred was frantic to try something different.

Alice remembered the pine turpentine that Assanushque had given them the day after his fall and suggested that they use it on Jeremy's wounds. Assanushque had gestured to them that the Indians used it to cure desperate wounds. They began to dress it every day with the turpentine and crushed inner bark of the white pine. Assanushque taught them that even in the winter, the sap from the pine or other evergreens could also be gathered as a remedy to aid in improving difficult breathing.

They begged Assanushque to come look at their handiwork with the medicine she brought them, but she would not go into the house. Eventually, Jeremy's leg healed to everyone's great relief. But Assanushque must have moved on. The last time they ever saw her was a week after the day she brought the healing remedy that cured Jeremy. As quickly as she came into their lives, she disappeared, never to be seen again. Alice had grown quite attached to her and the fascinating lessons she shared about the treasures from the wild. Alice was alive like never before and animated with a different way to view the wilderness.

The summer felt particularly bright and optimistic. Alice sat on a stoop near the garden and observed the marvelous display of beloved English Canterbury bells that was now taking hold at the edge of their dwelling. The beautiful little red, cylindrical flowers were inviting hummingbirds to play on this day. Alice thought that they, too, were starting to finally settle into this new world that had strangely become home. She was deep in thought about so much that had transpired since her arrival.

Alice had continued to help Winifred sell herbal remedies on market days without further incident. They persisted in experimenting and creating herbal formulas for themselves and their customers. Alice hadn't seen Assanushque for a while, but wondered about her fate often and remembered her teachings and offerings of native herbs with gratitude.

Next to the Canterbury bells was a patch of beautiful bee balms, a native flower also blooming in bright red with its own offerings for the busy hummingbirds. Alice finally felt happy and at peace. Time passed as each new season bestowed surprising blessings. Alice had already stayed for over three years with the Holmans.

Chapter 7

SALEM, MASSACHUSETTS BAY COLONY, 1639

Overall, life was full with the Holman family. Their small farm was still growing and taking shape, with the initial pains of establishing it well behind them. Their lives became more comfortable as they got to know their new home better and adapted to a colonial way of living. Newtown grew and its name was changed to Cambridge. Alice had acclimated better than she thought she would. She loved Winifred and the children she helped take care of.

But even so, the end of winter started to drag and depress her. Alice missed the Tinkers. She still thought often about her cousins. The girls would be older now, with their own children. John, too, would be a grown man of the world. She grinned, remembering the twinkle in his eye. She felt guilt at the thought of not being fully content with Winifred, but her first loyalty had always been to her family. Ultimately, she knew that her place was with them. In her mind, the time had already elapsed too long. The Tinkers would always be a part of her, and she could not live without that part of herself any longer.

A couple of years after her arrival in Cambridge, Alice heard that most of the Tinker sisters had moved from Dorchester to Windsor in Connecticut Colony and that Mrs. Tinker was in Salem. She became distressed that she had not been able to connect with them while they were still living in the Bay. Aching to see them, she decided that waiting was no longer an option. Her resolve was strong to seek out and visit Mrs. Tinker at the first opportunity. She was determined to do it as soon as early spring was underway.

⸺∞⸺

Alice arrived in Salem on a brisk early spring day that was gripping stubbornly onto winter. She rode to Boston in a cart with another servant named Michael, who dropped off harvested goods from an adjoining farm. He stayed with her there until he could find and place her on a shallop that was bound for Salem that day. Other colonial passengers on the shallop helped her find the home of Mrs. Tinker once the small boat arrived.

Alice was not sure what to say to her. It had been many years since they last saw each other, but Alice decided to overcome her shyness. She was her cousin, after all, and she needed to find out about reuniting with the rest of the family. Winifred had been so kind to her and taught her so much. However, she needed to see the women who had always been her family and resolved to find them again.

⸺∞⸺

It was a strange feeling to see Mrs. Tinker, the family matriarch. When Alice first caught sight of her, she was in her yard overlooking a side garden whose vegetation was still dead except for the last of some root vegetables. She looked slightly older but was overall unchanged except for the dullness of her dress. She was directing her servant to find the last few parsnips and carrots hidden there that were sprouting again. As Alice walked closer, Mrs. Tinker heard someone coming and quickly turned around. The look of surprise was evident on her face.

"Alice? Is that you, Alice? After all this time? What has become of you? You look distraught. Are you well, dear?" she questioned her as she placed her hands on her shoulders and looked at her with a quizzical expression.

"Aye, Mrs. Tinker. 'Tis I, your devoted girl, Alice. I could wait no longer to find you and know of the Tinker family. I had word that you finally moved to the Bay with John," explained Alice.

"Come inside then. Let us talk by the warmth of the hearth. John has gone to England again on business for Mr. Winthrop and several other important men. It is an honor that he has been chosen to handle the affairs of such prominent men, including Mr. Keayne, whom you are well acquainted with from the ship," Mrs. Tinker highlighted.

"Please enter, Alice," she gestured her into her modest house.

Alice nodded. They entered her simple colonial home that was still light inside even though the sun had started to move towards the western horizon. Though the home was meager by an English merchant's standards, it was still more spacious than most other dwellings in Salem, despite the intention of its owner to stay only temporarily. One servant girl, Prudence, prepared a bed for Alice on the second floor while the other servant girl, Hope, continued to prepare a simple pork roast with stewed carrots and parsnips she picked earlier for their main meal of the day.

Mrs. Tinker released the servants for the afternoon so she could talk with Alice in private without the hindrance of their incessant eavesdropping followed by gossiping to the fellow neighborhood servants. One always had to be careful. Here in the colonies, the ruling clergy and elite commanded the populace to follow strict ecclesiastical codes. It was better not to have her every word scrutinized while talking with someone she knew from her previous existence.

Mrs. Tinker had not been raised in a stringent religious environment. It was true that she adapted to godly teachings before coming to New England, but she never completely embraced their stark way of existence. The last years in New Windsor, England were in steady economic decline, and she and her family turned to the New World as a way to rebuild their fortunes.

"Have you adjusted to the severe ways of the godly people, Alice?" she asked, but did not stop speaking.

She wanted to express what she honestly thought to someone from her past.

"Godly ways are still curiously strange to me, Alice," she divulged and continued, "Most of our family moved to the colonies more for financial prospects than anything else. Of course, there are exceptions. Some of my sons-in-law are more godly in their views. Especially Thomas, and William to a much lesser degree," she explained.

Alice was surprised by her act of disclosure. She nodded her head in understanding.

Robert Keayne, the merchant who immigrated to Boston and the long-time trusted friend of the Tinker family, was the one who introduced her to the ways of the Puritans along with her son-in- law William.

"After losing so many family members over the years, including both of my husbands and a cherished son and daughter, and even your mother, I turned to godly ways of thought as a way to restart my life. In my grief, I supposed the new religious guidance might move me in a fresh direction after so much loss and melancholy."

She paused and shook her head.

"But I never expected to be a part of such an unadorned and plain way of living. I am truly startled at the extent to which these reformist magistrates rigorously enforce such a multitude of strict rules and severely discipline the masses," she revealed.

Alice nodded and crossed her legs, feeling the contraband lace beneath her petticoats but not daring to say anything. She was still a bit nervous, yet relieved to be in the home of a familiar family member.

Mrs. Tinker continued, "I am thrilled that John was able to secure a position with Governor Winthrop. Yet, it is ironic that he should work for such a rigid man. Thankfully, John is respectful and knows how to keep his views to himself. I understand that the Governor's son is much less severe in his beliefs."

Once Mrs. Tinker had relieved herself of her scandalous thoughts, she focused on Alice and inquired about her new life in the colonies.

"So please tell me, Alice, where did the Holmans finally settle?" she asked Alice.

"Cambridge, ma'am."

"And have they been good to you Alice?"

"Yes, ma'am."

"Alice please, you must tell me all about it," pleaded Mrs. Tinker.

Alice bit her lip. She looked intensely at Mrs. Tinker before telling her the full story. Her elder cousin was the key to her future in the colonies.

Alice and Mrs. Tinker caught up over several hours. By the end of the evening, they decided that Alice would stay with Mrs. Tinker and help her to prepare to move to the new town of Windsor in the Connecticut territory in the Great River Valley. Mrs. Tinker wanted to move there as soon as John finished his business in England over the course of the next year. She was anxious to join several of her daughters and their children.

Communication was sent to the Holmans explaining that Alice could not come back because her family greatly needed her service at that time. Eventually, compensation was given to them as well. Alice quickly became part of Mrs. Tinker's household once again. But it was only temporary as a result of meeting a man named John Young.

Mrs. Tinker introduced them shortly after Alice's arrival in Salem. She brought him home for dinner.

"Alice," Mrs. Tinker called to her, "Please come meet John Young. He is the young man whom I was telling you about the other day."

Alice saw him and understood that he was the man she was supposed to marry. John Young was a slightly older carpenter, like her father had been, and was once a servant himself. He was strong, solid, quiet, and had a mild disposition.

"Nice to meet you, Goodman Young," she said as she curtsied before him rather clumsily.

It did not seem to bother John Young. He sensed that she would be good for him.

"I am glad we could meet. Mrs. Tinker has told me many wonderful things about you," he stated. He asked Alice about her time in the colonies and listened intently. He was a man of few words.

Mrs. Tinker seemed pleased. In the past, Alice had greeted all her attempts at matchmaking with disdain or rejection. But now she was sure that Alice was willing to take her advice. Indeed, Alice was polite and did not push him away.

"Alice seems receptive to this man," she thought to herself.

It was clear that a match would be looming. Regardless, it was time for Alice to marry. She was quickly approaching her mid-twenties.

After a very brief time, John Young proposed to her. He had lived a whole other life in London before coming to the colonies and knew married life was a needed practicality to survive the many hardships and challenges of the New World. He thought Alice was a gentle girl who was sweet in spite of being a bit awkward. He understood her awkwardness since he, too, was a bit uncomfortable showing his emotions.

"Alice," he began, "I know that we will be able to forge through this new wilderness together well. I think we will get along just fine should you take me as your husband."

Alice acquiesced and took his hand in marriage.

Theirs was a simple civil ceremony, as were all in the Bay. There was no feast or great party afterwards. A magistrate of Mrs. Tinker's passing acquaintance performed the marriage rite joining them together. It was a stark contrast to Margaret's great wedding banquet in England so long ago. Mrs. Tinker bought a few portions of cheese and made a sweet pie to mark their new life together.

After their marriage, Alice moved to John's little cottage on the outskirts of town. It was a tiny makeshift house that was nothing to boast about. Alice made do by cleaning it up and adding womanly touches: a spinning wheel at the hearth, the aromas of baking bread and simmering stews over the fire, and herbs growing plentifully outside the home in the kitchen garden and dried over the hearth.

Unfortunately, John and Alice's only neighbors were elderly and cross. Their children had died long ago. Alice could not relate to them, and she quickly became lonely for more human companionship.

After only a few short months of wedlock, Alice had her own daughter whom she dutifully and formally named Alice according to family tradition. However, Alice gave her child the nickname "Alissa", which she was commonly called. Mrs. Tinker came to help Alice in her labor with a servant. Baby Alissa had come early, too early to be considered respectable. Yet, Alice and John Young had not been intimate with each other before their marriage.

The baby was beautiful but very small and challenging from the day of her birth. Alice grappled with constant guilt. She thought that perhaps the baby's relentless bouts of crying and sickly state were a punishment from God. Alice spent long, weary nights up with Alissa, trying to appease her in whatever way she could.

It was difficult and solitary for Alice in her new situation. She had always been surrounded by the companionship of other women, and now there were none in her daily life. Mrs. Tinker was engrossed in preparing for her eventual move to Connecticut with the impending return of her son John and only occasionally saw Alice after Alissa's birth. Alice's existence with John Young became more isolated than she had expected or wanted, and she became quite lonely.

Mrs. Tinker told Alice that she and her new husband could also go to Connecticut if they wished, but indicated that they should wait until she made further arrangements in Windsor. With the help of her sons-in-law, Mrs. Tinker was certain that she could eventually find a simple lot to farm for them. She promised that she would organize it all in due time but, for the present, she encouraged them to stay in Massachusetts Bay.

After over a year of waiting, John Tinker finally returned. Mrs. Tinker sent Alice a message after she had left. Alice quickly became distraught when she realized that Mrs. Tinker had departed for Windsor. Alice did not expect her to leave without saying goodbye in person and was extremely disappointed that she was not able to reconnect with one of her favorite cousins, John.

She felt abandoned and alone. Fall commenced with cooler temperatures again, and the plant life that gave her spiritual sustenance went into slumber mode. John Young toiled long hours as Alice held together their daily life. But as time wore on, she became exhausted and dejected from the lack of support.

Gradually, a heavy cloud of darkness overtook every fiber of her being. Alice passed the long, brutal days in the Bay, working tirelessly for their daily survival.

The only chores that she relished were those that involved the care of her only daughter. She was depressed and could not seem to find her bearings. She missed her mother. She missed Winifred. And she missed her cousins. Her life was unfolding in a way that she had not planned for or anticipated. Alice concluded still that she needed to be with the only family she had ever known, the Tinkers.

It was not enough to be here with John Young. He had been accommodating enough and provided for her, but she needed to be with her near sisters– other women who understood her.

She carefully broached the subject with John.

"I must talk to you, husband. I know you have done your best to provide me with a good life. But pray, please understand what I have to say now."

He nodded obligingly.

"I am weary without the love of my cousins. I lived with them for most of my life. I must be with them again. I feel so alone without the regular presence of other women. Please dear husband, let us move to Windsor," she beseeched him.

"I see how unhappy you are. Honestly, I can no longer bear to listen to your constant sobbing. There are no strong connections here in Salem for me except work that I am still completing. If it pleases you, and there are work and land available to me there, then I am willing to go. I already had it in my head that we would go after Mrs. Tinker got settled and found us a nice piece of land," he responded.

Alice looked relieved.

"Thank you, husband. The day that our journey commences to Windsor is not soon enough."

John dutifully finished any projects and obligations that remained in Salem. Alice hoped Mrs. Tinker would let them stay with her or, better still, that they could stay with one of her adopted sisters until he could purchase their own home lot and farm.

It took several months after Mrs. Tinker left Salem before John Young was ready to venture on to Connecticut the following summer. The winter that year in Salem was long, bleak, and monotonous. Alice held onto the hope of going to Windsor the following spring or summer with all her might. She worked hard to bring Alissa and herself to a robust state of health before the journey commenced.

Chapter 8

∞∞∞

WINDSOR, COLONY OF
CONNECTICUT, 1641

As soon as the early summer journey towards Connecticut began, Alice's mood became lighter. She was ecstatic to be able to see her dear cousins in just two weeks' time, provided the journey went as expected. Alice carried her little daughter on her back as her husband, John, led them just a few steps ahead through the open hardwood and evergreen forests. Alice was grateful that John Young had agreed to take her to Windsor, where the rest of the Tinker family resided.

The trail they traveled, the Connecticut Path, had gotten its share of foot traffic over the past five years, with new arrivals from Massachusetts Bay landing every week in temperate seasons. Normally, it took only two weeks to reach Hartford from Cambridge or Dorchester, but they would cut off a day by stopping permanently in Windsor.

The trail had been in use for hundreds of years as a major route for the Indians that traversed that part of New England. The natives along the trail were quite friendly and frequently offered food or lodging in barter to travelers along the way. Several of the Indian villages had been in contact with white settlers for several years already. Occasionally, the forests opened into meadowlands or isolated agricultural fields, and Alice and her little family caught sight of local Indians attending to their newly planted cornfields.

Alice marveled at the many amazing natural features of the wilderness along the path. There were many streams and rivers that they had to ford *en route*, but some of them had stone bridges in place or else were very shallow at the crossings. The ancient, moss-covered trees along the path towered over them, standing firm and majestic as they advanced along their route. In some places, the forest floor was thick with luscious ferns, and other areas were alive with the last of spring wildflowers. They passed crystal ponds, hiked up gentle hills, and stayed and accepted the hospitality at Indian villages along the way. They were fortunate that the weather was pleasant and rainstorms were minimal.

Alice felt very elated to be outside, cradled in the noises of babbling brooks and a plethora of birdcalls emanating from the thick tree canopy overhead. It was uplifting to be away from the drudgery of everyday life. She loved meeting other people on the path and enjoyed hearing their stories. The trail ahead led to constant discovery at each upcoming curve in the path. They came across little waterfalls cascading over glistening rocks, saw an abandoned beaver dam at the edge of a stream, ran into curious American animals such as skunk and raccoons, and encountered whole hillsides of mountain laurel almost ready to bloom.

Two weeks of westward journeying were entertaining and passed quickly. Even little Alissa seemed more content. Finally, the Great River came glistening into view on a sunny afternoon. They were at the end of their journey. Windsor Village was only across the river. They could discern in the distance one large canoe coming to greet them.

As the canoe approached the small traveling party, it became clear that they were only boys of the village fishing for dinner.

They had already completed their tasks in the fields for the day. They wanted to take advantage of the remaining sunlight and rare free time to go fishing leisurely. They were determined to catch some salmon or bass.

"What cheer, travelers?" they shouted, requesting to know if they could be of assistance, not recognizing Alice or her family members.

"Greetings," shouted John from the opposite shore.

He introduced his small family.

"Aye. We've come to settle with friends and family in the fine village across the way. Are you acquainted with the Tinker family there?"

The boys looked at them and nodded in recognition.

Alice added, "That's the family name of four sisters. But their married surnames are Sension, Thornton, Hulburd, and Taylor. Their mother goes by the surname Collins since her remarriage, and their only remaining brother, John, is thus the sole person of the name Tinker if he is there."

Enthusiastically, the boys nodded their heads again. They knew all the families mentioned and would take them directly across the Great River in their canoe. The Young family carefully entered the crude vessel with the few sparse belongings that they owned.

The boys paddled past large floodplains of newly planted fields. Newly built homes were at higher levels just above these meadows in the far distance. The boys pointed out different landmarks along the way. It was a matter of minutes before they reached the opposite shore. The boys directed them further down the path that in a half a mile opened into the village green. Alice and John thanked the boys for their kindness and continued walking until they reached their final destination.

The time that Alice had anticipated and hoped for after many long years had finally arrived. She became anxious in addition to being excited. She wondered if they would greet her warmly after such a long time. Her heartfelt wish was that she and the Tinker sisters would be as close again as they had been so many years before. These thoughts remained unvoiced but loomed incessantly in her mind.

As they approached the town green, John Young motioned to an old man whom he saw sitting at a bench near what appeared to be a shop and asked him if he knew the families of the Tinker sisters. Other small businesses were also within view. The man quickly pointed behind him to the shop connected to a larger thatched home on the edge of the green. He explained it belonged to William Hulburd, the husband of Ellen Tinker, the oldest sister. The Young family soon made their way into the small commercial establishment where Ellen and her husband were attending to various projects.

Ellen quickly looked up in astonishment at the happy sight of her dear cousin.

"Why, cousin Alice! Aren't you a vision with a little girl and a husband! What a surprise! Truly a blessed surprise! And the child, look at her! There is no doubt that she is part of the family!" Ellen exclaimed as she hugged Alice and her small child.

Alice quickly made introductions, beaming with joy.

"This is John Young, my husband, and the wee one is our little daughter, Alissa."

She then turned to her husband.

"And John, this is my dear cousin, Ellen, and her husband, William."

John tipped his hat.

"I am pleased to finally know you," he said.

"We've come to join your family in the village if it meets with the approval of the town leaders. Alice missed her cousins and would hear of doing nothing else for months. Of course,

I will need to find some carpentry work and some land for farming if we are granted permission to settle," he added.

"We'll figure out all of those details soon enough, John. But for now, William, will you please be a dear and fetch my other sisters on Backer Row? They will be so pleased to see you, Alice!" explained Ellen.

Within a short time, the other sisters, Anne, Rhody, and Mary, arrived with their husbands and children. Everyone eagerly introduced themselves to those family members that they were meeting for the first time. The reunion was jubilant, and Alice felt more light-hearted than she had in a long time.

The men soon broke off and showed John Young their workshops and fields close by, allowing Alice time to catch up with her cousins.

"And what has become of the rest of the family? Did your mother finally come to settle here as I had heard?" asked Alice.

"Aye. Mother arrived last summer with our dear brother, newly returned from England," stated Rhody.

"And John brought our nephew, Miles Merwin, with him. You must remember little Miles, the son of sister Margaret. But you won't recognize him now. He is so grown," said Ellen.

Alice nodded, looking relieved that most of the family was together again.

"My brother-in-law, Nicolas Sension, has also just arrived from London. He and the others live across the Rivulet. They live with Mother so she can keep an eye on all of them," informed Mary as she chuckled.

The others laughed, too, knowing that Mrs. Tinker would do just that.

Alice was in a hurry to find out more. She had waited so long for this moment when she could finally catch up with her cousins.

"How long was your brother John in England?" asked Alice.

"Too long, I suppose. He expected to be there only a few months, up to a year, but had to wait almost two years until he finished his work completely. Even so, he did well with his business and legal dealings and gained much respect in the process from the governor and others he was representing," explained Anne.

"But alas, for all his success, he's still a single man," stated Rhody.

"Do you think he is happy?" asked Alice.

"Despite John's success, I get the sense that something is missing from his life, Alice. Perhaps that will change someday soon. Only God knows. We shall have to see. All I know is that Mother would like him to meet someone and settle down. She pressures him all the time, but he is not so easily persuaded," stated Mary.

"John knows his heart. He cannot simply be satisfied with a cold marriage of convenience. He is more sensitive than most men," Alice commented, softly looking away.

"Come, let us eat," called Ellen, changing the subject. "The meal is ready."

Sitting down to dinner late that afternoon, the sisters and their husbands described their journey to New England and later to Windsor. John Young was ready to learn everything.

William Hulburd, the wool merchant from Reading, England who set the trend for the rest of the family to settle in New England, returned to Dorchester a second time, bringing back his wife. Ann Tinker and her husband Thomas Thornton, a tanner, and sister Mary Tinker and her husband Mathias Sension, a chandler, followed them to the colonies that summer.

William stroked his beard and inhaled deeply. He recounted their earliest years in the New World.

"We settled in the town of Dorchester in the Massachusetts Bay with immigrants who were mostly from Devon and Dorchester, England."

Ellen spoke up, "Sarah, the youngest, came the same summer as you, Alice, but married as planned, settling in Scituate, Massachusetts with her new husband, Thomas King. Rhody, then widowed, and her two daughters joined us in Dorchester a year later.

"That's when I met this handsome one," said Rhody, putting a hand on the knee of her new husband, John Taylor, as he winked back at her. They were obviously quite in love with each other.

William addressed the newcomers, "At first, life in the Bay colony was good, but it quickly became too overcrowded. Ships were bringing hordes of other new colonists, who kept arriving in Dorchester and in other places with the fine sailing weather. We also realized the soil there was not as fertile as many of us had originally hoped. And further still, there was talk that John Wareham, our minister, found Governor John Winthrop to be too oppressive in his dealings with the colony."

"At the same time, the deadly pox took hold of many tribes, leaving Indian villages and farm fields empty and abandoned all over Connecticut. As a result, many Indian chiefs were willing to sell their land to new settlers," he added.

He paused and took a bite of fish stew.

"Led by our clergy, we decided that we would take advantage of the opportunity to seize and settle some of the empty land. We desired to make our claims before Plymouth Colony or the Dutch, who were already here, had a complete hold on this area," he further explained.

Mathias Sension elaborated, "There was already a trading house in place, started the year earlier by the Plymouth Colony at the confluence of the Great River and the Rivulet, the smaller river that intersects the Great River a few miles north from the Dutch House of Hope. Both rivers run through the current town."

"The Plymouth Trading House was the hub of activity. Indians came from all over the Great River Valley to trade in beaver pelts, furs, and corn in exchange for kettles, knives and other metal tools, cloth, and blankets. Some Indian tribes stayed. The Tunxis tribe planted and maintained crops in fields around the trading house at that time. Today, they remain in the area near Poquonock just to the north of the town."

"We, too, relied on the trading house to secure goods. We bartered or traded in coin and wampum for sugar, molasses, firearms, rum, ale, and cider," explained Thomas Thornton.

William continued their story, "Plymouth traders and the Dutch were not our only competition. The Francis Stiles group, representing Sir Richard Saltonstall, came to the area just days after we arrived. But there were only twenty people in Stile's party compared to sixty of us. The advantage in numbers allowed us to make our claim. Stiles had to negotiate for land located directly north of our own, a couple of miles up from the town green."

William took a gulp of ale and recalled their initial difficulties.

"The first winter here was so harsh that we journeyed by foot back to Massachusetts out of fear of starvation. Cattle and other livestock died that unforgiving winter. Had it not been for the local Indians sharing their corn and other staples for survival, many of those who did not return to Massachusetts Bay would have perished for sure. The supply shallops that had come along the coastline from Dorchester had either been lost at sea or were frozen *en route* up the Great River."

Thomas Thornton interjected, "While we were gone in the Bay again, Matthew Grant, the town's surveyor, drew up divisions in the land, laying the first lots in the Great Meadow and adjoining uplands. Those that stayed made shelters by digging into the sides of the hilly banks along the Great River to brave the winter. By the time our families returned, the properties on the Great River were given to those with origins from Devon and Dorchester. Our family was granted land on Backer Row a little farther from the Great River. For not having a lot on the Great River and, thereby, escape access from hostile Indian tribes, we and other first settlers of Backer Row were also granted lots in the new town green with proximity to the smaller river, the Rivulet."

William Hulburd spoke again, "Our newly settled town was named Dorchester in honor of the beloved origin of Reverend White, the minister who originally organized the Dorchester Company. It was through that company that most settlers in the town came with Reverend Wareham and Reverend Maverick on Roger Ludlow's ship, the *Mary and John*, from the West Country of England."

John Taylor, Rhody's husband, explained that he, Rhody, and her daughters, Anne and Hannah, came a little later to Windsor than everyone else. In fact, they were currently settled into the Hulburd's home lot on Backer Row in the cottage that William had built when he and Ellen first moved to town. The Hulburds had decided to stay in the town center near the green to live in their basic supply shop. Mathias Sension also kept his chandler's workshop on the green and Thomas Thornton kept his tannery there as well, but both preferred to live on Backer Row. It afforded them more space and home lots connected directly to those of other family members.

William continued with the histories of the early Connecticut Colony.

"Settlers were also leaving other parts of Massachusetts Bay to form new villages in Connecticut. Around the same time we came, Watertown was being founded and constructed along the Great River. Soon after, a group from Newtown led by Reverend Thomas Hooker arrived near the Dutch Fort of Good Hope."

Alice remembered when the group from Newtown left for Connecticut since she was living with and working for the

Holman family at the time, but she said nothing and continued to listen with great interest. She bit her lower lip, nervously wondering if she would ever run into anyone in the group from Newtown.

William resumed, "Our three villages were known as the river towns and formed a coalition of villages that relied on each other in this vast wilderness. In February of 1637, the names of our new towns were changed: Dorchester became Windsor, Newtown became Hartford, and Watertown was renamed Wethersfield by the Connecticut General Court."

Mathias Sension spoke, "When the court decreed that the town change its name from Dorchester to Windsor permanently, many of the townspeople viewed this as an affront. They became resentful towards us since we are largely from the area of Windsor and its surroundings back in England. They viewed us with suspicion and with mistrust, thinking that we had influenced the name change from their beloved Dorchester in favor of one honoring our own origins. The name change was viewed as a blow to the pride of their revered ministers and their cherished roots. They did not take kindly to calling the town Windsor instead of Dorchester. But they had to relent and follow the directive of the General Court."

As the men continued to educate John Young about the town's history, the women exchanged news of family marriages and children's births. They decided to plan for a family reunion the next day.

"Mother and John will want to see you!" declared Mary Sension.

"A celebration is in order. I will send for Mother and John to come over tomorrow. We can have a great feast starting in the afternoon in honor of your arrival, Alice! If there ever was a time to rejoice that the family is largely reunited, it is now. It is only Sarah and her family who are now missing. Perhaps we can convince them to relocate as well. But in any case, I am so happy that we are together again! I am so truly grateful that you decided to settle here and be near us!" she added.

"We should also mark the occasion of your marriage and the birth of your daughter with John Young," suggested Ellen.

"Oh no, please! Do not call attention to us in that way. My husband is very modest and would be upset by such a display. Please, nothing in that regard. I beg of you or I shall be in trouble with him for not stopping such a thing," pleaded Alice.

"As you wish, Alice," assured Ellen.

Alice brightened. "It is enough to rejoice in our reunification! Oh cousins, I have been yearning for this moment from the time we separated in England. You cannot imagine just how joyful it is for me to be reunited with my dear Tinker family once more," she cried, with tears of happiness trailing down her cheeks.

The other sisters nodded and hugged her again. It really was wonderful to be where she belonged. She was both nervous and eager for the reunion the next afternoon.

Chapter 9

WINDSOR, COLONY OF CONNECTICUT, 1641

Preparations for the reunion started early the next day. The Tinker sisters decided that Alice, John, and their daughter would stay with Rhody and her family in the original home of the Hulburds on Backer Row. As the sisters made pies and other delicacies for the family feast, they were more than happy to update Alice on any events that she had missed over the years or give their insights into the characters and personalities of the townspeople.

"Please tell me about life in your new town, dear cousins. Does it suit you well here?" Alice asked.

"It suits us for now. It's a beautiful little town set nicely between two rivers," began Mary. "But truth be told, most Windsor folk have never fully accepted us into the fold."

"Even though we have lived among most of the people here since our time in Dorchester in the Bay, they have treated us differently," clarified Ellen.

"Even before the name change of the town from Dorchester to Windsor," Anne chimed in.

"They try to be kind to us, but even after several years, we can still sense that they regard us as outsiders," added Rhody.

"For they knew each other in the West Country of England, long before they made our acquaintance."

"You see, unlike other settlers, we are the only people coming from Berkshire and other regions near London. The Devon and Dorchester folk have known each other for years, and they stick with each other. They think differently than we do. They are unable to understand the freer views and customs of London and New Windsor, England," explained Mary.

Alice nodded, trying to understand the dynamics of her new surroundings.

"They are country people who know mostly farming. They are extremely devout and strict in their religious beliefs," said Anne respectfully.

"But they are distrustful of those of us who come from a merchant background and the life of the big city," emphasized Rhody.

"They are good people but do not understand the ways of the larger world. They are simple people and have never experienced a grand and bustling city like London with its great guilds and halls," agreed Ellen.

Alice listened to her cousins' insights intently, eager to know more.

"Most townspeople are set in their West Country ways. For the most part, they are unreceptive to new ideas or ways of doing things," reiterated Rhody.

"We do not mean to discourage you in your new home, but life here can feel very constricting when compared to our upbringing. Mother often yearns for the life we once had with father," lamented Ellen.

Those from near London and neighboring towns such as New Windsor, England were also devout but were more in tune with the rhythms of commerce and the irreverent hums of a large city. They were acquainted with the latest introductions from the Continent and exposed to the customs of foreigners as well as many political or theatrical groups. They saw the need for tolerance in order to carry on with and widen their trading circles.

It was with these dynamics that tensions started to grow between the two main groups in town. The more metropolitan group from near London was in a distinct minority. After a time, the influence of that small group became more pronounced, especially when John Tinker strode into town, having just worked for the governor of Massachusetts, Mr. John Winthrop.

"Unfortunately, the tensions between us have only grown since our brother settled in the town. They don't trust him because he worked for Governor Winthrop. The governor's request to the town leaders to grant John a large parcel of property as a reward for exemplary service was grudgingly met."

John Tinker received two hundred twenty-six acres of property north of the main village not far from his mother's allotment. Indeed, working with the governor had been a boost to both his political and economic standing.

"John's allotment is on the southern edge of the Tunxis Indian territory called Poquonock near Stony Brook. It borders the banks of the Rivulet to the east. On it are large stretches of meadow and two ponds. It's beautiful but farther from the town center," explained Ellen.

"He does tobacco farming there with the Tunxis Indians but is still involved in diverse business dealings," spoke Mary. "He's so busy it's hard to keep up with him!"

John quickly became a gentleman farmer, amassing a group of servants to help him start experiments in raising tobacco with seed he purchased in Boston from a Virginia trader. He also invited his closest neighbors, the Tunxis Indians, to continue growing their crops in the meadow as they had done for hundreds of years. In exchange, they showed him and his servants how to plant and grow the newly acquired tobacco seeds from Virginia and tend to his new tobacco fields.

Many other settlers would have felt uneasy working directly with the Indians, but not John. He had met and talked to the Indian chiefs who tried to negotiate with John Winthrop and had also made the acquaintance of the Pequot servants in the Winthrop home taken in captivity after the war. And, he had lengthy discussions about Indian affairs with Winthrop's son, John the Younger, who also had a keen interest in Indian customs and relations. Eventually, he learned some of the dialect of Algonquian spoken by the local Tunxis Indians.

It was so interesting for Alice to see how her cousin had adapted so much to the new land. She always knew he would do well for himself.

The little group of women quickly finished their preparations for the reunion as they spoke of various topics. Everyone was understandably excited for the reunion to begin. This was the first time in several years that the Tinker family was almost completely together. The transition from England was finally over, and they could settle into their surroundings more securely as an extended family unit.

The day of the celebration was gloriously sunny. All the menfolk had finished their work in the fields or workshops early. The Tinker sisters and Alice had busied themselves to bake, roast, and stew a variety of dishes. Several pies were cooling at Rhody's house. People started to arrive in the afternoon and stayed well into the night. John Tinker, his mother Mrs. Tinker, Miles Merwin, and Nicolas Sension paddled across the Little River in a dugout canoe to reach Backer Row and Mary's house.

John Tinker knocked briefly and then opened the door quickly.

"Good day, dear sisters! Cousin Alice, I am so pleased to see you again!" he exclaimed.

He gave her a wink and then walked up to her and the young child she was holding. Dark ringlets framed Alissa's face.

"She is beautiful," he said, staring at her awhile and then glancing once more at Alice before enveloping her in a warm, familiar embrace.

"Mother just told us this morning about your arrival and of your role as a mother. Please introduce us and tell us all about it," John Tinker requested.

Miles, their nephew, bowed a greeting in her direction. Mrs. Tinker and Nicolas Sension had also just come in the door and greeted everyone as well. Mrs. Tinker was happy to see Alissa again and spent the rest of the night doting on her and her grandchildren.

John Young stepped forward.

"Nice to see you again, Mrs. Tinker." Then he introduced himself to the others.

"Ah, the famous John Tinker. Everyone has been talking about you and your great accomplishments. It must have been a real privilege for you to work with the governor of Massachusetts. I understand it's paid off well."

"That is what one would assume by looking at land or contracts," replied John Tinker and continued, "But there are always hidden costs to anything. So what are your plans now that you are here in Windsor?" he asked.

John Young explained his hopes to settle into his own small farm. He had the desire but not yet the experience to do it, as he had grown up in London and not a rural area. John Tinker assured him that he would be able to pick it up just as he himself had done. The other men in the room joined in sharing their experiences with farming. For many of them, New England had been the teacher of a whole array of new experiences including agriculture and animal husbandry.

Despite the move to be with her cousins, Alice was still not quite feeling herself. It was lovely to be with everyone here again, but she needed an excuse to be quiet on her own for a few minutes. Mrs. Tinker was holding Alissa, and Rhody had just come back with the first round of pies. Alice noticed and took advantage of the opportunity.

"Stay here, Rhody, and rest. I will fetch the other pies for you."

"Thank you, Alice! Isn't it wonderful that we are all together again?" said Rhody, hugging her.

"Yes, Rhody. There's hardly anything else that could be more wonderful," she said and smiled gently.

Alice excused herself and went to get the remaining pies from Rhody's house. The beautiful wild red columbines that Rhody had planted outside her door were in full bloom. A brilliantly-colored hummingbird visited them and gained sustenance from their nectar. The fresh air and scenes such as these always made Alice feel better. She sat down for a little while and then returned to the festive gathering with the pies, feeling at once renewed and refreshed.

Most of the family joked, laughed, and told stories well into the night. However, there was also a more serious thread to their conversation. William told the story of their experiences during the Pequot War to all who were listening. It was something the newcomers had to understand in order to fully grasp all the dynamics at hand in the town of Windsor.

William began after the sweet pies were served. He was a wonderful teacher of history and an amazing storyteller.

"Despite our differences with West Country town folk, we had to work with each other for our own protection. In those first insecure years of settlement, we were greatly concerned about Indian attacks by unfriendly tribes. The Pequots on the coast controlled the wampum trade with other tribes, and the colonists thought that they were becoming too aggressive. You see, in 1634, a trader by the name of John Stone was killed by Niantic Indians, near kin of the Pequots."

He paused and took a large gulp of beer before proceeding.

"John Stone was a Virginian and trader who had sailed his vessel to Massachusetts where he stirred up a good amount of trouble. He had a reputation for terrible outbursts of anger, a propensity for immoral behavior, and a fondness for carnal delights. When an unhappy husband found out that Captain Stone had been fornicating with his wife, the philanderer was brought before the General Court to answer for his misbehavior!"

He took another sip of beer and inhaled deeply.

The room immediately filled with lewd commentaries about Stone's depraved conduct, along with name-calling and laughter.

"Whoring scoundrel!"

"Perverted letch!"

"Mr. Ludlow, one of our leaders here in Windsor, was then serving a position at the court in the Bay. According to him, the trader became violently hostile towards the magistrates, stooping so low as to call Mr. Ludlow an ass! He so angered them with his blatant disrespect that he was forbidden to ever come to Massachusetts again under penalty of death."

William paused as his listeners chuckled and offered further irreverent remarks about Captain Stone.

"Shortly after the incident, he left the Bay for the Connecticut River Valley with his vessel, kidnapping and enslaving a couple of Niantic Indians whom he forced to be guides on his ship. Unbeknownst to the trader, the friends of the seized Indians were watching the event unfold and waiting to rescue them and extract revenge. They murdered John Stone and any remaining crew in their sleep, freed their fellow Indians, and then set fire to their craft."

His little audience groaned at the thought of it.

As entertaining as William's story was, Alice had a hard time focusing on it. She was lost in a daydream again until she heard the voice of her cousin John, also a wonderful storyteller, adding his own commentary.

"The leaders of Massachusetts Bay considered the incident to be a Pequot declaration of war, although they also had experienced negative interactions with Captain Stone. The Pequots assured them that Stone's killers had thought the ship to be Dutch and offered payment in wampum and furs for the murder. However, the colonial leaders refused the payment, and the incident was used as an opportunity to demand further Pequot territories. Bay leaders required that the killers be brought before English justice. The magistrates also required the Pequots to make a hefty payment in wampum and agree to trade only with the English, thereby severing all ties to Dutch traders. Sassacus, the Pequot chief flatly refused."

Alice regarded him thoughtfully and admired how distinguished and articulate her cousin had become, yet appreciated that he was still the same warm-hearted person he had always been.

William nodded at John and continued.

"As tensions steadily rose, our English side built a fort at Saybrook. We preferred to maintain a truce with the Pequots, as uneasy as it was. Most people here did not want war. We already had our share of challenges in settling a new town and keeping ourselves fed. The situation remained relatively peaceful until the summer of 1636."

"What happened next?" asked John Young. The others nodded for him to continue.

"Unfortunately, another trader, named John Oldham, was brutally murdered. Oldham had originally settled in Plymouth but was banished from that colony. He ended up in the Bay for a time despite shady propositions concerning land disputes and trading beaver without prior approval from the magistrates," William elaborated.

"He relocated finally to Wethersfield and often traded in the sound off the coast. Oldham was on his way to Block Island to trade on that fateful midsummer day when local Indians killed him. Cold-blooded murder!"

The circle of family members shuddered and moaned as William described the bloody details.

"To this day, the circumstances that led up to his assault remain a mystery. John Gallop, a fellow trader, was passing by in the same waters the next day and spotted Oldham's shallop. He noticed the sails looked peculiar and went to investigate. And there he found old Oldham lying in a pool of his own blood and his shipmates killed as well. The Narragansetts much later admitted responsibility, but the magistrates in the Bay again assumed it was the Pequots who were guilty."

William resumed his story, "Captain John Endecott and his men came from the Massachusetts Colony with instructions to kill all native men found on Block Island and take any Indian women and children prisoner. He burned and pillaged any Indian village he found along the coastline on his quest to find the murderers of John Oldham. Not surprisingly, the Pequots were enraged and they attacked the garrison in Saybrook mercilessly, as its builder, Gardiner, had feared."

He took a deep breath as Mary came and refilled his beer. The others waited for the rest of the story with bated breath.

"But the final episode leading up to war happened in Wethersfield the following spring. In further retaliation, Pequot warriors attacked planters in a field adjacent to the town, killing several and kidnapping two young girls later returned by a Dutch ship. Some say the Pequot did it as revenge for all the Indian children taken for ransom to get information about the traders' murders."

He paused and scratched his whiskers before finishing his thought.

"What infuriated us the most was that, as the Pequot escaped on the Great River, they sailed in barks with sails made up of the clothes taken from the newly dead. Fear and uneasiness gripped our river communities. We scrambled to make alliances with many other Indian tribes for protection."

John Tinker explained the situation.

"Sassacus was then leader of the Pequots. His brother-in-law, Uncas, had split away and started a new tribe that he called the Mohegans. In his rivalry, he sided with us English, as did the Narragansetts and sachems of smaller tribes. As a result, Sassacus found himself quite isolated before the war."

"Very true," said William.

Alice, still unable to concentrate on William's story, was now staring at her daughter, being held by Ellen at the other end of the room.

"With the looming threat of war with the Pequots, we, the people of Windsor, decided to build a stockade for protection. Those of us on Backer Row who had previously received land on the hill overlooking the Rivulet used it for this purpose," William spoke again.

Mathias Sension explained further, "We worked tirelessly to build a palisade made up of high connecting stakes. We fortified it on the inside and added a deep ditch around the outside to protect our simple fortress from any surprise Indian attack."

"All of us townspeople worked together until we finished it," elaborated Thomas.

"We left our homes on Backer Row for a time and built simple dwellings on our properties inside the palisade when the tensions of war were greatest."

"Those were very frightening times," recalled Anne. Everyone murmured in agreement.

Alice needed some air. She was too plagued by daydreams to pay attention to the story and left the room unnoticed.

"A war party was organized by Captain John Mason to deal with the increasing hostilities." said William.

Mathias Sension spoke up, "Captain Mason is an extremely religious man. He lives on the green next to Thomas' tannery. He was eager to lead troops into battle with the Pequots in what he considered a "holy war"."

Thomas Thornton nodded his head and spoke, "Aye, that Captain Mason is firm in his beliefs. A pious man who is certain of himself and the will of God."

"Please continue, William," urged John Taylor, Rhody's husband.

"He left Windsor in the early part of May that year. I remember it well," added William.

"He brought with him ninety troops made up of men from Windsor, Hartford, and Wethersfield. Thirty troops were from Windsor. Our Connecticut colonists joined forces with Captain Underhill and others from the Bay as well as Indian allies: Uncas of the Mohegan tribe and Miantonomo, leader of the Narragansett tribe, with his warriors. Plymouth declined to fight and soon left Windsor after the war."

William spoke seriously, "After our troops left, the remaining men here, including many of us, were on watch at all times for Indian attacks. We quickly became overly exhausted with so many young men gone with Captain Mason's forces. We had to double and triple up with other townspeople in the quickly built dwellings of our fortress so that everyone would be afforded protection and safety. And we dared not leave the Palisado without our guns."

"Indeed, it was a very uncertain time," stated Mathias in a somber tone.

The deep voice of William carried on, "Captain Mason was absent for three weeks and two days with his troops. When those men who were sent to fight in the war came back, they gave horrific accounts of Pequot families being burned to death in a predawn attack. One of our neighbors that fought, young James Eggleston, has not been in his right mind ever since."

He looked engagingly at his listeners and stroked his beard once more.

"The story was that they reached one of two Indian forts by an approach from deep in the woods behind the forts, not by the expected coastal way. The surprise attack began with the slaughter of the stronghold's defenders, followed by a fire set to the entire fort of elderly men, women, and children. Some say Mason chose a massacre instead of a fight with warrior Indians who were waiting for him at another nearby fort," William surmised.

"The sickening aroma of whole families burning alive inside their huts must have been so disturbing to young James Eggleston that he couldn't help but lose his mind," said Mary.

"Some say that the souls of the Pequot Indians that perished that day still come to haunt him and others," added Rhody.

Now everybody in the room was thoroughly spooked.

William continued in a low, serious tone, "Only two English died. In contrast, the young soldiers that came back recounted that there were so many bloodied natives lying on the ground, it was difficult to even walk through the mass of their corpses."

Ellen nodded and made her own contribution to the eerie conversation.

"Poor James. Such a sensitive, sweet young boy he was. The sight of it destroyed him, I say."

John Tinker nodded and said, "Reports were that the Indian allies who stood by at the massacre refused to participate and even remarked at how cruelly the troops led by Captains Mason and Underhill fought by refusing to spare the lives of even Indian women and children."

William described that last scene of the fight.

"Eventually, a force of over a hundred Indian warriors from their fort on the hill to the southwest saw the smoke of their burning sister fort and came to try to rescue friends and loved ones. But they were too late to the battle, and our soldiers were able to escape. At the perfect time, our English ship appeared and led our troops to immediate safety away from dreaded reprisals of the Pequot warriors.

"Captain Mason said that it was God's good providence. Others are not so sure. They say that hundreds of Pequot Indians died that fateful spring day of May the 26th, 1637," William solemnly finished.

Everyone paused to break for beer and stayed silent as they digested the story. Suddenly, Mary noticed that Alice was gone and asked,

"Does anyone know where Alice went?"

"I haven't seen her for a little while," acknowledged John Tinker.

Mary and Anne quickly went to look for her. Their brother, John, and Rhody waited a little while but were about to get up as well when Anne hurried back into the room.

"Alice is crying outside," shared Anne, visibly concerned. "Mary is with her."

"She's very emotional, that one," stated John Young matter-of-factly. "She has her bouts, and there's nothing you can do. She's probably just happy to see you again. She's hard to figure out. How about some more beer?"

Rhody and her other siblings stared at him incredulously and were about to speak, but Mary and Alice entered the room at that moment.

"Alice, my dear, what is happening?" asked Mrs. Tinker, carefully looking at her.

"Oh, 'tis nothing, ma'am. I am just so overwhelmed to be back with the family again. That's all. Please continue with your story, William. Don't mind me," she said as she took hold of Alissa from Ellen and kissed her.

"Aye, William, be a nice gent and tell us the rest," prodded John Young.

William looked at his wife questioningly and then the rest of his listeners. He was waiting for a nod of approval to make sure it was acceptable to continue.

Ellen and the other girls went over to Alice and hugged her tightly.

"We are so happy to have you back with us, Alice," they said.

"Yes. We are," confirmed their sibling, John Tinker, who smiled warmly at her and had just gotten up to embrace her again.

Ellen finally motioned for her husband to continue the story, but she and her siblings still continued to watch over their cousin Alice.

William obliged the others and concluded with the aftermath of the massacre.

"Mason and our government leaders did not rest until they were satisfied that they had decimated the Pequot completely. That summer our soldiers, led by Captain Stoughton, continued to eliminate any remnants of the tribe, capturing hundreds of refugee Pequot Indians. He and his party executed the men and made slaves of the remaining women and children. Some slaves went to Indian allies, and the remaining slaves went to English families. The few enslaved men that survived were sent to Barbados and exchanged for African slaves."

William described a specific event in detail.

"A little further into the summer, leaders got word that the Pequot sachem, Sassacus, and some of his men had survived the attack at the fort and were living in a swamp with their families.

Thomas Stanton, the official Indian translator, successfully negotiated for the surrender of one hundred eighty women and children and two old men on the condition that their lives be spared," he explained.

"The remaining men in the swamp tried to fight but were outnumbered. Observers reported that many Indians that day simply gave up, huddling together as they were killed at close range. But their sachem, Sassacus, did escape with eighty warriors. They made their way to the Hudson to seek refuge with the Mohawks. However, the Mohawks thwarted their plan and murdered them. They sent Sassacus' head to Hartford to prove that he was dead."

William's listeners sighed at the thought of the grisly sight.

"I'll never forget the gruesome day they came back from that excursion in the swamp!" exclaimed Mary.

"Nor will I! I wanted to vomit at the sight," said Ellen as she shuddered.

William enlightened the others as to why the scene would elicit such a strong emotional response.

"Captain Mason and the other soldiers strode into Windsor that day carrying, in a shocking display, the heads of several Pequot warriors on spikes. And what followed was a most pathetic sight. The wives, sisters, daughters, elderly parents, and children of those defeated Pequot warriors, looking shocked and dazed in ropes and chains, were being led into the Palisado."

Alice, now calm and focusing on the story, winced as William recounted it. She remembered her friend, Assanushque, with a tear in her eye and hoped she had not met such a brutal fate. But she also recalled those ghastly heads of traitors on iron spikes placed strategically on the London Bridge, displayed to remind English citizens of the consequences of treason. This was all too familiar.

The final part of William's story continued, "The town leaders and some wealthier families happily took in the Indian slaves to ease their workloads. Captain Mason had told them that the Indian women would look upon the English as liberators from their slovenly and lazy Indian men, but it didn't work out that way."

"That buffoon wouldn't have the slightest idea about life in an Indian village and he certainly has no knowledge of relations between Indian women and their men!" John Tinker interjected.

Other listeners snickered, "Why would the sisters and wives or children of dead Pequot men embrace the very people that killed their loved ones? Why would they be grateful to be taken away from everything they had ever known to slave away at the hands of cruel masters such as Captain Mason?" questioned Mary.

Ellen added, "I felt such pity for them when I saw them on the town green being whipped for doing their tasks incorrectly. How would they even know how to do them? Our customs are foreign to them."

"What happened to the Indian slaves?" asked Alice, who had now composed herself.

"Do they still live in town with different families?"

"Nay," responded Mathias. "They all escaped within a short period of time. They didn't understand or care for our English way. The ones that couldn't escape because of injuries were mysteriously found dead. Many slaves said privately that they would rather kill themselves than serve us English folk."

"How could they anyway? These Pequot slaves often saw other Indian tribes come into town with the severed heads of their kin or friends. Our governments threatened to cut off trade with the allied tribes unless they paid tribute in this way," elaborated William.

"In September of the following year, all the New England colonies decreed the end of the Pequot War in a document called the Treaty of Hartford. It stated that the very existence of the Pequot tribe is forbidden. Even use of the name "Pequot" was outlawed at that time and may still not be spoken. Remaining Pequot Indians had to be called by other tribal names and blended with Narragansett, Mohegan, or Mohawk tribes. It became illegal for them to speak their dialect or practice their religion or customs from that day forth," explained John Tinker.

William finished the evening's story with one final thought.

"You don't hear much about the Pequot Indians anymore. They've died, run away, or become assimilated into other tribes. The palisade was taken down, and Captain Mason became a war hero. Now he's an important man in town and in the General Court. I am glad to tell you the story, but it's best not to talk of these things outside the family. There are some of us that have our doubts and misgivings about the handling of the Pequots."

"It's puzzling to see that, despite our Christian faith, our leaders thought it necessary to allow the violent deaths of Indian women and children," spoke John Tinker thoughtfully.

Indeed, most family members nodded their heads in agreement.

"Aye, don't speak of this to others in Windsor. You might stir up some needless trouble if you do," agreed Mathias Sension.

It was very late. Everyone gathered their things and returned to their homes. John Tinker, his mother, Miles Merwin, and Nicolas Sension stayed in different family homes on Backer Row since it was too late to paddle across to the other side of the Rivulet. Alice was relieved and yet intimidated to have a better understanding of this place she now called home, the town of Windsor.

With the perceived aggression of the Pequot tribe largely annihilated, the colonists moved forward. With their biggest threat to English expansion and colonial development devastated, the settlers focused on their survival and basic needs. The town of Windsor grew, as did all the towns of the colonies.

With time, the residents of Windsor became more self-reliant and resilient. The townspeople felt more secure and could write a new chapter in Windsor's history. They started to feel like the land of Connecticut Colony was their own. Connecticut had indeed become their home. As for Alice, she also felt like Connecticut was home after only a few short weeks of living in the midst of her family again.

Chapter 10

WINDSOR, COLONY OF
CONNECTICUT, 1642

"'Tis a fine thing to see the gristmill open for business again," shouted Mathias Sension to the miller as the busy man hoisted a large, open sack of corn onto his shoulder and fed it into the hopper.

The splashing of water and turning of the large waterwheel, along with the noise of the running stone and gears right next to him, made it difficult to hear. He put a hand behind his ear, gesturing for Mathias to speak up.

"Good morrow, Goodman Howard! Happy to see the mill is running again!" Mathias strained to say.

He nodded quickly and smiled before going back to his many tasks. He had two apprentices also doing various jobs to keep the mill humming.

The gristmill had been closed for two days to clean and dress the millstones. After three weeks of constant use, the granite stones had become too smooth and needed to be sharpened. With it being the end of harvest season, the men were all pleased to see it operating again.

They did not mind standing in line and waiting their turn. Some waited outside, enjoying their pipes of Windsor-grown tobacco as they gazed at the moving waterwheel or across to the millpond that was dammed and controlled by the flow of water through a series of sluiceways.

The constant din of the mill's machinery was a glorious sound, and the wall of men waiting in line at Reverend Wareham's mill was a wonderful sight for it meant that farming in Windsor was finally thriving. It was a relief to the settlers that they no longer had to rely on the Indians for their corn or on their ancient methods of pounding it.

John Taylor voiced his elation.

"Glad not to be pounding corn with a bent tree into the end of a log," he chuckled as he looked around him, reveling in the modern methods employed at the mill.

Small and large gears connected to the main shaft of the waterwheel outside. They were turning in many directions, with the end action of making the running stone turn and grind the grain against the bedstone. It was truly marvelous.

John Taylor was a part-time sailor and a farmer. He owned a very small lot in the Palisado that he bought for possible business ventures but also lived on Backer Row with his wife, Rhody, his two stepdaughters, and his sons.

Thomas Thornton was also sitting with them and voiced his opinion about the matter.

"We toil hard every day. I don't mind it being a little less cumbersome. We've plenty to do even with the mill working!" Thomas Thornton spoke loudly. "In any case, it must be the Lord's plan, with the mill belonging to our pastor," he laughed.

"What I'm most appreciative of is not relying on Pyncheon or his Indian friends for our corn," said Mr. Porter, who was passing by.

"We've done well now since we dealt with the Pequots. Still got to mind your back, but at least we can breathe a little easier," added Mr. Loomis, Mr. Porter's neighbor and brother-in-law.

In addition to making their lives simpler, the mill filled an important social function and became a meeting place for the men. As they waited for the miller to grind their harvests into more usable forms, they caught up on the news of the day.

John Young was also waiting his turn in the gristmill. He took some local tobacco offered to him and lit his pipe, listening to the conversation until he spied John Tinker.

"What cheer, John Tinker?" he approached him.

"Are you faring well in our town?" asked John Tinker politely.

"Aye. The town is growing. There's a great demand for new housing. I can scarcely keep up with the work." As a carpenter, John Young was busy at his trade as well as working his farming allotments.

He and John Taylor together bought and divided a plot of land from William on Backer Row. Rhody and John Taylor continued to stay in the Hulburd's original home. And John Young built a new cottage of simple design and small proportions for his little family on the other half of the former Hulburd property.

"What are you building lately?" John Tinker questioned him to make small talk.

"There's a new tavern I'm just finishing along the outskirts of town by Hartford way. It should be serving libations very soon. The tavern keeper is also a brewer and is using barley grown in town and milled at this very mill."

"That sounds pleasing," John Tinker responded. "How are my cousin and the little girl?"

"Ah! Just fine as usual. And you, John Tinker, pray what have you been up to?" he inquired.

Before he could respond, the miller interrupted him.

"Tinker! Your grain is ready!"

"Pray, pardon me. I shall speak with you sometime soon. I must be going to bring Mother her cornmeal."

In truth, John Tinker was relieved to be on his way. There was something about Goodman Young that he did not care for.

"Aye. I imagine you will. Greetings to our friends on your side of the Rivulet, Miles and Nicolas. And, of course, your mother, too."

John Tinker nodded. He departed with his sacks of meal, having already paid the required 1/16th tithing in grain, as well as an additional tithing to the miller for his services.

As the town men discussed events of the day, the busy miller and his apprentices kept working. Goodman Howard used all his senses to ensure that the stones were not rubbing together and burning their meal. Taking time to smell and feel the finished cornmeal, he was able to assess its quality and the possible need to adjust the width between the grindstones.

The conversations continued as the Windsor men discussed numerous local topics.

"So I see the ferry across the Great River is finally in place."

"Aye. Now it won't be so difficult to get to my livestock on the other side."

"If the town could just do something about improving the road to Hartford. 'Tis a dismal sight. So difficult to travel because of its stumps, ruts, overgrown vegetation, and mud. Better to travel by water."

"Aye," many of the men agreed.

Consequently, there were several shallops that went to and from Windsor. Sometimes even larger ships were seen, too.

"It is a challenge not to be discouraged. Seems like nature has no trouble at all wiping out the fruits of our labor."

The speaker was referring to the town bridge that had been built over the Rivulet to connect the two sides of the town. It had easily washed out in a large storm and flooding earlier that year.

One of them thoughtfully inhaled tobacco smoke from his pipe.

"Aye, 'tis true, but with time we'll get through. So much growth has already occurred in just a short time."

Elias Parkman was in town after several runs up and down the coast with his shallop. On this day, he entered the mill in hopes of finding grain to transport and sell to other locations in Connecticut. He spotted his neighbors from Backer Row and quickly joined in the banter.

"What cheer, neighbors!" he heartily greeted them. He turned to Thomas.

"So what have you been doing of late, Thomas?" he asked.

Although Thomas Thornton had taken up farming in the New World, he never left his trade behind in England and eventually started a tannery on the corner of the Palisado next to the properties of Captain Mason and Walter Fyler. His home lot with his wife and their children was on Backer Row next to the Youngs and the Sensions.

"I'm happy to say the tannery is finally coming along. 'Twas so difficult to start because of a lack of animal hides."

"Aye, but you're a diligent man, Thomas. I knew when more animals came from the ships you'd have your hides, and work would pick up," responded Elias.

"And that it has, except for occasional lulls," Thomas replied. "With the orders for leather from the cobbler and the tailor, I have two apprentices now, not just Miles Merwin as before."

Mathias Sension nodded in understanding. It had been difficult to start his fledgling enterprise in the colonies as well for similar reasons.

"Aye, the work is better now for certain. But I suppose we needed the time to feed ourselves!" he surmised.

They all laughed in agreement, even though the hungry times were really no joking matter.

Mathias Sension worked in London as a chandler but developed his trade and shop slowly in the colonies for the common reason of scarcity of raw materials. Tallow, the animal fat used in his candle-making operations, was initially in very short supply.

"I just started being able to get tallow for candle making, but the need is still greater than what I'm able to make. When we were in Massachusetts, I tried to make do using bayberries to make the candles, but it was tedious and it hardly produced anything."

Out of necessity and survival, he fabricated ovens and branched out into baking as an added trade. He also made soap for sale. Mathias had always been an adaptable man and found it easy to seize opportunities when presented to him. Some of his older boys helped him with the business. Others were apprentices to various tradesmen in town.

At Mathias' side stood William Hulburd, another brother-in-law.

William became a shopkeeper of basic commodities and filled a rudimentary need for basic supplies after the dismantling of the trading house. His brother-in-law, John Tinker, acted as a middleman by greeting ships at different ports in the colony and obtaining much-needed merchandise for William's little trading exchange.

"It's a wonder the town didn't falter more after we lost the fur trade to Pyncheon and then the trading house to Matthew Allyn," added William.

After the Pequot War, the Plymouth Colony leaders, seeing that the group from Dorchester already dominated the town, decided to leave Windsor altogether. It sold the last of its property, goods, and servants to Matthew Allyn, a Hartford merchant and resident at the time. Instead of keeping the trading house functional for Windsor, he decided to take it apart and build a large home with it. The action angered many townspeople, but there was nothing they could do about it, and William Pyncheon in Springfield had already been granted sole rights to trade with the Indians for furs.

"It was a dirty trick of that Allyn, but we survived," Elias agreed. "We've finally got the beginnings of a great little town. We've got the blacksmith and barber on the green. We've got skilled woodworkers and cabinetmakers."

"And a fine gristmill!" Thomas reminded them.

"Aye. Indeed!" concurred the others against the steady din of the mill's moving parts and the rhythmic turning of its impressive water wheel.

By the end of the day, they left with their sacks of meal in tow and their heads filled with the latest news of the town.

———

Just as the men established themselves, Alice and the Tinker women took hold of their own purposes in family and community life. Alice quickly started kitchen and herb gardens from seeds she brought with her from Salem and those she obtained locally. In a couple of years, she had a fairly complete apothecary. Alice also planted some native species that she came to adore. A trellis of sweet American honeysuckle quickly took root and provided her with much delight. It was full of bright little red trumpet flowers that she loved because they attracted hummingbirds.

For Alice, connecting to the Tinker sisters again was one of the best parts of settling into her new town of Windsor and one of the greatest gifts in her life. Being raised in the same household, they continued to be like real sisters, even though Alice was a distant cousin and had been a servant.

As she made her medicines from her new garden and took forays into fields and woods to gather native herbs, Alice began to learn more about her environment. As the seasons changed, so did she, gradually becoming more comfortable in her surroundings. She slowly acquainted herself with the plant beings in the wild marshes and forests. Even though she did not know most of their names, they were like her neighbors in another world outside her otherwise regimented life.

"Alice, you have a way with fairies in the garden. They must love you to help it be so full and lush," said Mary.

"Yes, a true green thumb," agreed Rhody. "Your mother passed her skill down to you."

Rhody and Mary were sitting next to Alice's bursting garden.

Alice beamed, happy to be noticed and appreciated for her talents.

"Rhody, Mary, please come with me to the forest. You must see the rich splendor there."

They both looked at her a little warily.

"The men don't like us to go there. They say it's too dangerous. What if a wolf attacks or an Indian takes advantage of us when no one is looking?" warned Rhody.

"Nonsense. It's beautiful there. You must see what I've found. Please come with me," begged Alice.

The other women looked at each other mischievously.

"Yes, let's. Show us your green treasures then, Alice. We can ask Anne to watch the babies, for I know she would never venture out," suggested Mary.

"The older ones can watch the other younger ones," added Alice.

Rhody shrugged. In spite of her usual independence, she needed a little more prodding.

"Just a short time, Rhody. And only near the edge of the woods. Scarcely farther than where we normally pick berries," encouraged Alice.

"It's agreed then. I cannot deny my curiosity," Rhody conceded.

Once they settled their children with Anne, Alice led them to the edge of the forest, where she quickly found a barely discernible path under the trees. The forest gave way to a different type of scenery that was lush and wild.

Spring had passed, but the wild cabbage-like plants sitting low to the ground remained.

"I know those strange plants. They grow close to the stream near the house," pointed out Mary.

"Aye," Rhody recognized them, too. "They have the stinking maroon-colored flowers in early spring."

Because the flowers smelled so awful, they came to be known as skunk cabbage by the next generation of settlers.

Alice explained to them, "A sighting of the rotten-smelling flower marks a time to start looking for the delicate white-petaled flowers of the red puccoon."

She scanned the forest floor and found an older weatherworn leaf. She pulled it out of the ground and showed them its roots. When broken, they appeared to bleed like a fresh human cut. Soon the roots would be ready to gather.

"Assanushque taught me to treat certain skin problems and sore throats with it. But red puccoon is very powerful, so great care is needed to use it in a weakened tea," she said, then added, "Indians also use the root to make a red dye."

She explained to them how its flowers were low to the ground and only lingered for about a week. Their leaves folded around their stems like infantile hands growing into larger, more mature hands as the spring and then summer wore on, long after the little flowers' white petals had been blown away by winds.

A few steps beyond, Alice spotted its sister plant, the yellow puccoon, that awoke from its winter slumber slightly later in the spring. Dainty greenish-yellow flowers had transformed into bright red berries. It was interesting how it, too, was low to the ground as if to safeguard its valuable root.

"Soon it will be time to gather its bright yellow roots. 'Tis binding in hot and wet conditions to balance the humors to a drier and cooler state of health."

She explained how Assanushque powdered the root or made a tea out of it for eyewashes, mouthwashes, and gargles. It also soothed and dried weeping, inflamed wounds or other conditions of an inflammatory nature.

The women took a few more minutes to linger and glance at the variety of plant life Alice pointed out. As they returned near a stream, Alice also showed them tall plants with hollowed-out stems and tiny yellow or orange flowers in full display on the sloping hills above the riverbanks. The sensitive flowers coiled back if touched and came to be known as touch-me-nots. She showed them the fresh sap inside the stems that was cooling and soothing enough to stop an itch.

It was also at this same time that the lush, deep purple berries of the elderberry shrubs along the river would offer their marvelous bounties for use in jams and medicines to treat scourges of a febrile nature. Mary and Rhody recognized them, too.

" 'Tis a great gift to find elderberries also growing in the forests of the colonies," Mary stated and thought of their familiar uses back home in England.

Late August was alive as well with other new delicacies for their eyes in the form of the flowering of snakeheads with their beautiful pink and cream flowers in the flood plains of the Rivulet. Later settlers would see them and think of the heads of turtles instead.

At the same time, the bright red, petite and delicate blooms of cardinal flowers harkened passers-by in canoes to explore the riverbanks where they grew. Their colors earned them their name, just like the brightly red-colored birds that would sing to each other in the woods. These were just a small sampling of the treasures that the woods offered.

"Alice, look! A beautiful bouquet of flowers in the hollowed-out hole of that old tree!" exclaimed Rhody.

"Curious," said Mary.

Alice peered into the tree and grinned.

"Ah, sweet treasure left from a dashing knight of the forest as tribute to his Earth queen. I have seen stranger things," she laughed and changed the subject. "The sun keeps moving farther west, Rhody. We must be going," she added as she gestured to the sky.

Alice, being mindful of the time and Rhody's initial hesitations, did not keep them in the forest for long. They slipped back to the fields on the edge of the woods and rapidly picked wild raspberries and placed them into baskets before going home. Alice's green treasures had put them all into good moods and eased their worries.

"Thank you, Alice. The flowers were beautiful. But I still won't be going there on my own. 'Tis a bit too wild and strange for me," spoke Rhody.

Mary looked at Alice seriously and approached her, placing a hand on her shoulder.

"Alice, it's comforting to me that you know so much about this wilderness already and that you are able to apply what you have learned for the rest of us. I would like it very much if you were my assistant midwife. I'm confident in your soothing ways."

"Yes, Alice, you've already used your skills to help family members. And with all of us singing praises about your medicines and abilities, other neighbors have started to call you to their sickbeds. You might as well help Mary, too," reasoned Rhody.

Alice paused and smiled sweetly at both of the women she loved dearly. She had only one child and hence more time to be of service to others. She had also found herself and her calling ever since Winifred and Assanushque had mentored her. She knew it was time to give back to her community.

"I suppose I will," she said.

From that afternoon forth, she became Mary's assistant and a folk doctor in the town. What Alice gathered from the wild places and her gardens went into her medicines with a prayer for healing and a sentiment of gratitude. Her successes in treating common illnesses and conditions earned her a trusted reputation as a healer. She seemed to be much more successful in her attempts than even the doctor, Bray Rossiter. But no one voiced these opinions too loudly. Soon, Alice's advice was sought out by an even larger group of community members.

As much as Alice wanted to help others, she struggled to overcome her shyness. But as she dutifully went to the sickbeds of those that needed her, her desire to be of service to others became stronger than her timid nature. She remembered what her mother and Winifred taught her about treading carefully and humbly so as not to offend those in power or call too much attention to herself.

She was also weary of her intuitive abilities and her gift of sight at times. As a child, she remembered the stories of those who were misunderstood and persecuted for their gifts. It was a new world and a new time, though. She thought that perhaps now that the godly were in a new land, things would be different. A new religious experience was the whole reason that opportunities had arisen to go across the sea in the first place.

Consequently, the most fundamental development in the town of Windsor and every reformist town in New England was the construction of the meetinghouse. Alice realized this and was mindful that it and those at its pulpits were central to everything else.

Inside the meetinghouse were the oratories of proud pious Puritan men that gave the reasoning for all their early actions in the new land. They justified their forays into the wilderness to create new places dedicated to God. And they justified their brutality in wiping out whole Indian nations as the providence of God and His will against the heathens. They were resolute in their righteousness and their convictions. They, like good shepherds watching over their flocks, would be on guard against wolves and Satan in his many forms.

Chapter 11

WINDSOR, COLONY OF
CONNECTICUT, 1642

S amuel Eggleston scaled the stairs to the belfry of the simply-
constructed meetinghouse early in the morning. One day,
perhaps in the far-off future, a foundry in Boston would forge
a new bell. But for now, drums, and occasionally a trumpet,
called the townspeople to meeting. He went out to the platform
and began beating his drum at the level of the thatched roof
and cupola to alert the townspeople that it was time for lecture.
Steadily, he pounded out the message, pacing along the planking,
until he was sure that all were warned to come promptly to the
weekly Sabbath ritual.

Alice and the others quickly ate the last of the morning's
meal of sampe, pulled on their coifs, and heeded the drummer's
call. Sitting in the meetinghouse on this mild, warm September
day was more tolerable than being there in chilly winter.

For Alice, her family, and her cousins, Backer Row was only
a short walk away from the meetinghouse. They joined other
families, single tradesmen, and servants and blended into a unison
file once they heard the end of the drum's call. Several men
carried arms for protection. Some villagers came by horseback

and carefully tied their animals to the block outside before the sermons began. Mrs. Tinker, John Tinker, Miles Merwin, and Nicolas Sension often came together in their dugout canoe farther upstream on the Rivulet. The Backer Row part of the family usually waited on the town green for their relatives from the other side of the Rivulet before entering the meetinghouse together.

"Mother, where's John?" Rhody asked, inquiring about the whereabouts of her brother.

"He went to trade in Boston again. He was expecting some special shipments from London last week," replied Mrs. Tinker.

"And when is he returning?" his sister Mary questioned her.

"It should be any day now."

"Did he go with anyone else?" asked Alice.

"Thomas Hopewell, his Indian assistant."

"What kind of shipments, Mother?" Ellen prodded her.

"I don't know, girls! I'm sure he'll tell you all about it when he gets back, which should be any day now."

The meetinghouse doors opened and most Windsorites dutifully filed in.

"Come, we must not dally or we will end up like poor Goodman Ponds over there," Mrs. Tinker said, tilting her head towards the stocks.

Nearby on the town green, the whipping post, the pillory, and the stocks stood as a reminder for all to meet their requirements of honoring the Sabbath and adhering to the godly principles taught in the meetinghouse throughout the week. On this particular day, an unlucky sinner was serving his punishment, dejected and humiliated, as Sabbath attendees passed. Benjamin Ponds was an unfortunate servant who had stolen from his disgruntled employer. The exposed thief hung his head in shame before the crowd. No one envied him. Passersby either ignored him or spoke severely to him with their chastisements.

"That will teach ye to keep your hands in your own pockets."

"For shame! Taking what's in the coffers of others!"

The affluent and highly ranked members of Windsor never found themselves in such humiliating positions. Instead, they deliberated secretly and were given fines for any offense they had committed, thereby avoiding public displays of disgrace. Embarrassment bestowed to the ordinary citizen was agreeable to them, but they hid their own improprieties from view.

The Tinker clan quickly filed past the disgraced servant. The meetinghouse they approached was constructed in simple, unpainted clapboards that were starting to turn grey. Between leaded-glass windows along rectangular walls, gruesome bounty heads of wolves were freshly tacked to outside walls, leaving grisly splatters and trails of blood. Alice tried not to look at them as she walked on the steppingstones toward the entrance. They repulsed and sickened her.

As she and other villagers slowly filed into the meetinghouse, they glanced at the most recent notices stuck to the entryway doors. Tattered announcements of impending marriages, property or livestock sales, hangings, and other town events provided the news and gossip of the day.

Inside, the meetinghouse was stark and bare. The only furnishings were a simple communion table and chairs in front of the pulpit. It lacked plastered walls, curtains, or adornments except for one large dominating eye painted high on the pulpit.

The unmistakable, all-seeing eye of God was placed there to remind the congregation that God and his religious representatives were watching their every action. Its purpose was to jolt them to be mindful of their thoughts and the pureness of their hearts. Alice found it unnerving. The eye, the ever-powerful eye-carefully watching and waiting for humanly lapses and weakness.

Alice took her place on a bench on the right-hand side with her cousins. Their men sat separated from them on the left side, as dictated. Alissa sat on a stool in front of her mother but soon ended up in her lap. Other little girls did the same with their mothers. The tithing man, Ezekiel Sexten, directed younger boys to the gallery steps where deacons and elders could closely monitor the youths' boisterous behavior. Older children and servants sat high in the galleries. Every pew or bench in the meetinghouse had been carefully arranged and assigned. Those of greatest age, position, and wealth sat in the front. Deacon Gaylord and Deacon Henry Clarke positioned themselves near the pulpit with Elder John Branker, Elder William Hosford, and Elder John Witchfield. They faced the congregation and sullenly and suspiciously watched their movements.

The tithing man, Ezekial Sexten, scrutinized the small crowd gathered there and made sure everyone was seated and in their proper places. Then he gestured to the pastors. Reverends Wareham and Huit entered solemnly, wearing their skullcaps and full capes, accompanied by their wives. The Windsor townsfolk stood up in deference as they entered, awaiting the signal to sit down again.

After the clerical procession into the meetinghouse, doors were closed, and no one was allowed to leave. The congregation had become devout prisoners of faith and religious captives of the Sabbath. Sentries were posted outside to guard the townspeople as they prayed in case of Indian attacks.

The stage was now set, and the gaze of the all-knowing eye escaped no one. Reverend Wareham turned the hourglass and commenced his endless sermons. The cleric read from his notes, animated about the sins he attempted to save his flock from. And they, in turn, listened intently to the dedicated leader who had led them there.

"What is the Seventh Commandment? What does the Bible say?" he questioned.

Reverend Wareham frequently paused and stared intensely at his congregation. They respected him. His burdens were great when he brought them to a better land. His co-minister Maverick in Dorchester and his own wife had both died in the Bay, yet he remained strong in guiding them to the lands in Connecticut once called Matianuck. When a deadly smallpox epidemic wiped out multitudes of Indians and left much of their fertile land almost vacant, it confirmed to the pious pastor a need to build this settlement and devote it to the Almighty.

Despite the high regard bestowed on him by his community, Reverend Wareham seemed uncertain of himself and his own salvation. He was prone to long bouts of depression and sometimes denied himself the same communion that he gave to his followers. Perhaps he blamed himself for the deaths of his first four children, who were born early and died before they were a week old. They had always weighed heavily on his heart. Their deaths were like a punishment from God that had always made him wonder how he could have been a more unwavering and faithful servant.

"Thou shalt not commit adultery. In essence, thou shalt not compromise the chastity of thy neighbor or thyself. God demands of us that we preserve not only the chastity of ourselves but also the chastity of our neighbor. The act of adultery brings a dark stain upon oneself and thy neighbor," he cautioned.

"Matthew 5:28 teaches us, 'But I say unto you, That whosoever looketh on a woman to lust after her hath committed adultery with her already in his heart.'"

Seated next to the pulpit, Reverend Huit nodded with each pronouncement made by his senior minister. Ephraim Huit was the replacement for Reverend Maverick. The previously prosecuted cleric had fled Warwickshire, England and escaped punishment by coming to the colonies with his wife, Isabelle, their daughters, and his nephews, Daniel, Henry, and Joseph Clarke.

The congregation in Windsor and Reverend Wareham were immediately impressed by his energy, stamina, and drive on behalf of the church when he preached a sermon the day after he arrived. They quickly decided to ordain him teacher of the church by the end of that year.

Alice wondered how many times his head would bob in agreement to Reverend Wareham's assertions. She and others on Backer Row knew him all too well. After his arrival, Ephraim Huit was allotted and bought property in the Palisado and a home lot on Backer Row from Sergeant Thomas Staires. He resided at first in the Palisado, but when the threat of Indian attacks diminished he spent most of his time at his home on Backer Row, where he kept a watchful eye over his neighbors.

"With unmarried persons, this sin is termed FOR-NI-CA-TION!" the minister emphasized.

Just then, a loud snicker followed by an uncontrolled guffaw echoed from the boys sitting on the stairs leading to the gallery. The tithing man quickly responded in kind by slamming his two-foot cane onto the skulls of the guilty parties.

The deacons and elders were more than happy to assist him by glaring at the boys in such a way that ensured the smoldering of any lingering laughter.

Once the meetinghouse became completely silent again, the pastor continued.

"Deuteronomy 22:28-29 notes, 'If a man find a damsel that is a virgin, which is not betrothed, and lay hold on her, and lie with her, and they be found; Then the man that lay with her shall give unto the damsel's father fifty shekels of silver, and she shall be his wife; because he hath humbled her, he may not put her away all his days'."

The boys on the stairs could barely contain themselves. The sermon was more entertaining than most.

The minister paused and inhaled deeply, finally releasing an exaggerated sigh.

"The Bible cautions us that for those who are married or at the least betrothed, the term used is A-DUL-TERY and the same punishments are given to both for this sin," he warned.

"From the holy words of Proverbs 6:32, the Lord hast warned, 'But who so committeth adultery with a woman lacketh understanding: he that doeth it destroyeth his own soul.' Marriage is the covenant of God only. Thus an adulterer breaketh his sacred pact with God by breaking the bonds of the marriage contract. As doth the Lord admonish in Corinthians 6:18, 'FLEE FORNICATION. Every sin that a man doeth is without the body; but he that committeth FOR-NI-CA-TION sinneth against his own body," appraised the pastor from his exalted place high on the pulpit.

It was too much for the naughty boys on the stairs. Uncontained laughter flowed like beer from a newly tapped barrel. Once more, the tithing man harshly revisited their bruised skulls with the unbridled rapping of his knotted cane. The deacons and elders stood and scowled to threaten them as a last warning against future wicked intrusions.

A few minutes later, with the order of the meetinghouse once again restored to an oppressive stillness, an undeterred Reverend Wareham continued preaching.

"And yet again in Deuteronomy 22:22-24, we find, 'If a man be found lying with a woman married to an husband, then they shall both of them die, both the man that lay with the woman, and the woman: so shalt thou put away evil from Israel. If a damsel that is a virgin be betrothed unto an husband, and a man find her in the city, and lie with her; Then ye shall bring them both out unto the gate of that city, and ye shall stone them with stones that they die; the damsel, because she cried not, being in the city; and the man, because he hath humbled his neighbor's wife: so thou shalt put away evil from among you.

This is a great sin, as may appear in that it is the punishment of idolatry'."

Alice did her utmost to stay awake through long lectures but often became quite drowsy. It was only Alissa and her constant fidgeting on her mother's lap that kept her fully awake. Turn after turn of the hour glass, she struggled to keep her eyes open and her mind pious as Reverend Wareham read the notes of his sermons one page after the next, frequently looking at his audience in a stern yet animated fashion.

"And as for the children begotten of this sin and marked with such a stain, they may not enter the church as it sayeth in Deuteronomy 23:2, 'A bastard shall not enter into the congregation of the LORD; even to his tenth generation shall he not enter into the congregation of the LORD.' The adulterer maketh his family shunned from his community'." He stared at the congregation, holding up his pointing finger and continued lecturing for the better part of an hour.

When the lively and admonishing lecture finally ended, Reverend Huit stood and spoke to the congregation.

"The tithing man will collect the obligations of each household."

Ezekiel Sexten signaled for the head of each family to file up to the tithing box in front in order of their rank. The community dutifully contributed, as they were required to do. They placed an array of coin, wampum, and mostly promissory notes for farm or other goods that slowly paid back the costs of construction of the meetinghouse.

"We shall sing Psalm 6 in reflection of our human weaknesses," Reverend Huit instructed. The deacons and elders were the only ones with songbooks and took turns reciting their verses with the congregation singing verses back to them. But try as they might, without musical notes or guidance, the resulting sound was a howling cacophony.

"Lord, in Thy wrath, rebuke me not."

The congregation repeated the same words in an unsettling disharmony.

"Nor in hot wrath chasten me."

"Pity me, Lord, for I am weak."

They dutifully recited each verse in an eerie echo.

And so it continued for many minutes more.

Finally, the last verse sung, Ezekiel Sexten opened the solid wood doors of the meetinghouse. The pastors allowed for an intermission from the services, a welcome midday break. The men, women, and children of Windsor filed out for a brief respite from threats of eternal damnation.

Nooning was the joyous reprieve between the sermons when families gathered for a midday morsel. In winter, it was a time when the congregation warmed up at someone's hearth on the Palisado Green.

On this day, the Tinker sisters, Alice, and their families followed their usual habit of meeting at the Hulburd's home. Ellen had baked spiced cakes for the gathering and quickly made refreshing drinks. With great relief, they chatted and gossiped about the community events of the week. But the time spent socializing between sermons was fleeting. In what seemed like a very short time, the beating of the drum summoned them back to the meetinghouse for further scriptural instruction.

The heavy doors slammed shut again with a thud, and everyone resumed their places. Once more, the hourglass turned. Once more, the reverends read and lectured from the scriptures of the Bible. Boys fidgeted and girls daydreamed. Dogs slept at their masters' feet, and the church elders monitored and surveyed the faces of the faithful.

The ministers, Reverend Wareham and Reverend Huit, hoped that their sermons had helped their followers come to grips with their sinful and wicked ways. At a minimum, the clerics desired that their congregation be ready to start another week of work dedicated to God. Their highest aspirations were to help their congregation surrender their hearts more fully and dutifully to their Creator. Pastors, deacons, and elders did their best to keep the followers on a righteous and devoted path.

For Alice, the time moved on slowly and painfully. She was unaware that others in the meetinghouse felt the same way. And she dared not ever voice these sacrilegious sentiments. She resolved to be more devoted and virtuous the next week but could not deny the relief that came when it was time to open the doors again.

A soft breeze blew. The gentleness of nature was welcome after hours of harsh words from the pulpit. The time following sermons was lovely and sacred for Alice. She had a precious few hours each week during which she was not toiling in the fields, laboring over a hot fire, or tending to some kind of chore in general.

After sermons, her daughter enjoyed playing with her cousins. John, her husband, met with other men in the village to discuss various affairs. Freed from the cooking of Sunday's meal, the womenfolk in town took advantage of the time to gossip amongst themselves. It was the one time of the week that Alice sometimes took leave of her cousins' company and ventured into the forest.

It was not possible for her to go into her beautiful woods every Sunday, but as often as she could, she invented an excuse to be there. Others feared the forest. To them, it was the place of savages, the untamed wilderness where the Devil himself abode. But for Alice, it was different.

She felt great comfort, peace, and tranquility to be amongst the majestic trees and curious plants of a lush new world. The forest here seemed to pulsate with a magical energy that could draw one deep into the realm of other realities, realities where anything was possible. Her spirit felt free among the trees, hidden from the ever-watchful eye.

Alice carefully and eagerly slipped away, being cautious not to be noticed. The time she had to delight in her special place was limited.

In a wooded grove of rich evergreens, a giant Sycamore stood firm near the riverbank. Its trunk was thick and multi-colored with a hollowed-out knot. Uplifted by the whispering wind, its leaves swayed towards her, acknowledging her presence. At its base, red cardinal flowers opened in ecstasy to satisfy a beautiful hummingbird searching out nectar for its sustenance.

She sat among them in a bed of ferns and waited for the renewal of her spirit. Nothing soothed her being more than the sweetness of this calm and mesmerizing place. Such was her bliss that a moment easily transformed into an hour or more.

She arose from the bed of ferns, pulling her hair back tightly and then placing it under her coif. She allowed her bare feet one last sensation of touching the mossy carpet below before pulling on her stockings and slipping on her shoes again. Finally, she was ready to commence another week of toil and sacrifice.

Chapter 12

———— ⬬ ————

WINDSOR, COLONY OF
CONNECTICUT, WINTER 1642-1643

Winter was fast approaching. As much as Alice did not want to be closed inside for the winter, she was looking forward to socializing with her cousins in their cloth-making circle. Soon, the women had more time for gossiping, sharing stilling recipes, and giving advice. The friendship, laughter, and tears between them made the cold, harsh winter pass a little faster. The bitter chill in the air seemed to dissipate with a roaring fire, creating hands at work, and jubilant laughter. Alice often lost herself in the stories, the memories, and the jokes shared by all. The circle made the reality of her life a little less severe.

As they resumed weaving, spinning, and stitchery together, they infused the cloth they made with love, laughter, impressions, concern, teasing, tears, and secrets that they shared.

The Tinker women and their cousin took advantage of the fledgling colony's desperate push to encourage homespun cloth production. Precious cargos of linen, hemp for cordage and sails, and other textile goods came too infrequently from England to meet even the most basic colonial needs. Herds of sheep used for wool were also in scarce supply. The Tinkers did their best to help fill this void for textile goods through their own cloth-making efforts.

Even though it was mandatory that every home have a spinning wheel and every woman and child spin fiber, the Tinkers were more expert than most. Large and small spinning wheels that produced both wool threads and smaller ones of flax and hemp graced their homes. The sheep, brought with them from solid Berkshire County stock, grazed in the Pound Close between the Palisado and Backer Row and gave them plenty of wool for their weaving endeavors.

Because of their upbringing with a textile merchant father and the influences from the region where they were raised, they had specialized knowledge about spinning, weaving, and fabric production in general. At a very young age, they learned how to spin flax into fine linen thread and how to card and process wool into many kinds of cloth.

They met at each other's homes in the Palisado or on Backer Row, bringing their spinning wheels, embroidery, or wool to be carded. At the Hulburd house, they often weaved upon a much larger and more complicated loom. In the early years of Windsor, it was the only large loom in the town. Occasionally, other members of the community came with their processed yards of flax thread and requested that the Tinker women weave them into cloth.

Their daughters were also part of the circle. They came to learn everything a young woman needed to know about cloth production, including dying fabrics or carding and preparing wool. Their hands were also busy at the spinning wheels or simple looms. They learned various skills of stitchery and embroidery and often practiced for hours on their samplers in anticipation of being matriarchs of their own homes one day. There, they came to assess through their mothers' insights their roles within the town and the strengths or deficits of possible suitors.

Sometimes, the Tinker sisters' brother, John Tinker, came to visit, often bringing their mother from the other side of the Rivulet. He relished telling them stories about his various travels, multiple trades, and working with the Indians.

John often took what they produced, their finely spun flax or wool and woven cloth, and brought it to Boston to trade for other commodities. At times, he used it in barter when he traded with the Podunk, Tunxis or other Indian tribes. He was technically not allowed to trade such needed materials with them since William Pyncheon possessed sole rights to trade with the Indians at his trading post in Springfield. But on such a small scale and at such reasonable rate in wampum and beaver furs, he could not resist.

Thomas Hopewell, John's assistant and translator, was a lone young Nipmuck Indian man who had no kin left. He helped John in every way and was a valuable resource. He had known the English since he was a young child and was familiar with their peculiar ways. For survival's sake, he started trading with them.

It was during such a transaction that he met John and decided to work for him on his large tobacco plantation as well as assist him in trading with other natives. John was more pleasant than most of the English he encountered, and soon they had developed an odd and unusual friendship for the times.

One chilly day at the end of February, when snow still lay upon the ground, John decided to stop by and pay a visit to all his sisters and his nieces in the weaving circle. John had decided to take a short journey when the snows started to abate and wanted to see if they had any finished cloth or thread that he could sell for them. They were working at the Hulburd house where the big loom was set up. They had already dyed some carded wool a rich indigo color and spun enough of it to weave an ample amount on the large loom in the previous month. John would be happy to see that a small supply of fine indigo flannel material was ready for sale.

John knocked on the door from the frigid cold and then quickly pushed it open in haste to join his sisters in the warmed air by the hearth.

"Good day, dear sisters, lovely nieces and, of course, our fair Alice and her lovely daughter," he grinned.

"What are my favorite ladies working on today?"

John was warm, personable, and outgoing. He was also very kind and caring. His sisters loved to dote on him and welcomed his boyish presence. His mother did not understand why he had not yet chosen a wife. But John was independent and was always involved in many enterprises. His mother was resigned to wait impatiently.

He looked over at Alice. She was creating a very fine needlepoint with a hummingbird and bright red wild bee balm flowers.

"Ah, so your head is with the birds and the flowers again, Alice. You'd be a little red flower yourself if you could," he laughed.

Alice looked up and gently smiled. A small tingle chased up her spine.

"In honor of your fine flower, Alice, I have a new story for all of you today. Another little gem that Thomas Hopewell told to me. The Indians have many legends and tales about every plant and animal imaginable. Sometimes the same story is told in more than one tribe in different versions. Today, dear ladies, I have a sweet one for you. Can you recall the little pink slipper-like flowers that grow near the pine and hemlock groves at the middle of May until the beginning of June? They look like little moccasins. Well, the Indians have quite the legend of how some of them came to be."

All eyes were on John. They loved the stories he told about his adventures and his encounters with the Indians. "Tell us, John. Pray thee, tell us!" they begged.

John smiled. "Dear ladies, I give you *The Legend of the Moccasin Flower* as told by Thomas Hopewell from a tribe he encountered in the northwestern regions on his travels."

Everyone was silent now. They looked up from their looms, their spinning, and their needlework, intent on hearing every word describing the mysterious world they were so curious about.

"It is the story of a young Indian maiden who admired and looked up to her brother."

He winked and then began his tale.

"Many winters ago, along the banks of a great river, there was a tribal village. In this village lived a brother and his younger sister. The brother was being trained by the elders of his tribe to be a messenger who would communicate with other nearby tribes and also act as a courier. He was talented at everything a young brave needed to know. He could track and hunt animals with great skill, stalking them in silence, and he could swim effortlessly like an otter. His younger maiden sister loved him and yearned to do all that he could do. She was not sure what to do in her own life, so she followed him everywhere. He tolerated her constant presence and when he was patient, taught her the many skills that he knew, especially how to be a messenger and tread softly on the trails to other places through the woods."

John looked around the room to enjoy the wonderment on the faces of his dear nieces and continued.

"One day that winter so long ago, some people in the village fell ill. A sickness had quickly ravaged their entire community and left debilitating fevers and increasing weakness. The illness wore on, and soon the villagers had depleted all their local medicinal cures. The elders of the village were concerned and wanted to send the young Indian brave to fetch more medicines from an old healer woman across the great frozen river. But winter raged on with howling winds and unrelenting snows. Unfortunately, even he suffered from the ravaging illness."

"What happened next, Uncle John?" pleaded little Anne, the Thornton's daughter.

With a hushed, serious tone, John explained.

"Panicked to see her dear brother ill, as well as many of her other beloved family members and friends, the young Indian maiden desired to make the treacherous journey herself. She pleaded her case to the village elders and asked that they send her in his place. They were hesitant at first but had no other choice, or the whole village might suffer further danger or probable death. So they sent the Indian maiden in the thickest of animal furs covered from her head to her feet, including a warm coat, leggings, and winter moccasins."

The room was silent as the girls listened intently to John's story.

"It was bitter cold, and a winter storm stirred as she traveled, but the courageous maiden stood up to the ferocious winter winds and, step by step, made her way towards the village and its revered old healing woman. The daring maiden crossed the solidly frozen river undeterred as the ice crackled under her feet and the wind whipped. She could see the village fires burning in the distance and persevered onward until she reached the opposite shore."

John looked around the room again. Everyone was entranced with his borrowed tale. They were no longer looking at their weaving of indigo flannel but at his animated face, and imagined the Indian maiden trudging through the snow. A look of relief came across their faces as they found out that she had safely forded a narrow portion of the river. Farther upstream, the determined maiden succeeded in reaching the healing woman and her greatly needed medicines on the other side of the frozen waters.

He continued, "The young maiden was wrapped in warm bear furs and placed by a fire in the healing woman's hut. There, the young maiden told the story of the suffering of her people and felt rushed to return to them. The old woman bade her to rest for the night. She offered to send her back with young warriors in the morning after the storm had passed. The healing woman encouraged her to accept the warriors' assistance in making her way across ever higher snow and thick ice."

John took a breath and resumed, "But the young maiden, after briefly napping by the fire, awoke when the hissing wind stopped beating against the hut. She quickly dressed in her warm, dry clothes. She slipped the pouch filled with dried medicinal herbs prepared by the medicine woman around her neck and underneath her coat. She then set off into the cold winter night. She was concerned for her people and, despite her fatigue, forced herself to return that night with the medicines that were so desperately needed."

"Did she make it back to her village, Uncle John?" sweet Sarah Sension asked, determined to know the outcome without further delay.

He answered, "This time the snow was deeper, and she struggled at first with each footstep. Then she remembered the lessons her brother taught her about swimming like an otter. She pretended that she was an otter and that the snow was water. She danced through it in the swimming motions of that animal. It took her many hours, and eventually she lost her fur-lined moccasins in the snow. Her feet became frozen and bloody, but she stubbornly strode on with absolute determination until finally, in the early hours of the morning with the eastern sun rising, she reached her village."

Every little girl in the room seemed visibly relieved as John elaborated.

"The tribe heard her stumbling into the village and ran to her. They carried her to her hut where they warmed her and rubbed healing salves into her feet. The herbs she brought saved the villagers from their illness and they would be forever grateful to the young Indian maiden."

He paused again to glance at his enraptured audience.

"In the spring, her brother went with her to help find the missing moccasins on the shores of the meandering river. They searched the woods and the shores along the river for several miles. They never did find the moccasins, but instead, at the place of every step the maiden had taken where her bloodied and injured feet had left a mark, there was a pink moccasin flower in its place. A beautiful flower to commemorate the drops of blood shed by the feet of a courageous maiden's journey to bring healing herbs back to her people."

Ellen sighed and said, " 'Tis a beautiful story, John. Exquisite flowers to mark each step of her hardship and sacrifice for her family and her community."

"I do love your stories, Uncle John!" cried out Priscilla, the oldest child of Anne.

Hannah, Anne, Sarah, and Alissa nodded and giggled in unison. The pack of cousins adored their Uncle John.

"I want to be an Indian maiden!" cried out Hannah.

"Now, John, mind yourself, or you're going to make these children tempted to run off with the Indians," scolded his younger sister Anne as she smiled at the same time.

"Now, little sister, don't even let the magistrates hear you joking like that, or they'll cast their big eye on you and your children. It appears that a good many of our English are quite drawn to the Indian way of life. Many indentured servants and others have gone off to the woods to be with the Indians and live amongst them. They find their way of life to their genuine liking. So much so, that the magistrates have devised a new law against it which is now a part of Connecticut's Code of Laws."

"And what would they do to a person if they found him running off like that?" inquired Rhody with curiosity.

"Would they hang someone in the gallows for living with the Indians?" asked Sarah.

"Nay," responded John.

"Should a person go settle with the Indians and take on their customs and their way of life, the colony would hunt them down and force them to be imprisoned for three years as a punishment for their crime. The accused criminal might sit in the house of corrections being visited by minister after minister. Finally, he might go free after convincing the clergy of his belief in the godly doctrine again and acknowledging the evil ways of the heathen Indians. And of course, should that person still be determined to follow what they call a "profane course of life", they might make him undergo further corporal punishments or fines." He shook his head.

"What crimes do people commit to actually hang from the gallows, Uncle John?" asked Sarah, Mary's oldest daughter, in a very serious and hushed tone with her eyes open wide.

She barely breathed again until she heard his response.

"Murder, witchcraft, adultery..." answered John.

"You ladies have nothing to fear," he chuckled, "for I see no ability or desire of a murderous vein here. But I'd mind how some of you have a sweet way with how you treat your animals. If the magistrates see how they love you and follow you around, you might be accused of having a familiar and being a witch! And, hopefully, no one here should be gifted with ever knowing anything that could be construed as sight or foretelling. Why, that might also get you in a cauldron of trouble!"

He didn't call Alice out by name, but he looked at her and winked.

She shook her head and grinned, always amused by his antics.

"Enough of this macabre talk," playfully chastised Mary.

"Children need not talk of dark things such as ways to warrant a place in a hangman's noose at the gallows! Hopefully, the magistrates will have their wits about them now that we are here in a new world and will not be accusing good and innocent healing women of being witches, as in days past in the more superstitious corners of England," she added seriously.

The children continued to listen intently, and the older women nodded. Soon John took some of the sturdy indigo woolen cloth they created and bid farewell to all the women. The sisters, Alice, and the nieces continued with their weaving, stitchery, and spinning. Many offered commentaries and further tales spawned from the earlier story and discussion. Even from a distance, the constant hum of the spinning wheels and notes of laughter could be heard by passersby.

Chapter 13

WINDSOR, COLONY OF CONNECTICUT, 1643

Everyone on Backer Row and in the Palisado was excited, especially the Tinker sisters and their dear cousin, Alice. Ellen was about to give birth to her third child.

Her first child, John, had died as a baby from smallpox. His little body could not withstand the ferocity of that disease. His mother and aunts had tried every herbal remedy they knew to balance and align his humors again. But it had been too late and, sadly, they lost sweet John. She named her second child John after the first. It was often the custom to name new children the same names as the ones that had previously died. And now a third child, who everyone thought to be a girl, was about to be born.

Ellen woke up William, her husband, sometime in the middle of the night. The moon was full but had only partially traversed the night sky.

"Go get Mary and maybe Ann, Rhody, and Alice a little later," she said.

"The first pains are here."

Even though her sister, Mary, had a place in the Palisado, her family liked to stay closer to their crops at their home on Backer

Row. John mounted his horse and took the quiet night ride to reach her in a matter of a few short minutes. It was quite close by.

Mary Tinker Sension was Ellen's younger sister by only two years. They were inseparable since childhood. She remembered playing together in the flower garden of their home in England, picking lavender and calendula flowers with the view of Windsor castle in the distance. They learned to cook mince, savory, and fruit pasties together; to sew and spin on the wheel together and help mother in the stilling room make herbal water and salves as well as ale and cider for the household. When their father died, he named them both to inherit one of his tenement houses in Berkshire. He knew they would have no trouble sharing responsibilities.

Mary was a ball of energy. Her personality was that of fire which lighted up a room and attracted people to gather around her. She was personable, a hard worker, and took naturally to midwifery. She just knew what to do around mothers and children. Having a brood of her own, she voiced the perfect words to get a tired mother to muster up the final strength she needed to deliver her babe at the very end of her labor travails. No one in the village could soothe a crying infant as effectively as Mary. She had a way about her that could be grounded and businesslike yet very friendly and comforting.

Mary learned about midwifery from her mother-in-law, Joan Sension. Joan had been a midwife for many years near Silver Street and St. Nicolas Cole Abby in London. After Mary and her husband Mathias married, they moved close to his mother in London. Joan took her under her wing immediately. She showed her many things: how to turn a baby that was feet first, how to coach a mother to go on when she felt she could not, how to position a mother and coax a baby to come, which herbs to use to keep labor going and which herbs to use to help stop bleeding.

Sadly, there were things that only God could control. And when God wanted to take a baby or a mother away for His own,

He did. And He did it too often, in her opinion. But of course, she never voiced this sentiment publically.

Mary heard someone calling her name with excitement, in addition to an impatient knock at the door. She knew it was William and jumped to her feet to assist her sister. She had been lying awake at that very moment, worrying about her. She had hoped that this anxious knocking would have come days before.

She was afraid that her sister was becoming far too large. She noticed as early as two months previously that the baby seemed to be a little too big for her calculations, but she shrugged it off as being just a mistake on her part. Then, in the last month, Ellen's belly seemed to grow overzealously. She had given Ellen small amounts of weakened tansy and rue tea to bring forth labor earlier. But the baby was stubborn.

To make matters worse, she lingered too long inside her mother's womb, way past the time that she was supposed to come out into the world. This only added to Mary's worries. She knew this could delay the process and add not just hours, but days to her sister's labor. Even though Mary did not speak about her concerns to her sister, she was secretly apprehensive that something was not quite right. Alice, too, had sensed the same complications but was unsure what to do.

She grabbed her delivery bag with the birthing stool and rushed to the door.

"Yes, William Hulburd, I hear you and I am ready. Let the others rest awhile for I've a feeling that this labor will take some time. Let us go now and check on Ellen. How is she now?" Mary questioned him.

"She is excited and happy. But the pains this time are mostly in her back and a little more difficult for her to handle than those of the other births. However, she is strong and complains little," stated William.

They hurried along with the horse at a brisk trot and were back at the Hulburd home quickly. Mary lovingly greeted her sister, Ellen. She was still in good spirits and smiling between the pains. It was difficult to know for sure just by looking at her because Ellen was always so brave and so stoic. Dear, sweet Ellen was the fearless leader of the Tinker sisters, being the oldest surviving one. She was mild-mannered, kind, devoted, and steady.

Mary opened her delivery bag. She took out butter and lathered her hands to check Ellen's labor progress. The needle, thread, and scissors would not be necessary for a while. The baby's door into the world had partially opened, but Ellen was still not quite ready to deliver.

Soon daylight started to stream into their home, and the cadence of the village roosters helped to awaken the contractions further. William went dutifully, as instructed, and retrieved the others: Rhody, Anne, and Alice. Soon Backer Row and the homes in the Palisado were abuzz with the news of the goings-on at the Hulburd household.

Once Alice arrived with the other sisters, she quickly helped Mary to take out the childbirth linen and hang the privacy curtains around the bed frame. Mary had made a nourishing broth with boiled eggs and was giving it to Ellen when the others walked in. Ellen took only a little of the broth. The pains were getting more intense. Mary encouraged her to keep moving around until her water broke. The baby still seemed high in the womb and somewhat wedged into her back.

Anne and Rhody were mostly there as supportive sisters, but Alice, even though she was almost like a sister to the Tinker sisters, was here as official assistant to midwife Mary. Just as Mary's mother-in-law Joan had taken her in and taught her the ways of birthing babies, Mary adopted Alice into her own practice. Mary saw potential in Alice and already knew of her healing propensities, both natural and learned, from her previous mistress in Cambridge.

As Rhody and Anne were helping Ellen to walk around the house, Mary could not help noticing Alice's somewhat nervous demeanor. She wondered if she, too, sensed trouble regarding this delivery. For all her secrets, Alice was much more transparent than she knew. She was paler than usual today and extremely quiet. And when she spoke, it was brief and to the point. It was as if she had seen the spectre of something she did not want to see.

Mary suggested that Anne and Rhody take Ellen outside to the garden. Perhaps a brief time in sunshine would help take her mind off the intensity of the contractions. Besides, she wanted to be alone with Alice to help decipher what was going on.

It was already late afternoon. Ellen had been having pains since the middle of the previous night. Mary had buttered her hands to check if the baby had come down any further and to find out if her labor was progressing before the other sisters went out to the garden.

Even though Ellen had labored for hours, she had progressed no further, and the baby appeared not to move, despite both midwife and assistant encouraging Ellen to keep moving. Together, midwife Mary and her assistant, Alice, had felt Ellen's belly and assessed the baby's position. They had both noticed the fruity smell of her urine, a sure sign that the baby had been overly eager to eat within the womb.

"Dear Alice, you are not quite yourself today. You seem somewhat out of sorts. What can you be thinking? Does it have to do with Ellen and the impending birth?" inquired Mary.

Alice froze. She did not want to admit to what she had seen in a vision just two days before. Cursed visions. She questioned why they burdened her so. She didn't want to keep horrible secrets in situations she could do nothing about.

"The baby is big. The baby has been greedy for its mother's nourishment as it is sweet. I fear we may have a difficult time coaxing this one to come out," she stated with great concern.

Mary suspected there was more but she did not prod further. She herself did not want to hear words for which there was no recourse.

Mary knew she must call her mother, Mrs. Tinker, to the bedside because she would want to comfort her daughter, laboring Ellen. Mary sent Mathias, her husband, to fetch Mrs. Tinker and her brother, John. She hoped that perhaps her mother could add something to the situation that would make it better.

Eventually, the waters broke, and the labor became even more intense. The infant was still pushed into Ellen's back, which caused her even more pain despite attempts by Mary to turn her. Ellen was shaking and sobbing.

She felt as if she were riding tumultuous rapids in an angry, boulder-laden river. With each labor pain, she sensed her body thrown against the rocks along the river's edge and knew with a feeling of doom that she was heading for a treacherous waterfall from which she would not survive.

She wondered if she would receive God's grace and if she would be saved like so few others. She oscillated between hope for the next world and the utter despair of eternal damnation.

Ellen was lying down in bed, being attended to with sips of broth and soaked cloths upon her brow. The baby did seem to come down a little farther, so hope did not escape the little group of women entirely. But by the next morning, Ellen failed to feel the baby's movements. Even jostling the baby from the outside of Ellen's belly did not cause the unborn infant to stir.

The exhausted women started to take care of distraught Ellen in shifts. Their daughters Priscilla, Sarah, Hannah, Anne, and Alissa had also come to help sooth their aunt. By nightfall, the baby still had not moved again, and neither Mary nor Alice could prove that the baby was still alive.

Ellen lost all strength to go on at the thought of having lost her child to the tumultuous rapids. She saw her child's head smashing against the boulders, and now she would be next. She started to drift off to another place. Mary and Alice tried to give her several herbs that would help to expel the dead baby, but to no avail. The baby had gotten so big that she was literally imprisoned inside her mother's womb.

Outside, the rest of her family had gathered to pray, along with some neighbors and the town minister, John Wareham. John Tinker, her brother, had finally come from the other side of the Little River from his allotment on the edge of Poquonock bringing their mother, Mrs. Tinker. His Indian assistant, Thomas Hopewell, had paddled them downriver in a dugout canoe, following Mathias Sension as soon as they heard the news.

John Tinker briefly went inside, where he saw Alice. Mrs. Tinker was already inside, carefully stroking her suffering daughter's hair.

"Here, Alice. I brought something for my sister. Thomas Hopewell found the medicinal roots that you requested. He dug out both black and blue cohosh. He said Indian women use them often in childbirth."

She nodded in agreement. He put his hand over his heart, stared into her kind face, and found comfort in her understanding embrace. Then she gratefully took the herbs from John's hands and stared back at him with hand over her heart as if to say she also understood the concern he had for his sister, Ellen. Even though she was a distant cousin, she saw Ellen as her sister as well. If only they had used these herbs days earlier.

For two more days, Ellen lay there in her childbirth bed, becoming weaker and more pallid with each passing hour. William Hulburd consulted Dr. Rossiter to see if anything else could be done to miraculously save his spouse. However, after seeing her, the physician's only course of action was to shake his head apologetically.

William came in and held his wife's hand for hours as he prayed for her with the women there. He knew it was the last time he would ever be granted to touch her or see her beautiful face. He prayed she would be one of God's chosen ones and that her life had been pious enough for His liking.

Ellen was distant. She had already disappeared into a gruesome dream. Her skin became very warm and then hot by the end of two days' time. She eventually did deliver the dead baby who by this time was deteriorating and already slightly decomposed. It was a little girl.

Once delivered, Ellen bled uncontrollably, and there was nothing that Mary or Alice could do to stop it. They had already tried administering several herbs and massaging the womb, but the bleeding was too heavy. As the sun started to set early that evening, Ellen Tinker Hulburd, the oldest of the living Tinker sisters, passed to another world. She was the first of her sisters to come to an untamed New World and the first to leave it. And now the Tinker family had to come to grips with what just happened to their beloved sister and daughter. And William Hulburd would have to learn to live without his gentle wife at his side.

Silently, William Hulburd felt tortured. He went over and over in his mind the last gasps of breath taken by his beloved wife and the depleted, expressionless look on her face, the look of one who has come to terms with her own unremitting death. He made a vow never to forget it and always to remember her in those last moments as she was trying so desperately to bring their child into the world.

Mary was filled with great sadness. She felt responsible for what had happened. The blow was exceptionally hard, as she had lost very few mothers prior to Ellen's death and a scant number of babies. She questioned if there was something else she could have done to save her sister and her stillborn daughter. She told herself that she should have tried just a little harder to coax the baby to turn and perhaps the extra effort would have led to a joyous outcome instead of a tragic end. Simply heartbroken to lose such a dear friend and sister, there was no way for Mary to deny it or ever forget her.

Alice made a secret vow to herself that day. She decided to become more forthright if she had a vision that could mean the difference between life and death. The days before Ellen's labor, she saw her father, the late Robert Tinker, and Ellen's deceased first son, John, standing in front of her with outstretched arms. Alice didn't say a word, fearing it would cause too much pain for so many she loved. But she also knew that it would probably be of no use to anyone. In the future, in just those cases where she felt a warning could mean the difference between peace and peril, she resolved to be silent no longer. She did not feel like she would be thwarting God's will in doing so but acting as an angel to keep someone safe.

The funerary sermon for Ellen took place a day later. Reverend John Wareham gave a long sermon in which he expounded on the nature of death and the sure suffering of most. He talked little of Ellen's virtues and the traits that her family loved. It was of very little comfort and instead evoked much anxiety in those listening.

Late in the afternoon, a somber procession made its way to the burying ground. Even there, expectations of godly society dictated that everyone behave in a composed and controlled manner. Ellen's lifeless body and that of her dead child were thrown into a prepared grave without much fuss or tarrying. Her young son, John, and other children were forced to look at his mother so they could understand death. Ellen's friends and family took one last look at the plain stone at the head of her grave before filing back to the Hulburd home where simple food and drink awaited them.

As was the custom, once at the Hulburd home, family and friends were finally allowed to release their normal inhibitions. Family members sobbed. They cried. Everyone was intoxicated on beer and ale, including the children. It was an emotional frenzy rarely tolerated but certainly needed. Ellen was already greatly missed.

Chapter 14

COLONIES OF CONNECTICUT, NEW HAVEN, AND SAYBROOK, 1645-1646

R hody wearily remembered the warning. Alice had clearly seen peril for the great ship that was to take off from New Haven that autumn to deliver goods from the colonies to London. Establishing trade from Connecticut with England was crucial to its development. Her husband, John Taylor, and seventy others had signed up for the task of sailing with that great ship.

John Taylor agreed to become part of the sailing crew because he needed to return to England to take care of various personal business matters. Her brother, John Tinker, had committed to helping stock the ship with hides, beaver pelts, wheat, corn, and plate from the colonies. She pleaded with her husband not to go on that early crisp Windsor morning, but he would not hear of it. He recognized her many bouts of anxiety and dismissed this episode as just another case of nerves.

Rhody met John Taylor in the colonies just as she was getting accustomed to life without her first husband, Thomas Hobbs. Thomas was respectable, stern, practical, and pious. He was a wonderful and committed father and husband. He had always taken care of her every need and organized their life precisely in a definitive and respectable course.

With Thomas Hobbs, she had two lovely daughters, Anne and Hannah. They were still very young when he died in England. She felt quite lost without his stability and strength and would have fallen apart were it not for the vast support of her large family. It was easy for her and her daughters to follow them to the New World. She could not imagine getting on with her life without them.

Rhody, of all the Tinker children, was the most sensitive, the most strikingly beautiful, and the least sure of her way in the world despite her strong, intelligent mind. Her nerves had always gotten the better of her. She was unique and always a little different.

So it was coming from this situation that Rhody met the love of her life, John Taylor. He was drastically different from Thomas. He was adventurous and virile. He proudly found his place in the world as a sometimes sailor but had also settled in Windsor to try his hand at farming. He stole her heart from the very first few moments she saw him. He seemed wild, brash, and exciting. His attractiveness lay in the fact that he was passionate, strong, and unafraid of the world around him.

They had two sons together: John, who was five and little Thomas, who was one. She treasured her time with him and their family life together, and could not bear the thought of losing another husband. She already felt fragile from the loss of her daughter, Anne, the previous year and was still trying to recover from the death of her sister, Ellen. She did not think that she could endure another tragedy.

John Taylor was to meet that morning with Elias Parkman, his neighbor and a mariner. He owned a shallop that provided transportation between the New England colonies. Also meeting them was her brother, John Tinker, who was friends with both.

John had amassed supplies for the ship as well as goods to sell to England and was transporting them on Elias' shallop. Elias and John Tinker needed to leave that morning so that they could return in time to help John Winthrop Jr. on his trip to survey for a new location to start a colony along the Connecticut coast in former Pequot territories. Finally, they carried goods and personal supplies into the small seafaring vessel awaiting them on the Great River.

The family gathered at the river for their farewells. As John Taylor said his last goodbyes to his stepdaughter, his sons, and his distraught wife, Rhody, she realized that even if her husband came back well and sound, she would have to wait many months before she saw him again. She did not want to let him go. Her sisters, including her cousin Alice, were there to give her support and send John Taylor off with good wishes. Alice tried to keep a cheerful face, but her expressions betrayed her. Rhody wanted to go with him badly but knew that she must stay behind to care for their children.

The day was crisp but bright, and the waters were calm. Soon Elias Parkman, the captain, John Tinker, John Taylor, and other passengers were on their way down the Great River toward the Colony of New Haven. At the mouth of the Great River, they passed the Colony of Old Saybrook and then continued along the coastline until they reached New Haven.

Preparations were underway for the great ship to sail under the command of Master George Lamberton. Goods were slow to arrive, and the ship was not nearly full at the date of its planned departure. There was no choice but to wait. The ship had to stay in port until the loading of cargo was complete. It would not fare well for the Colony of New Haven to send in its first commercial venture from the New World only a half-laden ship.

John Tinker arranged for his brother-in-law to stay with Captain George Lamberton until the cargo was filled and they could set sail. Unfortunately, the winter started early that year. It was the coldest year that anyone could remember since the initial settling of the colonies. As a result, goods were even slower to come in, and investors bemoaned their situation.

The early freeze and poor weather became a problem for Elias Parkman and his friend, John Tinker, as well. They could no longer travel up the Great River back to Windsor to meet John Winthrop the Younger, as it had abruptly frozen in several places. There was no way for Elias to navigate back up the ice-laden river without damaging his shallop seriously.

Instead, they sent an Indian messenger to Mr. Winthrop, hoping that he would receive the message and be able to make other plans to get to Saybrook Colony. They had no choice other than to meet him there. At the same time, he hoped his sister, Rhody, would stay calm and intercept Mr. Winthrop for news when he passed through Windsor. Indeed, he had requested that Mr. Winthrop stop at the Palisado Green and inform his family of his activities.

John Winthrop the Younger had already started out on his voyage. When the Indian messenger caught up with him, he was staying at William Pyncheon's house in Springfield. Upon receiving the message, John Winthrop was disappointed. But he knew the weather was out of his or anyone else's control.

Nevertheless, he was determined to make his way to Saybrook and from there explore the easterly region of Nameaug, the former territory of the Pequot tribe. He grudgingly resigned himself to travel there overland instead of by water. It was an important journey that could not wait. He felt strongly that Nameaug might be suitable for a new plantation. The idea became more fully formed the previous summer when he spent time on his island of Coninecut, just six miles from the shores of that territory.

He had been looking forward to working again with John Tinker, who had served the needs of his father well just a few years before. He did not see him as often now that he had moved to Windsor to be with his large family of sisters and his mother. However, they saw each other on occasion when John came for business in Boston. John gladly agreed to continue his service as an agent and assistant to the younger Winthrop with his new endeavor.

It was a frosty and cold Monday morning when Mr. Winthrop reached Bissell's Ferry, just a mile north of the village of Windsor. There he waited at the ferry site for quite some time before crossing the Great River. Goodman Bissell was taking care of business in the town green but came as soon as he was alerted.

Mr. Winthrop finally rode into Windsor a couple of hours later and was greeted by members of John Tinker's family waiting for him at the Palisado Green. Word had gotten out that he was coming. They were anxious to ask if he had heard any news of John, for they knew that he and Elias Parkman should have returned to the village themselves by now. Rhody was understandably both eager and anxious to find out about the great ship's departure in New Haven.

"Greetings to you, Mr. Winthrop, esteemed sir! We hope you are faring well on your voyage to our fine village and these parts of the Connecticut Colony. Pray stop a while and tell us of your journey. We are only sorry that my son, John Tinker, is not back from New Haven Colony as yet." spoke Mrs. Tinker on behalf of her family.

She had been helping her daughters with some winter tasks. Alice was with them as well.

After several proper introductions and after he had made sure to make the acquaintance of the entire Tinker family, John Winthrop spoke.

"I received a message from your son, John, yesterday, Madame. Through an Indian messenger, I learned that he would not be back in Windsor for a while."

Rhody appeared especially horrified upon hearing these words.

Mr. Winthrop must have understood, and replied.

"Oh, nothing to worry about. The shipments of cargo for Master Lamberton's new ship have not all arrived yet. The Company of Merchants is still arranging the last of the supplies. I was told to tell Goodwife Taylor that her husband will stay at Master Lamberton's home until they are ready to depart."

He looked directly at Rhody.

"Your brother, John, will send more messages later when he has more to tell."

"But why are John and Elias Parkman not here to greet you and escort you to Saybrook as previously planned?" inquired Mrs. Tinker.

"They cannot travel upriver now because of the early onset of winter. The rivers and streams have partially frozen in many places, and they have no clear passage up the Great River. We will travel overland to reach Saybrook Colony and meet your son, John, and Goodman Parkman there. Then, we can start to conduct the business of surveying Nameaug. God willing," responded Mr. Winthrop.

Mrs. Tinker nodded.

"Aye, and by His good graces," she offered.

"Please do come and sit at the hearth of my daughter Mary's house with some ale. It will warm you and give you strength for the rest of your travels."

"Thank you kindly, Mrs. Tinker. But we were so long delayed at the ferry that we dare not stop longer. We must try to reach Hartford by nightfall and I fear from reports we are receiving from other travelers that the Windsor highway to Hartford is not well maintained," responded Mr. Winthrop.

"Of course, Mr. Winthrop. Please be on your way with God's protection then, but take some wares that we made for you. It would give me great delight. And please tell John that his family sends their regards," exclaimed Mrs. Tinker.

"And a good day from Alice...and John Young as well," stammered Alice.

John Winthrop looked up. She did not look like a Tinker, but clearly their cousin was close to the family. She had compelling but mysterious eyes that elicited a strange sensation of recognition. It was somewhat confusing because he could not place making her acquaintance before that day, but somehow he knew that meeting her in that moment was significant.

However, his mind quickly got back to the task at hand. He knew he must move on to Hartford with haste. John Winthrop graciously accepted the mincemeat pasties and apple tarts given to him by the Tinker sisters and their mother before continuing on his way. He promised to keep them updated.

Another ferry helped him and his assistants cross the Rivulet. He and his assistants continued on to Hartford through the Plymouth Meadow until Matthew Allyn greeted them and guided them to the proper highway that led to Hartford. The markings were confusing, and it would have been easy to go astray. It was already nightfall when they reached Thomas Ford's inn in Hartford, where they stayed for the next couple of days.

Mr. Winthrop left Hartford on November 19th. He thought he would try one last time to procure a boat in Hartford to take him to Saybrook, but the water was low and the river frozen. He left his horse in Hartford and hired an able Indian man from the Mohego tribe to carry his gear, as he would have to ford small streams with his traveling party. They traversed the frozen wilderness, stopping one night at the home of the prominent and friendly Indian, Seancut, whom he knew from his dealings with Mr. Pyncheon and other traders up and down the Great River.

The next day they arrived at Saybrook, the colony that he had helped to found and patiently waited there for the reunion with John Tinker. He noticed the boat of Elias Parkman coming in to shore, trying to dock just two days after his own arrival. Unfortunately, due to continued ice buildup, Elias could not go into the shallow harbor and had to anchor eastwardly from the mouth of the Great River at a distance closer to Coninecut Island.

The following day, Elias Parkman, along with John Tinker, Goodman Williams, and several sailors, finally came ashore to Saybrook on a ferry. They left the boat anchored and manned with three remaining sailors. That night, the wind became fierce, and the rain beat down sharply out of the sky. The rainstorm lasted the entire night and well into the next day. The strong swell did not allow them to sail across the river's mouth the entire day. It was too treacherous.

The old friends greeted each other warmly and were visibly relieved to successfully meet again despite the severe weather. John Tinker dined with John Winthrop the Younger that night. They talked of Mr. Winthrop's overland trip and his meeting John's entire family. In the course of the conversation, John Winthrop felt compelled to ask about Alice.

"Who was the young woman standing there in the Palisado Green with your family? She has light blue eyes. She seemed extremely shy, but is eerily familiar. How would I know her? She was introduced as a cousin, but there is something else."

John Tinker answered, "That is Alice Ashbey, sir. At least she was, until she married John Young. She is a distant cousin of my mother, but grew up in our household. She assisted another family in Cambridge, but moved to Windsor with her husband, and is really more like one of our own family. She is well versed in the healing arts, sir. She has a gift, albeit not as educated as your own. You may have heard of her in that way or seen her another time with our family. In any case, she is lovely and kind."

"I see. Well, it is of no great importance now. I was simply curious," he explained.

"We must continue to discuss the main subject at hand, the question of Nameaug as a possible new settlement."

They exchanged ideas and went over the best possible approaches to take. As the wind finally eased, they decided it best to sleep for the night in order to be ready to proceed to Nameaug at dawn.

The first order of the day was to find Elias Parkman's ship. From the village, they could no longer see it anchored in the distance. Elias Parkman and his sailors set out with the sunrise to look for it along the shore. Mr. Winthrop, John Tinker, and the rest of the traveling party made their way down the coastline a little while later.

Soon, excited sailors greeted them and explained the fate of Parkman's shallop. Her anchor had lost hold in the storm, and gusty winds tossed the vessel to shore and onto a sandbank with large rocks. Luckily no damage was visible. However, Elias Parkman had to stay behind and deal with his shallop, and again Mr. Winthrop was forced to go overland to reach his exploration goals in Pequot territory. John Tinker joined him on his trip to Nameaug but returned to Saybrook instead of Boston once they concluded their business.

—⁂—

Elias Parkman rescued his shallop with his sailors' help during a high tide. They chipped through the ice but finally tied the vessel up in the Saybrook Harbor. It was still too frozen to head back to Windsor, so they waited in Saybrook, where Elias met up with John Tinker once more.

It was already December, and still the news John heard from Saybrook was that the New Haven ship was still in port. John decided to wait in Saybrook a little longer, for surely Master Lamberton's ship would leave on her maiden voyage sometime soon.

He did not want to return to Windsor until he had more specific news for his family. The thought of facing his sister, Rhody, without knowing what had happened to her husband's ship was not plausible. Besides, several weeks had passed, and surely the cargo would be ready at any time. Day after day, they waited until eventually they heard the news about the ship at the beginning of January.

—✲—

Despite numerous delays and the most difficult New England winter ever experienced by the colonists, the small ship of one hundred tons, with a cargo worth five thousand pounds, finally set sail at the beginning of January 1646. Her master, George Lamberton, and a diverse group of passengers, including some of New Haven's most prominent founders, felt a mix of both anxiety and relief as they departed for England. With the harsh weather, the ship's crew sawed ice away from their path for three miles before casting out to sea.

In addition, observers stated that the ship was either poorly constructed or had been stocked of its cargo incorrectly, for it was weighted and tilted to one side as it began its journey. Master Lamberton's attitude was one of dread as they sailed away, not fully trusting the seaworthiness of the ship. On shore, Reverend Davenport did not seem much more hopeful when he led a prayer accepting that God's intentions might well be to take away the lives of all the passengers on the journey back to England.

With the startling news of such a worrisome departure, John Tinker did his best in the telling of the story to leave out any dark details that might bolster his sister Rhody's fears. It was best to stay calm and not worry her needlessly. No one could know anything until the first ships of spring arrived from England with news.

Spring slowly came that year and with it the arrival of ships from London. No one had seen the ship that had left from New Haven. There were no tidings of friends or relatives that had departed from icy shores in the maiden ship the preceding winter. Family members prayed and beseeched the Divine to give them some sign of what had happened to their loved ones and friends.

Finally one day in June, an associate of John Tinker in New Haven gave him a curious story about seeing the missing ship in "phantom form." Just south of the harbor, many inhabitants of New Haven had seen an apparition of a ship on the horizon in the calm after a storm before sunset one evening.

The townspeople were convinced that the ship they saw looked exactly like theirs that had vanished. She had the same dimensions and the same sails. There were three tall masts that in a moment snapped and became snarled in her sails and cordage. Most thought they saw the keel of the ship sinking into the ocean. And then, with a thick cloud of smoke, she was gone, devoured by the sea. They took it as a divine revelation as to what happened to their loved ones and together with their minister gave thanks to God for the message that finally put their questions to rest.

In Windsor, the Tinker family stood somberly with the news of the probable death of John Taylor on the "phantom" ship. Rhody screamed hysterically when she heard the news.

"I knew it was a doomed ship from the beginning! Alice knew, and I knew, but no one listened to us!"

She carried on for hours as though she had lost her mind. She cried for days and could not leave her home. The love of her life, her perfect match, was lost at sea. She would have gladly thrown herself into the sea to be with him if she could have. Her sisters and her mother had to watch carefully over her.

Alice was plagued by fits of depression. She hated to see her cousin suffer so and wished that her words of foresight had helped Rhody. Instead, they acted to connect her to her own intuition and her sense of something foreboding.

Rhody had been powerless to change her husband's mind about going to London on the New Haven ship. She felt hopeless, as did Alice. Alice silently cried to herself and questioned the purpose of her gift of sight when those who could change their fates for the better would not listen to the information foretold.

Rhody became superstitious and more religious in her grief. The ministers had warned that no good could come from such a thing as foretelling by cunning women. In her despair and depression, she started to question if Alice had her best interests in mind.

The part of her that was so deep in grief was now prone to fear. And that fear made her look at her cousin– the cousin that had been like a sister, the cousin who was always there for her, with a darkened, disillusioned view. On her better days, she knew that such thoughts were ridiculous, but in her deepest states of fear she trusted Alice less than she ever would have thought possible. She questioned whether Alice's clairvoyant abilities had opened the doors to contact with dark forces responsible for harming her family.

She and others started to think that Backer Row residents were cursed. Indeed, in just the previous two years, their beloved minister Reverend Huit, had met his death quickly, followed by the death of his wife, Susanna, leaving their children orphans. Deacon Henry Clark, his nephew, took charge of the children at their home on Backer Row. But ultimately, the reverend and his wife could never be replaced and were greatly missed by their orphaned children and the Windsor congregation. Those deaths were a prelude to the deaths in Rhody's immediate family. She could not help but wonder who would be next.

Chapter 15

⬡

WINDSOR, COLONY OF
CONNECTICUT, 1646

E arly one chilly winter morning, Alice left for the village center to sell her eggs at William Hulburd's market. Once inside the general store, she immediately took notice of a finely dressed, middle-aged man of obviously higher rank with a displeasing and rude countenance. He had just finished arguing with the clerk about a price charged for an item there.

As he turned briskly to walk out of the store with a hostile scowl on his face, he bumped into Alice, tipping over her basket of eggs, small inanimate victims in the wake of his wrath. Enraged by his failed negotiations with the store clerk, he stared at her briefly, grunted, and then stormed out of the establishment. He left her to gather any unbroken eggs from the floor by herself without the slightest apology or offer to make amends. She had not seen this unpleasant man around town before and hoped he was only a stranger passing through. She shrugged the incident off, but her mind refused to let it go.

Ever since her encounter with the disgruntled man in Hulburd's market, Alice felt uneasy. She couldn't place exactly why. But deep down she knew it could not turn out well. She failed to remember or recognize Matthew Allyn from the streets and market of Newtown in the Massachusetts Bay Colony where she worked for the Holman family. His dark brown hair had prematurely morphed to grey, and the lines on his face were noticeably engraved. He was much skinnier now than his previously plump self.

He had been the richest man in Newtown, a merchant from the southwest of England. He owned more land than anyone else there. He was considered to be of lesser gentry in England and acted accordingly. Proud and arrogant, he gave the attitude that the world should be laid out before him. He was used to getting what he wanted and was vengeful if it didn't happen right away.

Newtown was now called Cambridge and was no longer at his feet, nor Hartford either. Matthew Allyn had alienated and wronged too many people in both places. In Cambridge, the people had demanded of the Connecticut Court that he be sent back as a prisoner for debts he owed and damage he had caused. He never went back. He never found himself in jail. Those large reserves of land, property, and wealth must have soothed some ruffled feathers.

In Connecticut, his reputation earned him few friends. An excommunication proceeding against him took place in Hartford after quarreling with his church's pastors. Despite appealing his case, he was ousted from the congregation led by Thomas Hooker and Samuel Stone. It was the same church that Alice briefly attended with the Holmans in Cambridge. The Connecticut General Court members were all too familiar with his extreme urge to litigate fiercely against his neighbors. Allyn's name was often brought forth several times in a single Court session either as a plaintiff or a defendant.

And now that he was in Windsor, people were not quite sure what to think of him. He was the person who had bought from William Holmes of the Plymouth Company the Plymouth Trading House near the confluence of the Rivulet and Great Rivers at the time that Plymouth decided to relinquish all their claims in Connecticut. Mr. Allyn, a merchant, bought it initially with hopes to discourage commercial activity in Windsor, in favor of boosting trade in Hartford. As a Hartford resident at the time, he could have benefited from the increased Hartford trade. In addition, Mr. Allyn refused to pay taxes to Windsor. He claimed he owed Windsor nothing on the grounds that Plymouth had sold him the land.

With an attitude of spite, Mr. Allyn deconstructed the trading house and used the lumber to build his own home. It was an impressive home for a frontier town and substantial enough to be the largest home in Windsor. It was two stories high and painted outlandishly in bright red with two big staircases at the entry. It was a very grand home for the young town of Windsor and clearly ostentatious enough to alert others to his vast wealth and influence.

Even though she could not quite remember him, there was something about him that Alice did not trust. He seemed quite ruthless and capable of manipulating any situation or any person to maintain what he had or to accumulate more power or wealth. He recently moved to his property at the old trading house site in Windsor to escape the exclusion from daily life that he had dealt with in Hartford since his excommunication.

In reality, Matthew Allyn needed to prop himself up in the eyes of those who had influence in Windsor. He was ambitious and greedy for recognition and position but still had to prove himself as a new resident of the town. And people continued to have their doubts about him because the trading house issue was not yet resolved.

The townspeople also wondered about the details of his excommunication in Hartford. He would have to earn his seat in the Windsor meetinghouse by flattery, bribery, and proof that he was really an advocate for, a protector of, and benefactor to the town. His sour attitude towards his fellow human beings had to shift, at least in outward appearances, if he were to achieve the measures of success he so craved.

Alice chided herself to stop worrying needlessly. If only she were able to see into her own life as well as she could see into the lives of others. She hoped that her feelings were of no consequence and resolved to forget the encounter.

Unfortunately for Alice, Matthew Allyn remembered her. He never forgot the faces of those that dared go against him in any way. Alice looked exactly the same as she had when she lived in Cambridge and sold herbs in the market, the same herbs that his wife bought against his wishes and gave to his young son. He had been infuriated with Margaret, his wife, for giving little Thomas supposed medicines from a lowly servant girl. He had always blamed Alice for the child's illness that ensued shortly after taking them. He would bide his time for his revenge, reassuring himself that these matters must be dealt with carefully and patiently. But eventually he would find the right time to exact his own personal justice upon her.

Chapter 16

WINDSOR, COLONY OF CONNECTICUT, WINTER AND SPRING 1647

The late winter and early spring of 1647 proved to be fatal for many residents of the fledgling village of Windsor. The townspeople were an industrious lot. They were gradually able to support themselves largely through farming, cloth making, and raising their own livestock. But even so, winter was a cold and hungry time.

Food stocks were low, and many people, especially children, were not as nourished or hearty as they needed to be in order to brave a serious illness and survive. A horrible fever had come through the village and infected the families of people living there. The effects of the illness were even more chilling than the frigid winter itself. The worst of the disease seemed to cluster around Backer Row and those that lived in the Palisado. Especially hit hard was the Tinker family.

Many people who became ill did survive, but many others did not. Windsor townspeople called upon Alice Young frequently for her healing abilities and her knowledge of herbs. She was exposed to the illness so much that her body had built resistance to it. People became ill in a widespread pestilence of influenza.

However, there were other illnesses that easily took hold as people's constitutions weakened with the onslaught of constant disease, cold, and malnourishment. Alice tried her best to attend to anyone who needed her help, but her resources had become depleted over time.

Even the town doctor, Bray Rossiter, lost a child from the illness that spread like wildfire. People began to question why the learned doctor could not prevent the death of his own child yet the modest herbal woman continued to avoid illness, as did her daughter and husband. The doctor and others started to eye her with suspicion. Of course, Alice's family was really not protected any more than those of other villagers. Her extended family, including her cousins, shared a large portion of the hardships caused by the uncontrolled illness and subsequent loss of life.

On Backer Row, the scourge gradually found its way to the Sension household. Young Sara Sension, who had been such an enthusiastic participant in the cloth-making circles, was struck down by the fever, too. After days of putting forth as much strength as her little body would muster, she succumbed to its fatal effects. Mary was inconsolable at the loss of her oldest daughter, but she was grateful to Alice for trying to help in the best way she could. She knew in her heart that it would have been much worse if Alice had not tended to her other sick children who had just enough vigor to survive.

However, the pestilence kept spreading throughout Backer Row. The illness had become too rampant in the village, like an untamed wild horse for which there were no reins. The announcements of the passing of loved ones melded together into days of endless grief. A makeshift morgue on the edge of the burying ground held the dead bodies together in the long embrace of death and winter until the ground was no longer frozen and burials could be made.

Most families were affected in some way. One of the Hoyt boys died, as did Anne Porter, the wife of the prosperous colony official, John Porter, and sister of Mary Loomis, Joseph Loomis's wife. Week after week, people heard the names of the next victims. John Orton passed on at the end of winter. Susannah Hannum died toward the end of the same week. The illness took pity on no one. Bray Rossiter, who was also the first town recorder, continued to write down names in his book of records, "the child of George Phelps died, the child of Anthony Hawkins died," with no seeming end in sight.

One overcast and dreary day as Alice was preparing to tend to the sick, she realized that the illness had depleted most of her herbal stores. Her cures had helped many Windsor neighbors, but she still needed many more. Unfortunately, what she could gather at this time of year was very limited and consisted principally of barks and superficial roots of saplings. Her usual supply of pickled elderberries and yarrow had run out.

The herbs and simples most needed at this time had already saved the lives of others. She inquired all over town to see if other women had extra supplies in their pantries for the medicines that she needed most. Most others had also used up their supplies or were unwilling to share them, lest they become necessary in their own households, because the dark cloud of death that hovered over the town had still not passed.

With her traditional European herbal simples depleted, Alice turned to the American herbs that she learned about from Assanushque. In desperation, she went out into the cold with a sharp knife. Her hands bled and cracked as she worked to free medicine from the frozen Earth. Eventually, she was able to gather roots of young hemlock saplings. She cut them into pieces and boiled them in beer to make a concoction to bring down fevers. She also used dried Indian sage that she had gathered in the previous summer. With it, she made strong infusions to cure fevers as well. Also in her native apothecary were dried wild geraniums as another remedy for the fever so plaguing her village.

Some people began to eye her with suspicion as she came to rely on the Indian physic more and more. They were strange medicines that they had never seen used this much by an English woman.

On the Sabbath, the preacher John Wareham chastised the congregation. He gave his judgments from the pulpit.

"Were it not for the sins of this community, God would never have allowed such a scourge to take place. It is the sinfulness and wickedness of those that have not obeyed the Lord at all times that has invited in this menace. It has come to purify the village and humble those that would dare affront the Lord with their lack of respect and their evil ways."

Sitting on her bench in the meetinghouse, Alice tried to make sense of it. The most recent victims of this disease, whom she had tried to nurse back to health, did not appear to her as being disrespectful or irreverent in any way. Yet, who was she to say what was in someone's heart? She bowed her head in silence and continued to untangle in her mind the judgments and pronouncements of the preacher.

In due time, Reverend Wareham also struggled to come to terms with the wrath of God when two of his own children caught the fever and died. Young Samuel, the minister's only remaining son, and his daughter, Hepsibah, quickly became victims of the calamitous disease. Dr. Rossiter, who tried to treat them, was powerless to help. The reverend and his family became engulfed in the realities of their cruel and final outcomes.

By mid-March, snow and ice still covered the ground, refusing to thaw. Alice worried, as did many others, when or if the disease would stop ravaging the village. Most families kept to themselves as much as possible, in quarantine, and some even skipped the obligatory lectures normally required every Sabbath. Most of the congregating in those times took place around the sickbeds of loved ones.

It was out of this fearful and desperate atmosphere that Alice learned the horrible news of the fever coming into the Thornton's home. Alice was quite concerned because cousin Anne was now early with child and was not feeling well herself. It became impossible for her to care for all of her children who had taken ill. She was feeling so poorly herself.

Anne's two girls, Priscilla and little Anne, often spent time with Alice's daughter. Alice loved Anne, yet of all the Tinker sisters that were so much a part of her life, Anne seemed the most remote. Anne was two years younger than Alice. Perhaps it was the attention that the older sisters bestowed on Alice that made Anne a bit insecure. She was not sure. In any case, Anne was a warm, caring woman, and Alice loved her.

She thought a bigger part of the distance had to do with her husband, Thomas. Thomas was also from the middle of England in a town along the Thames, but he had become more and more religious and rigid in his beliefs since coming to New England. He started to serve on some of the government panels and intermingle with the Dorchester group more than ever before. The colonies had changed him considerably from the young man he was in his London years.

Anne Tinker was very young, naïve, and impressionable when she married Thomas Thornton in New Windsor, England. Her sister, Ellen, and Ellen's husband, William Hulburd, introduced them. She looked up to Thomas from the start and seemed to hang on his every word. He could do no wrong. She was a very dutiful wife and did not find either following him to New England or obeying his daily decisions for the family objectionable. Whatever Thomas said was golden and not to be questioned.

As Thomas became more entrenched in the more conservative views of the Windsor townspeople in later years, Anne followed suit, developing a stronger bond with the church and renouncing many of the more open-minded views of her upbringing. If Thomas asked her to follow him to the ends of the Earth, she would have unquestionably obliged his wishes.

Anne was a very loving and warm mother, and she doted on her children. They and Thomas were her entire world and the absolute center of her life. She relished her time with them and loved being a mother. For Anne, the loss of a child felt even more devastating than for most mothers. She tirelessly rallied around her sick children despite utter exhaustion. Being with child, she found it was even more difficult to stay up all night with them for days on end, catering to their desperate needs. At one point, she also succumbed to debility and sickness but luckily recovered.

Neighbors and family tried to come over whenever they could to ease her burden and sit around the children's featherbeds in rituals of prayer. But with so much sickness abounding not everyone was available to help. They were nursing their own sick children. When Alice saw their need, she readily volunteered to be of service in the Thornton household.

However, at that late time in the course of the dreaded illness, she knew she had little to offer as far as medicines. The only abundant remedy remaining was the hemlock cut into pieces and boiled in beer. Alice looked sadly at her hearth in the little one-room cottage and remembered the many bunches of herbs that she had dried and hung from the ceiling rafters. She gathered the scant amount left with a heightened sense of urgency. The many pots of herbs prepared last summer were also empty. The pestilence had successfully outlasted her medicinal supplies.

The illness started to rage in the Thornton home by the time Alice came to help them. Priscilla was already desperately ill and in bed for several days. The other older children, Thomas and Anne, had recently taken to their sickbeds as well. There was still a cold chill in the air that seemed to seep into the very bones of those who were ill.

Alice crossed the threshold to the home where others were now weary of going lest they spread the scourge to their own families. Tending to their ailing children preoccupied Rhody and Mary. Only Mrs. Tinker could be there to help as well. Alice came with her few remaining herbal simples in hand and looked into the bleakness of the parlor with great concern.

"Priscilla falls in and out of wakefulness," spoke Mrs. Tinker. "She cannot seem to shake the fever. The other little ones are scarcely much better. Please do what you can to help them, Alice. Anne sleeps in the chair next to them. She is exhausted."

"I'll help as much as I am able, ma'am. Pray it is not too late," Alice responded.

She quickly proceeded to give Priscilla sips of the hemlock in boiled beer, accompanied with compresses of a wild geranium decoction.

"Now dear, listen to cousin Alice. Let the fever go. You need not hold on to it any longer," she soothed.

Priscilla moaned in response, having awakened slightly.

Alice covered her in thick blankets and placed her near the fire with the help of her father. She hoped that she would sweat out the disease. The remedy helped to bring her some relief but ultimately could not stave off her entrance into the other world. "Her body is already so weak," Alice lamented. "I wish I had been here sooner."

As Priscilla slipped toward unconsciousness, occasionally screaming out in delirium, she confused Alice with a dark angel that wished to take her from her parents.

"Pray, leave me, dark angel. Let me stay with my loving parents! I wish to stay. Do not bother me!" she sobbed.

" 'Tis just the fever, dear. Do not fear. You are safe next to your mother and father. 'Tis only the angels of Christ that hover over you," Alice consoled her.

Eventually, Priscilla became more peaceful.

"Mother, Christ has come for me. I'm not afraid of death anymore," she murmured.

Seeming to have forgotten what she said about Alice earlier, she smiled at her cousin and the faces of her parents and grandmother one last time. Finally, she fell asleep and never woke again.

Thomas, her father, was shaken. Priscilla and he had always shared a special bond. She was his most pious and spiritual child.

In his despair and memories that followed days after the event, he would remember Alice as saying, "You need not hold on any longer," instead of her actual words. Those terrible thoughts were immediately followed by Priscilla's cries of the dark angel coming to take her from her parents. These were the specific memories that would haunt him forever.

The rest of the children quickly fell to the sickness as well. In a last attempt to fight the fatal enemy, Alice gathered sassafras roots, boiling them in beer and used what little residual elecampane Anne had in her own supply. Alice normally added licorice and anise followed by mint and a little wormwood, but she was also out of these important ingredients. Unfortunately, the remedies were not their usual strength because of her empty herbal cupboard. They still brought relief to the children so they could die more peacefully, but she could not save them from their fates. She thought that it would have been presumptuous to think that she could have saved them anyway.

Thomas, Anne, and young Samuel died one after the other, much to their parents' horror. Anne kneeled and prayed. She begged and pleaded for hours at a time at her children's sickbeds, desperately hoping for them to be saved, but to no avail. Thomas, in his grief, started to view Alice with suspicion.

She was using Indian physic that he had never seen or heard of. Thomas wondered about when she would have had the occasion to make contact with the savages. It was a mystery to him why she would have sought them out. He questioned how she knew them in such an intimate way that she would have knowledge of their heathen medicines. He reasoned that since they were in league with Satan, she might be, too.

Anne had always been prone to an exaggerated imagination, and her husband easily seduced her in her grief into thinking that perhaps Alice did not have the best intentions. So deep was Thomas in his grief and his despair that he even thought he saw the face of the Devil hovering next to Alice in the firelight as she pronounced the death of his last sick child, young Samuel, who was just two years old.

The sorrow in the Thornton household knew no bounds. The rest of the Tinker family rallied together to help Thomas and Anne in their horrendous distress. In a matter of a few days, the Thornton family was reduced in size from five children to one. Of all the families in Windsor village, they were the ones to have suffered the greatest losses.

People noticed that they lived next door to Alice, the supposed healer who had helped them in the past but who had failed in keeping her neighbors healthy this time. They questioned why she used those roots and barks that only the natives, the heathens, knew about.

They even entertained the thought that it might have been her intention to do harm. Their steadfast representative of God, John Wareham, had also lost two children. And even the town doctor had lost a child while Alice's own household was unaffected by the pestilence. Unsettled and unvoiced terrors started to manifest and point to maleficence as the cause of this devastating situation. People wondered and whispered behind closed shutters. The stage was set for the fruits of fear to ripen and for an opportunist to seize control for his own selfish aspirations.

Chapter 17

WINDSOR, COLONY OF
CONNECTICUT, SPRING 1647

"Listen to me. It's true. Alice Young is a culprit and criminal. She ran away from her contract of indentured servitude with the Holmans. Everyone there was talking about it. It was she who nearly killed my eldest son when she sold her herbal poison to my wife in the market in Cambridge. After I approached her, she bore false witness against me to the family she was working for and others in the town so that the townspeople questioned my character! She is a troublemaker and liar," stated Matthew Allyn defiantly.

Of course, he had everything to gain from his tale, while Alice had everything to lose, including her life. It was an impossible situation for her. He was very wealthy and powerful, and, in their eyes, she was nothing more than a female servant who had broken her contract and almost killed someone in the past with her questionable medicines.

"But how do we know she is lying?" inquired John Porter, who was now serving as a Windsor representative to the Connecticut General Court.

No one quite trusted his neighbor, Matthew Allyn. But Mr. Porter was vulnerable and wanted to think there was a logical explanation for the loss of his wife and so many others in the town recently.

"It's bewitchment, I tell you. I remember her in Cambridge. She was working for a woman, Winifred Holman, who played around a lot herself with things that others might construe as magic. Alice was her servant, but they interacted more like sisters in a coven. She worked for Goodman Holman, too, but she ran away, as wayward and wicked as she was. I was in Hartford already at the time, but my contacts told me of such things. The talk was that she ran away because she must have been with child. That's how you may be certain she is lying. If she ran away and shirked her duties as well as became with child, she is the one not to be trusted. So you see, she framed me and almost murdered my son. Her word is as good as devil's spit," he explained.

"He, the Great Demon Lucifer, saved her from shame and punishment for her sins. And now, she has been working for him ever since to repay the hidden debt that immersed her evil life. And that poor husband of hers, John Young. She must have bewitched him, too, by enticing him to marry her. She's given him no children either! And now, she's been creating trouble everywhere the eye can see in Windsor."

"How do you know this for sure?" asked John Porter. He was becoming more curious.

"Look at everything that's happened! How many people have died? Not just with the fever now, but before as well. She has afflicted almost every one of her neighbors on Backer Row, even those that have acted as her protection from the winds of righteousness in the past."

He continued and gave examples of all the untimely deaths of those on Backer Row. And then he expounded on all who had perished thus far in the current crisis.

Matthew Allyn knew he now had the undivided attention of Mr. Porter and Mr. Loomis. With a little more convincing, he knew he could bend them to his will and his way of viewing the situation. Indeed, if he could convince these two powerful men of the town, they could be the ones to convince everyone else. He would reclaim a false innocence for his crimes in Cambridge, become an exalted hero of the town, gain acceptance into the church in Windsor, and undo his merchant rival, the Tinker family. This was a most fortunate opportunity.

"But certainly, the Tinker family will protect her as they always have. And as we all know, they themselves have taken great favor with the Winthrops," explained Joseph Loomis.

Joseph Loomis also served many important positions within the town. He lived next door to his brother-in-law, John Porter. They were related through two sisters from the White family. John had married Anna White, and Joseph had married Mary White back in Essex, England. Upon coming to Windsor in 1639 with Reverend Huit, they were granted large tracts of land based upon their status and their wealth in the Plymouth Meadow, near Allyn's lot, the site of the former Plymouth Trading House.

"It seems to me that we need to make the Tinker family understand and see who she really is. Our best path to success I feel would be through Thomas Thornton. He has started to serve on some government panels and knows us. He is mindful of his faith and is eager to rise to higher ranks within this community."

"Even though he is a part of the Tinker family by marriage, he has just lost four of his children and is in the midst of trying to come to terms with that horrible tragedy. We must pressure him to see the probable truth. He is also a friend and next-door neighbor of John Young, Alice's husband. Perhaps he could be counted on to spy on Alice and talk to John Young about what is really going on in that household," proclaimed Mr. Porter, who had now convinced himself of the logic of her guilt.

Of course, he viewed her guilt through the lenses of his own grief.

"Aye. 'Tis a splendid plan. But I beseech you to wait until John Tinker is out of town or busy with projects on that large property of his. I heard some talk that he might be visiting Pyncheon soon," remarked Mr. Allyn.

"We do not need his interference. He tends to be on alert for the whole family."

"And we could also entice some other neighbors to keep watch over Alice to see if she shows any signs of cavorting with Satan," added Mr. Loomis.

"She should be secretly followed to find out if there are any supernatural activities or secret coven meetings."

"Alright then. We will study the matter further, Mr. Allyn, and talk to the right people," stated Mr. Porter.

"Fare thee well, Mr. Allyn. Next time, we will show you our witch-finding manual that family from our home in Essex recently sent to us," explained Mr. Loomis.

"Pray, we will talk soon!" affirmed Mr.. Porter.

"Aye. So pleased to hear you understand the gravity of my argument," Mr. Allyn slyly smiled.

"Fare thee well. We will meet again soon, and you will tell me more about the witch-catching book," added Mr. Allyn, who was now quite pleased with himself.

And so by the means discussed in their meeting, they got to Thomas Thornton. So devastated was he from the loss of his children that he yearned for a way to explain his pain. He shared his story about Priscilla's fever-induced hallucination of Alice as a dark angel and the words Alice spoke to Priscilla that he heard incorrectly, thereby misinterpreting their substance. They urged him to speak with John Young to find out what he could be persuaded to tell.

"Thomas, the evidence is quite compelling. We must find out as much as possible to make our case. You must speak to John Young. Tell him he may be an accomplice to a crime if he does not cooperate," they advised him.

"He must either stand with justice or face his own demise."

The next day Thomas walked over to his neighbor's cottage. The weather had started to become fair, and spring had finally announced itself through the blossoming of many flowers coming out of their slumber. The fever that spread havoc through the town weeks earlier was starting to subside.

John Young was getting ready to prepare the soil in the family vegetable garden by the fence that adjoined both their properties, but a native honeysuckle vine that had spread everywhere hindered him. It was just starting to bud with red trumpet flowers. Thomas approached him.

"John, I must speak to you about Alice. 'Tis important, man. You must know the whole village is talking suspiciously about her actions during the pestilent times of late. There are a lot of things that do not make any sense. John, you must cooperate and be honest about what you know, or the magistrates will have you convicted as an accomplice to possible murder. It is very serious," Thomas stated, gingerly testing what John's reaction would be.

John turned pale. He looked down at the ground.

"Damn this unruly vine. It's everywhere now. Alice transplanted it from the edge of the woods in the little meadow shortly after we moved here. She tended it carefully, and now it's out of control. She says she loves how the hummingbirds come to feed from the red trumpet flowers. It's a nuisance to me now," he stated and started pulling at it frantically.

"John, please, I can't imagine what might be going through your mind right now. I know she is your wife, but you must talk to me. Please, John. We've been friends since you moved here a few years back. Is there anything unusual that you need to tell me about Alice?" he questioned.

John kept uprooting the vines with ferocity. Silence ensued. Finally, Thomas joined him until his neighbor was ready to talk. John was now covered in sweat.

He looked at Thomas and said, "You say Alice is in trouble. What has she done, Thomas? Tell me that."

Thomas explained why folks were suspicious of her in light of all the events and deaths that had transpired since they moved to Backer Row. People were apprehensive of her sight, her use of strange native herbs used mostly by heathens, and the way she put her hands on people recently when they called on her to help doctor them.

"People are starting to think she is a witch," Thomas blurted out bluntly.

"If you want to save yourself, John, you really must be honest about what you know," he said as he thought about the story Mr. Loomis recounted of a pregnant and desperate Alice running away from her employers in Cambridge.

They had both worked persistently as they talked and the vine that was such an annoyance was almost ripped out completely.

"I don't understand what I can possibly say, Thomas. Alice has her quirks and her crying fits, but she has never said a mean word about you or any other. I know of no maliciousness that she took part in," John Young reiterated.

Thomas Thornton pressed him.

"I do not believe that. There are too many events that support another truth. Speak what you may, John, but the fact is, if you side with Alice, they will call you a witch as well. We have been friends ever since you moved to Backer Row. I am dead serious now. You will perish if you are hiding anything that would stand in the way of her conviction. They have the mindset and the power to find out what they need to know."

John Young was silent, still not knowing what to do. Thomas continued to pressure him and revealed that he had overheard parts of a recent argument coming from the Young household. Finally, he conveyed the Cambridge rumor that he had been privy to from Mr. Loomis and Mr. Porter.

"Please, John. This may be your final chance to save yourself. I am telling you this as a friend. They will hold you as an accomplice to murder!" implored Thomas.

Finally, John relented. He realized that he could not protect himself and Alice simultaneously. He was conflicted about what he was about to do but he saw no other choice if he were to survive.

"If you must know then, Alissa... Alissa.... I don't believe she is my child. I had nothing to do with any of the strangeness you speak of. I am innocent in all this," he insisted.

"You will cooperate with the magistrates then?" Thomas asked.

"Aye. If that is what must be," he uttered softly as he looked at the heap of vines on the ground ready to be burned.

The rest of the men also came and pressured John Young. He collapsed from the constant barrage of questions. He blurted out the most damning evidence possible against his wife. He told them that Alissa was indeed not his daughter. He said he could not be sure whose child she was. He explained that Alice was desperate for marriage when she met him, so he took pity on her and married her.

Reverend John Wareham was out of town. He had gone to Massachusetts to participate in the Synod, an exercise in devotional principles written by many congregations of Puritan churches. Reverend Thomas Hooker was in Windsor covering for him. He left his congregation to Reverend Stone in Hartford to help out his friend.

Matthew Allyn could see that this would further advance his plan. Surely Thomas Hooker had heard about Alice deserting her employers in Cambridge and her obligations as an indentured servant. He would have friends there who could help corroborate the rumors that were being told about her.

Once Thomas Hooker understood who she was and the lies she was involved with, Matthew Allyn had a chance of falsely proving his own innocence regarding the criminal matter he engaged in years before in Cambridge. He thought that if he played his strategy correctly, the clerics would overlook his excommunication in the church, and he could regain the respect he craved within the community. He wagered that this plan was the best immediate way to gain personal power and influence in colonial politics and business matters again.

Matthew Allyn thought that Reverend Wareham would be grateful for his part in weeding out such a horrible envoy of Satan, for he, too, had suffered the loss of his own children, Samuel and Hepsibah. He and his wife were also in grief and surely hoped to find explanations for what had happened.

He remembered the sermons given by the good Reverend Wareham, who beseeched the congregation to search in their own lives for the evils they had committed against God. The minister was certain that God unleashed this epidemic to punish the people of Windsor for their sinful ways. Mr. Allyn reasoned that Reverend Wareham would certainly be relieved that soul searching had been done, and an elaborate answer had been provided to explain the recent dark events. Matthew Allyn thought that the minister would be especially grateful to him for being the one to provide answers.

Chapter 18

WINDSOR, COLONY OF
CONNECTICUT, SPRING 1647

The rumor in town was that someone of importance was thinking about filing a formal complaint against Alice Young with the local magistrates. Windsor townspeople blamed her for many of the deaths that followed the influenza epidemic. They did not understand why her medicines and healing worked in the beginning for some and then made things utterly worse in the end.

There was much confusion within the Tinker family. They had loved Alice like a sister, but there seemed to be so much loss. Anne Tinker Thornton, for her part, was the most confused of all. She had known Alice since the day she was born, but Anne was now overwhelmed with grief. She had lost four children within the span of a month. It seemed as if her grief knew no bounds. Her husband, Thomas, was equally tortured by the loss of their beautiful children. Even so, Anne would never have suspected Alice.

She did not think Thomas was capable of it either until one day some of the townsmen started to point out some obvious "facts". Alice had been in close contact with all of them and was not sick herself. Her daughter was not sick as well. They seemed to have some sort of protection from becoming ill even though the illness plagued everyone else in town. Her remedies and healings were largely effective in most situations. But, for some reason, she could not or did not want to help in this situation. Indeed, it was strange how Alice's own household was unaffected while the one next door was so greatly touched by this latest scourge.

Someone had reported seeing her in the woods on the Sabbath. Other witnesses pointed out how many men had died on Backer Row since she came to live there. Giles Gibbs had died just before she arrived, but his widow, Katherine, had a difficult time raising several of their very unruly children.

Next door, there was the home of Revered Huit, whose arrival they had greeted with such great joy. Everyone bestowed great respect on him. He had been such a wonderful helpmate to the Reverend Wareham. But he died, as well, from a situation no one quite understood, leaving his wife and her several children on their own. His wife also died within that year.

Adjoining his property was the home lot of the Sensions. Alice had also gotten along well with both Mary and her husband, Mathias. But they, too, had lost a child recently. Beautiful Sara, so full of life once, had also recently passed. Even so, Mary and Mathias never believed that Alice was capable of hurting anyone, especially not capable of murder!

It was the Thornton household next door which felt more pain than most when their entire family was nearly wiped out by the deadly disease. The more the other men talked, the more Thomas started to question Alice's motives and looked more closely at the possibility that was largely being suggested. They insinuated that Alice, because of her presumed contact with the Devil, made everything in her presence turn sour.

Next to Alice on the other adjoining property was Rhody. Rhody had always been a trusted friend, but things were strained with her after Alice predicted that her husband, John Taylor, would die on Master Lamberton's "phantom" ship. Rhody was always aware of Alice's gift of sight and had appreciated her information. But now, she started questioning everything. Why did everything seem to be falling apart around Alice, yet she was unaffected by the wave of sickness that had passed? Why were the others exposed to tragedy, but she was not? The more she listened to the chatter and ranting of the townspeople, the more confused she became.

Alice, for her part, had noticed that something was definitely different in town. Despite the calendar inching closer towards summer, there was an eerie chill that lingered in the air. Some of her sisters seemed more distant with her, but what was even more startling was the icy imprint of a stare that she felt on her back as she passed by other neighbors' homes. She could not explain it, but she didn't like it.

The next day was the Sabbath. In the meetinghouse, there were more stares and more perceived distance. People seemed uneasy and on their guard. Much to her shock, she realized that the preacher giving the sermon was Thomas Hooker, whom she had known from Cambridge.

All of a sudden, the hairs on her arms stood erect. Another strong personality was there from her past in Cambridge also. It was the rude man in the Hulburd's trading house who was now sitting in a pew for the first time in Windsor. She finally recognized him. It was none other than Matthew Allyn. He was the wealthy trader in Cambridge who had tried to accuse her of nearly killing his eldest son with the spring tonic that she had sold to his wife, Margaret, in the market so many years previously.

Alice nervously fidgeted as she remembered what happened. Alice and Winifred had both manufactured the remedy together. It was a formula that boosted health and acted to clear the body from the sluggishness of the winter, rejuvenating it for spring. It was highly nutritive and consisted of early simples such as dandelions, nettles, cleavers, and chickweed. Winifred sent Alice to the market to sell it on her own since she was busy at home nursing a sick child.

Alice looked up at him again. There he was, staring at her in a calculating way.

It finally struck her. True to his threats in Cambridge, when he grabbed her roughly by her arms and violently shook her, he would make sure she paid a high price for his son's past illness and especially for holding her ground that day he tried to scare her. He would finally get his revenge for that incident. Matthew Allyn ignored the fact that his child became well again and suffered only shortly. Alice looked at him with dread as she recalled the shocking episode in excruciating detail.

After Mrs. Allyn gave her children the spring tonic, one child, the oldest son, Thomas, took ill. Matthew Allyn demanded that his wife tell him what she had administered to his child. When she identified Alice and the spring concoction, Matthew Allyn flew into a rage.

He stomped over to the Holman farm where Alice was kneeling down gathering herbs from the garden. He grabbed her arms tightly in an admonishing and threatening grip. He bullied her and threatened her, becoming even more violent and enraged. Allyn's accusations that the remedy had caused his son's illness were unfounded, for many others in Cambridge bought the remedy and received benefit from it. Furthermore, Alice had no problem telling him so. She knew the care that she and Winifred put into all their herbal preparations.

Matthew Allyn's real motivation to intimidate Alice lay in the fact that his wife had trusted a simple remedy made by an uneducated servant girl in direct opposition to his wishes and his status.

He told Alice, "You should leave town before someone is killed!"

Alice screamed out and defended herself.

Winifred heard the ruckus and ran out to the garden to help her young servant. Even though she was furious, Winifred maintained her composure and calmly but firmly told him, "Leave Alice alone and vacate this property at once."

He glared menacingly at them both with a parting threat.

"Listen carefully to me now. I swear I will bring your maidservant before the magistrates. You have not heard the last of me!" he hissed before abruptly departing.

For days, Alice worried that she would get in trouble with the authorities, but Winifred assured her that Matthew Allyn frequently engaged in battle with half the town and would soon be preoccupied with someone else. Luckily, his son improved, and he had no time to follow through with his threats. Alice relaxed a little after no further disturbances took place.

Matthew Allyn left for Hartford with Reverend Hooker and other new settlers to the Connecticut River Valley shortly after the altercation. Winifred and Alice were both relieved that they no longer had to deal with him. However, he never forgot the servant girl that dared to defend herself, and vowed that he would show her to her place if he ever got the opportunity again.

As Alice thought about her past, she realized there had to be more. She could sense it. He knew something else as well. He glared at her as if he were a victor and would deal with her as a spoil of war.

The preacher's oratory now turned to restitution to God for the many sins engaged in prior to the epidemic. The sad consequence that ensued involved the precious loss of several souls, including the lives of young children.

Reverend Thomas Hooker carried on.

"God always knows the careless vanities and improprieties of his flock. These sins can never be hidden from Him. And they will always be punished accordingly."

He forcefully advised that they do penance for themselves. He implored them to share their sins with all present in the meetinghouse. Many of the congregation did so in accordance with what they were asked. But Alice could not. She felt as if many were expecting her to, which disturbed her even more.

Alice felt extremely uncomfortable the rest of the time she was there. The remaining sermons of the day were all of a punitive nature. She felt like a pressure was on her chest and she could barely breathe. She was relieved to finally return home that evening.

———

The following day, Alice was working in her kitchen garden with Alissa, tending to all those precious herbs that Winifred had taught her about so long ago. John was planting corn in the larger farm fields with some of the other neighborhood men. She was actually grateful for a respite from everyone but her daughter. She also took the time to start dough in the morning that she shaped into loaves with Alissa to bake into bread later in the day.

She imagined what Winifred was doing now and how her children had grown. She shuddered. There it was. She continued to have thoughts of Cambridge again. She lost herself in thought, the thoughts of life's journey and the many roads that journey takes. Once she finished most of her tasks, Alissa wandered next door to be with Rhody's daughter, Hannah. It was sad how she had lost most of her friends and cousins to the epidemic.

Suddenly, Alice heard the strong bird call of the whippoorwill. Such a bird always enticed her to follow his song. She left her bread to bake in a large covered kettle and passed through her newly planted kitchen garden. She dutifully followed the birdcall into the woods. She needed to meander away for a little while to quiet her mind in the last hours of the day. Following the voice of the whippoorwill in the forest would be a much-needed meditation.

Once in the woods, she went to her favorite sycamore and looked for her singing messenger. It was not long before the light in the woods became dimmer and it was time to take the bread off the fire and find her daughter. The sun was heading towards the horizon. In a couple of hours it would usher in the dusk.

The younger Gibbs boys rushed off to the home of Matthew Allyn and the other gentlemen, Mr. Porter and Mr. Loomis, as they had been instructed to do. They had been spying on Alice for the last few days. In a tumultuous fashion, they blurted out what they had just seen in the forest not far from the Young's home.

"Sirs, Goody Young was just in the woods meeting with a dark man. It was the Dark Lord. She meets with the Devil to plan her mischief."

"We must make haste to find Reverend Hooker at once!" triumphed Mr. Allyn.

They saddled their horses and met Pastor Hooker at John Wareham's home, where he was staying as a guest. The gentlemen sent the young men to round up the church deacons to meet them there as well. They successfully found Deacon Hoskins, Deacon Clark, and Deacon Gaylord. As many godly men as they could find were necessary to face off with a minion of Satan!

The previous evening, Mr. Allyn had visited Reverend Hooker with Mr. Porter and Mr. Loomis and prevailed upon him to remember Alice Young when she was a young servant girl for the Holmans in Cambridge. He exposed her story and awakened the recesses in Hooker's mind that pertained to any memory of Alice. She was the young servant girl who had dared fight against Matthew Allyn. She was the one who had run away from the Holmans in Cambridge and abruptly stopped her required time of indenture. For some mysterious reason, the Holmans had dropped any charges and pretended like the incident never happened. However, this last piece of information was so critical to the case that it had to be delicately exposed at the right time.

They also explained their theory of what was causing the deaths of so many in Windsor. They described Alice as a woman who was not a healer but a murderer, and argued that she must be arrested for murder and for witchcraft. They explicated that even though she had gone to the homes of many who were ill, she never became ill herself. She left young children to die while preserving the life of her own child. They implored that something had to be done about her and that it had to be done immediately. They pleaded that everything they had worked so hard to accomplish at this outpost in the New England wilderness would disappear if they did not stop her and her extremely destructive nature immediately.

Soon their distorted theories propelled fear into the minds of others and spread like wildfire, as gossip and fear so often do. Within an hour's time, they were across the river and marching with muskets and scythes in hand to apprehend the "witch". The crowd gained volume and turned into a mob by the time it reached the town green. People were in a frenzy to find and arrest the culprit who had caused their suffering.

An angry horde approached the Young house from all sides so Alice could not escape. Men were just returning home from the day's work in the fields. As they did, they heard the news and quickly joined in. When Alice first heard the uproar, she thought that an Indian attack had just taken place or that perhaps the Dutch were starting a war with the English to reclaim lost territories. She never imagined that the boisterous noise she heard was a mob directly heading her way in a fury to accuse her of murder.

As the crowd approached, Alice's heart sank. She grabbed her daughter and held her tight behind a corner of the hearth. There was no escaping now. Alice could feel the pulsating anger and palpable hatred in the pounding boots leading to her door. At first, the shouting seemed like a snarling growl with no specific words, but as the crowd approached the house, she started to hear what they were saying.

"The witch. The witch. Find us the Devil's witch wife. You will die, witch," they shouted.

As Alice hugged Alissa, she knew it would probably be the last time she would ever be able to hold her beloved daughter again. That word 'witch' gave her the unwelcome forewarning that she trembled to recognize. Her heart froze with fear and shock. She could not even fathom why or how this was happening to her.

Moments passed in terrifying slow motion to deliver a sure message of despair. The constable pounded on the door and then kicked it open violently. The magistrates, the deacons, and several townspeople were there. Alice was still cowering in the farthest corner of the hearth, shaking. She felt like a hunted animal. The constable spotted her quickly and ran over to her, forcing her to let go of Alissa. Her poor child was screaming, crying, and grabbing for her mother in a desperate attempt to stay connected to the woman who brought her life and gave her love more than any other.

"No! I want my mother! Mother!" Alissa sobbed for her.

"Goodwife Alice Young, you are under arrest for complaints of consorting with Satan. You are charged with plotting and carrying out the murder of your fellow townspeople," the constable announced.

She was quickly placed in chains and forced out of her home with nothing but the clothes she was wearing. Tears streamed down her face as she cried out for her daughter, desperately trying to reach her again.

"My child! My sweet child! Mother loves you. I love you, sweet child! Mary will come for you as soon as she hears."

She knew Mary Sension, more than anyone else, would be there for her daughter. As they marched her down Backer Row toward the constable's house, neighbors started to approach. Mary had already grabbed the little girl in a safe embrace.

"Alice, be strong! You are innocent! Pray, stay strong! I will keep the child safe from harm," she shouted to her cousin.

Anne and Rhody looked shocked, with tears in their eyes, not really sure what to think.

"Alice, Alice," whimpered Rhody.

Their children looked horrified and also cried out for their cousin.

"Cousin Alice is no witch!" staunchly proclaimed Mark Sension.

"No witch is as kind as our cousin, Alice!" reasoned Hannah, Rhody's daughter.

Daggers of insult, one more profane than the last, psychically and emotionally stabbed Alice's heart. It was difficult for her to keep her footing as the constable led her down the path toward the town center. She felt ungrounded and unbalanced. It was as if she were walking across a rickety old bridge between two worlds above a sickeningly steep gorge. She was being forced to leave the world that was filled with lush relationships and flowing love, kinship, and community and to enter a new world that was barren, lonely, punitive, and harsh. Right now, she hung over the vast gorge of despair, teetering with instability at every step she took towards her doom. She had never felt so heavy of heart or terrified in her entire life.

The jeers were coming from angry devils whose faces were not quite recognizable, yet they were similar to the kind faces of neighbors with whom she had once shared so much. The faces of those she toiled with in the fields, celebrated with at weddings, births, and feast days, and mourned with at funerals were suddenly lost to her. Fear had transformed their faces into ghastly creatures whose sole purpose was to harm her.

Not far from Backer Row on the edge of a throng of people, she saw John Young. This simple, quiet man who had been with her, living in the same house for eight years, barely looked at her. He only glanced up once and then hung his head in shame. He said nothing to comfort or defend her. He was like a stranger, too. He was also with some of the other men of Backer Row.

Thomas Thornton stared at her but said nothing. He seemed calm and at peace that she was being taken away, but Matthew Sension seemed to look at her empathetically and shook his head out of disbelief. She guessed that word had not yet reached the Tinker family members on the other side of the Rivulet.

Once at the town center, she was placed in the rough shed of Captain John Mason to keep her secured until the morning. As they threw her into her new prison, Alice noticed other chains. This was the private chamber where Captain Mason had kept his newly acquired Indian women and child slaves after the Pequot war. They were the victims of war that he thought he could tame like animals. She shuddered. Their sadness and hopelessness still enveloped this forsaken place.

Even though it was May, there was a chill in the air at night. She had not had her evening meal and was hungry, although she probably could not have eaten anyway. She spent the night huddled in a ball alone, with her tears and her hunger, lying on a dirt floor. One of the worst parts of it all was not knowing why they had placed her here or what crime she had committed. The only things that were worse were the constant worry about her daughter and the forced separation from her. She was unable to make sense of any of it.

Mary Sension ran to the Young home and hid Alissa away with her for the night. But by the following morning, she was placed in the care of Elder Hoskins, a church selectman. The Tinker sisters had offered to take care of her, but the town elders, selectman, deacons, clergy, and political leaders would not allow it, even though she was their flesh and blood. They were afraid of the Tinkers' influence on her. Besides, they had waited for this opportunity to shame and alienate the contingent from New Windsor, England, for a long time.

Elder and Mrs. Hoskins took Alissa and watched her with severity. She was tainted by the fact that she was the daughter of a supposed witch. They determined that she must at all times be exposed to the rigid scrutiny of the righteous. She had to be under the disciplined eyes of the chosen ones lest she fall prey to Satan's mazes of treachery. If they did not astutely watch over her, they thought she would easily plunge into impropriety and evil acts, as did her mother.

John Young, the man she had always thought of as her kind but distant and silent father, abandoned both her and her mother, saying that she was not his child to save his own skin. Her mother was accused not only of killing the Thornton children and others but also of adultery. Alissa was treated like a little bastard, accordingly.

That night there were rumors and talk in town about the proceedings scheduled to happen the next day, but no one knew for sure what would happen. The constable warned that everyone was strictly forbidden from speaking to Alice, and a man was put on guard outside the prison shed. Inside the shed, Alice waited in trepidation and sadness for the next day to come and for an explanation of the insanity that hovered around her.

Chapter 19

WINDSOR, COLONY OF CONNECTICUT, SPRING 1647

At promptly nine o'clock the next morning, Alice was brought to the meetinghouse to be placed before the town magistrates and deputies for an inquiry of her crimes. Her hair was knotted with bits of straw from sleeping on the floor of the prison shed. Shoulders hunched over and mostly looking straight ahead towards the ground, she felt embarrassed to be led before her neighbors as a feared criminal. Instead of being a part of them, she was alone, separate, and ostracized. Even seeing the faces of her cousins, who she knew loved her, was not nearly enough to bridge the vast divide.

A mass of villagers decided to watch the proceedings, and some of them decided to give testimony. At first, Alice looked around to get her bearings, but once she saw the grimaces and even the recoiling away from her, she stopped. People seemed genuinely afraid. Her gaze turned towards the wood-planked floor and the search turned inward.

They brought Alice before a long table in the front of the meetinghouse, where the current magistrate of the General Court for Windsor, Mr. Ludlow, and Treasurer to the General

Court also representing Windsor, Captain Mason, were sitting. The town representatives who were deputies to the General Court of the Colony of Connecticut included Mr. Porter, Mr. Clark, Mr. Phelps, and Mr. Stoughton. Reverend Thomas Hooker represented the ministry in John Wareham's stead, as well as Deacons Clark, Gaylord, and Hosford.

The town charged them to hear the complaints and allegations against her brought forth by the townspeople and to consider the need for further evidence of her crimes. They looked at her with serious and reprimanding expressions. The head magistrate, Mr. Ludlow, explained that if the evidence were sufficient enough, it might bring an indictment. She would then be sent to Hartford where the General Court of Connecticut would listen to the evidence as presented by the town's representatives. If she were arraigned, they would appoint a Particular Court and a jury to hear her case.

Mr. Ludlow asked Alice to stand as they read the complaint that several townspeople acting together had filed. This was the moment. The first moment that she might be able to try to comprehend how her life had unraveled so fast and so far.

"Alice Young, you have been brought forth on this day having been accused of having familiarity with Satan, and thus having conspired with him to complete his many works against this town and this colony, including sorcery, murder, and adultery. We will hear the testimonies from those that make these accusations. You may be asked to answer further questions concerning these allegations. This inquiry will determine if your case should be presented before the General Court in Hartford for a formal charge of witchcraft and criminal proceedings. Is this understood?"

Alice nodded, not uttering a peep, barely making any movement as the proceedings got underway. She fantasized that if she made herself silent and still, she would become invisible and slip away. Oh, what an escape from misery that would have been!

But brutal reality soon set in. Townsperson after townsperson came before the magistrates and deputies with a story of how Alice had bewitched their animal or caused a fire to go astray. However, the most serious grievances put forward were the supposed murders of some of those that died during the epidemic and the pattern of sorrowful deaths that occurred on Backer Row since Alice moved there.

Alice was deeply distraught when she saw the face of Thomas Thornton coming to testify against her. Pain inflicted by a former friend or neighbor whom she had once helped already stung her deeply. Yet, this pain was far worse. Seeing the face of a family member betraying her was like enduring the branding burn of a blacksmith putting hot metal to sizzle against her skin.

Thomas Thornton knew as he spoke that he would have to clearly distance himself, his wife, Anne, and his sister-in-law, Rhody, lest they all be under suspicion because of their strong association with Alice through family ties and shared activities as next-door neighbors over the years. The powerful leaders of the town had implied in private meetings that lack of cooperation could cast a shadowy eye of suspicion over his own household and that of the rest of his wife's extended family. He seemed to be the only one in the family to understand that fully.

Mr. Ludlow spoke, "Do you, Thomas Thornton, have evidence that would lead the gentlemen of this inquiry to believe that the accusations brought forth today against Alice Young are indeed warranted?"

Thomas Thornton nodded. There was no turning back.

"Aye, sirs. As much as it pains me to say, many of the unfortunate and tragic deaths happening on Backer Row only transpired after this woman moved in, which included the many deaths not only of men but also of children."

He pointed his finger at Alice. She was shocked now to learn about what this man really thought of her. It was so removed from the truth. Yet, Alice felt helpless to change his mind in any way. He was too far lost in delusion and fear.

" 'Tis as if she put a curse on the whole road."

He continued with his story.

"It started with Goodman Gibbs. He died just a few of days before she arrived, leaving Goodwife Gibbs with the sole responsibility for all her children. The children became unusually unruly after their father's death. Then, there's the early end of the Reverend Ephraim Huit. I know the town clearly loved the man. He was a good teacher but taken away from us all too soon, thereby leaving Reverend Wareham once again as the only minister of the church, doubling his burdens and responsibilities. A happy event indeed for Satan."

Thomas looked into the rows of people watching and saw his in-laws. Mrs. Tinker looked serious and rigid, as though she could barely breathe. John Tinker was shaking his head in disbelief. And his sister-in-law, Mary, was sobbing. Alice stood at her spot, looking down at the floor, dazed as if she were in another world, a dark nightmare.

Undeterred, he continued, "The event that bears the most heinous mark of a witch was the death of John Taylor. He, along with many other poor souls, met their early graves on the seabed floor. Alice had given forewarning to my wife, Anne's sister, Rhody, who was also John Taylor's wife, before the doomed New Haven ship had even departed.

"How else can this supernatural knowledge be explained?" he questioned.

Alice aroused from her daze. "No, Thomas. No! I did not want him to die! I tried to stop it!" she cried out.

"Silence, Goody Young! Only God Himself has the power to stop such things, unless, of course, the Devil had his part!" Mr. Phelps snapped.

"Indeed, Goodman Thornton. Please continue," interjected Mr. Ludlow as he gave Alice an icy stare. The other magistrates nodded in agreement.

He abided their wishes.

"I have seen Goody Young use and have great familiarity with the cures and remedies of the savages and I have seen, and others have seen, her use them just before several persons died. Anne's sister, Ellen, who died at her childbed, and my four innocent children were exposed to her poisons. She presumed to be healing when she was at once murdering!"

His untrue depiction of her awakened an anger that Alice had never known before.

" 'Tis a lie. 'Tis a lie, Thomas Thornton! I am not a murderer. God knows I am innocent!" Alice screamed at the top of her lungs, punching her fists into the air above her.

No one had ever seen Alice this rattled before. She always appeared a little shy and introverted. The display of rage only persuaded them further to think that she was Satan's consort.

The Windsor townspeople sighed, and some nodded in agreement, for they also had seen her skilled usage of such remedies. But, they reasoned, what she had presented as healing medicines were probably, in effect, really potions and evil toxins in light of the recent findings and events.

"Alice pretended to help us with the healing of our children from the horrible fever but, in fact, only brought her hexes. How is it that she was so unaffected by the scourge in her own house while the house of my family next door could suffer so?" he cried out.

He explained further, "There is only one plausible reason that her daughter did not take ill, while four of mine on the property next door perished."

"I see, Goodman Thornton. That is all. You may step down," instructed Magistrate Ludlow.

Thomas Thornton wiped a tear as he left the stand. The magistrates and religious leaders talked amongst themselves and then turned to Alice.

"What say you, Alice Young, about the use of these Indian remedies? Is it true?" asked the Mr. Ludlow.

She replied, "I used Indian remedies in good conscience and good confidence! I have seen these herbs do wonders, and I had already run out of most of my English simples with so much illness about. Thomas states lies! I loved his children, too."

She turned to the crowd and stared straight at Thomas.

"How could you say such things, Thomas, when I only came to help? I am innocent!" she yelled for all to hear.

"Your wife has been a near sister to me. Your mind is poisoned with lies! That is the only poison here!" she shouted again. She quivered as she spoke.

"Please...Silence, Goody Young. You have spoken enough!" admonished Captain Mason.

The Tinker family contingent that was there on Alice's behalf could not stay silent any longer. John Tinker stood up decisively and spoke.

"May I speak now, esteemed magistrates, selectmen, and clergy?"

John Tinker was the most educated and influential sibling concerning these matters. The panel of magistrates nodded and motioned for the crowds to quiet down. They were outwardly respectful, but inwardly hostile.

"Please, respected neighbors and friends, I implore you to stop your harsh judgments and think more logically. Alice does not deserve this horrible accusation. I speak for the entire Tinker family. He gestured to his mother, sister Mary, and her husband, Mathias Sension. William Hulburd, his deceased sister Ellen's husband, was also there and nodded in agreement.

"I even speak for my sister, Anne, who is paralyzed by grief and is horribly distraught without most of her dear children at her side. Anne and her husband, Thomas, cannot see clearly. Alice is not a murderer. My sister, Rhody, who is also not here, has been traumatized by everything that has happened. Taking away Alice has only made things more emotional and upsetting for her. She does not want Alice to suffer. We have all grown up together, and there is nothing that would make Alice evil like you describe. She has given much to this community, sacrificing her time and risking her own health to support others during the terrible sickness of late. Without her aid and assistance, more people would have surely died!" he shouted.

The crowd witnessing his soliloquy was visibly becoming disturbed, but he continued despite them. On the other hand, Alice was grateful to finally have an ally in the proceedings.

"She is not to blame for this latest scourge. It is laughable that anyone could have such power! She has never been a mean-spirited person and certainly has never had any type of familiarity with Satan in the past or presently! Thomas Thornton speaks utter nonsense!"

He glared sharply at Thomas. The crowd murmured in audible shock to see such a display of family division.

"Silence!" shouted Mr. Ludlow again.

Alice was relieved to have a cherished family member come to her defense. It was the only thing that made sense in the last several days.

Mr. Phelps addressed John Tinker.

"Of course, you are personally distraught as a family member, but you must understand that we are more capable of being objective in our assessment. However, we will consider your statement, Mr. Tinker."

It did not seem to matter that the loss of Mr. Phelps's own child during the epidemic might affect his personal ability to be objective.

John Tinker shook his head and stepped down. This is exactly what many townspeople had wanted: disharmony within the Tinker family. Other family members wanted to speak on Alice's behalf, but he could see it would be of no use. Their words could, in fact, become more incriminating if twisted and used in the wrong way, and could possibly implicate his sisters as well, because of their many associations with Alice.

As for Alice, his speech in her defense moved her to have the strength to get through the rest of the day. It may not have had much impact on the magistrates, but it meant the world to her.

Rhody had wanted to be there for Alice, but her heart was heavy, and she was afraid. She was also too vulnerable to show her face before the crowds.

As the day progressed, it became apparent that the most explosive and damning testimony of all was that of the boys who saw Alice talking to a dark man in the woods. When they asked her about it, she had no reply except to deny that she had met with the Devil. It did not matter what she said. Her lies and her truths would get her equally nowhere except for a space in a jail cell in Hartford, where they already determined to send her to the gallows.

After hearing all the testimonies of the day, the magistrates decided that more actual physical evidence was needed. They decided to convene at the meetinghouse in three days, once they had obtained more proof of her guilt. Everyone agreed that more specific evidence could help solidify the case.

Mr. Porter and Mr. Loomis were gentlemen from Essex, England and had recently become acquainted with the work of Matthew Hopkins. Matthew Hopkins was the Witch Finder

General in Essex. Their relatives back in Essex had recently sent them his new manual for finding witches. The name of the guide was appropriately, *The Discovery of Witches: in Answer to Several Queries Lately.*

In just a few short years, Hopkins had exposed and killed more witches in Essex than anyone had ever remembered. Certainly then, they thought his methods to be reliable and foolproof. Mr. Porter, as one of the town deputies and a former magistrate for the General Court of the Connecticut Colony, had put the book aside after its recent arrival, thinking that it might be useful one day if ever they tried a witch.

As accusations escalated against Alice Young, they took the time to share the manual with their colleagues in Windsor. Some of the town legislators and ecclesiastical leaders agreed that, indeed, it was only prudent to follow the procedural advice of Matthew Hopkins.

In his queries, Hopkins described in great detail the necessary steps that would produce the physical evidence and confessions needed to win a witchcraft conviction. They would need several days to try out his techniques. By employing the prescribed methods, they were hopeful that they could compel Alice Young to admit her guilt.

During the current day's testimonies, she had proclaimed her innocence repeatedly. And most of the Tinker family, except for Thomas Thornton, came to Alice's defense. An admission of guilt for the record would more likely result in a guilty verdict should her case go to trial.

As a result of this decision, a request was placed to form a committee of women to do a search for any marks of the Devil upon Alice's body. It was comprised solely of the spouses of the powerful men behind the table of distinguished town leaders. They would be called upon over the next few days. Judging the inquiry to be productive that day, the magistrates adjourned in the late afternoon hours.

Alice was led to her jail cell in the Mason shed once more, where she sat isolated and lonely on the dirt floor strewn with straw. The testimonies of the townspeople enlightened her. At least, she finally understood why they feared her, even if it was based on nonsense. They twisted her gift of sight and her healing abilities into something evil – into something that she herself would never practice. On top of those accusations, John Young had voiced concern that Alissa was not his child. She was being accused of murder, adultery, and witchcraft.

Her jailor threw her some meager pieces of bread that night with some dirty water and the bottom slop of an overcooked stew. It wasn't fit for a pig to eat. Regardless, it didn't matter to Alice. She had thoroughly lost her appetite and felt too sick to touch even the slightest morsel of bread.

Alice was tired and wanted nothing more than sleep. At least she could dream about her daughter and receive a few cherished hours of respite from this nightmare. Unfortunately for her, the magistrates had other ideas.

In accordance with the guidelines in Hopkins' book, they decided it would be useful to keep her awake all night. They tied her to a chair cross-legged and forbade her to shut her eyes. She was to stay in this one position for twenty-four hours to see if one of her familiars appeared in search of nourishment from a special teat. They took shifts throughout the night and hit her, kicked her chair, or screamed into her ear if she dared attempt to fall asleep. They interrogated her for hours on end.

Her only reply to their questions was, "God knows, I am innocent. You are wrong to treat me so. You will be the ones to face punishment."

Finally, in the early hours of the morning, when daybreak had shown itself on the eastern horizon, a sleepy night watchman saw the familiar animal approach Alice. It was a fat country rat that had snuck into the shed through a hole. It was scavenging for uneaten food when it happened upon the untouched slop given to Alice the night before.

The night watchman quickly assumed that it was a minion of Lucifer in search of its evil nourishment. Their plan had worked! The familiar had shown up as predicted! He quickly awoke the others and explained what happened. After much discussion, they all agreed that the next step was to have their wives search Alice for any signs of a witch's teat.

They continued to keep Alice isolated and without sleep for the greater part of the day until it was time to further their investigation. They gathered the wives of many of the notable men in town and brought Alice into a private chamber of the Mason home to allow the women to see Alice and her possible marks better.

To Alice's horror, she quickly discovered that part of this investigation included looking for signs or marks to see where familiars had suckled. Deacon Gaylord's wife directed the process that was carried out by her as well as the wives of other leaders involved. They forced Alice to undress so that she was completely exposed.

Alice had never felt so humiliated or lowly in her entire life. They lifted her arms and spread her legs, frantically trying to find some skin tag or mole that would proclaim her a witch and prove their theory correct. To Alice, they almost seemed gleeful in their search.

At first, they found nothing too suspicious. No moles, birthmarks, or extra nipples seemed apparent. Mrs. Gaylord and some of the other women promptly reported to her husband and other men who were eagerly waiting outside to hear their findings.

The men quickly consulted their Hopkins' manual. They admonished her to go back, but this time, shave all the hair from the hairiest parts of her body. Once they were exposed, they were to stick or cut her with sharp implements in these parts to see if a previously undiscovered teat would appear.

They were determined to get their evidence. Alice felt like a tortured animal. They afforded her no dignity and disregarded her modesty completely. Once the shaving was complete, they ran their fingers across her naked body, especially around her newly exposed private parts, looking with absolute scrutiny to find a hiding teat. They poked and prodded her with the little pins and a paring knife. Occasionally, they broke her skin with their probing instruments, causing blood to trickle.

It was barbaric, and they didn't even seem to know just how ferocious they were being. She wanted to kick them, to beat them off of her, to make them pay for what they were doing to her. She started to thrash about, and they had to hold her down to finish the task. They warned her to be still or the poking and prodding would be sharper and elicit more pain.

After many minutes of searching her body meticulously, after an exceptionally hard pinch, followed by the stabbing of a pin at the outer edge of her genitals, the women agreed that they had finally located the secret teat. They were exceedingly harsh, truly thinking that they were looking into the face of Satan's consort.

"Get dressed now!" they commanded.

"You can no longer hide who you really are."

"And you, all of you, cannot hide that you are really beasts, horrid, treacherous beasts," Alice whispered as she tried to hold back the tears.

With several cold stares and condescending glances at her naked body on the floor, all but three women left. Once she had dressed, they called for the men to come and bring her back to her depressing prison of the dark shed.

"Just as we thought it would be," bragged a deacon.

"Aye. 'Tis just that we found this out. Now she must sit for two more nights by herself alone in the dark shed except for a person on watch to keep her awake. Perhaps further sleep deprivation and isolation will warm her to the idea of talking and admitting her undeniable guilt," said a magistrate, thoughtfully following the protocols of Hopkins.

"And once and for all we will find out who the dark man in the woods was," chimed in another.

"It must have been Satan!" exclaimed the other magistrate present.

***

Two more days passed very slowly, with Alice getting scant sleep. They brought her inside the house again for questioning. She still had some strength, but soon, she was willing to say just about anything to end her torture and misery. The magistrates and clerics hammered her with questions. In the beginning, she kept insisting upon her innocence. But as time wore on, she lost her will to go on.

They attempted to discourage her and told her that no one had inquired as to her well-being. They told her everyone in the village had completely abandoned her. But worst of all, they told her that her beloved daughter was already adjusting quite well to Deacon Hoskins home and was forsaking her mother, relieved to be away from her and the Devil's grip. They promised her that they would destroy any inkling of Satan within Alissa through whatever firm means were necessary.

They tried to make her believe that the whole village was against her and she was indeed very alone, with only the Devil and his familiars as her companions. Even so, Alice remembered, as if in a dream, the whispering voice of one that loved her, encouraging her and letting her know that she was not forgotten. This was her last bit of strength. But even that wore away as the magistrates endlessly pressed her to reveal Satan's grand plan to destroy the new colony. They insisted for hours at a time that she admit her guilt. In the end, she was ready to do anything to stop her misery and just sleep.

Finally, dejected and hopeless, she came to terms with her fate. For Alice, a woman who had not a mean bone in her body, this cruelty was nothing she could ever fathom. She agreed to give them what they wanted.

She herself lied and said that it was Satan in the woods that the young men had happened upon. When they questioned her and proposed all kinds of imagined, fearful fantasies about demonic plans, she nodded in agreement. She could do nothing else that acted to satisfy them. She lied again. She admitted that John Young was not the father of her child, but rather a vagrant sailor whom she had known for only one night.

"Was this what they wanted?" she thought to herself.

She also started to question herself. In seeing the future, she wondered if she really did cause the death of Rhody's husband and all those other lost souls on Master Lamberton's "phantom" ship. She started to think that maybe it really was her fault that so many had died of fevers on Backer Row. She questioned whether she caused all this misery by her sins and her unresolved lies.

She thought in anguish that perhaps her medicine and healing ways were useless because she herself was so full of sin. Thus she relented and told them everything they wanted to hear. Yes, she had run away from the family of Winifred even though she loved her so. That is why the very healing Winifred had taught her had ceased to work. Alice sobbed. She was confused and just wanted this hell on Earth to end.

The magistrates and clerics were quite satisfied that their methods had worked so well. There was one more test that they could have administered. It was a final proof that could have been done to show that Alice was a witch. It was a water test, in which she would have been tied to a chair and then thrown into the river to ascertain if she would float. If she really had been a witch, she would have floated and been expelled by the pureness of the water.

However, it was decided by Mr. Porter that there was already ample evidence in her case to convict. Thus, they abandoned the water test and preferred to bring her back to the meetinghouse in the morning where they would make her reiterate publically what she had told them in private. A public confession was all that was needed to send her off to Hartford for a trial and probable hanging. The evidence was overwhelmingly sufficient.

The next day, a haggard and tired-looking Alice was brought in chains before the town leaders and clergy. They sat her in front of the meetinghouse facing the local magistrates and clerics. There, in the meetinghouse, in front of horrified onlookers, she recanted her innocence and acknowledged her pact with Satan and his murderous ways.

Chapter 20

WINDSOR, COLONY OF
CONNECTICUT, MAY 1647

The constable pulled Alice out of her prison shed the following morning. Disheveled and broken, she had no option but to comply. Word had gotten out that she was being sent to Hartford that morning for her possible arraignment. Several villagers gathered on the green near the Mason house, waiting for the next phase of the drama to unfold.

Alissa, who was now in the care of the Hosfords, overheard adults talking in the hall about the witchcraft case and her mother. With all her will, she snuck away and ran to the town center, hoping to find her mother and hug her. She knew they were taking Alice to Hartford that morning, and she intended to hold on so tightly that they would not have the chance to take her mother away from her forever.

Mrs. Hosford soon discovered that Alissa was nowhere to be found and headed to the village center to recover her. She saw her on the path ahead and followed her. Having caught up to her at the village green, she tried to take the girl away again. Mary Sension was there as well and quickly ran to the scene and stood between them. She sternly grabbed Mrs. Hosford's arm in a warning.

"Leave the child alone to say good-bye to her dear mother. At least give her that decency!" she scolded.

Mrs. Hosford was forced to acquiesce.

As Alice was brought into the daylight outside the shed, the villagers who had gathered on the green quickly noticed her. In an instant barrage, she was subjected to incessant jeers, mocking, and abuse. But none of it compared to the distress Alice felt at being separated from her cherished daughter. Her mother's intuition told her to look carefully for Alissa. She knew her dear one would be there on the green, seeking her out. When Alissa screamed for her, Alice instantly heard the anguished cry and instinctively and immediately caught sight of her. Once she laid eyes on her precious daughter, she was determined not to let go.

She followed her with her eyes. The eyes would safeguard their connection for as long as possible. She cared not if she slipped or fell, just so long as those eyes could continue to meet in a gaze.

Little Alissa pushed through the crowd with the strength of ten adults. She grabbed onto her mother's skirt and held on tightly before the constable forced them to part again. Alice took advantage of the brief moment Alissa held on and gave her daughter a kiss on the head.

"Never forget me, dear Alissa! Never forget the love your mother has for you! Never forget the purity of my heart and the goodness I have shown you. I love you, dear daughter! All else is lies!"

She screamed to her daughter above the gossiping din of the crowd. She was satisfied that Alissa heard her, and now she knew with certainty that her daughter saw her for who she really was. She knew the clerics had not poisoned Alissa's young mind. It was a bittersweet gift amongst the sorrow that abounded.

They led her past the Palisado Green and then steps away down to the Rivulet, where a shallop was waiting in the dark waters below. Her daughter followed the entire time, continuing to hold on to her mother's eyes with her own gaze. They both sobbed along the route and were determined to stay near each other. Mary Sension and her brother, John Tinker, had approached and held firm on either side of Alissa to shield her from the crowd. They tried to be strong but were tearful as well. Alice kept looking back at her daughter, Alissa, and her protectors.

At least the villagers felt enough pity for her daughter to allow them to do this. Her daughter, born out of love, had soothed her soul. But now it was time to get on that shallop, the shallop to deliver her to a judgment and probable death in Hartford. She was determined to keep her daughter's image in her mind forever. She focused with all her might to etch her features permanently there.

As they pushed her along the bank heading down to the river, Alice realized that the last moments with Alissa were about to end. At that instant, she cried out the most agonized scream she had ever let spring forth from her being. It was sorrowful and panicked. The pain was piercing and inconceivable. It reverberated and magnified on the ripples of the water. Her heart was ripping to shreds in one single instant.

Her child, her beautiful, fair-skinned lovely girl, was being taken away from her forever. Alissa was only eight years old. Alice questioned how anyone could do such a heinous thing as separate a child from her mother. It was all so unfair.

The constable pushed Alice into the boat. She could no longer see her daughter as the captain pushed the shallop from the shore. Alissa, now held back by the river, was prevented from running to her mother one final time. The connection was broken.

It didn't matter now. No need to keep proper composure. There was no purpose to it. Alice had lost everything. She screamed. She cried. She tried to absorb the last remnants of

Windsor's shoreline, especially the silhouettes of those whom she dearly loved.

Soon the shallop entered the waters of the Great River. The sail was up and the river current would swiftly bring the boat to Hartford in very little time. Normally, Alice would have wanted to savor the blue sky, the trees on the shoreline, the birds in flight, and the sunshine touching her skin, but she could not. She was dazed and shocked, trying to understand what had just happened to her. All thoughts went to Alissa. She wasn't even sure whom she had seen in the procession to the quay where the boat was waiting. She had been so focused on not losing sight of her child that everyone else disappeared from her mind except Mary Sension and John Tinker, who had acted like her valiant protectors.

The trip to Hartford was relatively short, graced by favorable, gentle breezes along the water route. Within an hour's time, Hartford could be seen in the distance. As the vessel approached the Hartford shoreline and pier, the Dutch fort ahead, just at the confluence of the Little River Ford and the Great River, loomed into view.

As she sat on the boat that fast approached the capital seat of the colony, she wiped the last tears from her eyes and mindlessly peered at the shoreline. She had no more energy to scream or fight. The fight was already over. It was clear to her that there would be no chance for justice in Hartford either.

Disembarking, Alice could see the meetinghouse up the hill, several roads in the distance. The jailer, William Roscoe, had come to apprehend his new prisoner at the dock and led her in chains to the Hartford prison, her last home for the remaining days of her life. It was conveniently placed near the town square just steps away from the pillory, the whipping post, and the execution block.

A throng of curiosity-seekers gathered to come gawk at the first witch of the colony. Despite their eagerness to hurl rotten food at her as well as insults equal to those that she received in Windsor, all she could think about was her abandoned daughter. She had many regrets looking back on Alissa's life. But her biggest regret was that she never had the chance to tell her who her true father was.

Chapter 21

HARTFORD, COLONY OF
CONNECTICUT, MAY 1647

The last time Alice had seen blue skies or starry nights above her was the day that she arrived in Hartford on the shallop at the beginning of May. Everyone was waiting for the spring session of the Connecticut General Court to begin. Alice languished in jail and rotted in spirit as she awaited her appearance and possible arraignment before the court.

Only the sight of Mary Sension and John Tinker, who had come to Hartford to visit her in jail, uplifted her spirits. Their presence and their gifts gave her great comfort. Mary brought her a featherbed, a throw rug, some blankets, and some food from home. John Tinker paid the jailor, William Roscoe, extra shillings for her food. At least, she would get a little bit better treatment than if he had not paid.

It weighed on all of them heavily that Alice's daughter had been taken away from them and that her husband had abandoned her out of fear. They were the only ones willing to come forward and risk their reputations. They knew it might ostracize them further from the Windsor community, but Alice was family, and they could not let her be completely alone.

Town representatives in Windsor had gathered mounting evidence against Alice. When the General Court of the Colony began its session in Hartford, the same Windsor representatives presented it to the magistrates, deputies, governor, and deputy governor for evaluation. Unfortunately for Alice, they found the evidence compelling and decided to arraign her. The case was then sent for trial with a jury in the Particular Court.

As she awaited her trial, the magistrates, influenced by her case, worked to rein in undesirable behaviors of the colonists and to stop the sins that pleased Satan so much. In the days before her trial, the General Court addressed several issues at hand that were crucial in bringing the populace better under their control. The magistrates reasoned that it was necessary to tighten rules and expectations for behavior to prevent citizens from going so far astray from the church and its godly teachings.

They quickly put in place laws greatly restricting the use of tobacco and alcohol. Colonists were prohibited from lingering in alehouses more than thirty minutes at a time. Tobacco use in public became strictly prohibited.

But the most telling laws that underlined the emotions and fears of the General Court were new laws regarding interactions with the local Indians. Whereas the colony's code of 1642 had clearly stated that settlers were forbidden from living with the Indians, the new law proposed to further limit interaction with local Indians within the English communities in Connecticut.

The magistrates admonished that intermingling with Indians corrupted the behaviors of the young colonists. Therefore, they acted to restrict the renting of property to natives for agriculture or other reasons. They hoped that this law would further separate the heathens and their ways from the minds of susceptible godly youth. They argued that Alice Young's pending case alone was cause enough to be concerned about this issue.

Alice's case was an experiment of sorts, being the first witchcraft case to be tried not only in the fledgling colony of Connecticut but in all the English colonies. Witchcraft had only become a capital crime in the colony five years previously. The court knew that her case would influence many future cases.

Alice was certain that her fate was already sealed and that she would not be treated fairly. From what she had seen and heard so far, no one was willing to believe her. She worried that others who supported her would also be viewed with suspicion.

With this in mind, she insisted that Mary Sension, John Tinker, and other family members not attend the trial. In fact, she forbade them to attend. She worried that only more suffering would come to the Tinker family as a result. She knew the verdict would be quick and decisive. She determined not to let the dark shadow of fear extend to the rest of the family. With tear-filled eyes, she uttered her last sorrowful good-byes to them the morning of the trial.

The Deputy General of the Colony, Edward Hopkins, Esquire, acted as prosecutor. The magistrates who presided over the Court and formed the judges' panel were Magistrate Captain Mason serving as foreman, Mr. Welles, Mr. Whiting, and Mr. Webster. The jury consisted of twelve men: six deputies of the General Court, as had been done in past Particular Court cases, and six other esteemed men from the colony who were not currently in the General Court. However, their faces were familiar and most had served on the court in some capacity at a previous time.

The trial also took place in Hartford. On that late day in May, Alice felt trepidation and dread at the same time others participating in her trial were excited and eager. The trial commenced when Captain Mason asked Alice to rise while he read the charges against her.

"Alice Young, thou hast done works above the course of nature to the loss of the lives of several people including children in the town of Windsor. The jury will hear all testimony. If you wish to bring forth your own witnesses, you may. The gentlemen of the jury will question you about evidence against you and require you to explain yourself or give more information. Furthermore, the court may call additional witnesses to bring forth evidence that has not yet surfaced. Is this clear, Goody Young?"

Alice nodded. "Aye," she spoke defiantly.

By this time, Alice knew she didn't have even the slightest chance of being found innocent. She recognized many of the magistrates who sat on the panel of judges. Captain Mason, who had treated her so cruelly already, was heading the trial. She recognized Mr. Welles and Mr. Webster from Cambridge. They left Cambridge with Reverend Thomas Hooker when it was still called Newtown. They also recognized her as the servant of the Holmans. Her heart sank when she first saw them, knowing that everything was about to be exposed and unfairly distorted.

Not only did the jury weigh the mountains of testimonies already presented by the Windsor representatives, but it also allowed further evidence to be considered that was pertinent to the case. They reviewed the many deaths on Backer Row, including the most recent ones of the epidemic. They went over her Indian apothecary, John Young's claim of not being the father of her child, the unusual prediction she made about the doomed "phantom" ship of Master Lamberton, and her encounter with "the Devil" in the forest as witnessed by two young men of Backer Row.

Mr. Hopkins, acting as prosecutor, spoke, "As the court can see, the evidence that the Windsor town magistrates, Mr. Roger Ludlow, and Windsor deputy, John Porter, presented is damning indeed. However, I would like to call further witnesses before the court. I think they will clarify the testimonies already brought forth, in addition to bringing further evidence which strengthens the claims for witchcraft done by the defendant."

"You may proceed," spoke Captain Mason.

"I call Dr. Bray Rossiter to the stand, doctor of Windsor and former member of this court," announced Mr. Hopkins.

Dr. Rossiter came forward. Once sworn in, he spoke distinctly.

"Alice Young has been practicing unusual and questionable medicinal acts since she came to Windsor six years ago. I have witnessed on at least two grave occasions her using the potions of the Indians, probably leading to the deaths of those she proposed to cure."

"Go on, good doctor," spoke Mr. Webster.

"Her own cousin, Ellen Hulburd, was having a very difficult time in labor. I was called upon to help. When I arrived at the Hulburd home, I noticed Goody Young concocting a medley of Indian roots called "cohosh." I have not known of any healing properties that can be derived from them. Ellen Hulburd died shortly after Alice spooned the mixture to her," he explained.

"Interesting. Proceed please," stated Mr. Welles.

"I was also called more recently to the Thornton home after further damage inflicted by her with more unusual remedies taught to her by heathens. She had gathered more roots and bark that she gave to the Thornton children immediately before their deaths. I find the defendant peculiar in her use and knowledge of heathen ways. These must not be trusted. That is all I wish to say." He bowed and stepped away.

Mr. Hopkins looked sharply at Alice and asked, "How did you come to know about the concoctions of the heathens, and why would you use these poisons on your fellow settlers?"

"It was only my desire to help the children and dear Ellen improve that led me to use these remedies. All my other English simples were depleted. I learned about the native remedies innocently from a kindly native woman in Newtown who came to sell her wares in the village there," Alice said.

"So you sought out this Indian woman...That is all for now, Goody Young!" commented Mr. Hopkins.

"The court is compelled to call its next witness, Reverend Thomas Hooker."

After coming forward and taking his oath, Reverend Hooker commenced his speech.

"Goodwife Young is no stranger to my eyes. I attest that I was aware of her as a servant girl by the name of Alice Ashbey in Cambridge when it was still called Newtown. She worked for the Holman family there. At first, people in town assumed that she was a daughter or younger sister of Winifred Holman because they appeared to be so close. The year after she arrived in the colonies, many of us here removed ourselves to establish this town, Hartford. However, I have kept close contact with many there and kept reports of the goings on of people who were once my neighbors. It came to my attention long ago that this servant girl had run away amidst many rumors. The town folk there were convinced that she was with child. No one knew what became of her until now, gentlemen. The runaway servant of the Holman family and Goodwife Young are one and the same."

There was an audible murmur among the jury and the panel of judges. Those that had come from Cambridge searched for recollections of her in the remote corners of their minds and memories.

"It is with great sadness that I vow and believe that she has sinned against God and our church. Only God knows for sure, but, if true, a pact with Satan would explain why many have perished in Windsor. Satan has been steadfast in his numerous crimes against the clergy. Reverend Huit became Alice's neighbor shortly after moving to Windsor. He owned land both in the Palisado and on Backer Row. He started out in the Palisado but, preferring more space, moved to Backer Row, where he also had a larger home lot."

Reverend Hooker wiped his brow and took in a deep breath before continuing.

"Shortly after moving there, the minister, loved by all, was dead! And, of course, with the latest scourge of illness in Windsor, Reverend Wareham, who is unable to be here today, lost his two beloved children, Hepsibah and Samuel. The consequences of these events for the church have been dire. The Reverend Wareham has now lost his only son, and furthermore he is left alone to shoulder all responsibilities for the Church of Windsor, a difficult task indeed."

Alice stared at him in disbelief. How could even he, the fair-minded Reverend Hooker, be led so far astray from the truth?

"I implore Goody Young to beg forgiveness so that she may be closer to God again, regardless of the punishment that she will endure," he finished.

"What else do you wish to say, esteemed reverend?" asked Captain Mason.

He nodded and made his last statements, "I must point out to the court that Goodwife Young has proven herself to be of unscrupulous character by her unclean acts and then willful avoidance of just punishment of those said acts. In addition, she abandoned the family that invested in her indentured servitude. She also lied to her community at her inquiry in Windsor about the parentage of her child, about her real intentions, and, the most damning lie of all, about her meeting with Satan in the woods. I was present and also witnessed this lie. She disclosed the truth only after town leaders compelled her to do so."

He paused and then continued, "The boys who reported her convening with the Dark Lord are trustworthy and have never been in any trouble themselves. Therefore, I have no choice but to repudiate her denials. She has made the choice not to do penance for her sins. She had been given many opportunities to reveal the truth but chose not to. Therefore, I must judiciously side with the principles and morals inherent in Biblical teachings. It is with great sadness that I acknowledge Satan has infiltrated the life of this woman and thereby many lives in evil and horrific ways. We must take action as directed by the Holy words of the Bible: *Thou shalt not suffer a witch to live.*"

He dejectedly stepped down, disheartened that the situation had come to such a tragic but necessary conclusion.

"I will not beg forgiveness for a crime I did not commit!" Alice retorted. "I have not made a pact with the Devil nor have I done any harm to anyone. You know not what you are saying!"

Mr. Whiting addressed Alice, "Goodwife Young, would you care to elaborate or comment on these incidents or the identity of the father of your child? I'm sure the court would like to know."

All she could do was stare at him coldly, red-faced with crossed arms, seething in anger. None of these self-righteous buffoons would ever be given the opportunity to see into the most intimate and sacred parts of her life.

They waited with bated breath for her answers but were only met with icy silence.

"And how do you respond to the good reverend's testimony of your character?" questioned Mr. Whiting again.

She was defiant and stared at them all in a way that made them shudder.

"Very well then. You have had your chance. The court calls Matthew Allyn to speak against the defendant," continued Mr. Hopkins.

Alice's heart sank as Matthew Allyn rose to speak against her. She was fully cognizant that he would have no mercy. Her negative encounters with him both in Cambridge and in Windsor were proof enough. She knew he would do nothing less than crucify her with his words. She could see the hint of a malicious smile on his face as he approached the jury and panel of judges.

Matthew Allyn addressed the court with the air of importance that only a man of wealth could know.

"Goodwife Alice Young placed a curse on me in Newtown soon after she arrived from England. She conspired to kill my son with her so-called remedies. Then she accused me of making up rumors about her to others at the market. Those false accusations greatly tarnished my reputation," he lied.

"The day I confronted her about her misdeeds, she also swore at me with a fierce and horrible curse. From that day forward, I have been met with nothing but difficulties and misunderstandings. I wish for the curse to be lifted. I wish for my name to be cleared from the horrible injustices done to me by her lies and her satanic influences," he added.

He inhaled briefly and continued, "This evil must stop. Let it be known here today that I was the principal citizen in Windsor who ferreted out this witch. Out of concern for my fellow man and fellow villagers, I reported her wrongdoings to Reverend Hooker and others who will indeed verify my claims. I helped the good reverend and other town leaders to recognize who she was and to piece together her crimes. I demand justice that can be served in only one way."

He paused and glared at Alice.

"Alice Young must hang for her injurious acts of witchcraft! I am grateful that she was exposed before further wicked acts of evil could take place!"

Again, audible murmurs of shock and astonishment reverberated throughout the room. His testimony was explosive.

She was once a timid and shy girl. But the injustice bestowed upon her had kindled a raging fire of indignation inside her. She hated these pompous, arrogant men who, in reality, knew nothing yet pretended to know everything.

"I am innocent! I am no murderer! God is my witness. I am no murderer!" she cried.

"Enough, Goody Young! Your outbursts are unacceptable. You already admitted your guilt. It is impossible to disavow your confessions. Now be silent!" shouted Captain Mason back at her.

"Liar! You are a repulsive liar, Matthew Allyn! I am innocent. God knows I am innocent!" screamed Alice in complete revulsion and disbelief.

Matthew Allyn enjoyed the moment. He would recall in later years this precise time when his fortunes flipped and he once again claimed the rightful power and respect amongst members of his community that he felt he so rightly deserved. There was no longer the need to say who he thought was the real father of Alice's child. The balance was perfectly set in his favor. There was no use in disrupting such a precise and delicate balance as this. After all, he had achieved his goals, and that person would surely suffer. It pleased him even more that he would suffer in lonely silence as his lover was sacrificed to purify the community.

The jury deliberated for only a short time. Alice was damned and she knew it.

The jury pronounced the verdict.

"Alice Young, thou are hereby indicted for not having the fear of God before thine eyes; thou hast of late years or still do give entertainment to Satan, the great enemy of God and mankind and by his help hast treacherously committed murder, adultery, and witchcraft for which, according to the laws of God and established laws of this Commonwealth, thou deserveth to die!"

Captain Mason, the head magistrate and foreman of the panel, insisted that it was fitting that she be put to death on the same dramatic day that the New England colonies defeated the Pequot Indians It served to send a strong message of defiance to Satan. Thus, Governor Haynes sentenced her to hang the next day, on May the twenty-sixth, exactly ten years to the day that the proud Pequot people were slaughtered in a bloody massacre.

Her execution took place on a Wednesday and sent shock waves throughout the colony.

The colonists wanted to show, indeed needed to show, that they were stronger than the Devil's malicious acts of evil. They had erased all signs of the Pequot in the Treaty of Hartford by legalizing an edict that declared they had no right to even exist. In the same manner, the magistrates agreed that after the hanging there was to be no more talk of Alice. No one was to speak her name, just as the Pequot Indians were never allowed to call themselves by their tribal name again. She was to be erased from their collective mind like she never existed at all. The magistrates of the time would not allow such a black tarnish on the soul of their Puritan experience to be seen by future generations.

After the verdict was read, Alice became numb and barely sensed her feet touching the floor. She felt as if she had already left the courtroom. William Roscoe pulled her by her chains and brought her back to the dreary prison cell. The executioner's block would be waiting for her the next morning.

Chapter 22

HARTFORD, COLONY OF CONNECTICUT, MAY 1647

Alice returned to her cell with a heavy heart. Her mind could barely grasp that it was her last night on Earth. The past few weeks in this despicable place had been horrendous in every way. The jail was putrid and rank. She could not find comfort here. Not even in an inch of the entire space. Instead, despair, fear, loathing, and dread filled her dreary cell. The dominance and brutality of the jailor was unquestioned.

Alice had cried every night. It had been so horribly damp in this awful place. She remained shackled in the dark, and the only light at night came from an iron grease lamp. It was dim even in daylight when only an occasional ray of sunshine would permeate the space through a single, small barred window. She had often thought about the monsters taking away her dearest daughter. For many days before the trial, she questioned the final unfolding of her fate with great anguish.

As she sat in the jail cell during the pre-trial purgatory, she had also fixated on the fact that John Young had betrayed her and confessed that he was not her child's father. Luckily, he had not gone so far as to say whom he suspected of being Alissa's real father.

Mostly though, she cried in despair that at the end of all her good works and sacrifice for her community, they perceived her to be nothing more than a witch and a murderer. It truly was a stabbing wound to her heart. She thought back with surprise and shock at how those in her town wanted to see her suffer and die. It was hard for her to accept that some of the people who wished her death so adamantly were the same ones whose children she had helped bring into the world; the same ones who accepted her help when family members were ill; the same ones that she sat with in the meetinghouse on the Sabbath.

Those that would have taken pity on her could not because, in doing so openly, they would fall under the suspicion of witchcraft themselves. Moreover, they were powerless to influence or protect Alice from what happened behind the secured prison doors.

The jailers had often woken Alice in the middle of the night. They would say that they heard Satan speaking to her. They hit her, shoved her to the ground, and admonished her every breath. She was bruised and broken. So great was their harshness that Alice was in a constant state of terror and panic. What the jailer and his friends did to her was more gruesome than any devil could do.

As she went through the process of the trial, remembrances and concern for her secret love also occupied her thoughts. She had known that he could not come forward. His whole family would have been in danger. It had been too risky. They would have been looked upon with suspicion. It would have been the ruin of their daughter and his entire family. As it was, his family was now at odds with each other, and their former unity was probably shattered beyond repair.

He had to stay alive. He had to find a way to stop this kind of madness from ever happening again. He had to ease the way for their daughter secretly and behind the scenes through his many connections. Alice determined from the beginning of this unjust ordeal that no one should ever know the true nature of their relationship.

So, on that last night, she was relieved that her spirit would no longer have to endure further torture, regret, sadness, or even longing. It was finally becoming clear that she was really at the end. Alice, in desperation, got down on her knees and prayed the most heartfelt prayer she had ever prayed.

"Please, do not give up on me, Lord. I may be vile and pitiful now, but please remember me as someone who tried to heal and help others for You. I know I am not one of your chosen, but please remember me. For I am weak now and I need strength. Taken so far from any friend or family, I beseech You, dear Lord, to take pity on my soul. They have whipped me and pinched me and stripped me to find marks of the Devil. I cannot do this any longer. I wish to die rather than endure this torture. I wish only to receive Your blessing, as unlikely as that is."

Suddenly, peace filled Alice for a time. Surrounded by a force of Grace, Alice became protected from the jailers who did not bother her that last night. She transcended her physical surroundings and suddenly became cognizant of many truths. She knew now that nothing could ever really destroy or harm her and that her spirit would live on and endure. Alice received an image of her daughter and sensed that she would never turn against her and would always maintain a memory of the love that they shared. In that instant, she knew that Alissa would have a life filled with love and affection.

She started to drift off to sleep, but it was a strange kind of sleep in which she still perceived herself to be awake. In the dream, she traveled to a beautiful place that she felt acutely aware of. She lifted up out of her still, battered body lying on the jail cell floor. Her soul seemed to float through the prison walls. She could see millions of majestic star diamonds in the night sky, reflected on the water below. Moon rays beamed down upon the Great River, shining light on gentle ripples of water. A steady breeze blew her soul like a sail upon clouds over flowing waters to her favorite place on Earth, a grove of stately hemlock and pine trees. Amongst their mossy bases many feet below, she saw them, the pink moccasin flowers. The light of the full moon illuminated them.

These whimsical pink, botanical ladies cast a glance toward the water's edge. They saw him, too. John Tinker pulled up in the dugout canoe. He was alone and was there to leave her one last gift. Walking towards the grove, he pulled out a bouquet of wild columbines. He placed them in the hollowed-out hole of their favorite tree. He lay on the mossy carpet and gazed at the moon and stars above, thinking of no one but her, his love, Alice. He sensed her presence with him. He felt it was almost as if she were really there.

Chapter 23

HARTFORD, COLONY OF CONNECTICUT, MAY 1647

John Tinker came into Hartford the back way, the way of the deep forest highway, in a flatbed cart with a couple of strong horses. He quietly slipped out of Windsor before daybreak the day of the hanging. He knew at that point in time that there was nothing more he could do to save his love – his secret love. To others, their relationship was that of distant cousins. To Alice and him, it was a great love, a spiritual marriage that no amount of strife or tragedy could ever destroy.

John Tinker had been her spiritual husband since the first time they had lain together in Cambridge. He had wanted her to be his wife since childhood in the Tinker home. But fate had been cruel to their love. It had caused physical distance and separation, but never stopped the longing or the deep affection between them. Of course, their biggest connection was their daughter, Alissa. He regretted that he would never be able to acknowledge his daughter for fear that his whole family might be in danger from the authorities.

The woods seemed especially alive that morning. Birds were hysterically calling out to each other and, as strange as it was, the sun was beaming vibrant rays of light. It certainly did not match his mood or the sentiments of his soul. The wild place seemed so much more hospitable to him than his present world, a world that would soon send his love to a harsh death for no wrongdoing of her own. He could not bear the thought of seeing her hang but he knew he must be there. She would look up to see if he was present. She would look to him for comfort. He wanted the last thing she saw to be a glance of reassurance and love. Perhaps, it would bring her at least a small measure of peace as she came face-to-face with the farthest precipice of her life, leading directly to death.

He arrived in Hartford before two o'clock in the afternoon, the allotted time for the hanging. Remaining at the edge of the activity, he observed the bustle and commotion on the square. The townspeople were excited to witness the first hanging for witchcraft in the colonies.

Alice did not deserve this notoriety. She was innocent: innocence caged for weeks in a putrid jail in Hartford; innocence shackled and abused and mocked; and now, innocence led in rags and chains to a noose hanging from a scaffold in the square of the meetinghouse.

For her part, Alice was relieved to have this nightmare end. She did not know what was in store for her but whatever it was, she could not change it. She no longer cared if she received mercy, but she begged God to be at her child's side and take pity on her. She begged Him to bless her and guide her. Life would be difficult for her without a sibling, mother, her cousins, and her father, even though he would be in the shadows, making sure she would be alright.

There was a heavy knock at the large wooden door of the jail. It was the bailiff, with the nasty smirk on his face she had come to dread.

"Well, what say you, Alice Young, whore of Satan? Are you ready to die for your wicked ways? The noose is hanging and ever so ready to take you straight to hell."

She did not answer. The very sight of him repulsed her, and she did not want him to affect her anymore. So she stayed silent and looked away.

She could hear the shouting outside. People were screaming and getting excited for the event to begin.

"Where is Alice? Bring Alice, concubine of Satan. Bring her out to die!"

The crowd hated her. They despised her even though most of them had never met her. Their anger was palpable even from inside the jail. They had never seen her embrace her child or help bring another's into this world. They only acted upon what they heard and what they were told. It was their fear that made them so animated in this arena. They wanted to see an emissary of Satan's evil network die, an emissary whom they perceived as a very real threat to their own survival. The ministers had preached to them that Satan could not and should not be allowed to make inroads into the settled lands of the Lord's devout followers. This was the sentiment that they all shared.

"No words for me, hey? Saving it all for your Dark Lord?" William Roscoe violently pulled her towards him with her chains. As he yanked her towards the door, she fell onto the straw and the dirt on the floor. Her face was covered in a mix of dirt and tears. They had reduced her to this. They had stolen her child, her dignity, any chance of happiness, and, now, her life. Just then a little mouse scurried by.

The bailiff laughed, "Your little familiar come to see ya off now."

In an instant, he opened the heavy wooden door that had been keeping her enclosed and isolated, and pushed her out into the light of day. As the sunlight hit her face, she squinted her eyes. She had mostly been in darkness for three weeks and was pale and awkward in the sun.

"Look at how the consort of Satan shirks away from the sun and light of the Lord," he mused.

She resolved she would be strong and defiant as she walked out to the hangman's noose. It was all she had left.

The next moments came together in a blur. The bailiff paraded her to the meetinghouse square past the angry crowd. There was a lot of shouting. People reminded her of packs of wolves stalking their prey. Their faces snarled, and their ugly teeth couldn't wait to take a bloodthirsty bite of her. They were menacing and unkind. Others stood by, bewildered that this was happening. They looked like they did not know what to do. She wondered if there were hints of sadness or remorse on these other faces.

The minister who had provided her with the final blow was there as well. Thomas Hooker stood front and center to watch her die as a testament to his congregation that the magistrates had fulfilled their roles in ridding New England of a satanic emissary. However, it was a bitter sight, and he did not relish it.

Matthew Allyn was also there at the right-hand side of Reverend Hooker. He, on the other hand, had a victorious expression on his face and seemed quite pleased with himself. He sensed that his fortunes would imminently change. People had already started to see him differently. He perceived himself as the hero-savior who alerted others to evil in their midst. He had no doubt that he would ascend to new political heights, amass new riches, and receive their welcome into the Church of Windsor for his deeds of salvation despite his previous excommunication from the church in Hartford.

Once standing at the platform of the scaffold, the bailiff unchained Alice. She surveyed the crowd, hoping for at least a token emotional expression of empathy toward her. And then she saw him at the far edge of the crowd.

It was her love. He held his hand over his heart. He looked straight into her eyes and touched her soul. She no longer feared death.

No one else noticed. They were too engrossed in the spectacle at hand. Even though she was traumatized and haggard from her ordeal, she could at least look into the eyes of one who loved her at the end.

Chapter 24

NEW WINDSOR, BERKSHIRE,
ENGLAND, 1627-1635

As Alice stared into John Tinker's eyes and he into hers, their memories merged into the tale of their hidden love story.

Alice recalled her life as a child in the Tinker household with John and his sisters. Alice and John grew up together. They knew each other well, without the normal fears and barriers that arise when two people meet. Alice became like a sister to the many siblings.

He was always so protective and caring of her. Never did there exist in her eyes a boy of a more endearing or sweet nature. The wonderful days they played and hid in the garden made her smile. She recalled the joy she felt every time John hugged her tightly. It seemed that he even invented games so that they could touch each other. Nothing in life felt more comfortable than to be in his arms. She learned that from a very young age.

As she blossomed into a young woman, their attraction grew into something more than just that of a fond sibling nature. Mrs. Tinker, his mother, sensed their growing passion for each other. She promptly sent John off to school, not only because of his lure to Alice but because of many other circumstances as well.

But distance and higher education did not stop their love and attraction for each other. Whenever he visited home, he sought Alice as a bee seeks out the pollen from fragrant flowers. He did whatever he could to be alone with her. It was during one of these visits that he kissed her in the more hidden part of the gardens. The world had never felt more exquisite to Alice than in that moment. Alice lit up every time she came near him and hummed more than usual in doing her chores.

Mrs. Tinker found their attraction obvious and put what she thought was a final stop to it by sending Alice to the New World with the Holman family. She thought that by separating them with the entire Atlantic Ocean and time they would both seek out more suitable mates. But it devastated John to find that his mother had sent her away. He became determined to find her in the colonies. The note she left for him the day she departed only fueled his desire further.

Alice recalled her despair that day she left the Tinker home. John was still finishing the last of his studies, and she was in agony that she could not say goodbye. Early on, when they sensed Mrs. Tinker's disapproval, they had learned to communicate through love notes exchanged in a metal container that they hid in a spot near the lilacs in the garden. On that day, the note she wrote for John put her heart on display before him as never before.

"Dearest John, your mother has sent me to the Massachusetts Bay Colony far away to earn my keep with another family. But I yearn to stay. I yearn to be in your outstretched arms for always. How cruel is fate that I should not be allowed to stay with the one whom I love more than anyone? I beseech you, please find me if you love me as well. Robert Keayne will help you to know where I am. I will dream of you every night and search the eastern horizon for your arrival every day. Please, my love, I implore you, do not forget me. I will surely not forget you.

Yours forever, Alice"

She called upon the spirit of her dead mother that day to help John find his way to her again, and she left some rose petals in the old metal container to infuse the parchment with the sweet smell of love.

Even though she was a servant, Alice was unique in that she had learned to read and write with the help of her cousins. Robert Tinker had insisted that his daughters be well educated, as children of a prosperous merchant. So as the girls learned how to read and write, so did Alice. The older girls had always doted on her and were equally attentive in their efforts to instruct her in letters. She was grateful that at least she had some way to communicate with John.

Mrs. Tinker wanted John to prosper and marry into a respectable, upper-class family. Alice was an obstacle to this plan. Even though she was her kinswoman as a distant cousin, she was still a housemaid of a much lower class. Mrs. Tinker hoped with all her being that John would find and meet a more suitable young woman to marry and bear children with.

As the months went by with no sign of John, Alice naturally wondered if perhaps his love was not as true as her own. What if he had been introduced to, and had fallen in love with, a woman from a prominent family, as his mother had hoped? Was she naïve to think that he would come find her? She tried to forget her fears and became increasingly involved with caring for the Holman children and learned as much as she could from Winifred about the healing arts.

However, within two years' time, Alice discovered that her fears were unfounded and that the passion they had for each other allowed them to rekindle their love. John came to the Bay and settled with his mother in Salem, where he quickly became involved in commerce. He swiftly searched for Alice, longing to find her again. His mother revealed nothing of her secret to him and remained evasive about Alice's history. It was through his dealings and conversations with Robert Keayne that he was able to find out more information, just as Alice had foretold.

He learned eventually that she was located in Newtown and was the domestic servant of William Holman, a husbandman, and his family. Alice remembered the unfathomable happiness she felt when she heard his distinctive voice the very first day he came to call on her.

He heartily knocked on the door, not wishing to waste even a few more precious seconds. Winifred walked over to answer the door.

"How odd that someone should come calling at this hour," noted Winifred.

Everyone was heavily involved in their morning chores. The caller wasted no time and briskly knocked again.

"Yes. I hear you. We are here and I am coming!" yelled Winifred as she pushed the door open. Alice came forward near the stairwell to find out who the caller was in case Winifred needed assistance.

"Good morrow, Missus. I am John. John Tinker, your girl Alice Ashbey's cousin."

He greeted Winifred with a bow.

"Good morrow, Mr. Tinker" replied Winifred.

John and Alice stared at each other intently for a few seconds, scarcely believing that the moment of their reunion had arrived. Once the blissful reality set in, they ran into each other's arms, comforted by a host of familiar and pleasant sensations.

"Alice! Dear Alice, is it really you?" questioned John, as he smiled at her tenderly.

"John! Why John, you've finally come! You've come and found me again. Bless you, John," cried Alice.

"Welcome, Mr. Tinker," replied Winifred. Your cousin is obviously very pleased to see you. I am Winifred Holman, the mistress of this little farm. Alice, I will make you both some spiced tea. Go on and take some time to catch up with your cousin," she said cheerfully as she winked.

The children surrounded them, asking John a slew of questions about where he came from and how he knew Alice. Alice beamed with delight as John played with them and patiently answered the questions posed to him. Soon, Winifred was serving them her delicious spiced tea and shooing the children into the garden with her, so that the cousins would have time to catch up on the news of their lives.

"Dear Alice, how I've missed you so. I was shocked to find you gone when I came home on break from my studies. Mother told me that you had made the decision to go to America. She told me that she couldn't remember the names of the people you went with and had no idea where they were going to settle. Mother and I settled in Salem, where I am involved in trade and law but frequently have business in Boston. I had been looking for you for some time in Boston and in Dorchester, where my sisters now reside, with no leads. Then one day, near the market in Boston, I came across Robert Keayne, our old family friend. He was the one who finally directed me to you," explained John, not taking his eyes off Alice.

Alice was still tearful and reached out her hand to him.

"I knew you would find me, John. I just didn't know when. I was hoping that you would still look at me in the same way you did in the gardens where we played as children. I am so happy that you did not forget me and that you can still look at me in that same way," she sobbed with joy.

John squeezed her hand.

"Of course I can, Alice. I still love you. I have for years and I know I always will. I knew you wouldn't just leave England without trying to communicate with me somehow. The only way you could have was through notes left in the old metal container," he chuckled.

"I've kept that letter close to me ever since you left," he spoke as he carefully pulled out the well-worn letter and kissed it.

Kisses followed to her hands.

"John, I too have remembrances of you. I treasured the gifts that you gave me through Rhody before I left England. Upon my departure, she whispered to me that they were from you."

Alice checked in every direction and then secretly lifted her petticoats to show him the fine silk ribbon and broad Flemish lace covertly woven into her skirts and undergarments.

"Oh, Alice!" he laughed. "I am so happy to see they meant so much to you!" he said, giving her a smile and a wink. He looked at her longingly and became quite serious.

"If only we could be truly alone together now," he wished.

John visited Alice as often as he could from that time on, not telling his mother. He sensed that she would disapprove and did not want her to interfere any further in their blossoming romance. He told himself that eventually his mother would come to terms with their relationship and have to concede defeat in her personal wishes for him.

Once John had introduced himself to the Holman family, he could often be seen on their little farm, calling on Alice. Winifred was fond of John and even encouraged his visits. In turn, John brought little gifts to the Holmans to ease his way into their lives and be closer to his beloved. Alice and John ate from the same trencher when he came to eat dinner, a sign of their fondness for each other.

They were permitted to meet privately because they were related as cousins. However, Winifred was intuitive and could recognize their budding romance. It gradually became common knowledge that they had hopes of being together and wished to be betrothed in the future. Everyone involved understood that Alice would finish working for the Holmans until John was in a stable position to marry her.

After several months of growing sexual tension and increasing attraction, Alice and John mustered the courage to ask Winifred and her husband, William, for their consent to be bundled together. Since Alice was an orphan and their servant, they were obligated to act as guardians on her behalf. Winifred convinced William to give the couple their approval and the Holmans honored their wishes.

On the designated Saturday, John came together with Alice in the long-awaited courtship ritual of bundling they were so eager to initiate. They were put to bed together in an upstairs chamber on a featherbed. However, as was the custom, the bottom half of Alice's body, including her legs, was kept hidden and chaste by a snug-fitting bundling stocking. At the same time, her body was exposed from her waist to her neck. In between the two of them, Winifred securely fastened a bundling board. The two lovers were allowed to tarry with each other through the night with the implicit understanding that they could not become more intimate than these devices would permit.

Alice felt splendidly at peace in John's arms. But the permission given to be only partially intimate with each other only kindled their passions further. The courtship continued under the watchful eye of Winifred for several months. Winifred and William were tolerant and allowed them several more days to bundle together.

Alice had completely given her heart to John and was hopeful that one day soon they could be together permanently. She wondered how long it would take before John became established enough to marry her and repay the Holmans the rest of the debt she owed them for her passage. She was blissfully happy until one day John came to her with a heavy heart and solemn news.

Chapter 25

CAMBRIDGE, MASSACHUSETTS
BAY COLONY, 1638

John continued to live with his mother in Salem at the same time he pursued his relationship with Alice. He visited her as much as possible while still taking care of his mother and his obligations to her. In their time apart, he also worked to create business connections for his trade as a merchant that would ultimately provide for Alice as well as for his widowed mother. He saw his sisters occasionally in Dorchester and then later in Windsor after they moved to Connecticut Colony. He was also an attorney and was starting to represent the affairs of others.

John had the respect of many men in professional circles, and soon his hard work was noticed. The renewed relationship with family friend, Robert Keayne, was a boost to his career since Robert had been highly involved in the financing of the Massachusetts Bay Company and, thereby, an associate of the governor himself, John Winthrop. Upon Robert Keayne's glowing recommendations and because of John's noticeable intelligence as well as his naturally amiable and warm personality, Governor John Winthrop asked him to be his personal representative in regard to the sale of his property and the resolution of personal affairs in England.

He also obtained several powers of attorney from other prominent New Englanders, including his mentor, Robert Keayne, and Thomas Lechford, another prosperous merchant in Boston, for sales of property back home in New Windsor and nearby Wokingham, Berkshire County. He was to go back to England and settle their affairs. It was autumn of 1638, and John knew that he had no other choice but to accept the offers for work from these esteemed men. His mother was thrilled by his opportunities and encouraged him to go. He knew that she would never forgive him if he did not. He felt obligated since his mother had invested so heavily in his education and was relying on him to make his mark for his family's benefit.

An opportunity like this might never come again and would certainly secure his place in the New England colonies. It would put him in a better position to marry Alice despite his mother's probable disapproval. His only hesitation was leaving Alice for several months.

It was a very tumultuous October day. Alice could not quite explain what was different about it. But she could feel something had changed. The blanketed clouds were moving by quickly. A small swath of light brilliantly shone through, giving it an atmosphere of other-worldliness, but then the rays of light disappeared rapidly. The small creatures were scurrying about with much excitement. She could hear a cacophony of different bird calls in flight. And every tree willfully released several leaves at a time, scattering them in gusty breezes toward the ground.

The day was one of the most lively she had ever experienced. It was a day of heightened sensitivity and extreme significance. When John approached, Alice was not surprised and knew immediately that something was indeed different.

"Alice, I come to speak with you today of an important consideration that is not pleasant, but necessary for both of us. The governor has implored me to go to England to settle his affairs and wishes that I leave on one of the very next ships bound for England this week. He has entrusted me with significant matters, as have other prominent men. It saddens me to leave now, but I know of no other way," explained John woefully.

Alice listened intently, trying to hold back the tears.

"Because of you, Alice, the past months have given me some of the happiest times of my life. I will come back to you. I promise I will, Alice," he said as he took her hands and looked through her eyes, touching her soul.

"Fare thee well then, John. I will be waiting for you. I will never stop loving you – ever," sobbed Alice.

John took hold of her face and looked at her intently again.

"Nor will I ever stop loving you, my girl. The months will go fast, and we'll be together again before you know it. And then it will be for always," he reassured her, smiling softly. They embraced one final time, and then he departed.

He hated to leave Alice again, but they both understood that it was necessary for their future. After all, they had endured long separations before and would withstand this one as well. Parting was sorrowful, but he was sure it would bring its rewards in the end. He had to turn his attention to focus on preparations for the voyage at hand.

Chapter 26

CAMBRIDGE & SALEM, MASSACHUSETTS BAY COLONY, 1638-1639

Unfortunately, neither Alice nor John suspected that Alice was newly pregnant with their daughter the last time they parted ways in Cambridge. It wouldn't be until a few months later, with the first movements of their child, that Alice realized what was happening.

Temptation had gotten the better of them both and they unfastened the bundling board the very last time that John spent the night with Alice at the Holman's farm. It would be a decision that they both regretted for the rest of their lives because, paradoxically, their union that night led to the undoing of any chance that they had to be together again.

At first, Alice thought her melancholy and moodiness were based solely on John's return to England and having to live without him for a few months again. Her courses did not come as expected, but she concluded that the new sadness and stress made her humors unbalanced. She tried to bring her courses back with teas of pennyroyal and rue, but to no avail.

Ultimately, she did not care. She plodded along in her newly dulled existence, lacking the same zest that she had found months earlier. All she wanted was to see John again. She drearily convinced herself that the rest of fall and winter would move slowly. She pulled herself up off her featherbed every morning and attended to the duties that the Holmans expected of her, but she felt as if her heart would break. She wanted to be more optimistic, but she sensed that she might never have the chance to be with her love again. There, amidst her dismal outlook also lay the fear that John would find another love more suitable to his station in life. She lamented to herself that she had nothing to truly offer him.

Winifred noticed that her young friend and servant was not the same. She lacked the joy she once had and even lost interest in her herbal studies. By this time, Alice herself had mastered much of her craft well. But when fellow settlers and neighbors came to the house to ask for help, Alice shied away, reverting to the quiet and sullen young girl that she had once been.

Alice sang less and wanted to sleep more. Winifred had a brewing suspicion of Alice's condition but decided to wait before she approached her about it. In truth, she was not sure what to do.

Penalties for children born out of wedlock were harsh, especially for those of the servant class. Eventually, Alice began to notice other changes in her body. Her belly was starting to protrude visibly outward. She chastised herself for not being aware of her situation earlier. With the baby's movement, she knew there was no other reason for her missed courses. She did not want to bring shame to the Holman home, so she decided that the only solution was to run away.

In addition, she had no way of communicating with John, save for letters. She did not know his exact location at the time and was afraid the correspondence would never reach him. She had little way of knowing that John was experiencing delay after delay in the proceedings taking place overseas. It would be many months more than they had both expected. So, not knowing what to do, she ran to the home of the one woman who she hoped would help her and also be her future mother-in-law. With mixed feelings, she said goodbye to her life in Cambridge and traveled to her near future.

She enlisted the help of Michael, a fellow servant who was going to market in Boston town in the very early hours of the morning before the sun had even risen. With tears streaming down her face and a heavy heart, Alice softly tiptoed out of the house and into the frigid New England air. She was to meet Michael in a roadside barn. From there he would hide her in his cart and take her to Boston, where she could take a shallop to Salem. He pretended to be her brother and helped her secure her passage.

Michael was willing to help her and, in fact, felt indebted to her because of the time she had helped to deliver him from a fever that brought him very close to death. He did not know why Alice was leaving the Holmans but thought it best not to ask since she seemed woefully distraught.

Alice felt like a criminal, hiding in the cart on the way to Boston. She was ashamed to leave Winifred under these circumstances. She had been so good to her, and now Alice had to leave her teacher and a woman she loved like a sister. She had to leave Winifred to struggle alone with raising six children and settling a farm with her husband, William. They had loved her and showed special kindnesses to her. How then could it all end this way? But what if she stayed?

She simply could not. At least if she distanced herself from the family, they would in no way be accused of having corrupt morals themselves. She thought about leaving a note for Winifred but it might be incriminating, not only to herself but also to her love.

"No," she decided with certainty.

It would only act to compound her mess into a larger problem with more human casualties. She knew what she had to do.

She thanked Michael profusely for coming to her aid and waved goodbye as the shallop in Boston was unmoored and its sails took up the wind. She was both dreading and looking forward to seeing her distant cousin again. If only it were under different circumstances. She arrived later that afternoon when the sun was still a few hours from setting. She hoped that Mrs. Tinker would be understanding of what she had to say.

Mrs. Tinker was very surprised to see Alice and knew immediately that something must be wrong for her to show up in the unexpected manner that she did. She wisely dismissed her servants for the evening so she could honestly and frankly uncover the reason for Alice's unannounced arrival.

Once alone, and the initial chit-chat out of the way, Alice proceeded to explain her situation to Mrs. Tinker with humility. But Mrs. Tinker was not pleased or accepting of what she had just heard. She was surprised and shocked to find Alice with child. Even though Alice had been part of the family, Mrs. Tinker was always a bit distant from her. Now, she chastised her and made her feel embarrassed.

"What are you telling me, Alice? You are with child? The child of my son, John! How can this be? Do you not understand how much shame this will bring to my family and the governor himself for that matter?" she screamed.

Her anger was fierce and palpable. Alice felt completely overpowered by her rage.

"Aye, ma'am. 'Tis my condition," she stammered.

"John Winthrop, our esteemed governor, turned to my son, John Tinker, to take care of his affairs in England. He has such a level of respect and belief in the abilities of my son that he allowed him to take care of his personal matters! And now you come along and tell me that you have permitted yourself to become pregnant out of wedlock!"

She continued, "He trusted John to be a man of good moral standing who would follow the godly code of conduct to the letter and was thus worthy to handle the governorship's many affairs and dealings."

"I…I am so sorry, ma'am. I would have wanted it another way. But there's no denying it. We do love each other, and the child is certainly his! Please, I beg of you, help us!" Alice pleaded.

"Why, you're not thinking clearly, Alice! Don't you see John's career will be in ruins and his name blackened if the child should be acknowledged as his! They will wait for him at the whipping post and be more than happy to strip him of any privileges he now has. And how do you think that will affect his family, Alice? And how do you think that will affect me, the mother of only one remaining son? As his mother, I have carefully and dutifully prepared him at every opportunity for success. He must marry another more suitable to his station in life, Alice. You must come to your senses or you will ruin everything!" implored Mrs. Tinker angrily.

"Besides, John will be in England for several months, if not more. From what I understand, there are many complications and, therefore, delays. He is also handling the affairs of many other influential men. There is no telling when he will come back. If you really love my John, you will let him go, and you will marry another man quickly and discretely!" she admonished her.

Alice was holding her head in her hands, with tears streaming down her face. She had been able to handle waiting for John for long periods of time, knowing that eventually they would be together. But this was too much to ask. Marry another and forget a life with John altogether? How could her dream to be with her love be slipping away so quickly? She frantically thought about the possibilities. She was panicked and realized she had very few options if what Mrs. Tinker feared was true.

"But what of your grandchild?" asked Alice meekly.

She continued to sob uncontrollably.

"I am not as cold as you suppose me to be at this moment, Alice. I will help you, but you must follow my instructions carefully and faithfully. You must do as I command if you hope to come out of this situation free of public shame and chastisement. I will make sure the child is cared for in exchange for your absolute silence and release of my son from any paternal responsibility."

A long silence ensued. Both women were extremely shaken for different reasons.

Finally, Alice spoke, "But who will marry me in my current condition? Surely tricking a man and lying to him will have worse consequences than punishments given for fornicating out of wedlock."

"Do not worry. I think I know of a perfect solution," whispered Mrs. Tinker.

Chapter 27

SALEM, MASSACHUSETTS BAY COLONY, 1639

Mrs. Tinker took Alice into her home for a time. She wrote to the Holmans and told them that Alice's family had an emergency situation for which they needed her immediately and indefinitely. She promised she would pay them for the rest of the time that Alice needed to work for her passage if they indicated the amount that was required. She apologized but hoped that the payment would satisfy the completion of her indenture contract. And she promised to deliver it to them in the very near future. Mrs. Tinker and Alice both hoped that word had not spread about her running away and that there would be no repercussions to deal with from Cambridge later.

But first, she needed to find a man to marry Alice quickly. There was no time for delays. Mrs. Tinker and her servants would help Alice through her childbirth ordeal. But Alice had to promise her the hardest thing of all – that she would never tell John Tinker that her baby was his child.

John Young was a man who had gotten into some private trouble concerning his attraction to men back in England and was sent over to the colonies after having been officially apprehended for the English crime of "buggery." The English state thought to send him over to the Puritans, where he would either change his sodomite ways or meet an early death. He was a carpenter by trade, so he was easily able to find work in quickly growing fledgling settlements, but "changing his ways" was not such a simple task. He was who he was, whether he had to contend with Puritans or not.

He came to do a carpentry job for Mrs. Tinker in Salem. She recognized him immediately as the friend of Nicolas Sension. Nicolas was her daughter Mary's brother-in-law, who had also found himself in the same kind of trouble before. He was the youngest brother of Mathias. Mrs. Tinker knew that Nicolas and his friends, including John Young, were from an area of London called Silver Street, where their sexual leanings were not as much of an oddity.

Most people considered these men's erotic desires and actions to be wanton behavior, but some Londoners turned a blind eye to them. The Sension family knew about Nicolas' preferences and grudgingly accepted him for who he was, keeping it a family secret. But in the colonies under Puritan rule, neither Nicolas nor John Young would have a chance to carry on as openly as they had done in certain districts in London. Sodomy crimes often ended with the terrible fate of execution.

Mrs. Tinker was certain that John Young would agree to marry Alice and pose as a father to her child. It would serve to protect her family from a truth that could destroy them as well as give John Young the protection he needed behind the institution of marriage. Surely, he would die if the magistrates discovered his true nature. In her mind, it was the ideal answer.

When Mrs. Tinker told her the plan, Alice was in genuine disbelief. She was shocked that Mrs. Tinker was actually proposing to marry her off to a man who preferred to be with other men. But in all honesty, she knew there was no other kind of man who would marry a woman several months pregnant with another man's child.

"Don't worry, Alice. He is a quiet man and a kind man who works hard and is simple to get along with. And the best part of it is that you needn't worry about him approaching you in bed for a lark or becoming intimate with you. He will make a fine husband, and you need not feel uncomfortable with him. He truly has no interest in women," stated Mrs. Tinker.

"As long as you keep his secret, he will keep yours as well," she continued excitedly, happy to have solved the problem.

In exchange for his silence, Mrs. Tinker agreed that she would buy him land once he assured her that he had kept his end of the bargain. No one must ever know the true nature of what had really transpired. Mrs. Tinker thought that once her son, John, found out that Alice was married and had a child with another man, he would relinquish his silly dreams of a life with her and find another woman who was a better match.

Alice grudgingly agreed to the plan on one condition. Mrs. Tinker had to allow her to settle in Windsor with the rest of the Tinker family. If Alice were going to go through with this sham, she would need to be surrounded by the loving presence of her cousins, the Tinker sisters.

Yet eerily, she felt as though she were making a pact with the Great Demon himself. She betrayed her own heart and became quiet and numb in order to move forward with her life and be strong enough to have John Tinker's child without his knowledge. If her sacrifice were for the best, she questioned why she felt so despondent. Guilt settled on her as an ever-constant burden and thickened each time she saw other villagers punished for the same crime for which she had not done her own penance. She had no idea how she would ever look John Tinker in the eyes if she ever saw him again. And Winifred...what would become of her dear mentor left to manage all the children on her own?

The remorse she felt when she thought of her was overwhelming. What should have been a very joyous time became a time of relentless mourning and grief.

When the baby was born, Mrs. Tinker made sure that Alice did not register her with the town. They lived in an area of many newcomers who did not know each other well, so no one realized that Alice's child was illegitimate. Mrs. Tinker was ready to soothe any suspicions with the explanation that the baby was born prematurely, if need be. It was believable since the infant was extremely small due to her mother's inability to eat for most of her pregnancy. Alice was too weakened by grief to bring even the slightest piece of food to her mouth. It was a miracle in itself that she did not lose the child.

Chapter 28

∞∞∞

SALEM, MASSACHUSETTS
BAY COLONY, 1639-1641

Mrs. Tinker was anxious to move and be with her daughters in Connecticut Colony. But she was waiting patiently for her son, John, to return before she did. She avoided revealing her plans to Alice or the fact that she had heard that John Tinker was coming home soon. She told Alice and John Young that she was quite busy with making arrangements for her relocation to Windsor. She created more distance in their relationship.

She explained to them that everything had to fall into place in Windsor before they could make their appearance. She promised she would send for them when a home lot became available. Alice lamented that she had to stay behind with someone who was a stranger to her. But Mrs. Tinker had helped her, and now she had to play by her rules.

It was awkward and strange for Alice to take up housekeeping with a man she did not know. They scarcely had a word to say to each other initially. Their conversations together were brief and perfunctory. They both tried to be kind and adaptable, but it was blatantly unfamiliar. Alice was naturally shy, and John tended to be a man of few words.

Consequently, they passed long hours together in silence, not thinking of anything else that they had not already said. Alice was grateful and relieved that her new husband showed no interest in their marriage bed. Mrs. Tinker was correct in her assessment of Alice's new husband's true nature and lack of desire for the opposite sex.

Alice wasn't sure how they would pass off their charade as a real marriage. There was obviously no spark at all between them. Many couples in those times married for love, but marriage for convenience and mutual economic benefit was not unheard of either. For most people that they met, John Young's and her relationship did not seem very unusual, but for those who knew her and loved her, the marriage might have seemed unbelievable. She feared that it would take more convincing than she was prepared to do once they interacted with family again in Windsor. She knew that she would need to remain quiet and vague about her situation in the best way she could.

John Young and Alice found and lived in a small cottage on the outskirts of Salem for several months, where John was busy with his carpentry work. He was away long hours working at as many jobs as he could find. Consequently, Alice spent many hours alone with a baby who was irritable most of the time. She found herself falling into a deep depression. It was impossible to shake the constant guilt she felt.

The days slowly added up to months. She hardly ever saw Mrs. Tinker. When Alice heard that Mrs. Tinker had finally left for Windsor without any word or communication, she became forlorn that she had been forgotten and abandoned. Life had evolved into an endless abyss from which there was seemingly no way out. She was barely able to function to perform the endless tasks that were required of her. She had always lived with the love and laughter of a large family, and the loneliness was too much to bear.

One day, in a moment of desperation followed by another miraculous moment of grace, she pulled herself slightly out of her darkness. She recognized that if she and her child were to survive, she had to change her outlook. She started to question Mrs. Tinker's promises to them. The more she thought about it, the more she convinced herself that Mrs. Tinker could not be trusted. She kept these concerns to herself and urged John to finish any remaining work in Salem quickly so they could make their claims in Windsor. If they were already there, Mrs. Tinker would have no recourse but to comply with the promises made previously.

In the meantime, Alice mustered all her strength and applied the knowledge that she already had to heal herself from her depression and to soothe her baby. She brewed catmint and chamomile tea several times a day and drank it to help calm and appease her child as well as pacify her own nerves. Alissa received its benefit through her breast milk.

She made for herself an uplifting herbal salve of rosemary that boosted her spirits and stimulated her mind to come out of its dullness and lethargy. Applying it routinely to her temples, she started to notice a lighter mood. In addition to this, she made teas of marjoram and mint that helped to strengthen her head and stomach, and encouraged her appetite to come back.

Slowly, Alissa started to improve along with her mother, and she became a happier child. She no longer cried through the night, which allowed Alice some more time for desperately needed rest. She was finally able to bond with her newly very cherished daughter and started to connect deeply with her.

By late spring of the following year, John Young had finished his last projects, and they were on their way to Windsor. Alice felt her remaining depression lifting further. They were welcomed and embraced warmly by her adopted sisters, who were surprised by, but supportive of, the most recent developments in Alice's life.

Ellen Tinker Hulburd, the oldest Tinker sister, and her husband, William, graciously invited them to stay at their property and home on Backer Row.

When questioned on their first day in Windsor about meeting John Young, Alice was evasive to her cousins and quickly changed the subject, trying to avoid any explanations or the need to lie. To her relief, they did not persist with their queries. However, Alice's biggest concern, how she would manage to see the love of her life, was also close at hand. The following day, at the family reunion, she saw her love for the first time in her new identity and role as Goodwife Young.

Chapter 29

SALEM, CAMBRIDGE, AND
WINDSOR, 1640-1641

After many delays and business endeavors, John Tinker returned to the colonies almost two years later. He inquired about Alice and his mother from other travelers to England but was unable to find out much information. He was concerned that Alice had not responded, nor possibly received a single letter that he sent to her.

The delays in property contracts had been maddening. The affairs that he was charged to take care of took months longer than expected, causing him to miss both spring and summer passages that first year away. Finally, as situations resolved, he decided to invest with several other financiers in a voyage of the ship named *Susan and Ellen* on his way back to the colonies. This time, he brought his nephew, Miles Merwin, with him. He had word that all his sisters except for the youngest one, Sarah, had settled in Windsor in the Connecticut Colony.

Once they reached American shores, they returned to his mother's home in Salem, where she had been waiting and was ready to move with them. Amidst his mother's protests, he sent her and Miles on to Connecticut without him, promising to come before the last shallop of the season departed. He gave evasive excuses of business that had to be completed, and then headed out to Cambridge.

He was eager to see Alice after so much time had transpired. He hoped that she received the letters that he sent to her describing his difficulties in England and the causes for his unexpected delays. However, when he arrived in Cambridge to seek out Alice, he quickly discovered that she was gone and, indeed, had never received the correspondence he sent to her.

Mr. Holman explained seriously, "Alice is no longer here." He looked quite reproachful.

He was stern and emphasized that Alice's sudden and unannounced exodus was a great inconvenience and hardship for his family, especially Winifred.

"When Alice left us so abruptly it was extremely difficult for my wife. We could not find a replacement for her very easily. The children did not understand why she left them without saying good-bye. They missed her."

Most women who traveled to the colonies to work were without families and secured their positions before they left England.

But Winifred was kind and told him calmly the story of Alice's disappearance. She also explained how his mother had written describing a family emergency that required Alice to be with them. She paid for the rest of Alice's passage and apologized profusely for the inconvenience in a quiet visit she paid to them to smooth things over. She was never trusting of the reasons Mrs. Tinker gave for Alice's departure and was still convinced it had to do with a secret pregnancy and fear of being exposed. However, she politely kept these thoughts to herself, not understanding how much John's own mother had kept him in the dark concerning those events.

John wondered to himself, "Had mother come around then? Was she supporting Alice until I could return? But why would she need her to leave her contract early?"

The more he thought about it, the more he realized that something was very wrong. His mother said nothing of this news upon his arrival in Salem. Further explanations were in order. Winifred started to speak. He looked at her in a daze.

"If you see her again, John, please tell her how much we miss her here and that I am sorry we did not get a chance to say good-bye to her. We wish her well," emphasized Winifred sadly.

"I hope everything is resolved in your family." She went to a small desk and pulled out the letters that Alice was never able to receive.

"Here are your letters to her," she said as she handed him a small stack of worn envelopes tied together with brown string.

As she showed John to the door, she whispered to him.

"Please John, tell her that I wished I could have helped her."

John nodded and bowed respectfully, and then hurried out the door to where his horse was waiting. He galloped on towards Salem town at a brisk pace, hoping to find out Alice's whereabouts and the truth. He was determined to catch the last shallop bound for Connecticut that day.

His thoughts were disjointed and scattered as he tried to make sense of the situation. His previous plan was to pay the Winthrops a visit before he left for Connecticut Colony, but he had to make haste and could not wait. He would write them a letter once he reached Windsor and express his regrets at not being able to meet with them before departing Boston.

John Tinker became increasingly distraught and anxious. He wondered why his mother neglected to tell him about Alice. It was extremely confusing. He thought that perhaps he had misunderstood something. There was nothing left to do but go to Windsor and confront his mother to discover where

Alice might be. He had to find her. He could not live without her any longer.

Once reunited with his mother and the rest of his family, he desperately confronted the woman who had been hiding information from him. His mother acknowledged that she had helped Alice. She tried to deliver the blow in a way that she thought would convince him of the need to move on with his own life.

She tried to manipulate and cajole him into thinking that Alice and this man, John Young, had fallen in love. She conveniently said nothing about their child together. He desperately strived to understand, but it made no sense based on their time together in Cambridge. He could not bring himself to believe it. He demanded to know where she was, but his mother feigned ignorance of her location.

Upon Alice's arrival in Windsor the next summer, John was happy to finally know where she was but shocked and disturbed to discover that she had arrived with her new husband and a baby girl! Seeing John Young for the first time only furthered his suspicions and doubts. He was so much older than Alice and a man of very few words. He was a carpenter by profession who had recently immigrated to New England. He did not seem like the man of Alice's dreams. John Tinker thought he knew her better than anyone. But he supposed that she probably gave up on him, not knowing where he was or if he was ever coming back from England.

Mrs. Tinker's plan might have worked had it not been for her son John's ability to clearly see his own likeness in Alice's child. He deduced by the age of the child that Alissa must be his own daughter. Slipping away unnoticed from the family celebration just a day after the Youngs came to Windsor village, he confronted Alice.

He carefully escaped from the family gathering celebrating the reunion when he observed Alice leaving. Waiting only a minute, he quickly caught up to her. He pulled her aside from the path on Backer Row when no one was in sight, forcefully grabbing her hand and leading her into Rhody's house where no one was home. He approached her frantically.

"Alice, look me in the eyes and tell me the truth as if God were asking you the question Himself! I already see and know the truth by looking at the child, but I want to hear it from your lips. Who is her father, Alice? Do not deny me the truth!"

He grabbed her shoulders, shaking her, and then collapsed into her chest crying.

"Who is your little girl's father?"

He suddenly turned so quiet that he could barely be heard.

"Who is her father?"

Alice stroked his hair. She had started to cry as well. After some moments of silence, she finally spoke.

"You are little Alissa's father, my love. She looks just like a Tinker. There is no denying it. I am so sorry, John."

These were clearly not the words of a woman in love with her husband. He stood up and put his arms around her, kissing her over and over again.

"You must tell me everything, Alice. I must know," he whispered.

"John, I had no idea what to do. Your mother told me that we would both suffer severe punishment and that you would lose everything: your reputation and any opportunity for advancement in your vocation, as well as endangering your own family's future. She was the only person that I could have turned to. I would have brought shame to Winifred if I had asked for her help. What could I do, John? Your mother arranged everything," she explained emotionally.

"But Alice, now I have lost something worse than anything you described, and so have you. I have lost something more dear to me than any of those things. I have lost my paternity rights to be acknowledged as the true father to my beautiful daughter, and we have lost our chance to be together openly with our family and in the community," he lamented.

The stark realization of what he described was brutally true. Alice wept uncontrollably.

"What have I done!" she gasped, looking straight into his eyes.

He held her hands.

"I blame myself, Alice. What could you have possibly done? I will carry this guilt with me forever. I brought this misfortune to your doorstep. And I will do penance the rest of my life in regret for my actions. I should have married you immediately in Cambridge, and this would not have turned into the impasse that it is now," he wept.

"John, you know that was not possible. The Holmans would have demanded that I finish my contract and, at the least, that you pay them for my passage and the rest of my time in their indenture. This was not yet possible."

"I should have found a way, Alice. Tell me, do you have any love for this man, John Young, whom the rest of the world calls your husband?" asked John Tinker.

"Dear God, I hope he is gentle with you," he added, not really wanting to think about it.

"John, the marriage is a lie. It is a marriage in name only. John Young is hiding from the truth as much as I. You needn't worry. He does not approach me in the bedstead and never will. He was happy to marry me in order to hide his true nature. He has never enjoyed the company of women. His feelings are directed in an opposite way," Alice clarified.

John Tinker looked relieved.

From that day forward, they carried on a secret relationship with each other. They developed their own private ways of communicating. John thought desperately of ways to resolve their horrible situation one day and hoped to figure out a way to undo all the damage that had occurred, if that was even a possibility.

Eventually, John Young bought the Hulburd property on Backer Row with the money secretly given to him by Mrs. Tinker. Alice was never certain if she would have fulfilled her promise had they not come to Windsor on their own. But in any case, she felt at peace with her decision to leave Salem sooner than Mrs. Tinker would have liked. She also saw that, despite the fact that Mrs. Tinker could be distant and calculating, she still wanted to see John's child grow up.

Mrs. Tinker was upset with Alice for coming to town unannounced before John Tinker had time to forget her, develop other more suitable love interests, and go on with his life. But there was nothing she could do about it, and she consoled herself in knowing that she was at least able to keep an eye on Alice. She knew her heart had softened at seeing John's child and was glad that at least little Alissa could grow up with her cousins.

It was easy for her to become more attached to her grandchild. Little Alissa's likeness to John was uncanny, and she could not avoid having feelings for the child. She was attentive to little Alissa at family gatherings and showed as much kindness to her as she did to her other grandchildren.

Ultimately, Mrs. Tinker thought that her plan had still worked. Alice had married someone else, and John had no other option but to marry another woman who was a more suitable mate. She was certain that no one from Windsor would be able to connect Alice to her past in Cambridge. And Alice had no choice but to continue to comply with the plan now that she was amongst her cherished adopted sisters again, and the false story of her reasons for marriage was already told.

Mrs. Tinker did not realize at the time that Alice and John had not abandoned their love affair at all. Once able to be near each other again, they passionately renewed it. She never understood the depths of John's love for Alice and his determination to make the mother of his child into his wife one day. What she did understand, though, was that her son seemed newly distant and even hostile toward her. She quickly sensed that their relationship would never be the same again.

Chapter 30

WINDSOR, COLONY OF
CONNECTICUT, 1641-1647

From the night of the family reunion, John and Alice carried
on a clandestine romance with each other. At first, it consisted
of momentary whisperings or intense glances across a room
when no one else was watching at family gatherings. Sometimes
brushing up against one another during the course of a chance
meeting at a sister's home or a brief, stolen kiss behind a shed
would satiate them for days. After all, they had waited years to
be together.

But as time went by, their yearning for each other and their
passions only grew. They planned their meetings carefully and
strategically, and secret communications slowly evolved with
time. They became more creative in their excuses to see each
other, increasingly clever in arranging rendezvous, and, most of
all, more daring in the risks they took to be together.

It was convenient for John that Alice lived on a property
between two of his married Tinker sisters on Backer Row. Anne
lived on the northern edge of the Young home, and Rhody lived
on the southern end. John used any excuse he could think of to

visit his sisters and their children. He gladly offered his assistance to any family project.

Eventually, they began meeting at a beautiful pine and hemlock grove hidden just out of view from a bend in the river. The grove was covered in a mossy carpet, near a confluence of the Rivulet and a smaller woodland stream. He left gifts and sent messages to her, placing them in the hollowed-out hole of a sycamore tree. At times when they could not meet, it was a place where they could both go to dream about each other and escape from the reality of not being together as husband and wife in the eyes of their community.

Their meetings would always remain forever vivid in her mind. Stepping into the forest, Alice felt instantly at home. As her lover, John Tinker, emerged from the shadows and kissed her softly, cradling her beneath the cathedral of trees, she knew she was whole. Theirs was one of pure love protected by a circle of life force in the form of vines, shrubbery, and trees. It was radiant love that caught the rays of the sun. It was a perfect love that was reflected in the majestically and beautifully flowering plants on the mossy forest floor surrounding their embrace.

If this was sin, there was no way to return to a state of piety in the meetinghouse. It was here in the bosom of the Earth with her love that she felt completely free, that she felt entirely one with the natural world again. It was only here that she could fully honor her true nature. In the constricting atmosphere of the village, she had to hide from her very humanness and pretend and deny who she really was. It was only here in this sacred spot that she could let go, finally unencumbered and unfettered from the cruel and unrealistic expectations of society.

On a beautiful June day when they could wait no longer, they held their own private ceremony proclaiming their eternal union with each other. The mountain laurels were in full bloom in what appeared to be little wedding bouquets. John offered one to Alice with his undying love. They vowed to stay connected to each other as long as they lived. Their only witnesses were passing birds, a babbling brook, and scampering squirrels. But it made no difference. Their vows to each other were even stronger than if they had human witnesses.

For them, meeting in the woods was their sacred time, all the more sacred since it happened mostly on the Sabbath. It was strangely exciting to know that what was sacred in their forest was sacrilegious and adulterous outside of its wild confines.

Savage love. Unbridled love. John gently guided her to their bed amongst the ferns on a cloak laid on hallowed ground. A sweetness and oneness ensued that caressed their beings to forget about any earthly bounds. They both yearned for more of it. If this were really the path to hell, even the angels would not have recognized it, for it so resembled the heavens and all their delights.

Because John lived intermingled with the Tunxis Indians in the Poquonock region of the town, he was often excused from Sabbath services or military drills. In actuality, his tobacco farm was only across from Simon Hoyt's on the other side of the Rivulet and, consequently, only a short ride downstream in a canoe to their sacred place on the opposite shore. As a trader and merchant, he often traveled and could meet Alice there when others assumed he was still out of town or had already left for his business dealings in Boston, Springfield, or other places.

She, on the other hand, had a more difficult time getting away to greet her lover. She had more obligations. But as her daughter grew and started to run off to be with her neighbors and cousins, Alice had a little more time to sneak off in between chores. The day that was the safest and easiest for her to leave was the Sabbath. On the day of meeting, most people would be enclosed inside the meetinghouse listening to hours of sermons, not ambling around the woods. Alice often feigned illness or weakness on the days she knew John would be in the forest waiting for her.

In those days, it was often said that winters were the hungry time of the year. For Alice and John, this took on another meaning altogether. Once the snows commenced, it was impossible to meet at their sacred place. It would have been too easy for others to track them and find out their secret. And just as fires were made bigger and more powerful at the hearths of each home during the cold time, their own internal fires ignited further with passion in anticipation of spring.

John Tinker hoped and waited for the day that John Young was no longer a part of the landscape and their lives. He reasoned that Goodman Young would either die a natural death, or he, John Tinker, would figure out a way to coax Alice's legal husband into leaving town. Exposing John Young was not an option. Goodman Young had too many secrets of his own that he could share. Besides, Alice would have been furious with her love for doing so.

She had developed an understanding and, some would even say, a friendship with John Young. For, in reality, he respected her and assumed no control over what she did. They worked together for their survival and mutual benefit. John Tinker realized that he had no other choice but to take time to devise a believable and foolproof plan that would lead to their own legitimate marriage recognized by the town and the courts. His ultimate goal was to be able to live in the open as husband and wife with the love of his life and the mother of his child.

To stay busy as he waited and prepared to be with her, John Tinker enthusiastically started many business endeavors in the hopes of creating a good life for his beloved and their daughter. His large tobacco farm on the banks of the Rivulet did well and occupied him often. The pitch and tar business he started with others in town was also a success. He looked for any business opportunity to thrive economically so that he could easily provide for his family. Everything he did, he did with Alice in mind.

No one understood why such a handsome and eligible bachelor never took a wife. Certainly he had traveled enough to have ample opportunity to meet many women. But his heart already belonged to Alice.

John Tinker had been a very patient man over the years. But as time wore on and his daughter grew, he became more desperate to find a solution to their dilemma. He spoke with Alice about his hopes to be together in their near future.

As they sat in their forest retreat, he intensely revealed his inability to wait much longer.

"Alice, this situation can no longer be as it is. My love for you has grown over time and will never diminish. We must find a way to be together openly as husband and wife once and for all. I cannot bear to live without you any longer. I have been a patient man, but my patience now wavers, and I must find a solution."

"I wish there were a way, John. With my whole heart, I wish for that. But what can we do? There must be something," Alice spoke.

John Tinker answered, "There is only one way that could be beneficial to everyone involved. The most obvious solution that comes to mind is to entice John Young with a better future. I will make him a financial offer that he cannot refuse. He need only comply by leaving town. The court will be obliged to give you a divorce on grounds of desertion. It is then that we will marry, and I will adopt Alissa."

One day, he approached John Young in the fields. He was attending to some crops by himself not far from his home lot. John Tinker hoped for a positive outcome to the conversation.

John Tinker walked straight up to him. He was so focused on the ensuing discussion at hand that he barely uttered a greeting.

"I know everything, John Young: the deal my mother made with you to marry Alice. I know everything about it. I know it all," John Tinker pronounced, hoping to set the stage for fruitful negotiations.

John Young was startled. He had not expected John Tinker to address him in such a way.

He eyed John Tinker cautiously and then said aloud, "So Alice was talking to you then. I have plenty of secrets of my own about the two of you as well."

"Of course, John Young. I do not aim to alarm you or threaten you. I only ask what I can do to make you take your leave of this place gracefully and without consequence. I have waited long enough. I need to be with Alice. I need to be with my child. I will pay you handsomely if you leave this place and never look back," pleaded John Tinker.

"It is not my problem, John Tinker. I cannot help you. I have been given land here and worked the land with my bare hands for many seasons now to build up its soil and establish my farm. You are asking that I leave it after having so carefully tilled it and preserved it."

John Young put down his hoe and wiped the sweat from his brow before continuing.

"You are also asking me to abandon my responsibilities and my civil contract to my recognized wife, thereby becoming a criminal in this colony. Do you think I could ever be granted my own land again after doing such a thing? What good would all your money do for me then? I am too tired to start anew in a faraway place. I also have other considerations now. How do I know that word would not get out about my own secrets if I left, furthermore causing the government to apprehend me as a criminal?"

He looked at John Tinker defiantly.

"No, John Tinker. I will not do it! I will not take this risk upon myself!" he answered with absolute certainty.

"I see." John Tinker lowered his head, feeling dejected and hopeless.

He had thought about this conversation for several months and thought it would be a turning point. It was, but not in the way he had imagined. It was he and Alice who would have to leave in order to be together.

For them, it was more difficult. John Tinker had many family members here and was more widely recognized throughout the colony. The penalties for Alice leaving her husband would be more severe for her as a woman. He was certain of this. If they left, it would be the final cutting off of all ties to family, community, and even the New England colonies. And this decision would not only affect two persons. It would affect three. Damn John Young anyway!

John Tinker was desperate to figure out a solution. Running away would take further time and planning as well as convincing. He would have to justify taking Alissa away from everything she knew in order for them to be together and to sacrifice not living in the open near his family as he had dreamed. They would still have to live in secrecy and be in constant fear of exposure. He grew bitter and knew he could never forgive his mother for all the hardship she had caused by her meddling and manipulation.

Once Alice became privy to their conversation, she also felt desperate. She pleaded with John Young for some resolution. But it only ended with fighting and arguments. As time progressed, it became clear that the situation was hopeless.

Chapter 31

WINDSOR, COLONY OF
CONNECTICUT, 1646-1647

It was not long after his definitive conversation with John Young that life unraveled tragically for both Alice and the Tinker family.

The following winter and spring, the family lost five of its members, all children. John was shaken by the loss of his favorite nieces and nephews who reveled in his stories and delighted in his jokes. The void was vast and endless for everyone who felt the children's permanent absence. The heartbreak that ensued brought even more misfortune.

Gross misunderstandings and the need to blame someone for the many catastrophic events that unfolded in Windsor led to the astonishing conclusion by many that Alice played a key role in the tragedies by use of witchcraft. John knew logically Alice was no more culpable of the crimes they suspected her of than the minister himself. But mass fear had set in and quickly invaded the psyches of many townspeople. Even John Tinker hated to admit that in a brief moment of confusion and grief he had wondered if the accusations could remotely be true. Ashamed of himself, he quickly found his way back to logic and the knowledge of his heart.

Soon the situation reached a boiling point. John tried to use common sense and reason in secret discussions and arguments pertaining to Alice with his brother-in-law, much to his disdain. As an observer of gossip and whisperings at the local tavern, he could see before his eyes how imaginations had gotten out of hand. And the trepidation about Satan's designs, evoked from the pulpit, only acted to fan the flames of fear.

John became frantic to find a solution. He knew he had to act quickly without letting on to anyone. So he decided to send Thomas Hopewell, his Indian messenger, that evening and have his beloved prepare to run away with him and their daughter. He had plenty of coin and wampum to start a new life. But many people were acquainted with him in New England, so they would have to flee into the wilderness, hiding out for a while, and then escape either to Virginia or the West Indies. From there, they would stay unnoticed with new identities or move back to England.

Their final destination was unclear. In any case, it was no longer safe for Alice in New England. He wanted them to be together. He was desperate for the plan to work because it was their last and only option.

The issue of protecting his family still reverberated in his thoughts. But he realized that some of his family members helped to bring this craziness to the point where it was. In a way, he was ashamed. He had done everything to prop up his family's position and bring them prosperity and had tread carefully in order not to tarnish their reputations. But his beloved was left to endure living with a man she did not love, being forced to live in a charade. It was an intolerable situation, and he had to dismantle it quickly.

Alice was in her house baking by the hearth late in the afternoon. The tensions were high in the village, and she needed a respite from the outside world. When Thomas Hopewell, the young Indian man who worked for John, started calling the familiar whippoorwill birdcall he had always used, Alice sensed that it was important. She quickly ran off to the woods to greet him.

Thomas Hopewell explained John's urgent plan to run away. They had to be discrete. She was to find Alissa and quickly prepare to leave the village forever. He said that he would be waiting in three hours' time with the dugout canoe at the side of the river when night fell. John Tinker would be with him. She was to gather her belongings and Alissa quickly, meeting them at the prescribed place on the Rivulet immediately after dusk.

Alice hurried back to the cottage, determined to escape with John and their daughter. She became lost in the alarm and urgency of her situation. Unfortunately, she was completely unaware that a couple of neighborhood boys had followed her into the woods and were spying on her.

Matthew Allyn and others had hired them in hopes of finding incriminating evidence against Alice. The boys had been secretly watching her every move in the previous days, waiting to see if there were some sign of a secret witch's coven or a clandestine ritual with the Devil in the forest. When they saw her standing next to a sycamore tree with the tall Indian man in the distance, they didn't recognize him.

All they saw was a dark man, possibly Satan, who was speaking to Alice in the wild forest. That was all the proof they needed. The fear in their minds left no doubt that he must be an envoy of Satan or even the Dark Lord himself! They ran promptly to tell the town magistrates, who apprehended Alice as a criminal within the hour. Escape was no longer a possibility.

John quickly recognized that something was amiss well before the appointed time near the riverbank. He had paddled downstream and hid the canoe in the woods near the river's edge with his gear an hour early when he saw activity farther downstream. There were several more canoes traversing the Rivulet than there normally would have been at this time of day during the week. He knew from the increased movement that something had to be going on in the town center.

With fear in the pit of his stomach and a feeling of dread, John Tinker went to investigate the happenings in the town. With heightened senses, he hurried across newly planted tobacco and grain fields on his way to Backer Row. As he came closer to the edges of the little Puritan settlement, he could hear the hectic cacophony of voices that would normally not be as boisterous at this early evening hour. He knew immediately that it was a bad sign of things to come.

As he approached Backer Row, his steps became more frantic and rushed. The Youngs' small thatched cottage looked abandoned. The front door had been kicked open and was completely ajar. No one was home even though a fire still smoldered in the fireplace. A crowd had trampled Alice's garden, and only the heavy boot prints of an angry throng of people were left behind.

His first thoughts went to Alissa. He panicked at the thought of his child and his beloved face-to-face with an irate mob. He had to find them at once. He ran to his sister Rhody's house and found her collapsed and crying at the table with her children.

"Rhody, what despicable act has just transpired here? Where are the Youngs? Where is Alice?" he demanded with impatience.

Rhody looked up at him intently.

"They say she is a witch, John. To where they have taken her, I do not know. Could it possibly be true, John?" she asked him, sobbing uncontrollably.

Even her question infuriated him.

"The world has gone mad. How could you even dare to pose that question? Don't tell me that our misguided brother-in-law has soured your mind against Alice, too!"

Rhody looked up at him blankly. Her hair was disheveled, and her eyes were bloodshot and swollen from crying. She was clearly conflicted. He nodded in disbelief and then ran out of the house, slamming the door in disgust.

Dusk had fast approached, and the skies were beginning to darken. In haste, he continued up Backer Row, scoffing as he passed the Thornton home. He was determined to find his sister, Mary, who he hoped was watching over his daughter. Of all his sisters, she understood Alice the most.

As the Sension home came into view, a soft light glowed through the small leaded-glass windows. He peered inside to see Mary's silhouette in a chair by the hearth, comforting his daughter who was in her lap. Mary's own little daughter, Mercy, slept in a cradle nearby. After a gentle knock, he slowly and carefully opened the door in a manner that he hoped would not disturb his little girl. Mary was softly stroking her hair with great care and humming a sweet lyrical but melancholy tune. It had the desired effect of lulling her to a calmer, almost sleepy, state.

John was able to discern that no one else was there. He realized that Mathias and the boys must have left for the town center to ascertain what had just taken place. Mary looked at him with compassion and anguish in her eyes. Her expression revealed an unsaid understanding and acceptance of his love for Alice. In reality, she had known for many years that they were forever intertwined. He had always appreciated the loving kindness and support of his older sister but never as much as in that moment. He softly mouthed the words, "thank you," as he gestured to Alissa and then departed for the town center.

As he raced down Backer Row, a flurry of unanswered and disjointed questions entered his mind. His primary concern was to find out the whereabouts of Alice and discover the dark plans that were being made for her. In a matter of minutes, he was running up the small hill towards the town green. He could see from the lit torches up ahead that there were throngs of people still milling about.

On a typical night, everyone would have been sternly reprimanded for the crime of "night walking." But this was no normal night. It was an unbelievable night that brought forth the first accusation of witchcraft in the colonies and all the pandemonium that came with it. And right in the horrid center of it was his love, Alice, being viewed as a consort of Satan.

Nothing made sense to him anymore. Shock hovered over him in such a surreal way that he thought it must have really been an awful nightmare that would end when he awoke. An innocent place inside him did not want to fully fathom or grasp the most disturbing thing he had ever encountered in his life–the vicious nature of his fellow man.

John passed the groups of people still talking animatedly on the town green as he approached the home of his brother-in-law, William Hulburd. Mathias Sension was there with his boys as well. They exchanged worried glances.

"Where is she? Where have they put her?" John demanded to know at once.

Mathias spoke first, "She's in the Mason shed, John. They will bring her to Hartford if they find enough evidence to convict her."

"I must see her at once. This is preposterous. There is no evidence because she is not a witch!" screamed John desperately.

William grabbed his arm. "John, please, you must know that the constable and elders have sternly warned everyone to stay away from her, lest they be accused themselves of witchcraft. The townspeople already view the Tinker family with suspicion."

Mathias insisted, "John, wait until everybody calms down tomorrow and we get a clearer idea of what is going on. At least, wait until everyone is sleeping. But you should know a guard is watching from outside the shed, making sure that she does not escape. He has strict orders to apprehend anyone who comes to her aid in any way."

John shook his head. His eyes looked dejected and his spirit was crestfallen with despair.

"I cannot leave her there alone. Where is her husband? The Young home looks abandoned. Did John Young flee?"

"We saw John Young and our brother, Thomas Thornton, together earlier. It appears that Thomas convinced Young to turn against Alice to save himself. I do not know for sure, but the magistrates have not gone after Young. He is probably now at the Thornton place, away from the leers of the crowds until things settle down," William explained.

"Ah yes, our brother-in-law, Thomas Thornton, has been unusually absent from us lately. Thomas voiced his ridiculous suspicions about Alice, but I never thought he would really accuse her. I know he was in complete anguish over the loss of the children, but we all were. What on Earth would make him speak against her? There is something else that is going on here," said John apprehensively.

"I have to go," John spoke, as he started to run off.

Mathias cautioned him, "Please John, remember my words. Do not incriminate yourself unnecessarily by getting caught abetting Alice."

It didn't matter. John was adamant not to leave Alice to her jail cell in Mason's shed without recognition that she was there. He had to give her words of support and comfort. He did not sleep at all that night but instead waited for a time when the guard might fall asleep. What he hadn't anticipated were the dogs on watch as well that first night of her captivity. Dejected, he realized it would be impossible to speak with her and resolved to make a stand on her behalf the next day.

Alice felt comforted yet alarmed when John stood up and spoke on her behalf in the meetinghouse. She did not want him to draw attention to himself or the other family members. She knew the evidence was already too overwhelmingly against her for his testimony to be of any use. That night as she sat tortured in the prison shed, she started to feel delirious but had a dream that he had come to speak with her. Once he was able to see her at the jail in Hartford, he explained that on the night the watchman had neglected to bring dogs, he had snuck over to the shed and spoken to her through the cracks. It had not been a dream at all.

Even in her darkest of hours, Alice was unable to show the world the spring from which she drew her strength. John Tinker was that spring. But the love they had would forever be hidden from view, unrecognizable except for the very likeness of their daughter's face. That love had never been allowed. It was concealed from public view. But there was no other choice but to hide the truth if his family, including his sisters, were to continue to live their lives in New England unhampered. In contrast, her motherly love for Alissa was accepted and open. It was there for all to witness. Alissa was her only testament to their love, and even that had been cruelly ripped away from her.

As Alice deteriorated in the Hartford jail, she was once again grateful that John Tinker had come to lift her spirits and take care of her in some way. But she became increasingly concerned that his presence would draw too much attention to the true nature of their relationship. He wanted to represent her in court, but Alice flatly refused, begging him to forget her and focus on nothing but making sure their daughter would be cared for.

Intuitively, she knew that the incriminating testimonies yet to come would expose her and lead to questions about the circumstances of little Alissa's parentage. She refused to allow the rest of the world to desecrate their love by having an open-door view of their relationship. She said good-bye to him before the end of her trial. She knew that it would not be a fair one and that the magistrates would cry out in feigned righteousness for a purification of their colony by blaming her for all the events that they could not explain.

Chapter 32

WINDSOR, COLONY OF
CONNECTICUT, MAY 1647

As Alice was being led through town, Mrs. Tinker peered from behind her daughter's shop on the edge of the town green. She was sobbing hysterically, steeped in deep remorse and regret. Mrs. Tinker was not pleased when Alice came to her in her early pregnancy. Alice and John had loved one another for years despite all she had done to "protect" him. She realized that had she just left them alone to share in the love they had for each other, her son's life would have ultimately been happier. Sorrow had filled his heart for too many years because of his own mother's actions. Alice Ashbey Young was the love of his life. The outcome of Mrs. Tinker's actions now weighed heavily on her heart, indeed heavily on her soul.

Alice had foreseen her late husband Robert's death. Alsie had also seen it coming. She tried to keep her premonitions to herself except for immediate family lest outsiders look upon her suspiciously. Dwelling in the same household, it soon became clear to Mrs. Tinker that Alsie had passed her psychic abilities on to her daughter. Perhaps it was this strange talent that scared Mrs. Mary Tinker the most.

Mrs. Tinker recalled how small Alice was when she was born. She never did gain a lot in size but grew to be a lovely young woman. She remembered her cousin's dying pleas for her to take care of newly orphaned Alice. She did so, as obligated. But as Alice became more mature, Mrs. Tinker started to sense an unbridled romance between her and John. She could not support this.

But now she wondered if Alice could have been a part of his life after all. Suddenly, her heart opened, and she realized that she, too, had loved Alice. The stark recognition of what she had done haunted her. She feared that John would never forgive her. She knew now that she could never forgive herself. She thought of Alice and her probable conviction and wept inconsolably.

Once Alice sailed to Hartford, to her future trial and probable doom, and the crowds started to disperse, John spotted Thomas, who had just entered his tannery. He grabbed him once inside his business in the Palisado. His sister, Anne, and their one remaining child were inside also. He thought he could have killed Thomas at that moment. It was only pity from the loss of his four children that saved John Tinker from committing such a passionate crime.

John spoke tersely to him, "Thomas, you know not what you have done. May God forgive you because I never will! Your betrayal of Alice and culpability in playing into the hands of those that would most want to destroy this family are too much for me ever to overlook."

He then turned to Anne. Anne looked very pale and had been crying for a while.

"Sister, this is nonsense. Alice loved you and those children. Now, because of your inability to see the good that was given to you in your time of need, you have also lost a brother," he said as he sadly gave her one last mournful look.

Indeed, the world had gone insane, and his brother-in-law had led the insanity against his wife's family. Never was John more acutely aware of how grief and fear acted to obscure the truth.

After speaking a few more reprimanding words to Thomas, he stomped off to confront his mother, who was hiding behind a window at the Sension shop. He shut the doors. Rhody and Mary and her husband, Mathias, were there also. They asked the children to go outside and wait until the adults had spoken.

He confronted his mother in front of his sisters and Mathias.

"How do you feel, Mother, now that Alice has been hauled off to Hartford as a murderous criminal?"

His voice was serious, more earnest and firm than it had ever been in his entire life. He was furious as he watched his mother tremble with guilt.

He continued, "I blame you for Alice's predicament and imminent conviction as much as I blame any town magistrate."

"But, John, I was there with you in the meetinghouse on her behalf. I have not spoken of her in bad faith, as did others. I stood with you, ready to defend her," she reasoned, desperately trying not to lose her son.

He spoke again, "None of this would have happened if you had just allowed us to marry and be happy. I could have protected her as her husband."

He knew that, with his clout and position, they might have left her alone.

"I hate the fact that you have put me in the impossible position of choosing and protecting either my family and my daughter, even though I can never acknowledge her as my own, or letting you all suffer by acknowledging my love and spiritual wife instead. Alice would still hang, but not alone since I would find myself at the gallows with her. It is an impossible situation, and the consequences of any and every possible action are too much to endure," he spoke fiercely. His hands were trembling.

He felt that, for his part, he would have to do penance the rest of his life. Never were human frailties and flaws revealed more clearly than in this shocking and deadly family calamity.

John chastised his mother further.

"All Alice ever wanted was to be a member of the Tinker family, and she was. She only acted out of love and helped whenever she could. The only thing that she had ever truly lived for was to be a part of this family. And we are the only family she has left. And what did you do, Mother? You abandoned her. You cut her off from the only people in this world who she knew loved her. She did not deserve this. She not only wanted to be a part of this family because she loved me but also because she loved all of you." He also glanced at his sister, Rhody.

"It befuddles my mind to try to interpret how you, any of you, could possibly allow yourselves to think that Alice was anything but faithful to all of you. She wanted your love and your acceptance as part of this family. She was so happy when she felt she had it for a time. But now look, Mother, at how all your manipulations have become a catastrophic disaster!"

Mrs. Tinker cried out to her son and begged his forgiveness. "Please, John, forgive your mother. I only thought I was doing what was in your best interests."

"What was in your best interests, Mother!" he corrected her as she sat whimpering in a chair.

Mary, his sister, told him, "John, we've known how you've loved Alice, so I cannot imagine how difficult this is for you."

Rhody was crying in a corner and nodded in agreement.

"I am so sorry as well, brother," she whispered.

John stated his appreciation to Mary and her husband, Mathias.

"I cannot tell you, sister, what it meant to me that you were there to comfort little Alissa. I draw much of my strength from you and Mathias. Thank you."

"Promise me you will not proclaim your paternity, lest the whole family be in jeopardy," Mrs. Tinker spoke. "Because you see, John, we all came to realize how much you loved Alice. Most of us even suspected the affair but said and did nothing. Please, son… I cannot bear the thought of them taking you to hang at the gallows. The loss of my five grandchildren this winter and spring was horrific enough. And now Alice… I am so sorry for her, John. Indeed I am, but the suffering and tragedies must stop somewhere. You must live," Mrs. Tinker pleaded.

"How will I live without my heart?" he questioned and quickly left to be alone.

Mrs. Tinker feared that the family had forever splintered. Several discussions had taken place privately as officials investigated Alice. She knew in her heart that her family would never be whole again. If her five grandchildren had died as a consequence of someone's sins, she knew they were her own.

William Hulburd, who had acted as her faithful son-in-law even after the death of her daughter, Ellen, and his remarriage, had come to speak with her. He explained to the family that the maliciousness of townspeople was forcing him out of Windsor. He no longer felt safe with his new family. As soon as he could get his affairs in order, he was moving to Hartford. People were accusing him of being a possible witch himself. They blamed him for selling his land to the Young family, allowing the so-called witch to reside among them.

Indeed, the whole family was under suspicion for associating with Alice. Life had become tense and difficult for all of them. Everywhere they went, they were looked at with suspicion. Her poor daughter, Anne, who was still grieving over the loss of her four children, had closed herself off completely from the rest of the family.

After Alice's conviction, John told his mother that he was leaving Windsor for good and hoped never to see her or his brother-in-law, Thomas, again. He could never forgive her and he could never forgive his brother-in-law who had lost his mind with grief. He knew a part of the problem had been Thomas' desire to gain piety and favor with the church. By doing so, Thomas thought he could make up for any sinfulness that, he concluded, contributed to the loss of his dear children.

Chapter 33

HARTFORD, CONNECTICUT, MAY 1647

Alice walked up the scaffold to the noose of her death.

"What say you, Alice Young?" cried out the Reverend Thomas Hooker, hoping that Alice would at least beg for penance in her last moments of life. He was greatly disappointed and chilled by her response.

Alice looked at the Reverend Hooker and vehemently denied using sorcery.

She reproached him, saying this, "You, Thomas Hooker, and others like you are responsible for an innocent death and the separation of a family. For your sins, God will certainly bring His wrath upon you."

Then she gave an icy cold glare to Matthew Allyn.

"And as for you, Matthew Allyn, the Devil has never known a better helpmate. One day, justice will find you. And when it does, my name will be cleared, and yours will be mud."

She abruptly turned away from them, took in a deep breath, and centered all her emotions to the one person in the crowd who mattered. With one last tender gaze at her lover, she put a hand over her heart and nodded. She knew she was loved. She knew that her daughter would be fine. She couldn't hear the mob's taunting or jeering at her anymore as the marshal placed her head inside the noose. She determined to focus only on the face of John Tinker at the edge of the crowd.

In an instant, the moment between her life and her death was viciously defined. Her body dropped as her neck snapped. When the savagery was complete, they threw her into a shallow pit near the outside edge of the burying ground not more than several yards from the meetinghouse square.

And so it happened that Alice was hanged as a witch in Hartford. Betrayed in Windsor. Hanged in Hartford. Killed in Hartford. Lost to this world and those that loved her. John Tinker grieved but had to grieve in silence. Those years of holding onto a dream that never came to fruition colored the rest of his life with disillusionment and sadness.

John Tinker hoped this would be the last case of its kind. But, realistically, he knew it would be a long time before the madness and fear that had taken hold would be subdued again. How many other blameless victims would die in this brutal manner? He was determined to find a way to protect the innocent from future witchcraft accusations.

Chapter 34

HARTFORD, COLONY OF CONNECTICUT, MAY 1647

The crowds had dispersed, but heavy clouds of hatred and fear had not lifted. John Tinker slowly and carefully crept to the open ditch where they threw his beloved Alice's body. It was so cold and lifeless. They discarded her with such little care or remorse. They left her to be nibbled on by vultures and rats. After all, in their stringent minds, no witch deserved a proper burial. John was one of the few people in the world who saw Alice for who she authentically was. At least those that loved her had been able to recognize the extent of her goodness.

He dropped to the ground and wept with unbridled anguish. The tears that fell ran down upon her face. They cleansed away dirt and misunderstanding in steady streams of compassion, love, and loss.

No one could see him now that it was late. Soon, the Windsor and Hartford townspeople would be dreaming of witches and their familiars. Soon, they would be looking for another witch whom they could blame for bad crops, a dead cow, or a child's deformity. The floodgates of suspicion and mistrust were now open, and ecclesiastical permission had been given to clear all evil impurities from their midst. How many more deaths and how many hangings would it take to rid New England of the dark forces that plagued her?

John carefully wiped the rest of the dirt away from her face and stroked her body, cloaked in shreds of tattered clothing. He carried a woven blue woolen cloth in his wagon, given to him by his sister, Mary. It was the same blue indigo cloth that Alice and her cousins had woven together in times of love, laughter, and sisterhood. He carried his dear one out of the shallow, muddy pit and carefully placed her on it. He wrapped the blue indigo cloth around his departed love and tenderly laid her in the back of his wagon. He would find the perfect burial place for her.

He hurried her body back to Windsor in the cart. He needed to reach his destination and make her burial before daybreak. His horses seemed slightly spooked from the strange noises in the forest on the road back but rode on with loyalty.

Finally, John reached the perfect place. He knew he could not bring her body to the town burying grounds. A grave made there would certainly be desecrated. He would also arouse suspicions if he attempted to cross the Rivulet with her body, for surely the ferryman would hear him in a boat and wake up.

Thus, the gravesite had to be far from the burying ground. It was a remote location, but he knew somehow that she would still hear God's call when He requested that His children take their places in Heaven. And just as John and Alice's secret wedding took place in a concealed corner of the rich and fecund forest near the flowing water of the Rivulet, so too would her funeral be there.

He dug the grave with steady frenzy. He didn't have much time. The first bird songs of the day had started. As first light approached the horizon, he quickly buried Alice in a grave facing east so that she could greet Christ when He came back for her. John did not doubt her salvation.

Then, with the increased light of day, he noticed them, the pink moccasin flowers in full bloom. They were Alice's favorite wildflower. They reminded her of the moccasins of the little girl in the Indian legend who sacrificed for her community out of love and compassion. He received his confirmation. This was definitively the place that would help her to be most at peace.

John scattered old leaves across the grave and placed a sandstone marker upon it so that he would be able to find her again. He intended to come back and plant more of her favorite wildflowers later.

In creating this burial site, John Tinker knew it was his last act as her husband. It was the only real action he had ever been able to do on her behalf as a spouse. But the church elders and magistrates would not have allowed even this one act of devotion. They would have frowned upon it and then demanded that it be destroyed. Fate had been cruel, but their love was not.

When he needed to connect to Alice's beautiful spirit, he could come to this revered personal spot along the river. Even though she was no longer on this Earth, he knew that their love had been strong and he hoped it would survive for eternity. With a last kiss to the sacred ground where his beloved was laid to rest, John Tinker slipped away before the sun could climb any higher on the eastern horizon. The wary townspeople were starting to stir. He dared not tarry any longer.

Chapter 35

WINDSOR, COLONY OF CONNECTICUT, JUNE 1647

The Reverend Thomas Hooker stood high in the pulpit, towering over the Windsor congregation. He continued filling in as a substitute preacher for the Reverend John Wareham, who was still in the Bay. He ruffled the pages of the prepared sermon that were before him, trying to find the power within himself that was once so familiar. It had been less than a month since Alice Young's death, but Reverend Hooker seemed noticeably weaker than ever before. He searched desperately to find any remaining vigor within his being. He was becoming wary of the future. He remembered her reprimanding words against him moments before her death. The dark cloud had not lifted as expected.

On this day, he chose to write a sermon based on the Book of Romans, 1:18. He commenced, knowing that he would gain strength as he read the scripture.

"For the wrath of God is revealed from heaven against all ungodliness and unrighteousness of men, who hinder the truth in unrighteousness…"

He stopped and stared at the congregation. Noticeably absent was John Tinker. He had already left town for Boston.

Several others were missing as well. Many of the remaining flock seemed inattentive and preoccupied. It fueled his anger and his determination to set his flock on the right path once more.

Something finally switched inside him, and he continued with his sermon, extolling the virtue of truth and the wickedness of deception. He underlined how it was impossible to be simultaneously a follower of Christ yet betray truth. He told the worshippers that one must have a sincere heart to profess genuine truth.

"If a man perseveres in opposing the truth, it argues he is under the power of corruption."

He thought of all the deception and lies that must have been told in this village over the past few years. God could not have been pleased. Indeed, the pastor was greatly distraught and defeated that one of the flock had strayed so far from the righteous path and directly into the clutches of Satan.

Eighteen days later, Reverend Hooker joined so many others in the afterlife that year by dying of the same destructive fever in Hartford.

As Captain Mason and other magistrates wished, Alice's name was forgotten over time, and she ceased to exist in the minds of future generations. Court records were destroyed. Even Governor John Winthrop in the Massachusetts Bay Colony wrote in his diary only "One ---of Windsor Arraigned and Executed at Hartford for a Witch."

There was no trace left of her existence except for one entry in another man's diary many years later. A man by the name of Matthew Grant, the second town clerk of Windsor, in recounting his town's history, wrote on the inside cover of his diary in the latter half of the 1600s, "May 26. '47. Alse Young was Hanged".

Chapter 36

BOSTON, MASSACHUSETTS BAY COLONY, SEPTEMBER 1693

Remembering the elderly minister's offer to be of assistance in the latest battle against Satan, the Reverend Cotton Mather called upon the old minister again. This time, there was a young woman whom he had taken into his care and who was being tortured by Satan. Margaret Rule was a seventeen-year-old girl who was a recent refugee from Maine. She and her parents came to Boston after hostile Indians attacked and destroyed their settlement.

The girl, already traumatized, was vulnerable to other negative forces. She complained that a witch on the street had cursed and pinched her. Cotton Mather had taken her into his home to restore her to a state of health and spiritual purity.

"Thank you, Reverend Thornton, sir, for coming to my home again to help us in our holy battle against Satan. You have heard of Margaret Rule, the latest victim in the witchcraft scourge of our time," Cotton stated.

"Some of our townspeople are now starting to say that we are not just in our assessments of the matters at hand. They would actually accuse us of stirring up false fears and creating the chaos ourselves. While these sentiments are preposterous, I feel it best to call for the help of my fellow ministers, especially those that have experience like yourself in these matters. We must bear witness and carefully scrutinize the signs that Satan has used to carry out his end through these witches."

He continued, "I pray that you will enter the chamber that I have provided to Margaret Rule and directly observe for us what you think is pertinent in calling out Satan. Please examine her carefully. I will need the testimony of what you observe to continue to make our case. I have also called another minister today. William Hudson should arrive shortly. But you may go in ahead of time and check on the child. She has had her share of fits. Indeed, her very spirit will be happy to be in the grace of another man of God".

"I would be happy to oblige, dear Cotton. We must not be taken off guard now," the elderly reverend answered graciously.

Reverend Mather showed Reverend Thornton to the sleeping chamber of Margaret Rule. The room was dimly lit. At eighty-seven, Reverend Thornton's eyesight and hearing were not as good as they used to be.

The room where Margaret Rule lay was simple and bare. It had nothing more than a featherbed and quilts and one small chest. It was on the highest floor of the house in the back near the eaves. Candles barely lit the chamber at all, with its one small leaded-glass window. Margaret stirred when he came into the room. She started to moan and thrash about. She was obviously quite disturbed.

There were small shadows on the wall from the flickering candles, and leaves rustled outside the window. The groaning emanating from Margaret, the crashing of branches against the window, and the creaking of the floorboards continued in such a way as to create a cacophony of eerie sounds, which undoubtedly announced the presence of Satan. The minister hesitated. Fear was rising to the surface from deep down in his being.

The next thing he thought he saw was quite strange. Was she rising up from the featherbed? Lucifer, the dark one, must be forcing her to move in such a way. He started to pray.

"Devil, be gone with you. May the Lord Almighty cast you away from this child," he proclaimed.

The lights of the candles flickered abruptly, and the room became even darker, as if Satan was preparing for an obvious assault. Was Margaret really being pulled by an invisible force toward the attic ceiling?

Soon there was a knock on the door. Thomas Thornton startled. It was Cotton Mather and William Hudson.

"How do you find her to be?" requested Cotton Mather.

"My good minister and Reverend Hudson, she is indeed tormented by the Devil!" answered Reverend Thornton.

The flailing, thrashing, and moaning in the featherbed nearly drowned out their discussion, as if Satan were giving a bountiful performance to let his presence be known.

"If you look ever so carefully, you will see how the Devil causes her to rise out of her bed from time to time. He does not let her rest," answered Thomas Thornton.

"Aye. How the Devil temps and tortures her! I will call in others from downstairs to witness this harassment. We must continue to make our case to the townspeople before they start to tire of fighting these bewitchments. For if we do not continue our noble fight, the Devil will win even though he is already considerably weakened," agreed Cotton Mather.

Soon, several others came to the room of Margaret Rule. She seemed to become more distressed as others entered the chamber. Reverend Thomas Thornton supposed it was increased torments to her by the Devil as the demon's rage mounted against those faithful Christians who were coming to stop him.

After a time, Margaret calmed down and went to sleep. Thomas Thornton felt that he could finally leave the room.

Downstairs, Cotton Mather had some warm ale and an empty parchment, a fine quill pen, and ink awaiting him.

"Dear Reverend, please be so kind as to rest awhile by the fire with some ale and contemplate what you will write as a witness to this remarkable event," stated Cotton Mather.

The Reverend Thomas Thornton gave a great sigh.

"Yes, of course, if that is what you wish," stated Thomas Thornton.

Timothy, Thomas' son, had arrived a little earlier. He observed his father yawning and fatigued.

"My father will come later to write his testimony after he has had some rest, esteemed reverend. He must take his repose. He needs to fortify his strength before contemplating this matter any further," pleaded Timothy Thornton.

Timothy knew that his father must have been thinking of Priscilla, the sister Timothy had never met, at that moment. Seeing Margaret suffering in the bed reminded Thomas of his daughter.

"Nay, Timothy. I am not tired, but I do think of your siblings that died just months before you were born. Seeing Margaret in her bed being so tormented caused me to think specifically of your sister, Priscilla," recalled Reverend Thornton.

Timothy understood. He had heard the story many times before in his lifetime and knew how emotional and drained his father became each time he recounted it.

"Please, Father. It is not necessary to talk of this now. It will only upset you further," begged Timothy.

"No. I must tell the kind Ministers Mather and Hudson about your pious sister, Priscilla, who had such a close brush with the Devil. She had often played and worked together with Alice's daughter, Alissa. She spent many hours in their home and, sadly, became close to them. But Priscilla had always displayed exceptional virtue. She was very pious and thoughtful for her young age and was quite curious about the afterlife. Eventually, she became largely concerned about her ability to avoid temptations and her own worthiness to enter God's kingdom. She tried to influence the other children to behave in virtuous ways and had even suggested that they keep a day of prayer together to overcome their ignorant and sinful ways."

He glanced up at Cotton Mather who was taking notes, as he often did in hearing those early histories of New England.

He continued, "She was only eleven years old when the evil sickness fatally enveloped her at our home in Windsor. Yet, the closer she came to her death, the more prayerful she became. In the beginning, she was afraid to die and found little comfort in her prayers."

Thomas Thornton wiped a tear from the corner of his eye and somberly resumed.

"She admitted to being bothered by Satan but said Christ was victorious over him in the end. She knew she would ultimately die but was no longer afraid of death amidst the many assurances from her affectionate mother, my dear departed wife, Anne. And so on the day of her death her body was greatly weakened. However, she was in a joyful state of mind when we told her it was the end of the Lord's Day. Thus, she fell peacefully to sleep for eternity and finally joined the Lord in His heavenly realm."

The old reverend looked frail and defeated as he finished his story.

"Soon, Thomas, aged thirteen, and then Anne, aged nine, followed their sweet sister into death. I am convinced they both became angels themselves. Samuel, who was two years of age, was also called to God's side. Alice Ashbey Young was there among us for years in our home and entwined in the lives of everyone in my wife's family. To think that we lost most of our children for lack of diligence in seeing evil's ways makes my heart mourn all the more. For that, I still cannot completely forgive myself."

The reverend shed a few more tears.

"Anne and I lost our entire family except for our little Mary, who was six years old. Timothy and the other siblings were not yet born," he quietly spoke.

"Dear Reverend Thornton, now I see how personal and tragic this situation was for you. Please, I beg of you to take your leave and get a good night's rest. You can write the testimony later," Cotton Mather said.

Timothy nodded at his father. The aged Reverend Thomas Thornton had no choice but to comply. He shrugged his shoulders, let his son help him with his cloak, and shuffled out the door into the cold night air.

Chapter 37

BOSTON, MASSACHUSETTS BAY COLONY, OCTOBER 1693

A few days passed before Timothy was ready to bring his father back to Cotton Mather's house. Thomas Thornton was starting to be somewhat forgetful and so was unable to insist on going back sooner. Margaret Rule had rapidly improved after their last visit. Cotton Mather released her back into her parents' care with careful instructions. Things seemed to be finally quieting down in Salem and other Massachusetts towns. Lucifer, the great demon and archenemy of Christ, had taken his retreat, according to Cotton Mather.

A writing table was carefully arranged for Thomas Thornton. The empty parchment lay next to the quill and ink.

The elderly reverend shook his head and wrote, *"We whose names are underwritten, do testify, that one evening when we were in the chamber where Margaret Rule then lay, in her late affliction, we observed her to be, by an invisible force, lifted up from the bed whereon she lay, so as to touch the garret floor while yet neither feet, nor any other part of her body, rested either on the bed, or any other support, but were also, by the same force, lifted up from all that was under her:*

and all this for a considerable while, we judged it several minutes; and it was as much as several of us could do, with all our strength, to pull her down. All which happened when there was not only we two in the chamber, but we suppose ten or a dozen more, whose names we have forgotten."

Thomas Thornton signed the document. William Hudson stood up. He quickly read the page that Thornton had written.

He continued to write on the bottom, *"William Hudson testifies to the substance of Thornton's testimony, to which he also hath set his hand."*

He also signed it and then handed it off to Cotton Mather. He glanced at the letter and smiled, replacing it on the table in front of Thomas Thornton.

The old pastor looked down again at the piece of parchment with the testimony. He was joyful that Margaret Rule recovered from her fits and apparitions. The Devil's influence seemed to be fading as time wore on. He took his leave with Timothy. Suddenly, he felt overwhelmingly exhausted.

That night, in his son's home that he shared, Thomas Thornton sat in silence at the fireside. He thought back to the days when he was the father of young children in Windsor forty-six years earlier. The Devil was just preparing to take a stand back then and to wage a war on the first generation of colonists.

He thought of his beloved, departed wife, Anne, and the many children they had together. He specifically pondered if she were now with his children who were lost in that time so long ago. Were his dear children, Priscilla, Thomas, Anne, and Samuel, under their mother's tender care again?

Perhaps his testimony and his influence on the Mathers and their writing and preaching had saved a few souls from Satan's recent plans. Hopefully, the information he shared in Boston with his church leaders served to save a few families from the suffering and loss he and his family went through so long ago. They revered and respected what he had to say.

After all, he was an elderly pastor who most colonists presumed was one of God's chosen. He had direct experience with Satan's first full-scale battle in New England, which took place in Windsor, Connecticut. This experience had taught him well, even though he was not in the ministry at the time.

The events of Windsor in 1647 had influenced and disturbed Thomas Thornton so profoundly that he and his wife, Anne, and their remaining children moved to Stratford that same year. In Stratford, he resumed life as a tanner. They moved in haste after Alice's death. The townspeople seemed to blame the Tinker sisters and their families for allowing Alice to come to their town. There had even been gossip implying that the sisters could be witches as well.

Those attitudes had made it impossible for them to stay in Windsor and grieve properly. They were also emotionally drained from conflict and turmoil within Anne's family, who were divided in their support or suspicions of Alice.

Life in Stratford was lonely and unsatisfying. Thomas served in governmental positions, but Anne missed having family around. They could never really get away from the family stigma of association with a witch. So in 1653, after many sorrowful and burdensome struggles in the New World, they moved back to England during the time of Cromwell's Commonwealth.

It was there that Thomas decided to fulfill a calling as a minister. It was an unusual thing for someone of his station in life to do, but he was determined more than ever that what happened in Windsor must be prevented from occurring elsewhere.

A few years passed, and they moved back to New England when the monarchy was restored under King Charles. It had become much more difficult in England to practice his strengthened religious beliefs and his ever increasing faith.

Ultimately, he and his wife, Anne, decided to move to the Massachusetts Bay Colony once more. They settled in Yarmouth, a whaling community, where he worked for many years as a minister in a congregation committed to converting the Indians to Christianity. He hoped it would be with God's favor that he turned the Indians away from their ancient heathen ways. These converted Indians became known as the Praying Indians. It was in Yarmouth that he lost his dear wife, Anne.

After retirement, he moved to Boston with his son, Timothy, where he became a respected member in Reverend Cotton Mather's church. As a retired pastor who had dedicated his life to making New England the dominion of God and not one of Satan, he often gave counsel to younger church leaders such as Cotton Mather. His advice concerning witchcraft cases had been firm and brutally honest, emphasizing the swift and decisive actions necessary to root out Satan again.

Yet, as he revisited his past, he could not quite shake a rather strange feeling of another kind. In their fervor to root out evil of all types and defeat Satan's armies, had they caused other families to suffer as much or even more? Why could he not quite explain what had transpired even though he desperately wanted to? There could be no room for doubt. He was certain that Satan was trying to trick him again.

Thomas was there in the meetinghouse square in Hartford the day they hanged Alice Young. He remembered how small she looked standing on the scaffold moments before her death. She no longer looked or seemed so threatening. He remembered how disheveled and pathetic she was and how remote the possibility actually seemed at that moment that she was responsible for all the chaos and misery that had occurred in Windsor over the past few months and even years.

He had been so sure that she was to blame for mass calamity, and now he was suddenly full of doubts. It was maddening how deceptive Satan could be. It was outrageous that he could orchestrate the shattering of a once-close family.

Then he remembered the specter of his brother-in-law John Tinker's last words ever spoken to him over forty years ago.

"Once your mind has become so confused as to see the face of the Devil in as caring and as sensitive a person as our Alice, you will, no doubt, find the face of the Devil in countless others. And it is this that I fear: not Satan himself but perceived devils that will cause more suffering, division, and death than any one Great Demon could ever do."

Thomas Thornton shuddered. Could John Tinker have been right?

Suddenly, a thought occurred to him, as if an act of simultaneous grace and damnation. If Alice were innocent, then he had not been guilty of failure to protect his family. There could not have been better surveillance of Satan's deeds. He was not responsible for the deaths of his own children by being less than vigilant. If he unburdened himself from guilt for not catching Satan in the act of harming his children, he could be more at peace with their deaths.

But what if those who died as witches might really have been innocent? Nay. It was Satan playing tricks on an old man again. It was better to leave it all alone. Either way, his heart would own the burdens of time and life.

Thomas was tired now. He was eighty-seven years old, and he was ready to go to his heavenly home if God chose to have him there. He had had enough of demons and of devils and was tired of battling Satan. He longed to be with those family members that he had lost so long ago. Perhaps, there amongst heavenly white clouds and singing angels, away from this dark New England wilderness, they could all be a united family again.

EPILOGUE

John Tinker could not tolerate living in Windsor after Alice's death and was estranged from many of his family members. He left Windsor almost immediately following the tragedy and took up residence in Boston, where he could be closer to major trade. He kept an eye on his daughter from a distance.

He did penance by marrying a dying woman, Sarah Barnes, in 1648, and assumed responsibility of her young daughter since he was not allowed to acknowledge his own. He then married a woman named Alice Smith, fifteen years younger than he, in the early 1650s and had several children with her. She had an illegitimate child after John died, but the court gave her the mere punishment of a fine only because of her higher social class.

John continued his relationship with John Winthrop the Younger and assisted him throughout the years, until his own death in Hartford, in 1662, at which time the state assumed his funeral and burial costs. He was highly respected at the time of his death and had become both a confidant and an important agent to the governor of the colony, as well as a public official of Connecticut Colony. Eventually, he told the story of his relationship with Alice Young to his friend, Governor Winthrop, in hopes of changing the face of witchcraft accusations.

Alice "Alissa" Young Beamon was put under the care of Deacon Hosford and his wife. She was not allowed to live with or associate with the Tinkers again. Deacon Hosford gave her strict discipline and tried to lead her away from evil influences. He brought her to Springfield with him and his wife, where he had a brief stint as a preacher. He later returned to England. She stayed and married Simon Beamon of Springfield, a shoemaker and a personal messenger of William Pyncheon. She bore many children by Simon, including a daughter named Alice. Eventually, she was also accused of witchcraft but was found innocent. She never found out the real identity of her father.

Thomas and Anne Thornton also left Windsor soon after Alice died. They departed in 1647, as soon as they sold their land to John Strong. The horrific loss of their four children was overwhelming for them, and they decided to relocate that same year to Stratford, Connecticut, with the financial help of John Porter through his son-in-law, Joseph Judgson. They were also concerned that Anne would be accused of witchcraft due to her association with Alice and the loss of her four children.

Thomas moved his family back to England in 1654 where he studied for the ministry. They had very little contact with Anne's family after Alice's death and none with her brother, John Tinker, ever again. Anne was saddened for many years not only by the loss of her four children but also by the loss of the family she grew up with. By the end of his life in the 1690s, Thomas was a revered retired minister in Cotton Mather's congregation in Boston and shared with Reverend Mather his personal stories of encounters with Satan. His hidden influence on Cotton Mather and his writings during the Salem witch accusations had a profound impact on fanning the flames of the witch hunts of that time.

Rhoda "Rhody" Tinker Hobbs Taylor Hoyt lingered in Windsor a little longer than her siblings and her mother, until she married her neighbor and fellow widower, Walter Hoyt, in 1651. After concerns about the resurgence of witchcraft gossip after the death of Henry Stiles, she convinced her new husband, Walter, to move to Norwalk, Connecticut, in 1653 and join her sister, Mary, and her family, who had already settled there.

Mrs. Mary Tinker Collins sold her property in Windsor in 1648 and moved in with her daughter, Mary Sension. She died shortly after from the grief of losing her son, John, whom she had forever alienated. The sadness at the fracturing of her once close-knit family by her treatment of Alice was too much for her to bear.

Mathias and Mary Sension initially left Windsor, in 1648, for Wethersfield, where he had a livelihood as a baker. However, the witch hunts there with Mary Johnson and initial witchcraft accusations of the Carringtons were too close and emotional for them to witness. Mary was concerned that she herself would be accused of witchcraft because of her association with Alice. Thus, they quickly removed themselves from Wethersfield and finally settled in Norwalk, Connecticut, in 1649.

William Hulburd left Windsor as quickly as he could, in 1647, for fear of being associated with witchcraft himself. People were suspicious of him for a while because he had sold his property to a convicted "witch" and her husband. He moved to Hartford for a few years but eventually came back to Windsor. The second time in Windsor was only slightly better than the first time, pushing him to relocate to Northampton, Massachusetts.

John Young was allowed to stay in Windsor for helping to provide evidence against Alice, but he had to sell his land and move in with someone else for proper supervision as a single man once again. He had a seat in the meetinghouse until he finally decided years later to move to Stratford, Connecticut. He died there, leaving a will that claimed no heirs.

Thomas Hopewell was the first Indian granted the right to settle in the town of Windsor. He tried to live in the Backer Row area, with several unsuccessful attempts at different locations there. He felt too haunted by the spirit of Alice Young and the residual despair that lingered in the neighborhood. He was prompted to leave Windsor altogether, moving to southern Connecticut. Backer Row became the least desirable of all the neighborhoods in Windsor after that time due to its sinister and ghostly history.

Matthew Allyn became a respected and longstanding selectman and then a magistrate in Connecticut Colony. He was welcomed into the First Church in Windsor not long after Alice Young's death.

His son, Thomas Allyn, accidentally killed a man named Henry Stiles due to carelessness in handling his firearm during a militia drill on the town green. Thomas was charged with involuntary manslaughter and was ordered to pay fines and be on probation from using firearms for a year.

This did not sit well with his father, Matthew. Since charges of witchcraft had already worked in his favor once and turned his own personal fortunes around, he thought to trump up charges against Lydia Gilbert in this case, allowing his son to be cleared of all charges of guilt. Lydia was convicted of the murder of Henry Stiles three years after the actual incident, even though she was not at the scene of the crime, becoming the second woman in Windsor accused of and hanged for witchcraft. All charges against Thomas Allyn were dropped and all fines paid to the court were returned to the Allyn family.

Winifred Holman always wondered what happened to Alice. She was shocked when she learned of her demise. Winifred continued to live with her family in Cambridge, teaching healing and apothecary skills to her daughter, Mary. After Winifred's husband, William, died, she and her daughter were also accused of witchcraft by a neighbor but were acquitted due to the numerous signatures of support from many of her other neighbors. She countersued with a defamation of character lawsuit.

Robert Keayne became a wealthy merchant in Boston. Despite his strict Puritan leanings, he was accused of cheating his fellow townspeople in Boston. He left a lengthy defense in his will and donated money for the first market building constructed in Boston. He founded the Honorable Artillery Company of Massachusetts and served in the Massachusetts legislature. The people of Windsor never found out if their town's name was changed from Dorchester to Windsor because of his financial investments in the founding of the Massachusetts Bay Company or if the Tinker family had an influence in the name change.

John Winthrop Jr. founded the town of New London shortly after his scouting trip in the former Pequot territories with John Tinker. Mr. Winthrop hired John to help him with various endeavors and to become his assistant while he was Governor of Connecticut Colony. He was greatly influenced by John Tinker's personal experiences with Alice Young's witchcraft accusations. Because of these and other reasons, he decided to halt the witchcraft insanity in Connecticut, as governor of the colony, by changing the rules for convictions in later years.

Reverend John Wareham continued to lead the Windsor congregation for another thirty-three years, until his death in 1670. His last years were beset with church controversies and melancholy. He was later referred to as "the principle pillar and father of the colony" by Cotton Mather in writings about the earliest Connecticut founders.

Dr. Bray Rossiter became the first doctor to perform an autopsy in the colonies. He assessed the corpse and cause of death of Elizabeth Kelly during the Hartford witch trials in the case against the accused woman, Goodwife Ayers. He also served in the Connecticut General Court at times.

Witchcraft accusations and trials in the Connecticut Colony continued until the year 1697. The last execution took place in 1663. In all, there were thirty-four accusations and eleven convictions, with deaths by hangings. Several people either fled or were banished from the colony. The accusations against Alice Young and her subsequent execution by hanging had a profound impact on the fury of witchcraft allegations and trials, not only in Connecticut but also in Massachusetts and other parts of New England.

AUTHOR'S NOTE

O *ne of Windsor* is a work of historical fiction. However, it is based on some actual people and the historical events that occurred in their lives. It is, in essence, a theory about what led up to America's first witch hanging and its aftermath but is embellished with literary inventions. During the research process, historical sources, ancestral records, and various maps were used. Other maps were created.

Within this narrative there are several factors at play that utilize some known theories brought forth about early American witchcraft trials, but another new theory is also proposed here. Most theories about early witchcraft accusations in America focus on the events that occurred in Salem, Massachusetts, in 1692-1693. However, some of these theories can apply to the earliest witchcraft accusation against Alice Young that took place in Windsor, Connecticut, in 1647.

In *Salem Possessed: the Social Origins of Witchcraft* (Cambridge: Harvard University Press, 1974), researchers Paul Boyer and Stephen Nissenbaum brought forth a social theory explaining the Salem accusations based on patterns illustrated in a town map. They showed that property and land disputes that fissured

Salem town from Salem village were at the heart of economic, religious, and social differences largely dividing villagers and town residents into accusers and accused.

Similarly in Windsor, maps on the following pages show two distinct groups, based on differing origins in England. The first group, the minority, lived principally around Backer Row. However, some members also settled on other properties elsewhere in Windsor. Comprised of extended Tinker family members, they originated from New Windsor, England, and nearby areas, including London. The other distinct group was from the West Country of England, the origins of Reverend Wareham, Roger Ludlow, Bray Rossiter, and others who came over on the ship *Mary and John*.

It is notable that the extended Tinker family largely dispersed and left the Connecticut town of Windsor either immediately after Alice's hanging or within a very short time. She had lived in the midst of this group on Backer Row and, logically, may have been a part of it. It is a possibility that the majority group in Windsor used witchcraft accusations to attack and fracture the minority group by using tragedy from illness and death as leverage.

Mary Beth Norton is another witchcraft scholar. She explains her psychological theory in the book, *In the Devil's Snare: the Salem Witchcraft Crisis of 1692* (New York: Random House, 2002). She argues that the witchcraft crisis of 1692 was a consequence of societal trauma and changes in psyche brought about by King Philip's War. Comparatively, the aftermath of the Pequot War, also an Indian war, may have been an underlying influence to some degree in the Windsor witchcraft accusation.

It may not be purely coincidence that Alice Young's hanging was exactly ten years to the day after the Pequot Massacre. Captain Mason played a major role in that war and ten years later was a Windsor resident as well as a serving treasurer in the

Connecticut General Court. It is also interesting to note that in the exact month of Alice's hanging several laws were enacted to chiefly restrict interactions with members of local Native American tribes.

Something else to consider in this scenario was the different views held regarding the handling of the remaining Pequots at the time of the hanging. John Winthrop Jr. was developing his plantation at New London. He worked closely with Robin Cassacinamon, leader of a small group of remaining Pequots, to help secure his success in the new settlement. It was in direct opposition to Captain Mason, who strongly felt that, in accordance with the Treaty of Hartford, the Pequots should cease to exist as a tribe. Winthrop and Mason were men who were often at odds with each other in their approaches and their beliefs. John Tinker, Winthrop's associate and quite possibly his assistant at that time, lived in Windsor, Connecticut, and was part of the minority group from New Windsor, England. Therefore, controversies surrounding the settling of New London and the subsequent differing views on handling the Pequots may have seeped into political divisions within the town of Windsor and contributed to the witchcraft accusation against a weaker member of the extended Tinker family group.

John Demos' work, *Entertaining Satan: Witchcraft and the Culture of Early New England* (New York: Oxford University Press, 2004) emphasized the psychological reasons for witchcraft accusations, not just pertaining to Salem in 1692 but to a wider array of witchcraft accusations throughout early New England. They may also have been at work in Windsor, Connecticut. Various fears about a variety of threats could have certainly been projected onto Alice Young.

Medical theories also play into a possible scenario for the reasons Alice Young was accused. We know from historical literature that an influenza epidemic took place in the year that

Alice was hanged. With fevers and infections, there is always the medical possibility of delirium. In a delirious state, any number of falsehoods could have been imagined and used to make an accusation.

One may also be able to apply some of the theory of Carol Karlsen from her book, *The Devil in the Shape of a Woman: Witchcraft in Colonial New England* (New York: W.W. Norton & Co., 1987) to the specific witchcraft accusation of Alice Young in Windsor. Even though her husband was still alive at the time of the hanging and she was not in direct competition for power in relation to property with men, she may have posed a threat to the only male doctor in town, Bray Rossiter.

In addition to these theories, I would also like to newly propose a geographical theory to explain witchcraft accusations and witchcraft fears. I believe that the witchcraft event that occurred in Windsor, Connecticut, in 1647 could have affected the outbreak of witchcraft panic in Salem, Massachusetts and surrounding towns in 1692-1693 through the writings of Cotton Mather.

In the field of geography, spatial diffusion theory states that a concept or practice can move a culture or people to a new location. The fear and panic that took place in Windsor greatly affected a man named Thomas Thornton, who later became a minister and, in his retirement, was a member of Cotton Mather's church in Boston. It was the same period, in effect, that Cotton Mather was writing *Wonders of the Invisible World*. The Prelude contains italicized direct quotes from this work. Cotton Mather referred to someone from over forty years earlier who had warned about the horrible effects of witchcraft.

Could this person have been Thomas Thornton, a man who underwent an extreme family tragedy in 1647 and was the next-door neighbor of Alice Young? My theory is that this is a strong possibility! In this way, this man took his personal experiences from the first witchcraft panic in Windsor and transferred them to Boston in his later years. As an elderly retired minister in Boston and a member of Mather's church, it is not unreasonable to assume that he could have influenced Cotton Mather, a young minister in his twenties, during the time he wrote his commentaries about the Salem witch trials. Many scholars feel that those writings acted to foment the spread of the witch hysteria from Salem to other Massachusetts towns. In this way, through spatial diffusion, it is possible that the first witchcraft accusation and hanging in Connecticut influenced the widespread witchcraft panic in Massachusetts over forty-five years later.

Many readers will want to know which parts of *One of Windsor* are fact and which parts are literary inventions. While I cannot go into complete detail here, I will share some of the key components of real history versus the fictionalized parts of the book.

Real people were the basis for most characters in the novel. It is only some minor characters that are not real, such as Assanushque or Goodman Humphrey, who represent people that could have easily existed from the time period. The characters and personalities of actual people and how they reacted to each other in the novel were based largely on educated assumptions derived from the real events and relationships in their lives as well as their actual status in Puritan society, when known. When information was not known, it was invented using educated guesses.

Although I cannot prove beyond a shadow of a doubt that Alice Ashbey, the maidservant of the Holmans of Cambridge, Massachusetts, was later Alice Young, my research into historical records indicates that it is a strong possibility. Also, in regard to the identity of Alice Young, there was the placement of the Young property. Its proximity to three Tinker sisters and their husbands as well as the sale of the property to John Young by another Tinker sister's husband caused me to question if there was a familial connection. That assumption was the cornerstone of this story.

John Taylor was lost at sea in real life at the same time the "phantom" ship disappeared. Family genealogies assume that he died on that ship. Henry Wadsworth Longfellow immortalized "The Phantom Ship" in a poem of the same name.

John Tinker really was an assistant to the Winthrop family, serving under both John Winthrop and his son. He also represented the affairs of Robert Keayne. He was a single man in his mid-thirties in 1647 and did not marry until 1648, a year after Alice's death. The *Winthrop Diaries* contain his correspondence with both Winthrops.

The ship manifest of the *Defence*, in 1635, listed both the Keaynes and the "Hoemans" as traveling together on a journey departing from London. The Holmans in this novel are the same family as the "Hoemans" based on family names and ages. Incidentally, Winifred Holman exists in the historical record as a healer and was also accused of witchcraft.

John Winthrop the Younger did take an overland journey through Connecticut and chronicled it in his diary. This book accurately reflects his travels and encounters, with the exception of meeting John Tinker's family in Windsor.

Historical records prove that Matthew Allyn originally settled in Cambridge, was frequently in court, and was excommunicated from his church in Hartford. He became a deputy representing Windsor in the Connecticut General Court the year after Alice's death. His son was charged with manslaughter in the death of Henry Stiles in 1651 but was cleared of all culpability three years later when a woman by the name of Lydia Gilbert was declared responsible for the crime by bewitchment. Some suspect that Matthew Allyn used his clout to clear his family's name in that case. However, it is not known if, in the case of Alice Young, Matthew Allyn had any motivations against her in real life or played any part in her accusations.

There are no historical records to indicate who transferred the witch-finding manual, *The Discovery of Witches* by Matthew Hopkins, to the New England colonies. However, its usage and methodology were noted in John Winthrop's journal describing the witch trial of Mary Johnson in 1648. Brothers-in-law Joseph Loomis and John Porter came from Essex, England, and therefore may have been responsible for the book's possible arrival in the New World a year earlier, 1647. It is feasible that the court used it in the witchcraft trial of Alice Young.

John Young stayed in Windsor longer than others who left Backer Row. If he is indeed the same man who died with the same name in Stratford, Connecticut, he claimed no heirs. His sexual orientation is unknown. However, the lengthy sodomy trial records of Nicolas Sension do shed light on attitudes toward homosexuality of that time and suggest the sexual orientation of the youngest Sension brother.

The Windsor magistrates, deputies, and deacons listed in the book really were in those positions of power in 1647. Furthermore, the laws mentioned in the book were actual laws and can all be found in James Hammond Trumbull's compilation of early Connecticut General Court documents, *The Public Records of the Colony of Connecticut 1636-1776*.

In describing the taking of captive Indian slaves by the English in the Pequot War, Captain John Mason states in his account, "they could not endure that yoke..." Although there is no specific record that he owned Pequot slaves, it is not a huge leap in logic to assume that, as leader of the Connecticut forces in the war, he would have taken his own personal Indian slaves.

Thomas Hopewell was the name of an Indian mentioned by Stiles that was allowed to take up residence in Windsor in the

1650s, where he had a lot on Backer Row. There is no known record of a relationship between him and John Tinker. However, John Tinker's land on the map represents what is recorded in the Windsor Land Records. His property was next to Tunxis Indian lands. It is quite possible that he did work with or befriend the Native Americans living on the adjoining property.

The italicized quotes in chapter thirty-seven are from Robert Calef's *More Wonders of the Invisible World* that was a rebuttal to Cotton Mather's work previously mentioned. The ensuing scene around it was a literary invention.

The majority of herbal remedies in the book, both Native American and European, were used at that time and can be found in Nicolas Culpepper's *The Complete Herbal,* or John Josslyn's, *New England Rarities Discovered.* Both works date from the 1600s. The remedies mentioned were just a small sample from a plethora of knowledge about herbal medicine from that period.

The beautiful tale about the pink moccasin flower is an actual legend from the Ojibwa tribe of the Great Lakes region that I adapted to the story. Although I was unable to find one from the New England region, it would make sense to me that one or more of the many tribes in New England would also have had their own legends about this remarkable and magical wildflower.

This section of the book includes maps of the town of Windsor. The Windsor map is based on research that I did and is an improved version of the *Map of Ancient Windsor* from the book, *The Memorial History of Hartford County* (Boston, 1886) by James Hammond Trumbull. However, I did not have time to research every resident from the period of the book. I only made adjustments to the map that reflected my own research into the characters of the book. Hence, I tightened the range of dates for the map, but there may still be inconsistencies for other town residents that I did not research.

The map of Backer Row in 1647 reflects a lot of research on the part of this author. The map reveals family connections of many of the Backer Row residents at that time and was also the basis for this book. The events that occurred during that year on that street provide a plausible theory of what culminated in the first American witch hanging.

Lastly, it is also important to note some inconsistencies in both the novel and history related to time and spelling of names. During the period in the novel, the English used the Julian calendar. The English and their colonies did not change over to the Gregorian calendar that we use now until 1752. Therefore, it is interesting that even though we refer to Alice's hanging as happening on May 26, 1647, and the Pequot War Massacre as happening on May 26, 1637, those events would actually have been ten days later by our current calendar and have taken place in early June.

Also of importance is the multitude of ways that names were spelled. There were no spelling rules in the 1600s, and the act of spelling a proper name was archaic and at the whim of the person writing. Thus, the name "Alice" could be spelled Alis, Alse, or a myriad of different ways. This also would apply to family surnames. For example, Hulburd was also found as Hubbard, Hulbirt, and more in the historical records. For clarity and simplicity, I chose one spelling and was consistent with it throughout the book.

The following pages contain all of the maps referred to: Backer Row, other Windsor maps, English origin maps, and the family tree. Please stay tuned for future research presentations and articles on this topic. Regular updates about this information will appear on the website www.oneofwindsor.com and the corresponding Facebook page.

Tinker/Merwin Family Tree

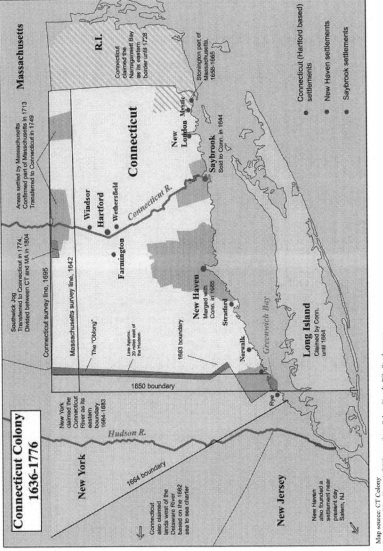

Connecticut Colony
1636-1776

Massachusetts

R.I.

Connecticut

New York

New Jersey

Long Island
Claimed by Conn.
until 1664

Hudson R.

Greenwich Bay

Southwick Jog
Transferred to Connecticut in 1774,
Divided between CT and MA in 1804

Areas settled by Massachusetts
Confirmed part of Massachusetts in 1713
Transferred to Connecticut in 1749

Connecticut survey line, 1695

Massachusetts survey line, 1642

The "Oblong"

Line Approx.
20 miles east of
the Hudson

1683 boundary

1650 boundary

New York
claimed the
Connecticut
River as its
eastern
boundary
1664-1683

1664 boundary

Connecticut
also claimed
lands west of the
Delaware River
based on the 1662
sea to sea charter

New Haven
also founded a
settlement near
present day
Salem, NJ

Windsor
Hartford
Wethersfield

Farmington

Connecticut R.

New Haven
Merged with
Conn. in 1665

Stratford

Norwalk

Rye

Saybrook
Sold to Conn. in 1644

New
London

Mystic

Stonington part of
Massachusetts,
1658-1665

Connecticut
claimed the
Narragansett Bay
as its eastern
border until 1728

• Connecticut (Hartford based)
  settlements

• New Haven settlements

• Saybrook settlements

Map source: CT Colony
https://en.wikipedia.org/wiki/Connecticut_Colony#/media/File:Ctcolony.png
(Accessed: May 2015)
Last modified by Yunliang Meng on May 2015
This map is free use.

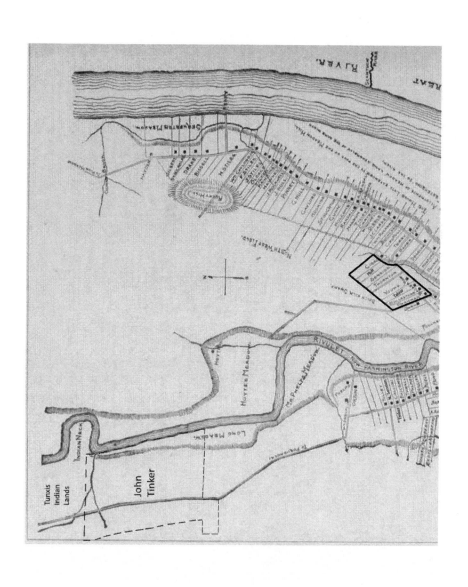

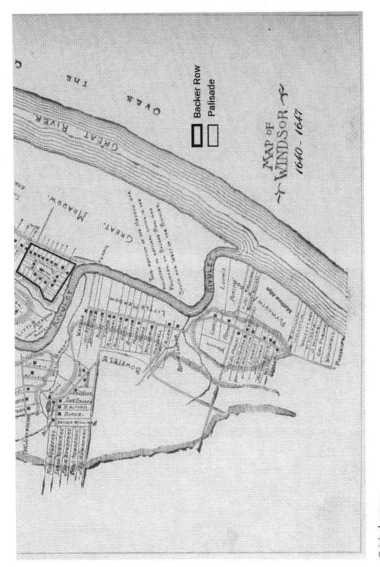

MAP OF
WINDSOR
1640 - 1647

Backer Row
Palisade

Original source:
Trumbull, James H. *Map of Windsor 1633-1650* [map]. Scale not given. In:
Memorial History of Hartford County, Connecticut Volume I. Boston, MA: Edward L. Osgood,1886, page 501.
Last modified by Yunliang Meng on (May 26th, 2015) with researched information from Beth M Caruso
Note: This modified map is free use for educational and research purposes. No copies may be used for profit.

1. Backer Row's Location in Windsor

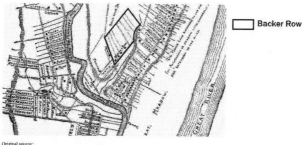

☐ Backer Row

Original source:
Trumbull, James H. *Map of Windsor 1633-1650* [map]. Scale not given. In: The Memorial History of Hartford County, Connecticut Volume I. Boston, MA: Edward L. Osgood,1886, page 501.
Last modified by Yunliang Meng on (May 26th, 2015) with researched information from Beth M Caruso
Note: This modified map is free use for educational and research purposes. No copies may be used for profit.

2. The Residents of Backer Row in 1647

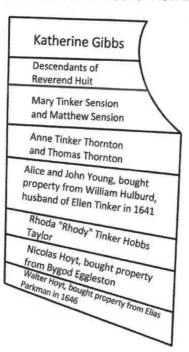

Note: The land parcels have been rotated 315 degrees clockwise.

Early Windsor Families

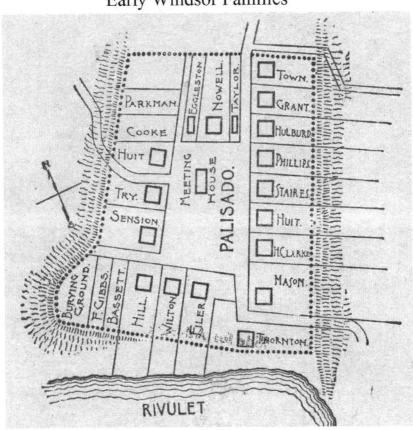

Original source:
Trumbull, James H. *Map of Windsor 1633–1650* [map]. Scale not given. In: The Memorial History of Hartford County,
Connecticut Volume I. Boston, MA: Edward L. Osgood, 1886, page 546.
Last modified by Yunliang Meng on (May 26th, 2015) with researched information from Beth M Caruso

England and Wales

Map source:
England and Wales (Pre 1974 County Structure) <http://www.barkerdavis.org/ScrapBooks/Gallery.htm>
(accessed May 2015).
Last modified by Yunliang Meng on (May 26th, 2015) with researched information from Beth M Caruso
Note: This modified map is free use for educational and research purposes. No copies may be used for profit.

Origins of the Majority of Windsor Residents in the 1640s

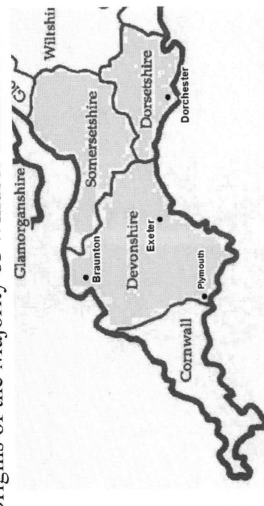

Map source:
England and Wales (Pre 1974 County Structure)
<http://www.barkerdavis.org/ScrapBooks/Gallery.htm> (accessed May 2015).
Last modified by Yunliang Meng on (May 26th, 2015) with researched information from Beth M Caruso
Note: This modified map is free use for educational and research purposes. No copies may be used for profit.

Origins of the Extended Tinker Family

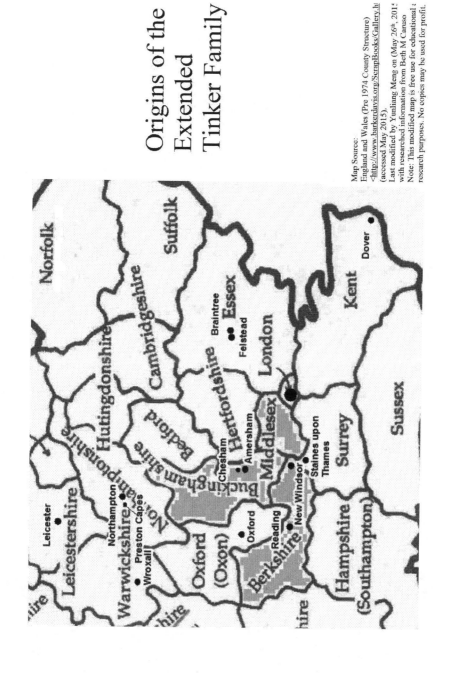

Map Source:
England and Wales (Pre 1974 County Structure)
<http://www.barkerdavis.org/ScrapBooks/Gallery.ht
(accessed May 2015).
Last modified by Yunliang Meng on (May 26th, 201:
with researched information from Beth M Caruso
Note: This modified map is free use for educational a
research purposes. No copies may be used for profit.

RESOURCES

To learn more about the Connecticut witchcraft accusations and trials, contact or visit:
Stanley-Whitman House
37 High Street
Farmington, CT 06032
860-677-9222
www.stanleywhitman.org
The Stanley-Whitman House and Karyl Evans Productions, LLC conducted a statewide survey in 2009 of primary and secondary materials related to Connecticut's 17th-century witchcraft trials. That survey and the research files are available to the public.

To learn more about the early history of Windsor, Connecticut's oldest town, visit:
Windsor Historical Society
96 Palisado Avenue
Windsor, CT 06095
(860) 688-3813
www.windsorhistoricalsociety.org
The Windsor Historical Society and its research library are open 11-4 Wednesday through Saturday year-round.

CONNECTICUT WITCH-HANGING VICTIMS

The following people were hanged for witchcraft in Connecticut Colony between 1647-1663:

Alice (Alse) Young of Windsor, 1647
Mary Johnson of Wethersfield, 1648
John and Joan Carrington of Wethersfield, 1651
Goody Bassett of Stratford, 1651
Goody Knapp of Fairfield, 1651
Lydia Gilbert of Windsor, 1654
Mary Sanford of Hartford, 1662
Nathaniel and Rebecca Greensmith of Hartford, 1663.
Mary Barnes of Farmington, 1663
More than twenty-three others were accused. Some were banished from the colony.

At the time of this writing, February 2016, the Board of Paroles in the state of Connecticut does not grant posthumous pardons. The Governor of the state of Connecticut has thus far not acknowledged the innocence of these witch-hanging victims in a proclamation. Nor is there currently a memorial to these victims. However, several citizens are exploring ways to turn these ideas or other forms of acknowledgement into reality.

To explore more about Connecticut's witch hanging history and find out what is going on in regards to acknowledging the state's witch-hanging victims, please visit the Facebook Page: CT WITCH Memorial or Connecticut Witch Interrogations, Trials, & Colonial Hangings Memorial.

AUTHOR BIO

Beth M. Caruso holds master's degrees in Nursing and Public Health. She had the honor of working with Karen hill tribes as a Peace Corps volunteer in Thailand. She also had the privilege to care for hundreds of babies and their mothers as a labor and delivery nurse.

She gained extensive knowledge and a deep love for plants through an apprenticeship with herbalist and wildcrafter, Will Endres, in North Carolina. She has continued to surround herself with plants through gardening and native species conservation.

Her latest passion is to discover and convey important stories of women in American history and has become an enthusiastic supporter of acknowledging Connecticut's witch-hanging victims. She lives in New England with her awesome husband, amazing children, loyal puppy, and cuddly cats. Beth can be contacted at www.oneofwindsor@yahoo.com.

ACKNOWLEDGEMENTS
"TEAM ALICE"

It took a whole group of people to help *One of Windsor* come to life and I am grateful and indebted to many.

To Susanne Aspley, long-time friend, author, writing coach, and editor. I am dead serious when I say that this book might not have happened at all if it were not for your encouragement from the first time I told you about the story. I am awed by your generosity, bravery, and incredible support. Many thanks.

A sincere thank you also goes to Dr. William Harris for copyediting this second edition. Your careful attention to detail was an essential part of this creative endeavor.

Lori Truly, accomplished artist, friend, generous and loving spirit, quickly tuned in to the spirit of Alice and the book, really capturing its essence. I was so grateful to have her as a part of this team.

I am also thankful to Claire Meucci who graciously created the lovely family tree. She is also a wonderful artist, supportive friend, and ever so humble about her wonderful talent.

Dr. Yunliang 'Phil' Meng is the geographer and GIS specialist from Central Connecticut State University who created all the maps you see in this book. He was also very generous, timely, and patient in helping me complete this project.

I am also thankful to Dr. Katherine Hermes, Chair of History at Central Connecticut State University who gave valuable feedback about the period that only someone with her expertise could do. As a professor and scholar with vast knowledge of Native American relations, colonial legal history, and Puritanism in 1600s New England, she helped steer me to create the most authentic story possible.

By the same token, I thank Lisa Johnson, Executive Director of the Stanley-Whitman House in Farmington, Connecticut, for her valuable feedback as well as kind and enthusiastic support. She has been a champion for the women and men accused of witchcraft in early Connecticut by encouraging their histories to be known through research of each individual case.

Thanks to the many readers, writers, and technical experts who either read the book and gave valuable insights, or gave their technical expertise during its development, including Jennifer Coe, Kathy Ryan Aries, Mary L Doyle, Cynthia W. Boynton, and Ed Kluska. Also, I give many thanks to staff members both at the Windsor Historical Society and the Town of Windsor, as well as Dan Hinchen at the Massachusetts Historical Society, for assisting me with my research efforts.

A very special thanks goes to friends Joan Meakin, Liz McAuliffe, and Tinamarie Finoia for their astonishing intuitive insights and support. Joan Meakin started all of this when she first told me about Alice. There were also many other friends and family members not directly involved with the book whose support I appreciate immensely. Thanks to all of you.

Equally important was the support of my husband, Dr. Charles Button, a geography professor at Central Connecticut State University, who helped connect me to important players in this project, spent inordinate amounts of time editing, and is collaborating with me to give educational talks. He was ever so patient as I disappeared into my writing world for hours at a time, leaving him to hold down the fort at home. Thank you from the bottom of my heart.

To my sons, River and Sky, you are truly amazing kids and I appreciate your support and enthusiasm. A thumb's up from you is worth a million more than from any literary critic. I hope you enjoy learning about your ancestors.

31461781R00226

Made in the USA
Middletown, DE
02 May 2016